GW00363480

About the Author

The author was born and brought up in Portsmouth, England and on leaving school at fifteen served an engineering apprenticeship before joining the Merchant Navy. He has been married to the same lady for fifty-three years and has two children, three grandchildren and one great-grandchild. He now lives happily in retirement.

Dedication

I dedicate this book to my mother and father who gave me and my brother a sound and loving upbringing, including for me, through the Second World War when times were very hard.

James Harley

CRIME ON A QUEEN

AUSTIN MACAULEY
PUBLISHERS LTD.

A CIP catalogue record for this title is available from the British Library.

ISBN 9781785541384 (Paperback)
ISBN 9781785541391 (Hardback)

www.austinmacauley.com

First Published (2015)
Austin Macauley Publishers Ltd.
25 Canada Square
Canary Wharf
London
E14 5LQ

Printed and bound in Great Britain

Acknowledgments

I would like to thank Shirley Lipscomb for kindly taking the time and trouble to proofread the original manuscript.

Also Alex Cracknell, whose contribution towards the publication of this book is much appreciated by the author.

And last but not least, to thank my loving wife Betty for her patience and understanding while I spent many hours writing this and other books.

CHAPTER 1

The alarm went off on the bed-side table at six o'clock, the time that James Royston had set it for the previous night. He had left it late getting to bed, spending time talking with his mother and father before venturing onto the second biggest liner in the world at that time, the Queen Mary.

After serving an engineering apprenticeship, he had spent three years as an engineer on cargo ships with two companies, both of which sailed out of London Docks. He had recently applied to join the Cunard Steam Ship Company who, with his previous engineering experience, accepted him as an Engineer Officer.

He was now twenty-three years old and wanted to get onto a more regular way of life and sailing out from nearer home in Portsmouth.

He arose, washed, shaved and got dressed, but not in the uniform he had had to buy himself because it was not supplied by the company. That was neatly packed away in his rather large suitcase. He sat and ate the breakfast his mother had got up to prepare for him as she had done for his father for years. After his dad had gone off to work in the Portsmouth Dockyard having shaken hands and wished his son all the best and given him some fatherly advice, it was time to say a fond farewell to the mother.

Before he picked up his navy blue uniform rain-coat, leather gloves and his now rather heavy suitcase, he turned to his mother and gave her a most loving hug. "Cheerio," he said with a catch in his throat disguised with a little cough. "It will only be for less than two weeks if all goes well," and with that went through the front door, out of the wooden gates that needed some TLC and down the hill to catch the bus that would take him to Cosham Railway Station. He stowed his case under the stairs of the double-decker bus when he got on and sat just inside rather than go upstairs, knowing he could manage without a cigarette for twenty minutes, the time it would take to get to the station? On arrival in Cosham, which is a suburb of Portsmouth, too large to be a village and too small to be a town, he made his way to the station. There he purchased a single ticket to Southampton Central and sat waiting for his train. Seeing that he had a while to wait, he thought he would get a newspaper, but being only a small station there was no WH Smith's news stand on the platform, but there was a paper boy just outside that he had spotted. He asked a lady on the platform if she would keep her eye on his case while he got himself a newspaper, and could he get her one while he was at it. She said, "No thank you, I have a magazine," but yes of course she would look out for his case. So James went out to get the Daily Mirror. He chose that because at the time, at least as far as he was concerned, it had the best sports coverage, which was his main interest. He had tried his hand at a lot of sports while at and after leaving school, so enjoyed reading about and keeping up to date with what was going on in the world of sport. So, armed with his newly acquired newspaper he returned to his suitcase and the young lady that was keeping her eye on it. It was quite a cold morning and very draughty with the chill wind blowing along the platforms. This was excuse enough for James to get into conversation with the young lady. Two trains passed through the station one each way, before the train both he and the young lady were waiting for came along.

They both got on, and, seeing he had already spoken to her, asked if he could join her on the journey.

She said yes that would be alright and so they found two adjoining seats. The young lady in question was about five foot four with light brown wavy hair and the most beautiful blue eyes. Being so cold she was heavily wrapped up so he could not judge what sort of figure she had, even when she loosened her coat before sitting down. Above the boots she was wearing she had shapely legs, what he could see of them. He was attracted to her mostly by her eyes; they were not just blue, but soft, with a hint of humour and intelligence. She was not heavily made up, obviously relying on her natural beautiful complexion. Her finger nails were well manicured and she wore earrings that dropped slightly. James wondered if the small diamonds in their gold settings were real.

They sat together, not speaking for a few minutes while the train with its usual 'puff puff' started out from the station, heading towards Portchester and Fareham; being a slow train it stopped at most stations on its way to London. Once they were under way, James introduced himself. She told him her name was Katherine. He said he was on his way to the Southampton Docks to pick up the Queen Mary, which was due to sail tomorrow afternoon. She said she was going on to London for an interview for a new job. "Will you not be a bit early arriving?" she said, "I didn't think the passengers arrived until the day of sailing." This brought a smile to James's face and a little flush of embarrassment came over hers because she thought she had said something she should not have done. "Why are you smiling?" she said, "Have I said something funny?"

"No, not really," James said, "I am an Engineer Officer and part of the ship's company, I only wish I was sailing as a passenger, especially if it was first class. What job are you going to interview for?" James asked, thinking it was probably modelling or the like.

"It is with a new in the market travel agency that have advertised for candidates for their organisation. I've always wanted to travel so thought I might give this a try. I wanted to be an air hostess but could not speak a foreign language which was one of the requirements and like you, would like to be on the liners, but they will not take me until I'm twenty six, which I am not; so if nothing else, if I get a job with a travel agency it will stand me in good stead when I am twenty six and apply to go to sea in some capacity."

As the train pulled in and out of the stations and the smoke from the engine passed the carriage windows, the conversation turned to where they lived and what schools they went to. James asked if Katherine had been evacuated during the war, to which she answered she had not and was glad she had not been. She said that they had been bombed out and that the house she lived in with her mother, grandmother and elder sister had been so badly damaged by a bomb that exploded about a hundred yards down the road, that they had had to find alternative rented accommodation; an upstairs flat near the Portsmouth sea front. She said they had been in the air raid shelter when the bomb went off and after the all clear was sounded and they immerged from the dug-out, they found the house was partly demolished and not a window intact. She said she was very young and could remember very little of the war or moving houses. They were still talking of the past when the train pulled into Southampton Central Station and it was time for them to say their goodbyes. Wishing each other all the best for the future, James especially wished Katherine good luck at her interview.

Lifting down his suit case from the luggage rack, James took leave of Katherine and left the train to try to find a taxi to take him to the old docks where the Queen Mary was berthed at the Ocean Terminal. On crossing over the bridge to reach the platform leading to the road, he dropped his ticket and had to put his case down to pick it up. As he picked up the ticket he noticed a pair of dark brown well-worn suede brogue shoes staring up at him. As he lifted his head his eyes passed the tweed turn ups of a rather baggy pair of trousers then to the matching jacket of a well-worn suit, flannelette type checked shirt and heavy duty, man of the country tie, along with a battered corduroy hat. He was a tallish man of about five ten and when he spoke he had a very thick Scottish accent. "Can I help you?" said the man, in a friendly way.

"Not really, I've only dropped my ticket which the ticket collector will want to see as I leave the station." James replied.

"Where are you off to? He asked, in an enquiring, rather than demanding sort of tone.

"As a matter of fact I am going to try and get a taxi to take me to the old docks and the Queen Mary," said James.

"That's funny," said the man, "so am I, should we travel together and share a taxi?"

"My name is James Royston, what's yours?"

"My name is Gordon Caligan and I have just come down from Glasgow to join the Queen Mary for my first trip as an Electrical Officer, I am pleased to meet you." They walked the short distance to the gate where the ticket collector took their tickets and out onto the pavement where other people were waiting for taxis. When it came to James's and Gordon's turn they both got in the back and James said, "The Ocean Terminal Old Docks, please, and the Queen Mary. "How many crew does that ship carry?" asked the taxi driver, as they started off towards the docks.

"I don't know off hand," James said, "but I do know there are eighty three Engineer and Electrical Officers of which we are two, why do you ask?"

"Only because I came on two hours ago and this is the sixth trip I have done from this station to the ship already, when is she due to sail?"

"At four o'clock tomorrow afternoon," James replied. The rest of the ten minute journey was completed in silence until they arrived as close to the ship as the driver could get. "How much do we owe you driver?" asked Gordon, who was first out of the car. "Make it half a crown, please, governor, and have a good trip."

"Thank you very much and take sixpence for yourself," he said, giving the driver a ten bob note. James had gone around to the car's boot where he waited for the driver to open it and lift out his case and Gordon's large and heavy travel bag. "I will square up with you," James said, "when we get on board, seeing we are going to the same place."

When they got on board they had to ask where the Chief Engineers Office was, and on finding it were told what they had to do and where their cabins were and after signing some forms, were told they had to sign on. They were told that would be in the second class lounge at eleven o'clock and given their respective cabin numbers.

Both James and Gordon went to their allocated cabins and arranged to meet back at the chief's office at ten thirty and go and sign on together. James found his cabin, a double in-board, which had up to then not been cleaned. There were unwashed pint pots and unmade bunks, one each side of the cabin and piles of fag ash all over the not too clean carpet. James was not very impressed having come from a home that was always spotlessly clean, but did realise it had to be cleaned at some time, he assumed by a steward and that it would then be better than being in the army. He did not attempt to unpack his case as he was unsure what part of the cabin furniture, wardrobe, drawers etc. would be his to use, especially as there were some cloths already in the cabin. He just left his case and raincoat on the cabinet between the two bunks 'before going back to the chief engineer's office to meet up with Gordon. He got there before Gordon and while he was waiting decided to find out what his job was going to be and anything else he could learn about what his next few hours and days might bring. So he asked the engineer in the office what he had to do after signing on and when would it be likely that the cabin would be cleaned up and the bunks made up with clean bed linen. He was told that after signing on he was expected to get changed into his overalls and report to the platform second in the after engine room, who would tell him what he wanted him to do, but that before doing that, it would probably be just as well to have his lunch in the engineers' dining room and then go down to the engine room. Regarding the cabin he didn't have a clue, not knowing how many stewards would be employed and in what order the cabins would be done. As a by the bye, James asked who the other engineer occupying the cabin was. Looking up a list, the office engineer said, "Oh! That will be Bob James who has done three trips and is due for some leave when you get back to Southampton. He's from Glasgow and a nice bloke, you will get on well with him as we all do and, when you see him, he will show you the ropes and give you all the advice you might need, especially if you like a pint."

"When will Bob be around?" James asked.

"He's probably down below, so you are likely to see him at lunch time when he comes up for lunch."

At that, Gordon appeared. "Are you ready for this signing on thing?" he asked, and turning to the office engineer said, "Have you got some directions for us then?" The office engineer directed them to the Cabin Class lounge and off they went to sign on.

After being asked a few questions, the discharge book was stamped for the forthcoming trip and retained, not to be seen again until he signed off in three or four trips time. That done, he waited for Gordon to finish his signing on and left together. It was the first time James had got to appreciate just how large the Queen Mary was. Once they moved out from the engineer's quarters and into the passenger domain it was like entering another world. Wide stairways clad in lush carpet, veneered bulkheads displaying wood from all over the world, brass work polished to perfection and space like you could not imagine on a ship. They took the lift, unmanned at the time because of course there were no passengers on board, up two decks and on exiting the lift followed the directions they had been given. Seeing that it was a bit early for lunch James and Gordon decided they would do a little bit of sightseeing. They decided to carry on going up in the lift one deck at a time, getting out, having a look round and then getting back in the lift for the next deck. They did not bother with the boat deck as they knew they would be required to report there the next morning for boat drill, already having been informed of this by the office engineer. They took the lift up as far as it went, before going back down again and back to their cabins, having arranged to sit together in the dining room.

It was when James got back to his cabin that he met Bob James for the first time. Bob was a tall dark man with a ruddy complexion who had surprisingly large hands and feet and a very broad Scottish accent. "Hellooo," said Bob holding out his hand. "Are you going to be my new cabin mate?"

"Yes, I think that is the general plan," said James, shaking hands.

"Sorry about the state of the cabin but John went on leave this morning and so we had a bit of a farewell last night that went on a bit late. Anyway, where are you from, is this your first trip and do you smoke and like a drink?"

"Portsmouth, yes and yes," James replied being a bit shocked at his new acquaintance's directness.

"Then we are going to get on like a house on fire," said Bob. "Pity about where you come from, laddie, but I won't hold that against ye, for I suppose I canny help coming from Glasgy. Being in port there is no steward served draught beer available but would ye like a bottle? I am going to have one before I go in for my lunch." James explained that he had arranged to meet Gordon for lunch. "OK," said Bob, "Go get him and he can join us and we can go in together."

James went across the ship to the starboard alleyway and found Gordon's cabin which likewise was a double in-board not yet cleaned; it appeared his cabin mate was not back from leave yet. They left Gordon's cabin and returned to James's and Bob's where introductions were made and the beer duly poured by Bob, who, while James was away, had had a quick wash and changed out of his overalls into his patrol suit. Over their beer Bob explained some of the ins and outs and do's and don'ts of life as an engineer with Cunard and the Queen Mary in particular. He explained that he could not speak entirely for Gordon, being electrical, but that he would soon find out from others anything he wanted to know that he hadn't explained. He said that the cabin would be cleaned in the afternoon and that he would take James down after lunch and introduce him to the senior second if he was about or the after platform second if he wasn't. "When you say the after platform what do you mean?" asked James.

"What I said," replied Bob, "for there are two engine rooms, one in front of the other."

"Oh!" said James.

"You will probably be the watch floater for this trip until you get more junior engineers come in behind you as time goes on, when you will go to platform junior then progress to the boiler rooms of which there are five."

Bob explained the machinery spaces and their layout and what they comprised of: two engine rooms, two generator rooms and five boiler rooms. "You will know what job you will be getting and the watch you will be on when the watch list goes up this afternoon."

Their beer finished, the three of them got up and made their way to the dining room, leaving the dirty glasses for the steward to wash up when he finally got around to cleaning the cabin. They went into the dining room where several men, already eating their lunch, acknowledged Bob who sat down at an empty table.

"There is only a skeleton staff on while we're in port so the service we get won't be up to much, but stewards have to have shore leave the same as everybody else, so we don't make a fuss about it and the menu is pretty basic as well," Bob explained, "but we will get served eventually." They sat there for about a quarter of an hour waiting for the steward to come to their table to take their orders. Bob ordered soup to be followed by fish, chips and peas and said he would have the cheese board to follow with a cup of coffee. James and

Gordon also had the soup, with James having sausage and mash and Gordon fishcakes and chips; they said they would choose from the sweet trolley. They were well into their meal when an engineer with two and a half rings around his well worn sleeve, obviously his working jacket, came over and asked who the new boys were and if Bob was looking after them. He introduced himself as Mike Chalmers one of the afterplatform seconds and shook hands with both Gordon and James after they told him who they were and said he would see both Bob and James down below when they had finished their lunch. After he left, Bob said what a good engineer he was and a nice bloke with it. During the meal the three of them talked about where they had served their apprenticeships and what sort of work they had done. James gave a quick resume of his and the sort of training he had received in the last five years and what it had been like on the cargo ships he had sailed on. Gordon said he had served his time in Scott's ship builders near Greenock, also going through the drawing office, but said he was employed mainly installing electrical machinery on ships being built in the ship yard, but also undertaking repair and maintenance work on ships coming in for refit. Bob told him who he thought he would have to report to after lunch and where the electrical workshop was situated. So when they left the dining room on the completion of their lunch, they all went back to their cabins to don their overalls and working boots prior to Bob and James going down into the engine room and Gordon to the electrical workshop. Bob and James's cabin still had not been cleaned but the steward was in the next cabin so they knew it would be done when they came up after the afternoon's work was completed.

Bob went off somewhere leaving James to find Mike Chalmers, the second he had met in the dining room. He found him helping another engineer doing something with a circulating pump, the biggest pump and electric motor James had ever seen. It was the one thing that had struck him directly when he had entered the engine room – how big everything was. He had worked on aircraft carriers and thought how big some of the engine and boiler room machinery was, but nothing like what he was seeing on this liner. Looking up from the floor plates to the engine room skylight casing was like looking into space, it was so high. Mike Chalmers looked up from what he was doing when James approached, and stood up. "Well, James," he said, "welcome to the Queen Mary and the after engine room where I have a little job for you; come with me." Mike took James over to where the condensers were for the after engines and introduced him to Barry who was already employed in checking them. The job was half finished when James arrived but he soon got into the routine of what was going on and was told they had to get the job completed within a couple of hours because all the tasks taken in hand by ships staff had to be completed that afternoon because they were due to start flashing up to raise steam at midnight.

Barry asked James what watch he was on, but James did not know because he had not seen the list yet. In the half hour they had until four o'clock, Barry took James right through the machinery spaces from the stern gland in the shaft tunnel to the water softening plant forward of number one boiler room. By the time they had finished and were ready to knock off for the day James's overalls were not white any more, in fact they were decidedly filthy and James was knackered. "Do you get changed in the changing room, Barry?" James asked.

"No, not while we are in port," replied Barry, "not while the dockies are on board: when things tend to go missing, but once we are at sea then most of us use the changing room." James thanked Barry for showing him round and for the tips he had given him.

James left the engine room with Barry, who said he was going to have a shower or a bath depending what was free and a lay down before dinner. James went to the notice board outside of the Chief Engineer's office to see what watch he was on and where he would be keeping it. Lo and behold, he found he was on the twelve to four and was being employed as the floater. He went back to his cabin, which had been cleaned, the bunks made up with fresh bedding and clean towels on the towel rails. He found Bob laying on his bunk reading and asked him if he had finished early. Bob said that he was in number five boiler room and that what had to be done was finished before four o'clock and so he had come up, had a shower and a shave and was chilling out before getting dressed for dinner. He asked James if he wanted a beer. "Yes, please, but after I've had a shower and got dressed if that's alright with you." This having been done, Bob opened a couple of bottles of beer and had taken the first swig when there was a knock on the cabin door. On opening it, Bob found Gordon standing there fully booted and spurred, ready to go down for their meal. "Want a beer?" Bob asked, "James and I are having one before we go into dinner."

"Yes, please," said Gordon, "but only if you come round to my cabin directly I can get some beer in."

"No worries," said Bob, "you will be able to get a case of beer tomorrow and the draught becomes available in the evening until nine o'clock." This said, Bob promptly poured another beer. They asked Gordon what watch he was picking up to which he answered, that he was on day work. This meant that he was to be available to do any electrical work allocated to him between eight in the morning and four o'clock in the afternoon. "You lucky sod," they said in harmony. James found out that Bob was also on the twelve to four; which was just as well because it meant they could bond as friends and also one wasn't waking the other in the early hours of the morning when they got up.

As at lunch time they sat together, but they sat with two more engineers tonight on a table set for six. Bob of course knew the other two and introduced James and Gordon. Both the others had just come off leave, so had plenty to say about what they had been doing during the last twelve days. James asked who was the platform second, on the after platform on the twelve to four and Bob pointed him out, adding that the senior second for the watch was at that table over there along with the other senior seconds. The dinner was more comprehensive than lunch, but still an in-port menu, unlike how it would be tomorrow night when they would be eating from the same menu as the first class passengers. The meal completed, James and Bob headed back to their cabin for a few hours' sleep before getting up at eleven thirty. James got himself into his pyjamas and climbed into his bunk with some difficulty; being short, he found it difficult getting himself over three drawers high. "Why don't you just pull out the bottom draw a little and stand on the edge of it, using it like a step?" suggested Bob, "It will be much easier to get in and out of bed." James tried this and found it worked fine.

Being only eight thirty, James thought he would have a little read before he went to sleep prior to being woken again at eleven thirty by the engine room store keeper to go on watch at midnight. The book that he had brought with him he was about half way through but wasn't really enjoying the story. He laid reading it but not really concentrating as he was thinking what the next five or six days were going to hold for him and what it was going to be like in New York. It wasn't long before his eye lids started to get heavy and drop. Time, he knew, to put the book down and turn the bed-head light out. He had had a long day and was not going to get much sleep before having to get up and carry out his first watch on the most famous ship afloat.

At eleven thirty the storekeeper knocked on the cabin door and went into their cabin, lightly tapping each of the sleeping men on the foot, enough to wake them but not to startle them. It was obvious that he had done this many times before, and quietly told Bob and James that it was time to get up. Although James and Bob smoked, they agreed that they would not smoke in the cabin, nor allow any visitors to smoke either, so were annoyed when the store keeper came in smoking and told him so. It was while James was washing his face at the cabin sink that he asked Bob why there had been so much mess and ciggy ash in the cabin when he first arrived, to which Bob answered, "Docking night is the exception." They went into the dining room for a cup of tea before going down below to start the first sea watch before sailing later that day. The port watch engineers who had been on for the previous eight hours were relieved and went up to turn in.

This being the first sea watch, everything had to be checked and prepared for raising steam and warming through the main engines. Now, the platform second was another Scotsman, this time from the East Coast, Dunfermline; a big man but with a gentle Scottish accent and the biggest mop of ginger hair James had ever seen. "I have to report to you, I believe," James said, addressing the after platform second. "My name is Jack Brooks, welcome to the Queen Mary's after engine room platform, young man," he said. "I suppose being your first trip, you want to know what your job as floater will consist of seeing there is no hand over." James didn't say he had been primed by Barry, but just took in all that Jack had to tell him. Jack called the platform junior over and told him to show James the ropes. "When you are sure of what you have to do, you can make your way through the machinery spaces right up to the water softening plant which is forward of number one boiler room so that when we get to see you will at least have some idea where you are going and who you will be meeting in what machinery space if you get a call. When you have done that, come back here and see me because I have a job for you."

When James had asked all the questions he could think of, he thanked Harry and worked his way through the machinery spaces, saying hello to the engineers as he went. It was surprising how long this had all taken, nearly two hours of the four had passed by the time James got back to the after engine room. "Have you seen all you want to see for now?" asked the platform second. "And is there anything

I can help you with regarding your job? For when you come down next we will be, or at least should be, ready for sea."

"Yes," said James, "seeing we do not get to bed until about five o'clock in the morning, do we have to go to boat drill at ten?"

"Yes," said Jack, "and if you don't attend you could be in big trouble." James thanked him for the information and busied himself until nearly four o'clock, by which time the reliefs had started appearing. James asked Harry if he knew the engineer that would be his relief and was told that his name was John White, a very tall skinny guy from somewhere in the midlands who was doing his second trip, but had been with another company before he joined the Mary. It was while he was telling James this that Harry saw his own relief appear, coming down the ladder from the changing room.

It was a little after four when John White showed up and, James thought, looking the worst for wear. With no apology for being late he came over to where James was standing and said, "I suppose you're the floater I have to relieve?" Smelling his breath James had a good idea why he was late on watch. His eyes looked as though they had just had a blood transfusion and if they looked that bad to James looking at them, what must it have been like looking through them? James noticed how black and dirty his overalls were and found out later that he came from the Union Castle line and had been on a diesel ships. "Anything outstanding to pass over then?" asked John.

"Not that I know of," said James.

"Then I will get myself lost somewhere and get my head down if I can, I'm knackered, after one hell of a run ashore."

"I don't really care what you do," said James, "I'm going up to have a wash and get some breakfast before having to attend boat drill."

"Sod that for a lark," said John, "I don't go to boat drills, standing up on the boat deck dressed like a dogs dinner in the freezing bleeding cold being expected to salute the bloody Captain. Not my cup of tea I'm afraid, he can go and kiss my ass."

"But you can get into trouble if you don't go I've been told," James said.

"I'll cross that bridge if I ever have to when the time comes. Anyway, get yourself out of here it's nearly half past four and if you don't hurry up they will clear the breakfast away."

By the time James got back to his cabin, Bob had already had his breakfast and was just getting into bed. "You're late up aren't you mate?" remarked Bob, "Where the hell did you get to?"

"I'll tell you when we get up," said James washing his hands and face ready to get his breakfast. When he got to the engineers' dining room, the stewards were beginning to clear away, but he was not too late to get bacon, eggs, beans, tomatoes toast and a welcome cup of coffee. He was not the last to go in for breakfast but was the last to leave the dining room. He went back to the cabin where Bob was fast asleep and so did not put on the cabin light to get undressed before getting into his bunk, tired out.

The cabin steward had obviously been detailed off to give all the engineer officers a shake for boat drill, those that were on the twelve to four and four to eight that is, although not many, if any, of the four to eight turned in when they came off watch. One of the exceptions, of course, was John White who had told James he was not going to attend. Both James and Bob got up had a shave and a lick round their face before donning their uniforms, grabbing their life jackets and making their way up to the boat deck. As it so happened, their nominated life boats were next to one another so for a while they were able to chat while other officers and the crew gathered. "I don't know which boats are being lowered today," Bob said, "but it will not be ours because they only lower them on the sea side in case of a falls failure. They normally nominate two boats to lower right down into the water but they might ask for the engines to be started on two or three boats on our side as well. This is one of the times when it is worth putting your full uniform on because as they come along, the deck officer running the boat drill usually asks the engineers in overalls or working uniform to start the boat engines." The Captain or Staff Captain, James didn't know which, with their entourage came along passing each boat in turn. The nominated ones already lowered to the boat deck level, where the officers on each boat threw off a salute, except as far as James could see, the majority of the engineer officers who, like him, when it came to his boat just said a very polite good morning to the Captain. The signal was given to start the boat engines and to lower the boats nominated on the sea side, complete with officers and crew. Although James could not witness this being done, as he was not on the sea side, he knew from what Bob told him that the boats lowered were let go from the falls and taken for a few minutes trip around off the berth before connecting up to the falls again and being re-stowed. All the boats re-stowed, the drill was completed and all hands were dismissed to return to their duties or whatever else they had to do. Bob said he was going to pop ashore and get a few bits and pieces before twelve o'clock and was not going to bother with lunch as he had had a good breakfast and would wait now until dinner at seven. James asked him if he could accompany him and share the cost of a taxi. Affirmed that that was agreeable, they both got changed back into civvies and went ashore.

It was twenty to twelve when they got back to their cabin where the pair of them got changed and went down below. While James stayed in the after engine room, Bob went through to number five boiler room, this time through the airlock doors that were now shut after passing through the forward engine room. All the boiler rooms were now coupled up and the engines warming through. Everything was ready to go. The engine room was now hot and the tunnel stunk, smelling like damp moss in a cave. The bilges where getting a little full now that everything was moving and pumps were running with small leaks, but they would have to wait until they had sailed and were well out to sea before they could be pumped out. While he was doing his rounds, part of which meant climbing over the turbines, he again realised just how big the Queen Mary was. On the after engine room platform the amount of gauges on the gauge board made your eyes boggle together with the size of the manoeuvring wheels, three for each engine making six in all; one for ahead, one for astern and the bypass, which was never opened and would only ever be if an emergency occurred and extra steam was needed to go to the HP turbine. Harry asked James what he thought was the most important gauge on the gauge board, which was a standard question for a first tripper. James hazarded a couple of guesses before Harry said, "It's the one right in the middle."

"But that's a clock," James said.

"That's right," said Harry, "that is the most important gauge among all the others; it measures time and if anything ever happens down here the first question asked is what time did it happen? I was caught with that one, mate, so why not pass it on, it's true." It was while he was on the platform that the senior second appeared. How was he getting on and was he settling in he enquired of James and was he looking forward to the trip to New York. James replied that yes he was getting on all right and yes he was looking forward to going to America for the first time. "Good," said Bill Moore, and with that, he put his gloves back on and went forward to the forward engine room. This watch was becoming very long due to James having very little to do. Jack Brooks suggested that he go around with Harry Oliver to see what he would have to do as the platform junior, as that would probably be the next job he would get when other junior engineers joined behind him. Harry showed James what he did while on watch and also showed him what he would have to do at the end of it when the twelve to four engineers would be retained on duty in the engine room, after being relieved, to man the manoeuvring wheels whilst the engine room was on standby, until full away was rung down from the bridge telegraph. There was also another telegraph that went through to the boiler rooms which indicated the movements being demanded from the bridge so that the boiler fires could be adjusted accordingly. This being why number two boiler room steamed number four and number three boiler room steamed number five. The combined boiler room steam pressure was controlled from number two and three boiler rooms and by phone from them to four and five. Bob had explained this to James during one of their chats.

It was just before four o'clock when the four to eight boys started coming down to relieve the twelve to four, including John White who was looking a little subdued. Standby rang down from the bridge, right on four o'clock as James was telling John that everything was OK as far as he knew and apparently the sailing time had been put back fifteen minutes to become a four-fifteen sailing. At seventeen minutes past four the first movement was rung down and, as if by magic, the Chief Engineer appeared, not the Staff Chief as had been expected. He was quite a small man in stature although big by reputation, extremely smart in his uniform with cap. He spoke to all the engineers and the greaser on the engine room platform in turn and had a word with James, recognising he was a new face that he had not seen before. He asked his name and if this was his first trip. "Yes, Chief," James replied and continued to concentrate on the job in hand, that of helping to manoeuvre the giant Queen Mary from her berth at the Ocean Terminal to the open sea. James would have loved to have watched the tugs nurse their charge from the berth pushing here and tugging there as well as the self-help forward and astern the ship got from her own four massive propellers. It took the best part of an hour before full away was rung down from the bridge and it was then the job of the four to eight to work her up to the revolutions required from the bridge for full ahead.

By the time James got back to his cabin he had been down below for over five hours and thought he and Bob deserved a proper pint when the draft beer became available at six o'clock. Bob came back to the cabin just as James was wrapping his bath towel around his waist to go and have a shower. "The beer does come on line at six, doesn't it?" James checked and said he would ring for the steward when he got back. It was after leaving the cabin and getting to the bathroom that he bumped into Gordon Caligan. He asked how he was finding things, to which Gordon replied, "Not too bad, but I will be glad when the beer is available, my tongue is just about hanging out to dry. Come to think of it, why don't you come round to my cabin and I'll get them in and bring Bob with you with your pint pots because I only have one in the cabin." When James had finished his shower and got back to his cabin, Bob was just going for a bath which he apparently preferred. James passed on the invite he had received from Gordon and started getting his uniform on ready for going in to dinner.

Just before six o'clock, James and Bob, complete with pint pots, went round to the port side alleyway to Gordon's cabin. They were both surprised to find Gordon was in a single inboard cabin and not having to share with somebody else like they were having to do, because they were very junior engineers. "How did you manage to get a single cabin?" James asked.

"I don't know," replied Gordon, "they were apparently scratching around for a cabin for me, then came up with this one and I wasn't going to argue, was I?" Right on six o'clock Gordon rang the bell for the steward and the three of them waited for his appearance, two of them sitting on the bunk and Gordon in his chair. It was nearly twenty minutes before the steward knocked at the door and came in almost buried under pint pots.

"What can I get for you gentlemen?" he asked, putting down the pots and taking out his list. "Sorry I have taken so long to get to you, but the other steward on with me has been put on other duties. I have to do the single outboard cabins first for they are the more senior officers and this is my third trip down to the bar so I am going as fast as I can."

The steward came back with the beer and gave them a little tip. "If you can manage to get your hands on another pint glass each I can get you two pints at the same time which will save you having to wait for the second pint if you want one." The three of them thanked him and now realised why he had so many pint pots on his tray. "I should have known that, being a third tripper, but I've not heard it before," said Bob, "but there you are, we live and learn don't we?" The chat between them was all about what it had been like for all of them since Gordon and James had joined yesterday, until Bob asked James how John was when he relieved him.

"He seemed a bit subdued actually," said James, "why do you ask?"

"Well he missed boat drill this morning and has had to report to the Staff Captain for a right bollocking and the threat that if he misses another one without a very good excuse he will be dismissed from the company."

"When I mentioned boat drill to him he told me he was not going, that he never does, so maybe this will change his mind. He also wants to watch the drink. When he relieved me after my first watch he had been ashore and was well on his way, he said he was going to look for somewhere to get his head down."

"He will, have to watch out for himself," said Bob. "His senior second is far stricter on drinking than ours and if he's caught under the influence of drink he will have no mercy on him. I believe he had some form of accident a number of years ago that almost cost him his life due to an engineer being drunk and has never forgotten it."

They were going to pick up passengers in Cherbourg that evening, but luckily they would be underway again by the time they went on watch and would not have to do a standby. When they finished their pint, and there was only time for one, they went into dinner together. This time, now being at sea, they had the first class passengers menu to choose from. This was luxury. James was looking at dishes he had never seen the likes of before, let alone eaten. There were five or six starters, mains and sweets to choose from as well as all the other fancy stuff rich people are used to. The three of them ordered their meal from the table waiter who was in regulation dress and the tables were formally laid. It was like being in a different dining room. It was an eye opener and for this reason the engineer officers were expected to dress for dinner. Because there were over eighty engineers and electrical officers on board, they could not mingle and eat with the passengers but were expected to dress and conduct themselves as if they were. They were not expected to wear a monkey jacket, but their best uniform. The three of them left the dining room and decided to take a breath of air and a smoke before they turned in for a couple of hours kip. It was while they were up on the boat deck on their way to Cherbourg that James asked about what time they would be arriving. "I haven't seen the ETA but we should be in berthing by about eight o'clock, I think," Bob answered having done three trips before. "Last time it only took two or three hours to get the passengers on board and we left the same evening. Whatever happens we can't go alongside before time but will leave as soon as the passengers being picked up there are on board as Cunard won't want to pay berthing fees for any longer than they have to. By the time we go on watch we will be well and truly at sea."

Bob and Gordon decided they were going down to turn in, while James said he wanted to stay up in the fresh air for a little longer and see the ship berth, seeing it would not be long. The other two had only been gone about ten minutes and James had taken one turn round the deck, when a door opened and a couple of young ladies came out on deck. Noticing James, they came over to him and asked if he knew when they would be getting to Cherbourg? He said it should be within the next hour but couldn't say exactly because he did not know the ETA. "What's that?" asked one of the girls.

"Oh! I am sorry," apologised James. "That stands for Estimated Time of Arrival and while I'm at it, I don't know what time we're due to leave Cherbourg for New York. That is the ETD."

"I know what that is," chimed in the girl who had been slightly embarrassed at not knowing what ETA stood for. That will be Estimated Time of Departure."

"That's quite right" James replied, "I'm sorry I didn't say it in English."

"You're an officer aren't you?" asked the other girl. "What do you do on the ship?"

"I'm a junior Engineer Officer and my job is working in the engine rooms and boiler rooms."

"You say plural. How many engine and boiler rooms does the Queen Mary have?"

"Two engine rooms, five boiler rooms and two generator rooms," replied James, "and they are all hot."

"How long do you work in that heat?" asked the first girl.

"In two watches of four hours," explained James, "and the whole ship's company work in watches. That is, twelve to four, four to eight and eight to twelve. Twice in twenty-four hours, excepting for those on day work who usually work from eight in the morning until five in the afternoon."

"Would we be able to see the engine rooms before we get to New York?" asked the same girl. James did not know but advised they speak to somebody in the Purser's Office to find out if a visit to the machinery spaces was possible. After speaking to them for so long without knowing who he was speaking to, he asked them their names and told them his name was James. The one that spoke to him first, the one that didn't know what ETA was, said her name was Carol and that her cousin's was Susan and that they were going to New York to visit an aunty who was paying their fare.

"Are you travelling first class?" James asked.

"No," Susan replied, "but she has gone to the expense of booking us cabin class which I believe is second class."

"Would you have gone tourist class if you had had to?" James asked.

"You bet," butted in Carol, "I would have gone in a broom cupboard if that was the only way to get to see her, we think our aunt is very generous and are dying to see her again."

"How long has she lived in America?" James asked.

"About four years now. She went out there with her boss, at the time, as his personal secretary supposedly for two years but when he returned to England at the end of his contract, our aunt had been head hunted by another company and remained there as the managing director's personal secretary. It must be a well-paid job as she was getting a very good salary when she first went to the States and I cannot see her taking a reduction in pay to stay on. Anyway, she's going to take a weeks' vacation, as she calls it, while we are with her and we will spend the other week doing our own thing. We only have two weeks holiday a year and we are using it all up in one go, but we are looking forward to it and it should be a great time." James enquired what jobs they had. "I am a trainee short hand typist for a solicitor," said Susan.

"And I am a telephonist," said Carol. Would they be able to meet James and perhaps another engineer up in one of the bars sometime they asked to get to know each other? James had to tell them no, that the engineers were not encouraged to socialise with the passengers and if caught in a passenger's cabin they could be sacked; but, if the weather was OK he might meet them here tomorrow evening about the same time if that was alright.

By this time there were a lot of passengers on the deck to witness the Queen Mary arriving in Cherbourg. Looking at his watch and realising he had been talking to these rather lovely young ladies for over half an hour and now feeling tired, he decided it was time to bid them farewell and hoped he might see them tomorrow. They said they hoped so and moved off to join other passengers looking over the boat

24

deck rails. James made his way down to his cabin and finding Bob asleep, climbed into his bunk without disturbing him. He lay thinking for a while about Susan in particular who was just about his height in the stylish high heels she was wearing. He was pleased too that neither girl was too heavily made-up. He hated women who plastered their faces with heavy lipstick and makeup. Carol was quite nice but being a bit taller was not quite so appealing to him. He was hoping to see Susan again before they got to New York, but that would only be if she was on the deck as they had discussed.

CHAPTER 2

The next thing James knew he was being called to go on watch, which was not the best thing he could think of doing, but he knew if he didn't get up there and then he would fall back to sleep and have Bob shaking him. As he made to get out of bed, Bob went straight for the kill. "Where the bloody hell did you get to, I was going to suggest we have a bottle of beer before we turned in? I waited for nearly half an hour and seeing you were not back by then I thought sod it and got into my bunk. Where did you get to?" James said he had been approached by a couple of passengers just before he came back down and stopped to talk with them. "They must have been interesting to keep you away from your pit, I thought you were tired."

"I was until I got up into the fresh air," replied James, "and then I didn't feel so tired any more."

"Who were these passengers then?" pressed Bob, not letting the subject close.

"Oh! Only a couple who were doing their first trip to sea and wanted a few questions answered," replied James, now pulling on his shoes. "Are you going to have a cup of tea before we go below or are you going to have some breakfast as well?" Bob said he would see what there was available and make up his mind then. What was on offer to eat wasn't much so they both just had a cup of tea and decided they would have a decent breakfast when they came off at four.

The ship had left Cherbourg at ten o'clock so James must have gone to sleep before that because he did not feel any movement, but was glad he had not been required to do a standby, either going into Cherbourg or leaving. He realised there could not have been many passengers boarding as they were only alongside for a couple of hours before leaving again. By the time he came off watch they were heading towards the Bay of Biscay and the likelihood of some bad weather. James had been warned before he even came to sea that the Bay of Biscay could have some of the roughest seas anywhere and by the same token could be like a sheet of glass and foggy. When he got down to the after engine room and made the change over, all was well. They were up to their cruising speed and everything was steady, only the thrust bearing on the starboard outer propeller shaft was showing a bit of heat but nothing to be concerned about. The watch went without incident and no call came from a boiler room which Jack Brooks commented on, saying that it was unusual to go through a watch without the floater being called through to the boiler rooms at least once. He warned James it would not be like that for most watches. James met Bob on the way up and suggested they have breakfast before they turned in because his relief had told him they were heading into some bad weather and so they could get some sleep before the ship started chucking around. They both washed their hands and changed into their patrol suits in the changing room and went straight into breakfast. The fried eggs looked like rubber so Bob had some scrambled egg on toast with beans and James had bacon, sausage and beans, then they had coffee. They were both in bed before five o'clock with Bob saying how much he hated the twelve to four and give him the four to eight any time.

It was about eleven o'clock that James woke up feeling as though his bunk had come alive and was trying to throw him out. The ship was rolling and feeling as though it was sailing over a ploughed field. Looking over, Bob was still fast asleep probably because he had been in bad weather before. They must be in the famous Bay of Biscay already thought James, just his luck not to have it calm on his first crossing. He wondered how the girls he met last night were feeling if they were awake. He laid there in his bunk until the store keeper came to wake them, then got up and dressed ready for the second breakfast of the day. Bob said his relief had been quite right, the weather was going to deteriorate as they got to the Bay and he wondered whether it was going to get worse before it got better. They didn't have long to wait, for by six o'clock, apart from having a couple of warm plumber blocks and the thrust bearing from the night before, the bilges had to be pumped, which Ken Morris, the eight to twelve engineer, had not done because he felt sea sick. This was James being put to his first test. Was he going to feel seasick or was he going to be alright? He was still pumping the bilges when Harry Oliver, the platform junior, came to him and told him he was required in number three boiler room. James had not finished pumping the bilges so Harry said he would keep an eye on them while James was in the boiler room. Harry thought the job was to mend a gauge glass but he had not taken the message so didn't really know, Jack had told him to go and find James and send him through to number three boiler room. By the time James got back to the after engine room things had changed somewhat, for when he got down to the tunnel he found a fire hose gently spraying water on the thrust bearing which had got considerably warmer and Harry had done this to keep the bearing at a safe temperature. The bilges too had water splashing about because the ship was now rolling so heavily the bilge pump kept drawing air and losing suction. James was still not feeling sea sick which is more than can be said about his relief. John White came down twenty minutes late after having been given a second shake, and was not too happy about having to go on watch with the weather so bad. "This is the worst bloody weather I have ever been in," he complained, without even a hint of an apology for being late on watch. It was no good James getting up tight about it, but he made up his mind he would not forget it. By the time he got up for the twelve to four breakfast, what little appetite he had was no longer with him. As well as the duty steward not being very obliging, he found out later that the steward had been given the job of going round to all the outboard cabins of the engineers on watch to shut the port hole dead lights as well as being on duty for the twelve to four breakfast, so he just had a cup of tea and some toast which he did for himself in the toaster and after a quick wash turned in. Bob was already asleep or at least James took it that he was, as he did not say anything when he went into the cabin and put the light on.

James found it hard to get to sleep even though he was dead tired; the only reason he had not gone for a shower was so that he would not wake himself up. The sea was very rough now and he wondered how the two girls he had met last evening were finding it, he hoped that later, after dinner that evening, he might see them again if the weather got better; as it was at the moment, anyone going on deck would be mad, unless of course they were intending to commit suicide. It must have been nearly six o'clock before he finally got off to sleep after getting out of his bunk to get his life jacket which he used to wedge himself in bed to stop himself rolling from side to side which was keeping him awake. It occurred to him that the twelve to four was not a very good watch to be on as it was all sleeping and not much socialising. You go on watch at twelve noon until four in the afternoon, have a bit of time to yourself until about nine o'clock which includes having a meal, then apart from being on watch from midnight until four in the morning the rest of the twenty-four hours is back to sleep or that's how it seemed. Next trip he hoped would be much better as it was usual, according to Bob, that you change watch from trip to trip going forward meaning he would be on the four to eight leaving Southampton next time.

Whatever the noise was, James never discovered, but it was near enough and loud enough to wake him up with a start. "What the bloody hell was that!" he said, putting the light on over his bunk. He looked over to Bob who was also awake and sitting bolt upright in his bunk.

"What's the time?"

Looking at his watch, that James always wore in bed, "Christ, it's only half past nine. I don't know what that noise was but now I'm awake I'll have to go for a piss." Bob, still half asleep, asked James why he had his life jacket in his bunk, was it because he thought the Queen Mary was going to sink in the night?

"No," said James, "but it made a good wedge to stop me rolling about, as I could not get to sleep before I put it there." On explaining this, he got out of bed, put the life jacket back on top of his wardrobe and left the cabin to go to the toilet. He went back to the cabin and got his towel because he decided he would have a shower before getting dressed because it would be useless trying to get back to sleep. When he was dressed, he told Bob he was going to see what the weather was like. He realised it would be too rough to go outside so decided to go up to the promenade deck where he would see via the huge windows what the sea state was and to see if there were any passengers around. He went up the main stairway rather than using a lift to the prom deck and met not a soul. He saw a couple of bedroom stewards along the passageways but not near enough to even nod to. He was surprised when he got out onto the prom deck however, for there were quite a number of older looking men and women who were obviously out for their morning constitutional walk, not walking in a straight line but rather like drunks walking home after a good session. Looking through the windows, James could see the roughest sea he had ever seen; the waves must have been fifty to sixty feet from top to bottom with the spray from their crests flying everywhere. Being an engineer and not a deck officer, he didn't know what the conditions actually were but thought they must be in about a force eight or nine gale. As big and heavy as the Queen Mary was at eighty one thousand tons, she was still being thrown about by the sea. James assumed that those passengers who were out walking the deck were either not feeling sea sick, being good sailors, or used to rough weather; their fellow passengers remaining in their cabins probably feeling the worse for wear. Before going back to his cabin, he took one last walk round, passing some seamen who were just starting to scrub the prom deck, whether all of it or only a section he did not know. If it was all, it was going to be an all day job he thought, not that he was over fussed because being in hot machinery spaces in this weather was no fun either.

The adverse weather continued right across the Bay of Biscay and into the Atlantic Ocean. For over thirty-six hours the storm lasted, albeit some times worse than others and in that time there had been a lot of internal damage such as crockery and glasses. Eating in all the dining rooms throughout the ship had accidents of some sort, passengers with their meals in their laps, those brave enough to go for their meals, that is, and a nightmare for the chefs and galley staff in the main galley and other areas where food was prepared. Anything that was not bolted or tied down was liable to move, fall or smash. The doctors and nursing staff were at full stretch to keep up with the sea sickness and injuries caused by men and women falling and breaking bones. They were half way across the Atlantic with the sea calm, when, at five o'clock in the morning, the ship's sirens began to sound as she hit the bank of fog. The call came for the twelve to four to turn out for fog standby. The watertight doors were closed throughout the ship. Those port holes that had been uncovered were duly recovered again with the deadlights and at regular intervals the sirens were sounded; all this for a bit of fog. At eight o'clock the watch changed and the twelve to four went to their beds while the four to eight engineers continued with the fog standby. James became a very tired and unhappy bunny. He started getting irritable, which was not like him, but he was so tired, what with not being able to sleep very much, even with his life jacket wedge, and now another three hours down below, he was getting a bit fed up with himself. After grabbing what became only a few hours' sleep, he was back down below doing another four hours. The weather was improving he could feel it and by being very busy the time passed quickly, or that is how it felt.

While having his shower, James wondered if a walk on deck after dinner would bear any fruit as he would like to see the girls he had met the first evening, Susan in particular. After his shower, a couple of pints with Bob and Gordon and a decent dinner, he said he was going up for some fresh air. Bob said he was going back to the cabin to do a bit of studying as he wanted to get his seconds ticket as soon as he could and by not having a National Certificate had to pass part "A" first. Luckily for James, Gordon was not interested and said he was going to go to the wardroom for a game of table tennis. James went back to the cabin with Bob to get his cap which had to be worn on deck when in full uniform. He went straight to where he had met Susan and Carol, but there was no sign of them but it was nice in the fresh air, although getting dark. He made a couple of circuits round the boat deck when a little way ahead of him a door onto the boat deck opened and Susan appeared closely followed by Carol. They looked both forward and aft as they got out onto the deck and spotted James immediately. It was as they walked towards each other that James noticed Carol had her arm in a sling. They all stopped by the guard rail between and below two of the life boats. James's first question was what Carol had done to her arm and how did she do it. The two girls started to giggle and Carol flushed up a bit when she said she had broken her arm and did it falling out of bed. "When was that?" James asked, being a little concerned. "Is it going to spoil your holiday?"

"Not on your life," said Carol, "the break is in the forearm and the doctor told me that the plaster will not hamper me, but of course it will have to remain on for a few weeks. It's a clean break and therefore there should be no complications and it should not keep me off work when I get home. It's my left arm and being right-handed I will be able to push in and pull out the connecting lines and also be able to write OK."

"Apart from breaking your arm, Carol, how did you both get on in the bad weather?" They had found it very uncomfortable but neither of them had been sea sick although by the same token they had not eaten anything either until lunch that day.

"Did the ship have to slow down in seas like that?" Susan asked. "And what was it like in the engine room?" James answered with a shrug of the shoulders saying that people might think that because the engine room is low down in the ship virtually at the very bottom of it, there is not the same effect as the decks above, that the higher you go the worse it is. Well, that is true especially where the rolling is concerned because the higher you go the longer the arc is and the further you travel, but there is quite a bit of movement down below, plus there is the heat and smells to contend with. He said how tired he had got due to not being able to sleep very well but that he would soon get back to normal now that the weather had improved.

"I know you are going to New York to see your Aunt, but don't know where you come from," James said. "Being cousins, do you live close to each other?" Susan explained that her mother and Carol's father and the aunt they were about to visit were all brother and sisters and that she and Carol lived about eight miles apart, closer if you take the little ferry, Carol on Hayling Island and herself in Portsmouth, Copnor Road to be precise.

"We are quite a close family and were hoping another cousin would be joining us on this trip, but she couldn't get time off work, also, she lives in Manchester and although we speak quite often on the phone we do not see her very often." As the darkness closed in, the wind, the little that there was now of it, started to get very cold and so the girls said they were going down to get a drink in their warm lounge and listen to a chap play the piano that was ever so good. They said good night to James and Susan gave him a little peck on the cheek behind her cousin's back as she turned through the door which they had come out on deck through. Just before Susan shut the door, James asked if he would see them tomorrow night same place, similar time and got a 'Yes' in answer.

James took another couple of turns around the boat deck, cherishing the small kiss he had received from Susan and wondered how far it might lead if only an opportunity arose. By the time he decided to go back to the cabin for a bit of sleep, it was pitch dark and, even in his uniform, now very cold. When he got back to the cabin Bob was reading in his bunk and, looking up from his book, asked James where the hell he had got to. James just said he had been up on deck to get some fresh air and had got talking to a couple of passengers. "I take it they were blokes," said Bob.

"No," replied James, putting his uniform away in the wardrobe, "as a matter of fact it was a married couple on their honeymoon. We got talking about New York," he lied. "Like me, they have never been there before and wanted to know what it was like."

"So what did you tell them?" enquired Bob.

"The conversation just went on from there until it started getting dark and cold and they went back to the lounge where there was some entertainment on, and I came back here."

"Are you going to continue reading?" James asked climbing into his bunk.

"No", said Bob, "if we don't turn the light out now it will hardly be worth going to sleep at all for the store-man will be putting us on the shake in two and a half hours' time." James, although tired, could not get to sleep straightaway thinking of the kiss he had got from Susan, small as it was, but had just dosed off when the store man knocked on the door before opening it and telling them it was half past eleven and time to get up. The pair of them got up and licked their faces round in the sink before getting dressed to go down for a quick cup of tea. It was while they were drinking their tea, not sitting down for there wasn't time, James remarked to Bob what a bloody silly time of the day it was to go to work. Bob's reply was to just think of it as being on the night shift for four hours. It might be said that it had not taken James long to start getting fed up with the middle watch, as it was so fondly known, and it could be that, as time went on, he would get fed up with all watch-keeping, but only further trips would determine this as the watches changed. Going down to the engine room, it occurred to James that he only had to do this three more times and he would be in New York and that he might get to see Susan one more time.

He woke at ten-thirty, the first time during the trip so far that he had had such a decent sleep. Bob was not awake yet so James went about washing and dressing as quietly as possible, knowing Bob could have at least another hour's sleep if he wanted it. James thought he would go out on deck to see what sort of day it was and what was going on. The weather now being fine and the sea relatively calm, there were plenty of passengers out in the fresh air, most, if not all, probably looking forward to tomorrow afternoon's arrival in New York.

Getting back to the cabin, Bob was up and ready to go for a late breakfast, yet another breakfast they had to face and actually commented on having two breakfasts and one dinner a day; albeit that the breakfast coming off watch at four o'clock in the morning could hardly be called a proper meal. They ate their breakfast and followed it with a cup of coffee. They both had a cigarette and sat chatting for a while. It came up about what were they going to do while they were in New York for two full days and a few hours. Bob said he was going to the seaman's mission where he could get a drink and a bit of entertainment the first night in and intended going to Radio City to see a show the second night. "What's Radio City?" enquired James having never heard of it before, "Is it far away from New York City?"

"It's only the biggest theatre in the world," replied Bob, "or at least has the biggest stage, and is only a stone's throw from Times Square. I am sure there is a show on there this time we're in, do you want to join me and a couple of the other engineers?" When James asked if it would be alright to bring Gordon along, because he had asked what they were going to do in New York while they were in, Bob said, "Of course he can, that will make up a group of about six which will be a good number. The seaman's mission is free to go in as long as you have your Cunard pass or anything else you have to prove you are part of a ship's company. Radio city will cost us, but do not know how much until we get there to book our tickets."

"I will tell Gordon and see what he wants to do, for we both want to have a look round the shops while we are here this time." Bob assured James that shopping was no problem for they were open until well into the early hours of the morning especially in Times Square and along Fifth Avenue.

As the afternoon watch was coming to an end, James wondered if he would see Susan and Carol, perhaps for the last time that evening. He decided it was about time he washed his overalls that were looking very dirty with some of the jobs he had had to do since leaving Southampton. He went up into the changing room where there were two washing machines and found them both in use. The engineer that had just set the second one running advised James that being on the twelve to four, after the early morning watch was the best time to do his washing as at four in the morning there were not too many wanting to use the machines. James thought he would take his advice and do some washing after the first watch on the way home, but would rinse out a couple of pairs of pants and a vest in the sink in the cabin which he did directly he got back to it. "Funny you have decided to do that," said Bob when he came into the cabin, "I was going to do exactly the same thing, for I have just checked to see if a machine is free in the changing room and they are both in use."

"So did I," said James, "that is why I am doing this now."

"Get a move on then," said Bob, "so that I can do the same, we will have to make sure we get into the machines directly, the first morning watch is finished". His underwear washing finished, James rang it out as tightly as he could and took it to the top of the engine room and hung it over one of the hand rails along with other washing that was drying there; just those few items would not take too long to dry. Only having two pairs of overalls, it was them that he was wanting to wash, with them now being very dirty and sweaty they needed washing badly but there was no alternative but to wait until the first morning watch, unless of course he might get lucky and find a machine available before then.

His washing done, a bath and a lay down on his bunk and a read, James dropped off to sleep until Bob woke him asking if he was going in to dinner, adding he had rung the bell for the steward. James got dressed and when they were half way down the first of the two pints Bob had ordered, there was a knock at the door which was half open and it was Gordon. "Hi guys," he greeted them, "are you going in for dinner?"

"Yes," both Bob and James said in unison, "after we have finished our beer." Would he like a pint, James asked Gordon, to which he got a positive reply whereby James gave him one of the two pints left and topped up his and Bob's glasses from the other one.

"What time are we due to dock?" Gordon asked, making conversation. Bob replied he thought they were due in at about eleven o'clock in the morning or thereabouts.

"Could be that we will break watches, which will mean we go on day work hours before picking up watches again the day after tomorrow which should give us two evening runs ashore." They decided they would make arrangements with the others as to when they would leave the ship and go to Radio City and the seaman's club. They finished their beer and went in for dinner. There was no doubt about it, the first class menu that they ordered from left nothing out – there was just about nothing that you could not have with the exception of caviar, that was a delicacy for first class passengers only – not that it worried James who thought it tasted like small, fishy black currants. They had their dinner and at eight thirty James said he was going for a stroll on deck. Bob said he was going back to the cabin to study and Gordon said he was going to another lecky's cabin.

James was so pleased neither Bob nor Gordon had suggested they accompany him, or the other two sitting at the table with them during dinner. He went up to the boat deck where the evening was drawing in, in fact it was nearly dark but the sky was clear of clouds and there was barely any wind. It looked as if it was going to be a cold and star-lit night. The sea was calm and the moon was throwing its golden reflection upon the wash coming off the Queen Mary's massive bow. As James made his way along the boat deck to where he thought Susan and Carol should be, if they were already there, he was spoken to by a man who was with a small group of passengers who were having a discussion.

"Hi, young man, or should I call you sir, have we slowed down?" James replied that yes the ship had slowed down because it would otherwise arrive in New York early which could not be allowed to happen. The ETA had been given and so not to be berthing before that time it meant the ship had to slow down. It was while James was engaged in this conversation that he saw Susan come out of the usual door the girls used, but on her own. The passenger, after turning to the group and telling them he was right the ship had slowed down, thanked James for answering his question and wished him a good evening.

As James approached Susan, she moved away from the ships side into a shadowy part of the deck where the deck lights that had now been turned on, were not illuminating. As she crossed over into the shadow, James could see how nicely she was dressed in a lovely floral dress with a stole around her shoulders and not too high heeled court shoes. With her long dark hair she was very attractive and when he got up close to her the perfume she was wearing smelt delightful.

"Hello, Susan, why have you come over here and where is Carol?" James enquired.

"Carol didn't want to come tonight and I have moved out of the wind," was Susan's reply. James thinking there was no wind to speak of and the two girls had been together every night he had met them. His suspicion was answered when she reached out and clasped James's hand and pulled him towards her. James, remembering the peck she had given him as she left him the night before, put his arm around her and gave her a proper kiss full on the lips, to which she responded. James, knowing that if he was caught in this way and got reported he would be in very serious trouble, cut the kiss short of what he would have liked, but enjoyed it all the same.

"What is this all about?" James asked pulling away just a little.

"We are getting into New York tomorrow and I will probably never see you again," Susan said in quite a sullen almost inaudible voice barely a whisper.

"Why do you say that?" James said thinking the worse. "You are going back to England when you finish your holiday aren't you?"

"Yes, of course I am," Susan replied, "but will you ever call on me or even telephone or write to me, when you could be meeting lots of other girls who will be sailing on the Queen Mary?"

"If you give me your address and telephone number and of course your surname there is more chance of seeing you again than as it is at the moment only knowing you as Susan, which is a name I like, by the way."

"It just so happens that I have written down the information you have just mentioned," said Susan with a little glint in her eye, "and of course I would like to have yours." James took the Queen Mary headed piece of writing paper from Susan and carefully folded it under where the writing finished and tore the paper as neatly as he could. He then went under one of the deck lights and wrote his name, address and his Mum and Dad's telephone number on it with the pen he always carried in his uniform pocket. This done, he moved back into the shadows that were now almost completely in darkness. He gave the piece of paper back to Susan and again cuddled her into a romantic embrace. It was surprising being such a nice night that there were not more passengers around on deck, but as Susan explained a lot of passengers would still be dining and then going back to their cabins to repack ready for tomorrow's docking. This sounded to James as being very plausible and very much to his advantage. "How long did you say you and Carol were going to be staying with your aunt in New York?" James asked.

"Two weeks," replied Susan, "all our annual holiday - why?"

"What ship are you sailing back on?" enquired James, not thinking.

"We are not sailing back," said Susan, "we are flying back, because to go by ship both ways would use up most of our holiday ten days out of the fourteen, by going there by boat and flying back we will be able to stay with our aunt for eight days or thereabouts, which is why I said I would never see you again."

Not wanting to miss a last opportunity to see Susan again, James said, "We are due to dock at pier ninety at just after twelve noon tomorrow and being on the twelve to four watch I will be down below as we call it, when we dock, but I want to see the Statue of Liberty for the first time as we start up the Hudson River, so if you want to see it too, I will try and meet you up here on the boat deck. There will be loads of passengers and some officers and crew up here so if we do meet it will have to look just a passenger-officer casual chat as if you were asking me a question. However, I will have to leave you by about twenty to twelve to get changed into my overalls and get down to the engine room; talking of that, did you and Carol get to see the engine rooms?"

"No, we were told it could not be arranged so I think we have missed out," said Susan.

"I don't know why that was," said James, frowning, "but then again being on the twelve to four it would be unlikely that I would see anyone anyway for they usually show passengers around before lunch, so I am made to understand, this being my first trip."

Was he going to stay on the Queen Mary for long, Susan enquired, to which James replied he didn't know. He told her he would like to get on a ship that went round the world for that is what he wanted to do – see the world. They were beginning to see passengers appearing now, after presumably finishing their dinner; men in their dinner suits and ladies very well attired. It was then that James asked Susan if she had been in for dinner, to which she nodded her head saying she had gone into dinner early and had left Carol still at the table. "What is Carol going to do?" James asked, to which Susan replied, "She wanted to come up here with me but I told her I wanted to meet you on my own if you turned up. I think she will do a bit of packing and then go to our lounge bar where I said I would meet her." Was she alright doing the packing with her arm in plaster, James asked, to which Susan replied, "Anything she cannot manage I will do when I get back to the cabin later tonight."

"I wish we could be somewhere better than this," James moaned, "but I do not know anywhere we could go, for as I have said, if I get caught with you I will be in trouble." Looking at his watch, which had a luminous dial, James could see it was now getting quite late and he had to say goodnight and break away from this beautiful girl. He told her it was time he had to go and hoped that he would see her tomorrow so they could see the Statue of Liberty together. He pulled her towards him and this time she pressed herself right into him. He could now feel her breasts which made the parting kiss even more passionate, this time he didn't care who came along and made the embrace last as long as he could, the smell of her hair and the scent she was wearing made leaving her tortuous but it had to be done. They stepped away from each other and James could see the tears running down Susan's cheeks but was just as upset at their parting. He looked out from where they were and, on feeling safe, said he would walk with her to the door she used to go back into the accommodation. He was very lucky, for as he went to open the door for her it opened and a Master at Arms came out.

"Hello, Susan," the Master at arms said, "I have been looking for you and what are you doing with this passenger?" he said looking at James. James had to think quickly on his feet or be in trouble so said that he was just being polite and opening the door for this young lady as he was passing. To this the Master at Arms gave a smile, he was a big man with a powerful looking frame, just as a policeman should be, for in fact that is what he was, a ship's policeman.

"I dare say some would believe what you have just said, but not me – so what are we going to do about this?" James didn't know what to say or what to do, he just stood there.

Susan then spoke up saying, "You are not serious are you uncle?"

"What?" gasped James, "This is your uncle?"

"Yes," said Susan, "This is my uncle Fred." Uncle Fred said he was usually on the QE but due to a Master at Arms being taken seriously ill just before sailing he was called off leave to replace him.

"You said you were looking for me," Susan asked her uncle, "why?"

"Because Carol has been taken down to the hospital again," replied her uncle, "and she has become unconscious."

"What has caused it and why did they call on you to come and find me?" Her uncle explained that the bedroom stewardess had gone into the cabin to turn their bed covers down ready for their return to the cabin for the night and found Carol slumped in the cabin chair, she asked her what was wrong and Carol told her to find her uncle Fred who was a Master at Arms. When he got to the cabin, after being

42

located, Fred had asked where Susan was, to which Carol said she was on the boat deck getting some fresh air; she then passed out. The stewardess called for a doctor and he went looking for Susan.

"You better get off back to your quarters," the Master at Arms suggested to James, who said he was sorry to hear there was problems and hoped that everything would be alright. The Master at Arms lead the way for Susan to follow him, but before she moved off after him she whispered to James, "I will see you in the morning as arranged." James went back down to his cabin wondering if anything would come of what had just occurred. He had wondered how it was that the girls had come out on deck through a first class passengers' door and realised it must have been due to their uncle Fred letting them through a segregation gate to which all the Master at Arms had a key. James had learnt this from some of the engineers who had keys they had cut from a segregation gate key carried by the deck engineers and deck electricians who have to go everywhere on the ship at any time and do not have to call for a Master at Arms to open them. He wondered if Susan and Carol had met Fred by accident or if Fred had known they were making the trip and made contact with them. Whatever way it was, James knew he had to be careful.

He got back to the cabin and turned in with only about two hours sleep to look forward to, and thought he had only just nodded off when the store-man came into the cabin and woke them up. James wondered if he would get another questioning as to where he had been, but Bob didn't say a word other than, "Are you going in for a cup of tea?" which suited James fine. He had his cup of tea, changed into his overalls in the changing room and went down onto the after engine room platform ready to take over the watch. For a good three hours he was busy but kept on thinking what had happened to Carol and how Susan was feeling knowing how close they were as cousins. It was nearing the end of the watch that James badly jammed his left hand the middle finger nail of which went almost immediately black and the pain was excruciating. He went over to the tap in the engine room and put it under the cold water which he was sure would help bring out the bruising but did not stop it hurting. Why, he did not know, but it must have been well over a minute before it started bleeding, but when it did there was blood going everywhere. He went to Jack Brooks and showed him what he had done and Jack immediately told him to get up to the hospital to see the duty nursing sister. James said should he see the watch out and then go, to which Jack told him no, he was to go then and not bother to change out of his overalls, which is exactly what James did. He got up to the hospital and saw the duty sister who called out the doctor. She cleaned the finger up and whatever she used; James guessed it was surgical spirit, but whatever it was it hurt like hell, so much so that it nearly brought tears to his eyes. While he was waiting for the doctor to appear James asked the sister if a passenger by the name of Carol had been brought in between eight and nine o'clock that evening. The sister said yes she had, did he know her? James said yes, he did know her and knew that she had been in before with a broken arm. Was she still there and would it be possible to see her, he enquired. "Yes, she is still here and no, you cannot see her." The conversation ended there as the doctor came in asking to see what he had been called out for at that time of the morning. The sister explained that the patient had quite badly damaged his fingers and that she thought stitching was necessary. The doctor looked at James' hand and immediately told the sister to get the needle and cotton out, as he put it. It was when they took the temporary dressing off that had been put on after the cleaning that James saw for the first time how much damage he had done to his fingers, especially the middle one; to say it was hanging off was an exaggeration but the wound was very severe and had to have stitches. How it did not bleed immediately he did it he did not know but it was a real mess. The doctor said he would give him a little local anaesthetic before starting the stitching which was nice to hear on

James's part, for it would stop the pain that was now very bad. It took the doctor nearly half an hour to complete the stitching and the sister to apply the dressing. James asked if he would be able to go back on watch and was told no and that if what he did needed two hands he would have to be stood down. When he explained the type of work he did the doctor said he would write a note to the Staff Chief Engineer notifying him that Mr. Royston could not continue his duties until cleared to do so by him. He asked James if he had ever had a Tetanus injection, to which James said, "No". The sister gave him the injection and half a dozen pain killers and said he was to go back to the surgery at ten o'clock.

"You will not see me but one of the other sisters and probably another doctor who will check your fingers and tell you what he wants you to do. Take two of those pain killers now and go back to your cabin and try and get some sleep." James enquired how he would let them know down below why he was not going back on watch. The sister told him not to worry about that, she would get word to them, and that to make sure he kept the dressing clean. James made his way to the changing room to change out of his overalls into his patrol suit before going back to his cabin, he thought he heard a noise but did not take any notice of it as he was in the changing room on his own, or that is what he thought. It was when he got back to his cabin and before taking his trousers off he always emptied his pockets out and put the contents on the dresser between the bunks. The pen knife and nail clippers were there and a couple of coins, but he was sure he had had a couple of pound notes in his left hand pocket --- they were not there. He went through his other trouser pockets, thinking maybe he had not transferred the money over, but they were empty too. He checked his wallet that he never took out of the cabin but kept hidden in one of the clothes drawers among his shirts, underwear and jumpers that he had brought with him for the trip and found the five pound, two one pound and the ten bob notes that should have been there and were. He was so sure he had put the two one pound notes in his patrol suit trouser pocket he could only conclude they had been stolen from the changing room. When he had got down to his under pants he had a wash as well as he could with one hand so as not to get the dressing wet. The dressing was not only round the finger but the outer bandage went nearly half way up his fore arm. He brushed his teeth but found squeezing the tooth paste out of the tube a bit awkward.

After a bit of a struggle he had only just got between the sheets when Bob came into the cabin and asked how his hand was. "How do you know I have got a bad hand?" James asked.

"Because I saw Jack in the changing room and he said you had badly damaged a hand."

"Yes I have," replied James, "and from what the doctor said I am going to be off watches for a few days. I have got to go back to the hospital and see the nurse at ten o'clock and she will tell me what the score is." Ten o'clock was about the time the Queen Mary was due to be passing the Statue of Liberty and he was looking forward to seeing Susan and hopefully Carol on the boat deck. It was about five in the morning by the time Bob had gone down for a bit of breakfast and got back to the cabin for some sleep. James was still awake when Bob got into his bunk for his fingers were throbbing and so painful, even with the two lots of painkillers he had taken. He didn't know what time he had eventually got to sleep, but when he came to and looked at his watch it was half past nine. He nearly fell out of his bunk trying not to hurt his hand more than what it was already. He looked in the mirror to see if he really needed a shave before he went to the hospital and on seeing it was not essential just gave his face a lick around with the flannel and combed his hair. He struggled a bit trying to get his shirt buttons done up using only one hand but could not manage the right cuff button at all. Getting dressed in his uniform was difficult, especially as he was trying not to waken Bob who would not need to get up until after eleven and was successful in his effort, as he closed the cabin door very quietly behind him. He could not manage to tie his shoe laces up so just tucked them down either side of each foot. It had been difficult getting his socks on and tying his tie and how glad he was that he had taken the tailor's advice and had a fly zip instead of buttons, but knowing he was going on deck after visiting the hospital he knew he had to be dressed in uniform and with his cap on. When he got to the hospital right on ten o'clock there were two nurses on duty, the tall slim one was with a patient, whoever he was, so James was seen by the shorter plumper one. "Ah! You look like the young engineer that came in early this morning and was seen by Mary and Dr. Cummings with damaged fingers – let's have a look at them. I am Jean, by the way, and the sister over there is Barbara and you are James, I believe." She started to unwrap the outer bandage as gently as she could, realising that the hand was giving James a lot of pain. As the bandage came off, James could see his hand looked very angry right up to the wrist. Jean said the next bit was going to hurt a lot because the dressing had stuck and had to be soaked off. She asked James how long ago he had taken the last lot of pain killers, to which he told her about half an hour ago, when he got up. It took Jean about five minutes to get the dressing off and expose the middle finger of the left hand; it was very badly swollen and looked terrible to James. The fingers either side of the middle finger were by now quite badly bruised and the nails going black "How on earth did you do this much damage to yourself?" Jean asked, "Because it is quite a bad injury." James tried to explain that an engine room floor plate that are steel and very heavy which he had to lift up had slipped and on automatically trying to stop it falling into the bilge had grabbed hold of it but it's weight was too much for him to control and it crushed his finger between it and a stanchion, but didn't fall into the bilge. How dirty were his hands at the time, or did he have gloves on, Jean asked. James explained that he had taken his gloves off just before the accident as he could not manage with them on and that his hands had become very dirty, but that he had put the one he hurt under a clean cold water tap as soon as he could get to it and just after his finger started bleeding. "Well, by the swelling I would say you have broken the finger and by the colour of it I would say it is quite badly infected, I am going to get Dr. Maiden to look at it." She went to the telephone and obviously called the doctor to the hospital from wherever he was. She only spoke for about a minute before going back to James and telling him the doctor would be there in about five minutes. While he waited, James asked if a lady named Carol was still in the hospital as she had been taken there last evening. Jean asked why he wanted to know and how well did he know her. He said he had talked to her and her cousin and it was her cousin who had told him she had been taken ill and was taken to the hospital unconscious. Jean said she was not allowed to tell him anything about it but did say that she was still in the ward.

James waited what seemed like half an hour rather than the ten minutes it took for the doctor to arrive. He looked at James's finger and said that directly they got into New York he must go to hospital for an x-ray and probably some treatment that could not be administered on the ship. The doctor was sure the wound was infected and said that he would give James a tetanus injection that would have to be followed up by two more at a later date. James said he had had a tetanus jab last night so surely wouldn't want another so soon after. Dr. Maiden said, of course not, but that he would have to have that one followed up later. It was quite a relief for James when the doctor told him he would make all the arrangements and to be back at the hospital about half an hour after the ship had tied up alongside. He told James he was not to do any physical work until after his visit to the hospital ashore and even then a decision would be made by him as to whether he would allow him to work on the return voyage, because it would be very unlikely he would be flown back to England. He said that he would give James a letter to give to the main reception desk in the hospital and that he would be requesting a report on James's condition which James would take to him. It was then that James remembered that he would not have an immigration card as it was his first trip and he put this to the doctor. Dr. Maiden made a phone call which from what he told him must have been to the Purser's office, for he told James that he should report to the Purser's office before reporting back to him at the ship's hospital.

After redressing his hand in much the same way as it had been done the night before, James was allowed to leave. He went firstly to the Chief Engineer's Office to let the office engineer know what was to happen to him and then went up on deck to see if he could find Susan. There were a lot of passengers on the boat deck as the Queen Mary approached the Hudson River with the Manhattan skyline on the ship's starboard quarter. James took one whole turn around the deck, trying not to bump into anyone, or make him-self conspicuous by his presence. He wasn't as smart as he would normally be, but to have shaved would have woken Bob up and he did not want that and it was shadow rather than really needing a shave anyway.

He was on his second circuit around the boat deck when he spotted Susan, who was obviously looking for him. Their eyes met and James indicated to her to move over to the hand rails under the boat she was standing near. She was still on her own of course so he was able to fall in beside her as though he was just there to see the Statue of Liberty as they went by it the same as everybody else. Directly James stood beside her she noticed his hand and asked what he had done to it. He said he had had to go to the hospital and while being treated tried to find out how Carol was. Susan wanted to know what they had told him and started to cry when he told her that they had more or less told him to mind his own business only that she was still in the hospital. Without drawing attention to himself, James could not do anything about Susan crying, though to her credit, it was very brief and she tried to cover it up by making out she had got something in her eye. She apologised to James but told him

Carol was still very poorly and was going to be transferred to hospital in New York directly they got tied up. She had been to visit her in the hospital; she was awake but the doctors did not know exactly what was wrong with her. "What do you think it might be?" James asked, just in case Susan had any idea what had caused her to become unconscious; did she think it could have been food poisoning?

"No it could not have been that because we ate the same thing – starter main course and sweet. However, Carol did meet a bloke the night before," she said, "who was a bit over friendly but who said he would see her again last night." She was alright when she left the restaurant and went back to the cabin where they parted and Susan went up to meet James, but after doing some of the packing she must have gone to meet the bloke and according to Carol had a couple of drinks. It was when she got back to the cabin after meeting him and having a drink that she became ill and passed out. "The doctors don't think it is alcoholic poisoning but something he put in her drink, but they cannot say what. Whatever it is it has had a very bad effect on her and it is going to spoil our holiday if they cannot find out what it is very quickly. Uncle Fred is doing his best to find the bloke but can only go on Carol's description of him for she did not know his name."

"Your uncle has obviously seen her then," James suggested.

"Oh yes," Susan replied "and if he finds him I don't fancy his chances, for Fred is very upset that our holiday is going to be spoilt."

By the time Susan had completely told James about Carol they were going past the Statue of Liberty. With the sun shining on it and the brilliant green against the blue sky she looked magnificent but seemed smaller than James had imagined, but then realised they were quite a long way away from it. Susan too was excited at seeing it but got upset again because Carol should have been there seeing it too. What was she going to do when they docked, James asked, to which Susan said her uncle Fred was going to go onto the dockside and try to find her aunt and explain what was happening. Fred and Freda were cousins-in-law and knew one another quite well. Although Freda would not be looking for Fred, he would know her when he saw her and intended getting her on board, which in his position would not be too difficult.

After passing the statue and Manhattan, the passenger numbers on deck started to thin out, especially those about them. Susan again clasped James's hand and squeezed it tenderly. It was as they were approaching pier ninety that a Master at Arms came towards them and on reaching them asked Susan if that was her name, when told yes, he said Fred would be with her as soon as he could which would not be long once he was told exactly where she was. "Shall I stay here with you or should I go?" James asked, because he knew he could get into trouble, but Susan said she had told Uncle Fred about him and he had tipped her the wink. He kept her company, chatting for less than ten minutes before her uncle appeared looking quite flustered. "What is going to be happening and are they going to have to take Carol to hospital ashore?" Fred nodded to James and suggested that he leave them now but promised he would find him later and let him know how things went. He asked what his cabin number was in the engineer's quarters and promised he would contact him. Susan said she hoped she would get a call from James at some time after her return to England and did he still have the address and telephone number she had given him. He said he had and that he would definitely contact her even if they couldn't meet between trips. She hoped his hand would heel and be better soon and she went one way with her uncle as James went the other.

James was worried, for he had no idea what was going to happen to him and even more if it was going to cost a lot of money, for he knew it would not be under national health. He went down to the cabin where Bob was ready to go down to the boiler room. He asked James what was going to be happening, to which he said he didn't know but would let him know when he got back to the ship and be able to say whether he would be doing the planned run ashore that night with the other lads.

James wondered if he should go to the hospital in uniform or his shore cloths and decided he would keep on what he was dressed in. They had been tied up for about half an hour when he went back to the ship's hospital to find out what was to be done with him. Sister Jean was still on duty and said that he was right to stay in uniform because that way it was proof he was ship's staff and an officer, and with the arrangements that were being made for him it would not cost him anything. That was all James wanted to know and waited as he was told to, as he would be collected and taken to the hospital ashore. He had been waiting only a little while when Jean came back to him and said it would be about an hour before he would be collected and there would be time for him to go up and get his immigration card if he went to the Purser's office, but to make sure he was seen right away because if he got in the queue he might be late for the hospital pick up.

James went up to the Purser's Office and explained his situation and was taken by one of the junior pursers to where the immigration was being done for crew members. The American Immigration Officer was very helpful and got him straight over to have his photo taken and within less than half an hour he had his immigration card and his discharge book that they must have got from whoever was holding it ready for him to be seen. He could now go ashore in any capacity either as a patient or tonight as a crew member. He went back down to the hospital to tell Jean he was ready to go whenever he was called for and as he waited he caught a glimpse of Carol being wheeled out in a chair wrapped up in a blanket. She saw James and gave a little wave but there was no opportunity to speak before she was gone. It was

52

only when he was picked up by an American male nurse and taken off the ship out to a waiting ambulance; unlike those in England this one was more like a long van. The male nurse told him there was already a patient inside but there was room for him together with the female nurse that was accompanying the other patient. James got into the ambulance and sat on a little drop down seat next to the nurse while the male nurse got in the front with the driver. It was after he sat down that he realised the other patient was in fact Carol, who must be being taken to the same hospital.

As the ambulance started moving off Carol realised it was James that they had been waiting for and could now speak to him. "What have you done to need to go to hospital?" Carol said. He told her he had had an accident and damaged his hand, but that it didn't matter about him, what was she doing having to go to hospital? The nurse sitting next to James obviously realised the two patients she was sitting with knew each other and so let them talk. "What was it that made you so ill Carol? You know Susan is worried to death about you."

"Yes, I know," said Carol.

"So is Uncle Fred. What happened then?" James pressed.

"How far is it to the hospital?" Carol asked the nurse, and when told it was about twenty minutes away she started to relay what had happened after Susan had left her to come up to the boat deck to see him.

"When Susan left the cabin I started packing my cases and putting some of her clothes out on her bed that I knew she would have to pack in her cases when she came back after meeting you. I finished the packing in about three quarters of an hour and went to the cabin class bar where I had briefly met a guy the night before who asked me if I would like to have a drink with him the next night. Seeing that Susan was with you and had not got back to the cabin when my packing was finished, I thought I might as well go and see if he was in the bar, knowing that if I was not in the cabin when she got back from seeing you, Susan would know where I would be. The chap I met the night before was there, and when he saw me he came over and renewed his acquaintance. He seemed alright, a bit flash perhaps and a bit big headed but other than that seemed quite affable to talk to. The silly thing is, I still don't know his name for I didn't ask him what it was. He asked me what I wanted to drink and I said I rather fancied one of the cocktails I had seen some of the other ladies drinking. He called a waiter over and when I told him which cocktail I wanted he ordered it for me and a large whisky for himself. We drank our drinks while we chatted and the cocktail tasted lovely, it had been a good choice. I asked what it consisted of to which he said he didn't know and called the waiter over. The waiter said it was the barman's speciality and that he didn't know exactly what went into it. My host asked me if I would like another and I said yes, and that he was being very generous. It was after going to the bathroom and nearly finishing my second drink that I started to feel funny and said so, but boyo said it was probably because I wasn't used to what I was drinking. He offered to take me back to my cabin to which I said I would be alright and could get back to the cabin on my own. However, he insisted and after picking up my handbag and stole we started heading to our cabin. I was hoping Susan was back by the time we got to it but of course she wasn't. It was when he started coming on to me that I began getting into a bit of a panic. I thanked him for seeing me back but asked him if he would go. At that time he had not got into the cabin but started to push me into it. He was getting heavy and I told him if he didn't get out I would start screaming. I was dreading what he was going to do to me, and what with the effort of trying to push him away from me and feeling by now quite sort of light headed, I must have passed out. I think someone must have come along for I don't think he did anything bad to me, but must have done a runner. I think I must have come to for a minute or so for I seem to remember a lady asking me if I was alright, it could have been the stewardess, I am just not sure." James told her what he knew about it which wasn't much, only what Susan had told him.

"Are you sure you did not catch his name and was he American, English or foreign by his accent?"

"He certainly had an accent but I am not very good at them, but it might have been a bit northern or perhaps a bit Irish, the only thing I am certain of is that he was not from south of London, wasn't American nor Scottish or Welsh." James wanted to know if it was possible he could have spiked her drink while she was in the ladies room to which she said yes she supposed so, but what with? "I think that is what they are taking you to hospital for to try and identify if he did put anything in your drink."

"Like what?" Carol asked. Turning to the nurse, she asked if that was why she was being taken to hospital. The nurse was very cagy with her answer by saying, it could be, but she had not seen any paper work and did not know what the Queen Mary's doctor had asked them to do. James was sure she would not have told her whether she knew or not. Carol asked James if he thought that is what had happened and James answered the question with one of his own, that being, did she think the bloke in question was well travelled, did he talk about all the places or countries he visited. "Well, yes, he did a bit but some of it could have been exaggeration, just showing off." James went on to ask about how old she thought he might be to which she said at a guess about thirtyish.

"Do you know what Spanish Fly is?" he asked Carol and also looked at the nurse. Carol said she had no idea but the American nurse said she had heard of it, wasn't it a sort of potion that aroused women's sexual desires, but had no idea what it consisted of or what any side effects were. It was just a thought James had, but of course had only heard about it himself from stories told by men who had been abroad talking in the pub. The nurse said she would mention it when they got to the hospital that was now only a very short distance away to whoever was going to examine Carol. As she was saying it, the ambulance slowed down and soon came to a stop. The driver and the male nurse got out and came round the back to open the doors of the ambulance and to get Carol organised to be taken into the hospital. You will come with me, Mr. Royston, as you can walk but Miss Armrod will have to wait for a porter to bring a wheel chair for we can't have her walking. James realised Carol would be being taken to a different part of the hospital to him so took the opportunity to say cheerio and that he would probably see her some time if she was ever at Susan's house when he called which he had promised to do during a leave, and hoped she would soon be out of hospital and enjoying her holiday with her aunt.

James, escorted by the mail nurse, was taken to the accident department where he had to hand over the paperwork the ship's doctor had given him. The male nurse said he would be alright now and made his way back to the ambulance. James was told to sit in a waiting area and that he would be seen by somebody fairly soon. He asked if he could have a drink of water and was told he could, but only a little. While he sat there for what seemed like an age with only nurses passing by, a man that looked as though he had run into a bus or had had a very bad fall right onto his face staggered in. He looked like a drunk or a junky but whatever he was he was carted away very quickly.

A rather large nurse, James guessed to be in her early thirties, dressed in a very smart uniform and white stockings, cap and shoes came out through the same door the drunk had been taken and went over to James and asked his name; when told it was James Royston, asked if he was the officer from the Queen Mary. James nodded and said, "Yes."

"You have to see Dr. Emil J. Shooter," she said, "he is very good with broken bones and limb injuries." She took him through the door she had just come through and down several passage ways before getting to a lift, "We are just going to take the elevator to the sixth floor where Dr. Shooter's office is and you should soon know what is going to happen to your hand." James was shown into a spacious wood panelled room where he was introduced to a little man with thinning grey hair and the biggest spectacles James had ever seen. His short white coat was spotless with a stethoscope folded in his pocket. James was surprised how deep and powerful sounding his voice was for such a small man, and in a very strong American accent said, "I am Doctor Shooter and I am going to have a look at your damaged hand, but before I do can I ask you how long ago did you hurt it and how did the accident happen?" James explained the same to him as he had to Sister Jean and told the doctor that it had happened about three o'clock that morning, it being now nearly four in the afternoon, about eleven hours ago. "How much pain is it causing you at the moment?" the doctor asked him, and had he been taking pain killers and what were they. James said his hand was hurting like hell, and that he had taken pain killers about two hours ago and that he still had two in his pocket. The doctor asked to see them and knew immediately what they were. Turning to the nurse he said, "All right, nurse, take him into the treatment room and start removing the dressing and I will be there in just a few minutes." True to his word, before the nurse had got all the dressing off the doctor was with them and looked closely as the fingers as they became exposed. "Oh!" the doctor said, "I think we have a good one here, nurse." He took James's hand, which was looking even worse than when Doctor Maiden looked at it, for it was almost twice the size of his other hand and looked very angry. Doctor Shooter calmly informed James that his middle finger was definitely broken but he was not sure if the ones either side were; they could just be badly bruised, he would know for certain after they had been x-rayed. He said the finger was poisoned and that the middle nail would have to be removed and maybe the ones either side. He turned to the nurse again and asked her if she would put a light dressing on the hand and take James down for an x-ray and that if she waited for the plate, she could bring it back with them.

The x-ray room was on the same floor as Doctor Shooter's office so they did not have far to go. When they got there no one was waiting, so James went in without any delay. The x-ray was all done within ten minutes and he found himself sitting outside with the nurse with whom he made small talk whist waiting for the negative to be processed. Only fifteen minutes passed before the radiologist came out with a big brown envelope and gave it to the nurse. The nurse and James retraced their steps and were back with Dr. Shooter within half an hour of leaving him. "Well, young man, let's see what we have got here and what work I have to do." He put the x-ray up to the light and said, more or less under his breath, "I see." He studied it for a good five minutes before he turned to James and said, "I am afraid I have got to operate on your hand and hope to save your middle finger. If I don't operate on it, and quickly, that is certainly what is going to happen, not to mention the possibility of your hand as well. I can see now why Dr. Maiden sent you here to me, because although I have unfortunately never been on either of the Queens, I am sure they would have had a job to cope with this injury with their hospital facilities. Stitching the wound has helped, but it is the infection that I am concerned about. I will arrange right now to have an operating theatre made available so if you will go with the nurse she will get you ready for surgery."

The nurse that had remained during the examination asked him to follow her and led him out of Dr. Shooter's office and back down in the lift or elevator as she kept calling it to the first floor. He was taken into a ward that looked to James just like a bed sitting room in England. It had a bed, albeit a hospital bed, two arm chairs, a sideboard type cupboard come dressing table with mirror over it, a wash basin and what James presumed was a toilet behind the door in one corner of the room. The room was carpeted with powder blue carpet and the curtains that would go round the bed if they were pulled matched those at the window. The room was warm although there was no radiator to be seen. James still wondered who would be paying for this luxury and asked the nurse who said she did not know - she was a nurse not an administrator. She went over to the chest of drawers and took out an operating gown and put it on the bed alongside the towels and asked James to get undressed as she pulled the curtains round the bed. His hand, which was now without any dressing on it at all, was so painful he didn't know what to do with it. The nurse had carried his uniform jacket and his cap when they left the surgeon's office and had put them on one of the chairs, leaving him to remove the rest of his clothes behind the curtain. He found this so difficult he had to ask the nurse for assistance. Again, it was the buttons that were difficult. When he was dressed in the operating gown the tapes, at the back of which the nurse had tied for him, he asked if it was possible to have some more pain killers but was told no, not prior to an operation. The nurse told James to lie on the bed and just relax, she realised he was in a lot of pain but the more relaxed he was when he went on the operating table, the better. After laying on the bed for half an hour or so and being very nearly asleep, a very tall man entered the room dressed in light blue operating gear with a stethoscope around his neck and some papers in his hand and told James he was Dr. Swan and would be the anaesthetist assisting Dr. Shooter. Dr. Swan asked James all the usual questions anaesthetists ask, confirming his full name, date of birth, and address, that James gave as the RMS Queen Mary, and then answered the questions if he was allergic to anything including anaesthetic, or had anything wrong with him that he should notify them of. When James said there was nothing, Dr. Swan said he was just going to give him a little injection that would make him start to feel drowsy in a few minutes but not to worry, they would be taking him down to the operating theatre in a few minutes to sort him out, as he put it. Being nearly asleep when Dr. Swan came in, it did not take James long before he was not just drowsy but fast asleep. He did not know another thing until he opened his eyes back in the room and bed that he had left.

James, on opening his eyes, recognised where he was but his head was in a jumble and he thought he was dreaming when into his eye line appeared Susan. His voice sounded very croaky and his mouth and throat was as dry as he had ever known it, this of course due to the anaesthetic. He asked, "Is that really you Susan?" he managed to get out, but before Susan moved towards him a nurse, not the one that had been with him before the operation, leant over him from the opposite side of the bed to what James was looking and asked him if he was alright and whether he felt sick. James, in a dozy sort of way, remembered what he was in hospital for and lifted up his left hand to look at it. He was surprised to see how big the dressing was and asked the nurse what had been done to it. She said Dr. Shooter would tell him when he did his rounds later on that evening. "What time is it?" James asked the question in general and both the nurse and Susan answered in unison that it was twenty past six. He tried to work out how long he had been out of the game but could not remember at what time he went to the theatre. He asked the nurse how long the operation took and she said two and a half hours. Susan by now had dragged an arm chair over to the side of his bed and before sitting down into it lent over and kissed him. "Could I have a drink of water please?" he asked, "My mouth is so dry." The nurse fetched over a small glass and poured him some cool water from a thermal jug, she put the jug down and her hand under James's shoulders to move him up and forward to put another pillow under and behind his head so he was almost sitting up to drink. The water was so refreshing he wanted more, but the nurse suggested that he drink little and often in sips so he did not make himself feel sick. He asked if he would be able to have anything to eat and was told no not until breakfast tomorrow. He now turned his full attention to Susan. "What are you doing here? I thought you were going on holiday with your Aunt Freda?"

"Yes, we are," Susan told him, "but Carol is still in this hospital and will be until at least tomorrow, so Freda is with Carol at the moment and I have come down here to see you then when I leave here I will return to Carol and at the end of visiting, Freda and I will drive the two hours to her place for the night and return here tomorrow to see if they are going to release her. I will call in to see you again then and find out hopefully what is going to happen to you."

"Have they found out what it is that made her ill?" James asked, to which Susan answered she did not know what Spanish Fly was but they had found something nasty in Carol's blood that should not have been there and was nothing to do with food poisoning, so he could be right. "I will see Carol tomorrow before I come to you so will let you know what they have told her." As she was getting up from the chair she asked James if his hand was still painful to which he replied he could not feel a thing. Susan said, as she kissed him again this time for longer and more tenderly, that he would. Susan picked up her coat and put it over her arm as she went out of the door saying cheerio and thanked the nurse as she did so.

James, being alone with just the nurse busying about, asked her if she thought he would be kept in hospital for long. Her answer was that he would not be kept in any longer than necessary, which did nothing at all to answer his question, but he would know more after the doctor had seen him later. The nurse had put a tray on wheels over his bed with the thermal water jug and the glass he had used onto it and warned him what she had said – not too much at a time but to drink it often. She said she had to see to other tasks but would be back before doctors rounds so would be there for anything James wanted. She asked him if he would be able to get to and from the toilet alright, and was there anything else she could do before leaving him.

James said no, there was nothing else he wanted at the moment unless she could get him a book or an interesting magazine to read, but not a newspaper. She said there was a bible in the room somewhere, would that do? Smiling, she said she would see what she could find.

It was approaching nine o'clock when the nurse returned, about ten minutes before Dr. Shooter, who was now dressed in a very smart lounge suit with a hankie in the breast pocket and a very smart red silk tie. "Well, young man, how do you feel?" he said, "I had quite a job to do on your hand. It was very badly poisoned and in such a short time, the bone of the middle finger was crushed as well as broken, the fore finger bone was broken and the index finger had a crack rather than a break. It was hard work setting it all up but I think when the swelling goes down and the bones knit, if you exercise your fingers after the stitches come out you should regain the full use of your fingers and hand. I must say that by sending you ashore to this hospital Dr. Maiden on the ship has saved your hand as much as I have, for you certainly did your best to lose it. From what you told me, it might have been better to let the floor plate do its own thing and get it out of the bilge or wherever it was going to go afterwards, rather than trying to catch it. All that said, I want you to take this letter back with you to the ship and give it to Dr. Maiden personally. Please tell him I will be back in the hospital at eight o'clock tomorrow morning and if he wants to speak to me he will get me on the extension number on the front of the envelope. I have given him that because if there is any complication, I will deal with it myself; not that I think there will be, but just as a precaution. Do you have any questions for me now before I leave?" James thanked the doctor for what he had done for him and asked when it would be likely he would be able to work again. The doctor said the only thing he was certain of was that he would not be working before the Queen Mary got back to Southampton. He had made certain recommendations and given some advice to Dr. Maiden, but of course it would be up to him what he did about it. "The only advice I would give you though is to wear working gloves in future especially when working on hot, dirty or heavy jobs. Whatever it was that got into the wound was very nasty, but the drugs we have used as well as the repair work I have done should have done the trick. I hope, for all the right reasons, I will not be seeing you again, James, but good luck for the future and it has been a pleasure meeting you." He put out his hand to shake James's, turned, and went to leave the room. As he got to the door, James thanked him again and said he might see him again if he came to England on the Queen Mary. Dr. Shooter smiled, opened the door, thanked the nurse and was gone.

"You are a very lucky man, James, for you have just been attended to by the best surgeon in this hospital."

James was woken by the first nurse he had met on arrival the day before, she was back on duty and asked James if there was anything she could do to help him get washed and dressed. He said he needed a shave, but of course had no gear with him. She went off to see what she could find in way of a razor and while she was gone James managed to go to the toilet and have a wash all with the use of only one hand. He wanted to clean his teeth but there was no toothbrush or toothpaste. Rather than worry the nurse again, he thought it wouldn't matter if they weren't cleaned for just a few more hours, but his mouth felt like the bottom of a bird cage. He had managed to get his underwear on and his shirt and trousers but could not get his socks on, do up his tie or tie his shoe laces. When the nurse returned she brought back with her, an electric razor, a toothbrush and paste and a packet of wipes, God knows where she got them but James was pleased she had. She helped him put his socks on, tied up his shoes and tied his tie as best she could under James's instruction.

"Right then," she said, "while you are shaving I will go and get you some breakfast – are you fussy or will you be satisfied to eat what I bring?"

"No, I am not fussy and I am quite hungry now but I would prefer tea rather than coffee if that is possible and could you do me a favour and bring me some strong pain killers as my hand is hurting like hell now that whatever the anaesthetist gave me has worn off." The nurse left and James plugged the razor into the socket by the mirror over the chest of drawers. It was a good razor and gave James a good shave seeing he always used a wet razor. He was reading one of the magazines the last nurse had managed to acquire for him when his breakfast arrived. The nurse apologised if it was a bit cold, but she had had to bring it from quite a distance. James thanked her so much for what she had done for him but she just said she was only doing her job. She told James not to get back up onto the bed but to sit in the chair and she would adjust the tray that had gone over the bed that had had his water on. James sat and ate the breakfast consisting of fruit juice, porridge, scrambled egg on toast, a small waffle with maple syrup and a cup of tea. He joked with the nurse by saying he would like to move in if the food was like this all the time, but would give it all up if only his hand would stop hurting. The nurse poured some water for him and gave him two painkillers, different from any he had had before, which she hoped would at least reduce the pain within about a quarter of an hour.

He told her he had read all the magazines he had been given, so was it possible that if he was going to be retained in the hospital until six o'clock, could she get hold of a book to read; she said she would do her best to find something suitable. After she left, there was a tap on the door and a cleaner was standing there armed to the teeth with everything you could imagine to change beds renew towels and clean and polish rooms, bathrooms and toilets, you name it, she had it on her trolley. Being black, her hair was very curly and close cropped and the earrings she was wearing were something to be seen; they were surely not real gold but they could be mistaken for it. She had on a very smart uniform and in what James took to be a West Indian accent asked James if it was ok for her to clean his room as he would be moving out of it later that day. He said, "Yes, of course, if I will not be in your way." She said not to worry she would work around him. She was about half way through her cleaning chores when there was another knock on the door, this time it was Susan.

"Hello, Susan," James said giving her a peck on the cheek.

"What is happening?" Susan first of all asked him how his hand was and was it still very painful.

"Not at that moment," he explained, as the nurse had given him some strong pain killers that had cut in and so his hand was feeling not too bad.

"What about Carol?" he enquired, "Is she going to be released today and have they told her what it was that made her so ill?" Susan explained that it was some substance that she could not remember the name of and yes it was something which can induce sexual desire and activity if used in very small doses. The doctor that was attending to her said that if the amount they found in her blood had been only a small amount more it might well have killed her, and if she had not been rushed down to the ship's hospital and the doctors not taken the actions they did, she could have gone into a deep coma and died.

"I wonder if they have found the stupid pervert who she met up with or if he left the ship before being identified?" Susan said she didn't know, but what she did know was that if her Uncle Fred got hold of him he would wish he had never been born.

So what were her plans now, James wanted to know. Susan said that when she left Carol she was getting dressed and ready to start her holiday with their aunt, and would be leaving the hospital as soon as her aunt had settled the hospital bill, which Carol should be able to claim back on the holiday insurance she had taken out before they left. Susan asked James what was happening to him, to which he replied, all he knew at that moment was that he was to leave the hospital at six o'clock and report back to the ship.

"And what then?" she wanted to know.

"I really am not sure," he said, "it will depend on what the doctor in this hospital has put in his letter to the doctor on the ship and what he will do about it. I will let you know the first time I speak to you when you and I are home." The cleaner was in the bathroom cleaning so James took Susan in his arms and kissed her tenderly and said, "Look after yourself and have a good holiday and remember me to Carol." With that she broke away from him and turned and walked out of the door, leaving James wondering when and if he would see her again.

CHAPTER 3

Having to leave his room that had been thoroughly cleaned and sitting in a lounge on the first floor until six o'clock wasn't really James's cup of tea, for although he had a book to read, killing time he found very hard going. He got terribly bored and took advantage of as long a lunch as he could stretch it out for. He was called upon by a nurse who asked him if he would follow her to an office and sign some papers that would finalise his treatment and ensure payment was made for it; not by him, he was pleased to hear. By the time he left the office after asking about arrangements for leaving the hospital it was quarter to six. He had been told in the office that a hospital car would be taking him back to the Queen Mary and that the driver would pick him up from the front entrance lobby at six o'clock, so would he go down there now and did he know where to go. He told them he knew where to go and thanked them for all they had done for him, giving back the book he had borrowed as he left. Still in uniform, albeit now with his jacket over his shoulders with only one arm down a sleeve due to the dressing and arm sling his left arm was in and carrying his cap, he went down to the ground floor entrance lobby and within five minutes a driver displaying a driver's security badge asked him to follow him to his car.

At six o'clock in New York the traffic was heavy with yellow cabs everywhere apart from all the other vehicles. It took nearly an hour to get back to Pier Ninety where the Mary was berthed. The driver got him as near to the ship as he could before letting him out. James gave the driver fifty cents as a tip and wished him well. As he drove off, James donned his cap and made his way to the passenger gangway at the bottom of which were two Masters at Arms. He showed his Cunard pass and was allowed to make his way aboard. As he entered the ship at the main lobby there was another Master at Arms, this time being Uncle Fred. "Hello sir," Fred welcomed him, for being an officer he had to do that. "I see they have let you out of hospital – how is the hand?" James said it was very painful but as well as it could be with what the hospital had done to it. He asked Fred if it would be possible to have a get together either in his cabin or if he preferred ashore somewhere when he came off duty, to have a chat about the Carol situation. He explained that he had to report to the doctor at the hospital as soon as he could but if they could meet somewhere he would appreciate it. Fred thought about it and said, "I come off duty at eight o'clock what about seeing you in the Market Diner across from Pier Ninety at nine o'clock." James said that sounded fine and would see him there.

He made his way down to the hospital and on arrival met yet another nurse who was younger than those he had thus far seen. She said hello and when James told her what he was there for, that he had to see Dr. Maiden, she said, "Will you just hang on a bit while I find out what I have to do, for I am the junior nursing sister and this is my first trip." She went over to the desk and looked in a book and going down the list turned to James and said, "Are you James Royston, an engineer?"

"Yes, that is me," James said.

"Alright then, Dr. Maiden has left a note in the book saying he is to be called when you report from the hospital ashore." She closed the book and picked up the telephone and on getting through explained that James was there and what was she to do. She was told that Dr. Maiden would be there in about ten minutes. Being observant as she was, she asked James how his hand was and what he had done to it.

James said it was a long story, but that he had managed to badly damage his hand and left it at that.

While they waited for the doctor, James asked her what her name was and how did she like being at sea if this was her first trip. She said her name was Jane and that she finished her training some years before in the Royal Hospital in Portsmouth, but decided she would like to try and see the world so applied to go to sea and carry on nursing and satisfy two ambitions. With no passengers yet on board, things were very quiet and so when Dr. Maiden came in, not in uniform, he was able to give all his attention to James. He asked him if he had the paper work he had been given at the hospital. James gave him all the paperwork and the letter Dr. Shooter said he had to hand to the doctor in person. Dr. Maiden took the envelope and opening it, read it very carefully. He either read it twice or found Dr. Shooter's hand writing hard to read for it must have been a good five minutes before he spoke. When he did, he said to James, "You have been a very lucky young man because according to Dr. Shooter, you have been very lucky not to lose at least a finger if not a hand and in getting Dr. shooter, you have had one of the best if not the best surgeon in New York if not America to operate on your hand. I could have done a job on it, but seeing we were so close to New York it was better that I leave it alone as far as an operation was concerned and leave it to someone who had more knowledge in that field and had far better facilities than we have on the ship. However, what are we going to do with you now? In his letter Dr. Shooter has been emphatic that you must not be employed for at least two weeks and certainly not using your left hand, which by looking at the dressing would be impossible anyway. So, I have two alternatives, I will put you on the sick, the same as I would in general practice ashore, and can either fly you home or with the Chief Engineer and Captain's approval let you remain on board as a passenger. Would you have a choice?" James did not have to think for very long and immediately plumped for remaining on board as a passenger.

"When would he know by?" he asked Dr. Maiden, as the ship was due to sail tomorrow.

"You will know by nine o'clock in the morning, which will give you plenty of time to get yourself sorted out and the Pursers to arrange a flight for you before we sail at two in the afternoon." James asked if it would be alright for him to go ashore tonight if he could manage to get out of his uniform and into some casual clothes, to which Dr. Maiden said yes, but to be careful with that hand and no alcohol.

"How are you off for pain killers?" he asked, and when James told him he only had two that the hospital ashore had given him, the doctor asked Jane to give him six more to see him through until the next morning. "I will see you here at nine and we will decide then what is going to happen." James thanked Dr. Maiden for all he had done and apologised for taking up so much of his time and left to go back to his cabin.

When he got there, Bob was dressed and ready to go ashore. "What's happening and how is your hand?" Bob wanted to know and was he going to be able to go ashore with the group. Bob apologised for not getting to the hospital but said it was impossible. James explained what had happened from start to finish and what might happen to him, but no, he would not be going for a run ashore with the boys but might go over to the Market Diner later on just to get some fresh air. Bob said it was a shame he had done his hand in as he knew how much he wanted to get to Broadway to see the sights at night time, but the accident was going to prevent it. Before they went ashore, all those that were going came round to see how he was and that they were sorry he would not be joining them. They set off at eight fifteen, which gave James only half an hour to get changed before going over to the Diner. Releasing his arm from the sling after getting his jacket off - that wasn't easy - and getting into a heavy jumper he had brought with him, he kept every other part of his uniform on. It did occur to him that it was going to be a job getting his shirt off, but as the nurse in the

70

hospital had got it on for him, with help he should be able to get it off.

He left the ship at ten minutes to nine and as it happened saw Fred coming down the crew's gangway as he got to it, so waited for him. They shook hands, for they were now on level terms, so to speak. Fred was nicely dressed in casual gear with a leather jacket and looked even taller than when in his uniform. It only took them ten minutes to walk over to the Diner where they managed to get a table for two in a corner. There were loads of the Queen Mary's crew in there, some of which looked the worst for wear. Fred asked James what he would like to drink and James said a white coffee please, because the doctor had warned him off alcohol. Fred said that was fine, but did James mind if he had a beer. When the waitress came over to take their order Fred asked for a white coffee and a beer and turning to James asked would he fancy a cheese omelette and fries, they were brilliant in there. James, having had nothing to eat since his hospital lunch, suddenly felt hungry and readily agreed to Fred's suggestion. While they waited for their order to come, they got straight down to talking about Fred's two nieces. James asked had he had any luck with trying to find out who the bloke was that was seeing Carol. Fred said that he was limited to what he could do as a Master at Arms but that he had been to the Staff Captain who had been as helpful as he could by getting the Senior Purser, Chief Steward and Doctor together with Fred into his day room to discuss the situation. Being so close to getting to New York, between them they did not have much time and with only Carol's description to go on to try to identify who the culprit was. Could it have been a fellow passenger or perhaps a crew member? But had it been a crew member, how could it have been done. If it was a fellow passenger there was now no way they could do anything about it for they were long gone and if it had been reported to the police there was not a lot they could do about it either for the same reason. The beer and coffee and the biggest omelettes James had ever seen arrived almost covering the plates, with really chunky French fries (chips) and some coleslaw, which James had never come across before. As they tucked into the delicious meal, James asked what, if any, theory Fred had. He said he had the feeling it was not a passenger, why he thought it was because on the Queen Elizabeth, his usual ship, he thought he remembered something similar happening a few trips ago. James put it to Fred that was it possible to find out if there were any crew members that were on the Mary this trip that were on the Lizzy on that trip. Fred agreed that James had a good point but how could it be checked upon.

"It could be checked from the Southampton office or head office in Liverpool if it came to it, but how long would it take to get the information back. If the Captain telephoned from New York, any names that were possibilities could always be radioed back while on our way back to Southampton." The thing was, Fred wasn't sure how many trips ago he remembered hearing about it, but as James said, if a check was made say four trips back they would be able to see if there were any transfer from one ship to the other. Fred agreed it could be worth trying and would get onto it in the morning before they sailed in the afternoon.

"What is going to happen to you?" Fred asked, to which James replied that a decision was to be made in the morning, that he would know by nine o'clock whether he was going to be flown home or remain on board as a passenger and in what capacity. They finished their meal, for which Fred insisted on paying for after ordering another coffee and beer. "It is quite funny," Fred said, "that here we are sitting here together when it is not usual for officers to mix with the crew, when only a few days ago I nearly reported you for associating with passengers in inappropriate ways. It was Susan in particular that got you off the hook saying that it was them that got you talking and that she had taken a fancy to you. She is worried to death about Carol because she thinks it is her fault that what has happened to Carol would not have happened if they had remained together, because of meeting you." James said he realised there was an element of danger but that by being in the open was not like being in a female passenger's cabin. Fred explained how it worked and that the deck officers and radio officers got away with murder on the quiet but engineers are another kettle of fish. Anyway, did James have any feeling for Susan?

"I think you know the answer to that, Fred," James replied and went on to explain how he would like to sort of carry on where they had left off on the ship, when they can get together whenever he is on leave.

They sat and talked about how long Fred had been at sea and what ships he had been on and James explaining about himself what little of him there was compared with Fred. They were just about to leave the Diner when a lot of shouting started down at the bar and it wasn't many minutes before the first punch was thrown and all hell broke loose. There was an emergency fire door adjacent to where they were sitting and Fred said, "Let's get out of here." They managed to open the fire door with the crash handle and, followed by a few other diners that did not want to get involved, started walking back to the ship. They had barely got across the road when the whaling sirens of two, not one, police cars came tearing round the corner and pulling up with tyres smoking as they screeched to a halt outside of the Market Diner. James was, as well as a little scared, quite excited at the goings on, just like how you see it in the movies. He asked Fred if it was a common occurrence, to which Fred replied, "Only when other company or nationality ships are in. When it's only Cunarders in, there is not too much trouble. What we have done tonight I have had to do before but only a couple of times. A lot of the cause of it is because some of the crew go and give a unit of blood and get five dollars for it, they then come back to the Diner and blow the lot on getting drunk. I don't know what sparked tonight's incident but it is always wise to give it a wide berth if you can." As they got back to the ship and the crew's gangway, Fred told James his surname was Baker and that if he asked any of the Masters at Arms they would always fetch him. James thanked him for the meal and the chat, saying the next meal would be on him and that he would be in touch if he was going back on the ship and not flying. If he did have to fly back, he wished him all the best and hoped he would see him again some time if he and Susan's romance progressed, which he hoped it would. They shook hands and went back aboard up their separate gangways.

By the time James got back to the cabin his hand was giving him so much pain he took three painkillers instead of the two he should have taken but thought it would not do any harm and would help ease the pain quicker. Bob was not back yet, as James expected he wouldn't be. He managed to get his jumper off and with even more difficulty his shirt. Getting the sleeve over the dressing was a bit of a job, James thought for a minute he would have to tear the sleeve to get it off, but eventually with a bit of patience managed without incident. Getting his shoes and socks off was easier than he first thought it would be and getting into his pyjamas meant leaving his jacket off. Not only did the pain killers do their job in easing the pain in his hand but he must have gone straight off to sleep and a deep one at that for he never heard Bob come into the cabin and then go out again when he realised James was asleep.

It was just after seven when the pain in his hand woke him up. He clambered out of his bunk being very careful to not knock his hand and went over to the sink and got a drink of water and took two more pain killers. Bob woke when he heard James running the tap to have a wash as best as he could with one hand. He got his underwear on, together with his trousers and the big jumper he wore the night before and his slippers. He wondered what would be thought at the hospital if he went dressed as he was, but knowing how difficult getting dressed would be for him they should give him the benefit of the doubt until his dressing was made small enough to make getting dressed easier. Bob, now being awake, decided to talk for a while. James asked him how his evening had gone and had they enjoyed the show at radio City. Bob said it was a good show and it was a shame James could not be with them and at the Merchant Naval Club afterwards. He said they had got back after midnight and were coming back to the cabin for a night cap but realised he was asleep so went to Gordon's cabin and had a couple of beers there. He hoped he did not disturb James for it must have been close on two o'clock by the time he turned in. James asked Bob if he was going to get up and go in for breakfast, to which he said yes he was as soon as he was washed and dressed. They went in for breakfast together at eight o'clock where James had cereal and Bob the full English. Bob asked what was going to happen regarding the trip home and James said he would be learning what was happening in an hour's time, if he was either flying home or remaining on board as a passenger. There was no way he would be working. They left the dining room together and went back to the cabin where Bob got ready to go down below and James got dressed again with Bob's assistance. He put his socks and shoes on and tied the laces and helped him get his shirt on, which was easier because James had got out a short sleeved white shirt. He put his epaulets up instead of his jacket which served the purpose of being in uniform. Bob said he was going ashore for a last bit of shopping before having to go on watch at twelve o'clock, so was there anything James wanted. He said he could get him some sweets; anything would do, even chocolate if that was all he could find.

At nine o'clock James was at the hospital where Jean and Barbara were both on duty. He said hello and that he was there to see Dr. Maiden to learn what was to happen to him. They said that Jane had mentioned about him coming, and why, as part of the hand over. Jean asked him what he would prefer to do, to which James replied, he didn't think he was going to have a choice but that the decision would be made for him. "I know what I would like but don't think I will have a say in the matter."

It must have been about nine fifteen when both Dr. Maiden and Dr. Cummings came into the hospital. Dr. Maiden went straight over to James and said, "You are staying on board ship and will be a passenger under my care, that is to say, you will move out of the cabin you are in to a single passenger cabin and will have to report to me every day to check your hand. The rest of the time you will be a first class passenger in every way. You can eat in the main restaurant, be entertained in the main lounge and attend whatever bars you wish to drink in, if you can afford it! By making this decision the Captain has stuck his neck out but, wants you to do a job for him in conjunction with the Masters at Arms. If you go up to the Purser's Office they will tell you what cabin you've been allocated and, when you've got all your belongings together a steward will transfer it for you. When that is all done, the Captain would like to see you at one o'clock in his day cabin and I will see you here at two so I can have a look at your hand. What do you think of those arrangements?" James said he thought he had come out of it well but, of course, had an injury he would have preferred not to have.

He went down to his cabin and got all his clothes, wash gear and personal possessions together and waited for the steward to come and pick it up. The steward wasn't very obliging or helpful, in fact, downright anti. James could only think he was to be his bedroom steward and being a member of the crew would not get a tip like he would expect from a proper passenger. He reluctantly transferred all James's stuff to the allocated cabin and just dumped it on the bed and settee that the cabin had. It took James a little while to sort it out and utilise the hanging and drawer space. He was wondering while he was doing this whether any other engineer would jump on the band wagon and try the same stunt, not that James would recommend it for his hand was hurting him badly. When he had put all his gear away, he decided that seeing he had a couple of hours to spare before he had to go and see the captain, he would ask to see the Chief Engineer and apologise for letting him down by leaving him an engineer short for the homeward voyage. He went to the Chief Engineer's Office and was told that he was engaged but that he could see the Staff Chief. This was agreed to and so James went into the Staff Chief Engineer's day cabin. James after saying good morning to the Staff Chief, Bill Richards, apologised for hurting himself and being the cause of an engineer short for the voyage home. Bill Richards was a big man and well respected by the engineers, even more so in some cases than the Chief, Ron Bright. They had both been with Cunard for many years hence their positions. Bill Richards asked James about his hand and how he had caused the injury and what had been done at the hospital ashore. James explained to him what good treatment he had had from the hospital and how grateful he was. "I believe you have to see the Captain at one o'clock, do you know what for?" James said he didn't and the Staff Chief didn't enlarge on it. Bill Richards thanked James for having the courtesy to come and see him and explain the situation. "I hope the word doesn't go round that you are having a bloody good time for others to think they will be getting the same treatment, so I would appreciate you keeping a low profile. It's only due to what the Captain wants you to do that this course of action has been taken and I hope what he wants to achieve is successful. Off you go and do a good job."

At one o'clock James reported to the Captain's day cabin where he was joined by the Staff Captain and Fred. "Sit down, gentlemen," the Captain invited, "and smoke if you must." Going on, he said, "Seeing it is coming up for lunch time, would you like a drink?" The Captain had a whisky and water, the Staff Captain had a gin and tonic, Fred had a small beer and James had a soft drink due to the pain killers he was taking. Captain Baron opened the proceedings by saying how upsetting it had been for him to learn that one of his passengers had had to be taken to hospital due to a serious incident on his ship. His reason for calling this meeting was to find out if the culprit could possibly be a member of his ship's staff. He explained that he had telephoned both the Southampton and Liverpool offices and was expecting a reply within the next twenty four hours. The information he had asked for at the suggestion of Mr. Baker, and he believed, Mr. Royston, was for the crew's lists of both ships the Queen Elizabeth and the Mary to be checked and any names that showed up as a transfer from the Queen Elizabeth to the Mary for this trip to be sent through to him. The other thing he wanted done was the reason he was retaining James, who would normally have been flown home as a result of the injury he had sustained to his hand. He turned to James and said, "You may not be able to work in the engine room because of your injury, but you can make a jolly good detective. I want you and Mr. Baker to work together to discover if we have a crew member abusing the passengers, as with Mr. Baker's niece. I cannot give you cash for any liquid entertainment you might have to purchase in way of investigation but you will be given my card that gives the barmen the authority to put the cost onto my bar bill, this, I may say, will be carefully monitored. If you buy a drink for yourself, Mr. Royston, you pay for it, but if it is as a result of doing what we are asking you to do then you can charge me. I want a verbal report from both of you each morning at nine o'clock and hope we can uncover something before we arrive back in Southampton. If a name or names come through from the Southampton or Liverpool offices that when followed up come to nothing we have not lost anything, but it could be a start. I am relying on the two of you to work together as much as you can without either of you causing suspicion from among the Officers and crew. Slowly, slowly catch the monkey is the name of the game, and let's hope we can have some success. It might of course be that the man we are seeking was a genuine passenger who is now long gone. Thank you gentlemen, you must now excuse me but I have a ship to sail." The Staff Captain remained with the Captain as Fred and James went out, James to go for his lunch and Fred to go on duty. He said he was pleased the Captain had been sympathetic to Carol's plight and hoped he and the young engineer could at least establish between them if it was a member of the crew who had carried out such a horrendous act; whoever it was, they had obviously over done the dose they put in Carol's drink and really wanted to go to town on her, for after all she is a very attractive young lady. Now that he was put on a sort of floating duty whereby he could be available day or night, and being able to have the whole run of the ship regarding First, Second and Tourist (Third class) passengers, there was a good chance if there was somebody, he and James between them should find him.

After finishing his lunch, James went up onto the boat deck where there were many passengers, most of them on the starboard side where they were waving to those seeing them off from the jetty. There were quite a number on the port side too but Pier Ninety-one was unoccupied. He took a slow stroll around the boat deck taking particular notice of young men who appeared to be on their own. It was so difficult only having a brief description rather than say a photograph to identify someone by. It struck James that the ship's photographer might have kept the negatives of the outgoing passengers in which case they might be worth looking at to see if anyone in any photos taken in cabin class state rooms could be the man they were looking to find. He went round the deck twice before deciding it was time to go down to the hospital as requested by Dr. Maiden. It occurred to James as he made his way to the hospital that if boat drill was held as they were going down the Hudson River, Dr. Maiden could not attend because he would be dealing with a patient; this would be good for James too, for if he had to see the doctor he could not attend boat drill either.

Dr. Maiden was waiting for James when he got to the hospital together with Sister Barbara. It was when he talked to nurse Jane the previous evening that he found out they preferred being called sister rather than nurse because their title was Nursing Sister. Dr. Maiden asked Barbara to remove the dressing so that he could look at Dr. Shooter's handy work. As Barbara took James over to a chair and drew up a trolley with instruments on it, three blasts of the ships sirens made them vibrate and rattle. She took a pair of slightly turned up nose scissors and started cutting through the layers of bandages that were protecting the hand and fingers, removing them as she went until she got to the lint, which she started to lift off with her surgical glove-covered hands. She was very gentle and asked James if he was alright as she progressed. When the last layer came off, Dr. Maiden called Dr. Cummings over, who was usually the night call out doctor but was obviously there to witness the work of a top American surgeon. The pair of them inspected James's hand, as did James himself, for it was the first time he had seen it since he went into the operating theatre. His hand was yellow from whatever had been put on it during the operation and black and blue from bruising. The little stitches could be seen on three fingers and there was what James took to be a splint either side of the middle finger. All his finger nails were in place but it was obvious that he would eventually lose the three black ones. His hand was still very swollen and even though the pain was not so bad now, it hurt a lot when the doctors touched it to look more closely. "This is going to heal beautifully in time and as long as you keep your fingers and hand moving as much as you can bear, when the healing process is complete you should regain the full use of it. Dr. Shooter has done a wonderful job and is worthy of the reputation he has got in America." The doctor told James he was to come in at ten o'clock each morning to have the dressing changed until they reached Southampton, when arrangements would have to be made for him to go under his own doctor. Sister Barbara set about redressing James's hand but this time cut down on the size, which would make it much easier for James to get his arm into a sleeve. When she had finished, it looked very tidy and much less serious. She asked him if he wanted any more pain killers, to which James said, "Yes, please, but only if what you give me allows me to drink small amounts of alcohol after taking them." Barbara said that what she was going to give him would be alright as long as he didn't overdo the drinking. James left the hospital thanking all concerned and said he would see them the next day at ten o'clock.

He went back to his passenger cabin and thought he might get an hour's snooze before he went for afternoon tea in the Veranda Grill. He kicked his shoes off and without removing any other clothing laid on his bed. He had brought a book with him that he was half way through but didn't read for long as the movement of the ship not yet up to full speed lulled him to sleep. He woke and wondered what the time was and if afternoon tea had started or was over but guessed it would not be yet. He glanced at his watch to find it was three o'clock. So he got up, changed clothes into what he thought would be appropriate, including soft shoes which thankfully did not have laces, and left the cabin. On his way along the passageway he passed the steward who had transferred his gear to the new cabin and if looks could kill James would have dropped dead there and then. He said good afternoon to the steward, who completely ignored him. Time would tell how things would be between them and what James would do about it if there became a need. He got to the Veranda Grill where there was plenty of activity, mostly passengers drinking wine and spirits from what he observed, but there were plates still available with some tab nabs and a few sandwiches left. James asked the waiter if he could have a coffee and if he could help himself to some food; the waiter said he would get his coffee and yes he was welcome to help himself, which he did. James found himself a table with two young chaps already sitting at it and asked if they minded if he sat with them. They said, "No," but that they would be leaving in a short while to get ready for tonight.

The waiter brought James his coffee as he was getting into conversation with the young men. His first question was where were they from. It appeared they were both doing an exchange with two universities in England. One was from Boston the other from Detroit; they said and after a short vacation they would be starting their courses in June before the summer recess. One was studying civil engineering and the other European history. They asked James what he had been doing in the United States which rather threw him for a few seconds, before explaining that he had to go to New York for an operation to his hand. They asked why it could not be done in one of the famous London hospitals and James had to think quickly again. "Oh, what I had to have done was very complicated and the expertise for the operation is only available in America," he lied, for the last thing he wanted them to know was that he was actually a member of the crew, albeit an officer. James asked if they had been abroad before and was told they had but only on holiday with their parents. Before James could ask them what countries they had been to they said they had to go now but would probably see him later. Before finishing his coffee, he had a good look round at the other passengers with a hope of remembering some of their faces if he met them in the lounge or any other part of the ship. He finished his coffee and went out onto the open deck where he saw Fred talking to a couple of crew members on one of the lower decks who must have gone out for a break and a cigarette. James would find out later what they had been talking about if it was anything important.

It must have been nearly seven o'clock when there was a knock on the cabin door and James shouted to come in from the bathroom. When he finished cleaning his teeth he went out to see if it was the steward who had come in to put his bed covers down for the night, so it was a surprise when he found Fred standing in the middle of the cabin. After asking him to sit down, James wanted to know what he was doing coming to his cabin and did anyone see him come in. Fred said that he was very careful not to be seen but thought it would be best if they could work out a plan of action, so to speak, so they could go in to the Captain on a combined front. James thought it was a great idea and the pair of them sat and drew up a plan including where and when they should meet to compare notes and try between them to cover as big an area of investigation as they could manage. James said he thought it best if they met each night in his cabin so they could go over whatever they had discovered during the day and evening, but to be careful of the steward looking after the cabins because he wouldn't trust him an inch. Fred said that if he saw him he would just say a disturbance had been reported and that he had been sent to investigate. So it was agreed James would find out what he could from the passenger side and Fred the crew, but this left the officers. James said he would do his best to tap them but didn't think an engineer could be the man they were looking for but of course they could not be exempt. James said they could meet tonight at eleven o'clock and have a beer or something as a nightcap before going to bed. Fred said that would be fine but it depended on how late some of the socialising went on and how big a group and what ages they were.

James thought it might be a good idea to go down and see if Bob was around as he did not want him to think he was being high and mighty because he was now sailing as a passenger and first class at that. He decided to put his arm back in the sling to make it look as though his injury was worse than what it was, although it was bad enough without pretending. Over the jumper, he managed to make the sling and put it round his shoulder and cradle his arm in it. He then went down to the engineer's accommodation and the cabin he had occupied with Bob. When he got there Bob was getting ready to go into dinner. "Want a beer, James?" Bob said, "I'm going to have one." James said he would like one so Bob pushed the bell to call the steward. "Well, mate, how is your hand now, I see they have moved you out - where to?" James told him the Captain made the decision on the doctor's recommendation that it would be better for him to keep his eye on my hand on the ship each day than fly me home. "I can't work in any capacity down below or anywhere else if it comes to that but must admit I prefer going home this way rather than having had to fly. All that said, I would have much preferred having not damaged my hand. Apart from the pain it's giving me, no one can tell yet whether I will ever get the full use of it again. I think the doctor on the ship is worried, that's why he wants to look at it every day on the way home." The steward knocked on the door and when he came in Bob asked for two pints, pointing to two pint pots over by the sink. The steward picked them up and put them on the tray he was carrying together with another six that were already on it, and left. When the steward had gone, Bob asked James if he was going in for dinner, to which he answered, "No," he would be eating in the first class restaurant with the passengers. James thought Bob was a bit envious of him going home as a first class passenger, but was trying hard not to show it. He asked if any of the others had said anything, Gordon, Harry, John or Jack Brooks. Bob said they had asked after him, but had not gone overboard about his situation. He said Harry and the eight to twelve floater were not too happy because they had to cover and do six on and six off until they got back to Southampton. James wondered if they would get extra pay but doubted it, they might be lucky to get an extra couple of days leave at layup time. Being his first trip, he didn't really have a clue but could do nothing about it anyway. The steward brought back the beer and put it on the chest between the bunks and Bob gave him the two shillings for it. "What do you do about tipping the stewards that look after the engineers?" James asked, and Bob said that he had spoken to the one that had just gone out who makes the beds and cleans up the cabins and told him he would give him a tip when he goes on leave. "That way I don't bother giving him something each time he does a beer run. I feel a bit sorry for the stewards who work for us because compared to the tips others get that work for the passengers, especially the first class ones, they get peanuts. Having said that, we usually get the new boys, whereas passengers, especially first class, get those that have worked for Cunard on the Queens for years." They finished their beer and James said he had to go, but promised he would come down again before the end of the trip. They tapped one another on the shoulder and James left.

When he got back to his cabin, he took his arm out of the sling and started to get himself ready for dinner. He decided the best he could manage for dinner dress was his suit so, getting it out and laying it on the bed, he then decided what shirt and tie should go with it, for although it would have to be the same suit each night, he could at least show a bit of variety wearing a different shirt and tie; this said, he only had three ties with him and one of those was his black uniform tie. There was no way he was going to be able to wear a dinner suit or white tuxedo or even a dress uniform he didn't have anyway. With the smaller dressing on his hand, he could now manage to get himself relatively well dressed, even doing his tie up. He was quite surprised how well he could now manage with all the fingers on his left hand covered up and hopefully would find it even easier when it came down to just having the three middle fingers covered and his little finger and thumb exposed. He would ask the sister tomorrow if this could be arranged. He had a wash rather than a bath or shower and then got himself dressed. He left the cabin at just after eight o'clock to go for dinner. Once again, passing his favourite steward who was seeing to the beds two cabins down from his. As he passed, he wondered if his bed cover would be put down when he got back, it also crossed his mind that the same steward was still on duty, and not the night steward.

He entered the restaurant and the Head Waiter, who was immaculately dressed, asked him what table he was on and when James told him he didn't know, he had to look it up from a list that was on a desk nearby. "What is the surname sir?" the Head Waiter enquired.

"Royston," replied James.

"No, your surname, sir."

"That is my surname," James retorted, "My Christian name is James."

"Oh, I am sorry, sir, how silly of me, I will just have a look". He found James's name at the end of the list written in by hand with the table number alongside and called a waiter over to conduct him to his table. When he got to the table, he found it was a round one that was laid up for six passengers, of which none had yet arrived. The table was dressed in the finest linen table cloth and table napkins, silver cutlery, crystal cut glasses, a very tasteful centre piece and top quality china wear. The table napkins were in a fan-like design and the whole table was beautifully manicured for wealthy people. Having never been in a top class restaurant at home, he had never seen anything like it before. The waiter asked him which chair he preferred to sit in and James chose the one that gave him the best view of the other diners. When settled, the waiter asked if he would like wine or a glass of water while he waited for the other diners on that table. James said he would like a glass of water while he perused the very extensive menu. The menu was exactly the same as the one they used in the engineers' dining room without the exclusions such as caviar. James was fascinated at the way some of the guests entered the room; some had gentleman and lady written all over them, then there were those who had money but were not gentry, then again there were those who thought they had money but had now come into the land of the big spenders. There was something about the mannerisms of the different groups that came across as they were shown to their respective tables. James had made up his mind what he wanted to eat when three of his table companions arrived, a father, mother and what James guessed at being a sixteen or seventeen year old daughter. The table waiter acted as cordially to them as he had done to him just a little earlier and just as he was about to ask what they wanted to drink, the remaining two, both ladies, James imagined in their sixties, turned up and were promptly seated in the same manner. The second steward who had accompanied the ladies joined the first one in removing the table napkins from astride the side plates and put them on the guest's laps. This done, the first waiter introduced himself as David and his colleague as Victor and said they would be their table waiters for the voyage to Southampton and that if there was anything wanted by any of their guests they only had to ask and they would do their level best to meet the request. They asked the table members if they could get them a drink while they studied the menu, then David beckoned the wine waiter who indicated he would be attending to them soon. James had the wife and one of the ladies sitting either side of him and thought he would start the introductions seeing they would be sitting together for the next five days. He said, "We know who the waiters are so why not each other? My name is James, who are you?" The father said his name was Henry his wife was Rachel and his daughter Helen. The lady sitting next to James said her name was Amy and her companion was Elizabeth. They each said hello in unison and James added he hoped they would all have a pleasant voyage and that it was nice to meet them. The wine waiter arrived at their table and politely asked who wanted what to drink and would it be in order to put it on their cabin account? They all said yes, including James, who did not want to be seen to be different from the others. They ordered their drinks from the wine list, the family having a bottle of red wine and a glass of fresh orange juice, the ladies a bottle of medium white wine and James a glass of South African red wine.

When the waiters came to take their orders, it was obvious to James that the table guests he was travelling with were accustomed to this standard of cuisine and the service they were receiving, for they all, including Helen, rattled off their courses in French whenever it was called for together with how they wanted it prepared. James was so pleased the waiter came to him last so that he would not embarrass himself. After ordering his meal, which he thought he did very well under the circumstances, he asked Amy about the trip she was making on the Queen Mary. She said her and her sister had travelled on the Queen Mary and the Queen Elizabeth a number of times as well as other passenger liners and passenger cargo ships over the years. They had been left quite a lot of money in their father's will and on his request were spending it seeing the world. She said they were on their way home after visiting South America and had arranged their homeward journey to coincide with the wedding of a great niece who got married a week ago in New York. James then turned to Rachel, who seemed quite reserved but was very pleasant with a slight American accent. He asked her what their trip was for, to which she said they were going back home for a holiday and taking Helen back to school in Surrey. She had been over with them for three weeks and now had to return to get herself ready to sit exams. James asked what they were doing in America and was that where they lived full time. Rachel said they worked in New York, she as a beautician, and her husband in banking. "I detect a slight American accent," James said, to which she replied that she had picked it up while staying in America with her father when she was very young. Her father was into mining and travelled extensively in the States giving advice and the knowledge and expertise to mining companies that sought it. "I stayed with my parents until I was seven years old and then was sent back to boarding school in England. When I didn't join them for holidays I spent time with my father's sister in Surrey, and that same aunt keeps her eye out for Helen now, in the same way she used to me. My husband works for the Bank of England but is employed as an adviser in the Bank of America. We usually manage to get back to London twice a year and Helen joins us once or maybe twice in America."

"I take it then you have a home in both countries?" James observed, to which Rachel said, "Yes," and her husband speaking across her said, "Yes, and have to maintain them both." It was then, just before the waiters brought their food that Helen spoke out for the first time, for up to then she had only spoken to her dad after a brief hello to Elizabeth who was sitting the other side of her. Looking over to James, she said, "What have you done to your hand?" James wondered when someone was going to ask this question and was prepared.

"I damaged it at work," he replied, "And due to the severity of the injury my company sent me to America where they are more experienced in dealing with the problem and in order to save me losing my hand." Rachel asked which hospital he had attended, "The one about fifteen miles from the docks," James replied.

"Was it the Mayflower?" Rachel went on. James thought that was the name, and asked why.

"Who was the doctor that attended to you?" Rachel persisted.

"Doctor Shooter," James said, "Do you know him?" Rachel said she did because he had operated on her foot when it had been crushed in a motor accident and that he was the best surgeon in America with a worldwide reputation. "I bet your bill wasn't cheap," she remarked, to which James replied he didn't know as his company were meeting it.

The first course arrived and as usual since his accident, James had ordered food that could be eaten with either a fork or a spoon, due to not being able to use both hands. While he had soup, the others had ordered really glorious looking starters. It was when they were about half way through them that there was a bit of a commotion on the far side of the restaurant. A man got up and started shouting something quite inaudible with a lady obviously trying to quieten him down. The Head Waiter went over to the table, which by now had drawn the attention of all the diners including James, and could be heard saying he would call the Chief Steward. By this time, whoever else was sitting at the table had become very embarrassed and were now also on their feet. James thought, this is a good start to the voyage, but at least it would make for good conversation among the passengers, especially the tables nearest the goings on. It took the lady that was doing the calming down nearly ten minutes to resolve the situation and when she did, her and the man causing all the trouble left the table with him leaning very heavily on her, obviously as drunk as a lord. By the time the Chief Steward arrived, the problem had been solved. The other table members had settled down and things seemed to have got back to normal. Elizabeth said, taking a sip of her white wine, "I wonder what all that was about?" Helen said she thought she had seen the man before somewhere but could not think where. It was Rachel who said she was sure it was a quite famous actor but couldn't remember his name. The waiters took their starter dishes away when they had finished and went for the main courses. When they returned they started serving the vegetables and when they got to Amy, she asked who the man was that had caused the commotion. Victor said, "It was the actor Steve Renton and his wife Judy Mendise. This is the second trip he has caused trouble like this, he is always getting drunk, it must be so embarrassing for his wife, but she seems to stick around. In actual fact, she is a better actress than he is an actor, but you would never think so the way he behaves. Last time he caused trouble was when he was going back to New York about six months ago and that was in the main lounge." Amy was quite put out by the actor's behaviour, commenting that who did they think they were and why should they be so temperamental. She said that Elizabeth and she were going to go to the cinema after dinner because they hated Bingo and she believed that was going to be played before the entertainment proper started. She wasn't sure what the film was but if they didn't like it they would go for a walk or give the library a visit before getting a night cap in one of the bars. The family said they were going for a walk around the boat deck to get some fresh air and help their meal go down. The mains eaten and cleared away, the sweets came to be followed by coffee but none of them accepted Henry's offer of a liqueur. As they left the dining room, the two waiters said good evening and started clearing the table, ready for laying up for breakfast.

James went back to his cabin to find it exactly the same as he left it, the bed cover had not been pulled down and nothing had been done to indicate that the steward had been in. As a matter of principle, if nothing else, he would confront the steward in the morning. The night stewards were on now and it would not be fair to get them to do what should have been done by the day steward that had something against him, maybe because he was only a junior officer and an engineer to boot. He would soon learn that he was taking on more than he could handle once James got going, which he intended in the morning, but for now, he had a job to do.

CHAPTER 4

James decided he would stay in his suit but took a couple of pain killers before he left the cabin as his hand was really painful. What he would have preferred was to have stayed in his cabin until the pain killers did their job, but wanted to get to the main lounge to see what was going on before making his way around the bars. What he thought of while he was sitting in the lounge was how many young single female passengers there were on board and how many there were in each class. As he was sitting there on his own with the lemonade he had ordered, he thought how nice it would be if Susan was sitting with him. He lit a cigarette, only the fourth one he had had all day, and just took in all that was going on. There were quite a few passengers smoking and drinking, he supposed waiting for the bingo to start. A table had been set up for the purpose and one of the pursers was standing by. Several young men caught James's eye, but all of them seemed to be with young ladies as couples rather than looking to chat them up. When the purser went over to the table he told the passengers that wanted to play that they could now purchase their bingo books and he would start calling in ten minutes time. He also announced that there would be live music to dance to at ten o'clock until midnight. James finished his drink as the bingo started and decided he would make his way around the bars available to first class and then, without being seen, use the key Fred had given him to open the segregation gate leading to the second class bars. The Veranda Grill was packed, you could hardly see across the room for smoke and the drink was flowing freely as far as he could see. He stood around for nearly half an hour without having a drink when a young woman approached him. "Hello," she said, "didn't I see you in the restaurant?" James said she had and asked her if she had enjoyed her meal. She said she had and asked him why he wasn't drinking. James said he was on tablets and showed her his hand. He asked her if she was on her own and was this her first voyage. She said, no, it was not her first sea passage but yes she was on her own and that she had gone to America three months ago with her work. She said she had flown over but was making a bit of a holiday going home. She said she had travelled by sea when she went to South Africa on the Edinburgh Castle but had more time on that occasion to get there.

"So I take it you are well travelled and not married," James said, to which she replied she had been married but with all the travelling her job warrants, it didn't work out. She was not as young as she looked, for when she said she was a foreign correspondent for a newspaper and the countries she had visited over the last ten years he knew she was a very mature woman that would know how to look after herself. He asked her what her name was and what newspaper she worked for, she just said her name was Joyce and that was all he needed to know. She said that if James was not drinking did he mind if she got herself a drink and that she might see him later. James thought that was a good idea and took himself off to a smaller bar where he found all men, dressed in dinner suits. Thinking this strange, he asked the waiter what was going on as there were no women present and felt a fool when the waiter said they were Freemasons. James beat a hasty retreat and continued to visit all the recreational places he could find where drink was being served until ten forty-five when he made his way back to his cabin ready for Fred's planned visit. It was as he got back to his cabin area that he bumped into Amy and Elizabeth and realised they were only two cabins down from him. They said they had sat through South Pacific again and enjoyed it as much as when they had seen it the first time, and had just come down from the Veranda Grill where they had a brandy night cap. James said it was very busy when he was up there and it still was according to the ladies. "We looked in on the main lounge too," Amy said, "and that was going well, the band sounds very good and there were plenty dancing."

James said goodnight as Elizabeth unlocked their cabin door and he reached his. He had asked the night bedroom steward to put four bottles of beer in the cabin, as he left for his tour of the bars and when he got the cabin door open saw the beers and the two glasses he had asked for on the coffee table. He noticed the bed cover was now pulled down so James could only assume the night steward had done it as it was not done when he came in earlier. He would thank him when he saw him. At eleven o'clock on the dot there was a knock at the door and Fred was in like a shot as soon as James opened it. Fred was not in uniform now but dressed very casually.

James invited him to sit down and pointing to the beer asked him if he would like a drink. Fred thanked him and said, "That would be very nice." James opened the beer with some difficulty, and sat down opposite his guest.

"How did you get on today?" James asked.

"There was too much to do and so many young people around, it was hard to sort out who was who quite frankly. Tourist class are buzzing with youngsters but I don't think the guy we are looking for would be interested in them, I think it will be first or second class he is after, that is of course if there is anybody?"

"I have had an idea," James said, "I want to ask the Captain in the morning if he can give us a passenger list so we can go through it and pick out the single women and single men. At least it would cut the numbers down and give us some idea which classes we should concentrate on." James, having said he had spent some time in the main lounge before going around the first class bars without seeing anything he would even consider following up, he said he realised Fred was looking at the crew but wondered, seeing him in casual civilian clothes, if it would be possible to get permission from the Captain or Staff Captain to mingle with the tourist class passengers when he wasn't on his Master at Arms duties.

They discussed what they thought they may be looking for in way of a clue into what the man might do to get the attention of a young lady. Fred said that was more in James's line as he felt that he was getting a bit long in the tooth for chatting up the birds and how to get them into bed. They agreed it would be difficult, but they could only see what there was to see and hope that they were in the right place at the right time to see anything that might set a trail to follow. They enjoyed the second beer before Fred said he would have to go and would see James in the Captain's day room at nine o'clock tomorrow morning. They shook hands and Fred was about to go out of the door when James said he would have a look out first; he stuck his head round the door and then beckoned Fred out. He put the bottles into the waste bin but left the glasses on the table, before slipping on his jumper and going down to the cabin class lounge to see how busy it was at midnight. He was quite surprised when he got there as it was still quite busy. Several groups of young people were sitting and lounging around, a few looking as though they would be having a hangover in the morning, but there was no sign of anything untoward and the bar must have very recently shut as there were some still drinking but the bar was shut and the security grill was down.

James made his way back to his cabin, once again using the segregation gate key, making sure there was no one around as he did so. He got back to his cabin at nearly quarter to one and with his hand now hurting like hell took two more pain killers, got undressed, set his alarm clock to seven o'clock and climbed into bed. The sea was calm so he had no trouble getting off to sleep and slept soundly until his alarm woke him. He went through the old routine getting his toiletries done and himself dressed. He thought how much easier it was going to be after the dressing was changed so then he would at least be able to use his thumb and little finger. Because he was ready to go to breakfast earlier than expected, he pressed the bell calling for a steward. After about five minutes the door opened and the steward came in and said in a very derogatory manner, "What do you want?"

James intended putting this man well and truly in his place so he began, "To start with, I want some civility and respect from you, and since when do you enter a cabin without knocking first and wait until you are told to come in? Secondly, why did you not turn my bed down like you do the other passengers and why are you so ignorant where I am concerned?" Whether the steward thought he was being macho or not, James didn't know, but he just said that James was only a bloody engineer and a junior one at that and that he could look after himself. James, keeping his cool, reminded the steward that he was sailing as a first class passenger and that he expected the same service and respect from him as any other passenger and that if he did not get it there would be big trouble. He must have been either stupid or have the thought that James was bluffing because is all he said was, "Fuck you," and walked out slamming the door behind him. Although only twenty-three years old, James had never been spoken to in this manner before and had no intentions of letting this steward get away with it. Before going into breakfast, James took a diversion and went up to the purser's office and asked how he could contact the chief steward. They said he could be contacted in his office and gave him the telephone number. Armed with this, he went into breakfast. There was only one at the table when James got to it and it was Helen. "Good morning, Helen," James said politely, "you're up early." She replied that she did not sleep very well probably due to the fact that she was excited about being on the Queen Mary and she was beginning to worry about the exams she had coming up. Asked why she was worried about the exams, she said that she had been out with her Mum and Dad enjoying herself, and had not done the amount of studying she should have and she badly wanted to do well and get some good marks. James put it to her that it was possible to study too much and perhaps by giving her brain a rest may be a good thing. She thanked James for being so nice and hoped he was right. Had she come straight into breakfast, James enquired. Helen said she had gone down to the swimming pool first but she was too early and they were cleaning it, so she went up on deck and had a stroll around. "It's a lovely day today," she said, "the sea is quite calm and there is very little breeze, but it is a bit fresh, if I get a deck chair out I will find somewhere sheltered." James had the usual cereal and fruit juice with some scrambled egg, tin tomato and beans - pretty boring, but easy to eat with just a fork. Helen ordered a healthy breakfast which she had not finished when James said he was sorry but he had an appointment so would she excuse him. She explained that she would not be on her own for very long as her mum and dad would be joining her shortly. As James got to the dining room door, who should be coming in for breakfast but Amy and Elizabeth. They exchanged greetings with a good morning, and James made his way up to the Captain's day room.

Captain Baron was sitting at his desk when James was ushered in by the Captain's Tiger (personal steward) and invited to sit down and offered a cup of coffee. As the Tiger was about to fetch it, a knock at the door heralded the arrival of Fred. He was also asked to sit down and if he too would like a cup of coffee. The Captain turned from his desk and said, "Good morning, gentlemen, I take it you are both well and raring to go. I am sorry I have kept you waiting but a ship's captain has more to do than just walk about being a captain." The coffee arrived on a silver tray with sugar and milk in their respective containers together with spoons and just a few biscuits. James and Fred had cups and the Tiger passed Captain Baron a mug with Captain Pug-wash written on it. "A gift from my Grandchildren, you know – I must use it or I will be in big trouble." After taking a couple of sips of their coffee, the captain said, "Right then, gents, let's get down to business. Did either of you have any luck last night, albeit it was the first night out so I suppose it would be difficult to know where to start?"

James said, "Before we start, sir, can I bring up a couple of things that might help us to achieve what we are trying to do." The captain nodded, so James went on to ask if there was any reply from the office regarding crew member transfers. The Captain said he had had a radio telephone call giving him the names they wanted and the dates they were transferred onto the Queen Mary. "So now, with the full crew list, including officers, we can highlight those we have on the list. I have already set this in motion, it should be in my office now." With that, he rang a bell at the side of his desk and when his steward came in he asked him to go along to his office and get the crew lists he had asked for. "What is the other thing you want?" the Captain asked, and James said, "Would it be possible for Fred to be allowed to be out of uniform and mix with the Tourist Class passengers as he was allowed to do with the First and Second Class ones?"

The captain thought about this for a few minutes before saying, "Would you not be recognised, Baker?" Fred said he didn't think so but it would be a good idea to try, as they both needed to be able to speak to the passengers as well as observe them, which would not be an easy thing to do in uniform. The captain gave Fred the permission. "What did you discover yesterday and last night in particular?" the Captain asked.

Fred said, "Nothing untoward, Sir, but maybe there could be a better result with the new arrangement." And James said other than the incident with Steve Renton the actor, and the dining room antics, there was nothing to report either. The Captain's Tiger brought in two brown A4 envelopes and gave them to the captain who said, "Thank you, that is all." When the steward had left the room the Captain gave them the envelopes and wished them luck until he would see them the next day at the same time.

James went back to his cabin, where he found nothing had been done as regards clearing up and making the bed. He had not seen the steward in the accommodation on his return but knew from seeing dirty towels and some bed linen outside other cabins either side of his that his cabin had been bypassed. He didn't ring for the steward but instead picked up the phone and telephoned the Chief Steward's number. The phone must have rung about four times before it was answered and when it was the person answering said politely, "Can you hold on for a minute, please?" James waited until the voice came back to him apologising for the delay and asking how he could be of help. James asked if the Chief Steward was in the office and would it be possible to see him. Again the voice said, "Hang on," before coming back saying the Chief Steward was available and yes he would see him if he came right away. James said he would come right away and that it was James Royston calling and enquired where exactly he could find the office. When told, he made his way straight for it. When he got there he found a large office, with two men manning it as well as the Chief Steward, resplendent in his uniform with three wavy gold rings on the arms. Addressing the Chief Steward, James introduced himself and asked if it was possible to speak to him in private. The Chief Steward, who was quite a slight man, thin on top with a very rosy complexion and a going blue boozer's nose, asked what it was that James wanted to speak to him personally and in private about.

The next room was obviously the Chief Steward's cabin, for he went over and opened a side door of the office and indicated to James to follow him. When inside and the door shut, James, not having been invited to sit down, explained the situation he was in excluding, of course, what he was doing, but that he was a ship's officer travelling as a first class passenger. He explained how it was that this steward had transferred his gear from the engineer's quarters and since then how he had treated him together with his final statement before leaving his cabin and slamming the door this morning. The Chief Steward at first seemed quite blasé about it with the attitude of, what did he want him to do about it? James said had he, the Chief Steward, been spoken to like it, what would he have done? Was it because he was an engineer, or just that he was ship's staff that made him react the way he has? "Whatever it is, if he is not reprimanded and warned of his future behaviour towards me, I will be taking it to the Staff Captain or if necessary the Captain. I respect people and wish the same respect in return. This man is badly out of order and if you do not do anything about it then it will not look good on you if and when I take the matter further, so it is up to you. All I ask is that you do not think I am bluffing as it appears your steward does. I do not know his name but I am sure you will find out who it is, so I leave it with you. I asked to see you in private to give you the respect you deserve as Chief Steward rather than going over your head and making the matter worse than it is and creating unwanted gossip." Whether it was the respect bit or the serious threat of being taken further James didn't know, but the Chief Steward seemed to change his attitude and said he would look into the matter and deal with it. James thanked him and left through the cabin door rather than the way he came in.

On leaving the Chief Steward's cabin, he headed straight to the hospital where he found Sister Jean available to remove his dressing, prior to Dr. Maiden looking at his hand. Jean asked him if he had used all the pain killers he had been given, to which he replied that he had only two left and that although he had a high pain threshold he could not do without them completely. He asked Jean if it would be possible to have the hand dressed so that his thumb and little finger would be exposed, albeit that they were still quite bruised. She said, "That decision would be made by the doctor after he had looked at it." Dr. Maiden came into the treatment area just as Jean was lifting the last bit of the dressing off, thus exposing the damaged fingers. Jean cleaned his hand so gently he could hardly feel her doing it, but after she threw the swab away the stitches could be seen and the swelling of the fingers had reduced considerably. Dr. Maiden took a good look at the wounds and remarked again at what a neat job Dr. Shooter had done with the stitching as well as the repair work that he had undertaken. "Looking at this now, James, I would say those stitches could come out before we get back to Southampton and start getting some exercise into those fingers. I don't want to see you tomorrow, but the day after." Jean asked the doctor if she could put a lighter dressing on as James had requested, to which Dr. Maiden gave an affirmative with the proviso that he was very careful not to knock it. James asked if it would be possible to use the gymnasium equipment or go swimming to which he was given a definite "no". He took the tablets Jean gave him and thanked them both before he left.

His hand felt a lot better with the lighter dressing but of course having been pulled about, albeit as gently as it was, it was giving him quite a bit of pain so he decided to go back to his cabin and take a couple of pain killers before finding somewhere on deck where he could finish the book he was reading, he could then go to the library and get another one. When he got back to his cabin it was getting on for eleven o'clock and it was still as he had left it. The bed had not been touched and the bathroom still had the towels in the bath as he had left them. He thought of ringing for the steward, then of telephoning the Chief Steward but decided to do neither until after he had lunch which, by the time he got back, would be close on two o'clock. He poured himself the last of the water in his thermal jug and took two pain killers, putting the remainder he had been given into a drawer. Leaving the cabin with his book, he went to find a deck chair out on deck, hopefully, like Helen, somewhere out of what little wind there was.

Before going to find a deck chair, James thought he would have a walk round the boat deck, just to see what was about. There were plenty of passengers up there being such a nice day, some playing shuffle board, a couple hitting golf balls into a net and one man dressed to kill in the most outrageous golf gear James had ever seen aiming in the opposite direction, driving what looked like brand new golf balls out to sea. Others were just lounging around or walking the deck. James noticed the actor and a lady, not his wife, leaning over the hand rail, both with a drink, talking. He decided he had walked the deck enough and went to find himself a deck chair. That was when he found Helen with her mum and dad who also had a drink in their hand as James acknowledged them. He found an unoccupied chair and asked the deck steward if he could find him a seat cover for it. The steward brought him one, for which James thanked him and asked if it was possible to bring him a gin and tonic with not too much ice and a slice of lemon. The steward went away and James settled himself down to have a read. Before the steward returned, and when James was well into his book, a voice said, "Hello," and in front of him stood Jane the young night nurse he saw when he returned to the ship from the hospital ashore. She said she had come out for a breath of fresh air before having her lunch, and that she had had a very quiet night and wasn't over tired, so waking earlier than usual, she had decided to get up. The deck steward arrived with James's drink, which he brought on a tray with just a few nibbles, and asked Jane if she wanted a deckchair. She looked at James and asked if he would mind, to which James responded, "Not at all."

She said, "Yes please, then," to the steward and when James asked her if she would like a drink she said she would like a straight tomato juice with a little ice. Jane said she wasn't sure whether she should be doing this as she was ship's staff. James knew that the engineers were not encouraged to mix with the passengers unless they were in evening dress uniform as was the case with all the male officers, but did not as yet know how the female officers were expected to dress.

"Anyway," he said, "if this is your first trip at sea and I am a patient I can't see anybody giving you the sack, and it won't be for long as we will be going for lunch soon." During the next half hour they told one another about themselves from where they both came, what schools they went to, why they chose the professions they had taken up and where they wanted to get to in life. Their drinks finished, they put their glasses on the deck by their chairs where the steward would see them and went down to the dining room together where they parted company. Amy was sitting at the table when James arrived and said Elizabeth, Rachel and Henry were up at the buffet getting their lunch. James, not realising it was a buffet today, said he had better go up and get his. When he got back with his salad, chicken leg, ham and a slice of ox tongue, the others were eating already. "Is Helen not having lunch?" James asked Rachel, who replied that Helen had had a very large breakfast and thought she would forgo her lunch. The rest of them had a glass of wine with their food but James abstained and had a cup of coffee instead. The ladies said they had a very lazy day up to then, spending most of it in the library and writing room catching up on some letter writing they had to do. "We know the post cannot be collected but they can be posted on the ship or directly we get into Southampton. We have more time here than when we get home after being away for so long."

After lunch, James decided he would go back to his cabin and have a lie down, as his hand had started hurting again now that the pain killers had worn off. He got back to the cabin just in time to catch the steward going through his drawers. "And what do you think you are doing?" James asked the startled steward, who was so intent on what he was doing did not hear James come into the cabin.

"Nothing," the steward said, "I was just putting your cufflinks that you had left on the table, back in your drawer," he lied.

"What was wrong with them where they were?" James countered. "You have no business going to my drawers or touching anything belonging to me, plus the fact my cufflinks were not left on the table, as I haven't worn them since I damaged my hand, I cannot get one into the button hole so do not wear either of them. I'm going to report you for trying to steal from me. I don't know what you were looking for, but whatever it is, you can explain when you're given the sack." With that, the steward knowing he had nothing more to lose decided he would have a go at James. He threw a punch that James managed to avoid but used the momentum of it with his right arm to throw the steward across the room where he hit his head on the base of the very heavy armchair and went spark out. James picked up the phone and telephoned the ships exchange and asked if he could be put through to wherever he could speak to a Masters at Arms. The operator said, "Hold on a second and I will put you through." And within seconds a voice said, "Baker speaking."

"What luck," James said, "that is you Fred isn't it?"

"Yes, who is that?" Fred asked.

"It's James. Can you come to my cabin immediately, I have a big problem."

"I'll be there in a couple of minutes," Fred replied and the phone went dead. James, wondering what to do, decided that if the steward came round he would not be able to stop him leaving the cabin and then deny he was ever there, so he got his dressing gown belt and tied his hands behind is back. It was much easier now his thumb and little finger were freed up on his damaged hand, and managed to tie his shoe laces together, though this was more difficult. The steward was just coming round when Fred knocked on the door and James opened it. "What the bloody hell is going on?" Fred wanted to know, "What's all this?" James explained what had happened and that he had called Fred to act as a witness that the steward was in the cabin with him and that he wanted Fred's advice as to what to do next. "I would suggest that you call the Chief Steward and the Staff Captain," Fred said, "in fact, I will do it from your phone here as I am supposed to be a ship's policeman," which he promptly did. By now the steward had come round and managed to get to his knees but as he tried to stand up to try to get away he fell over again due to not being able to put one foot in front of the other.

When the Chief Steward arrived, which did not take him long, he didn't like what he was confronted with and made it plain he was not happy with what was happening; he more or less implied, "not you again," to James. The Staff Captain was in attendance shortly after the Chief Steward and immediately took control of things when it was explained to him what had happened. The first thing he did was ask the Master at Arms to go through the stewards pockets, which contained three ladies rings, a man's gold watch, two pairs of rather expensive looking earrings and James's signet ring.

"Hang on a minute," James said, "can I have a look at that jewellery? I think I know who some of it belongs to, as I've seen them wearing it." Fred wanted to know which pieces James recognised and setting them down on his coffee table asked James to pick out his own signet ring together with two ladies rings and both pairs of earrings. "These belong to the ladies in the cabin just along the passageway. They are ladies who sit at my dinner table, that's where I have seen them. The two rings and that pair of earrings, belong to Amy and the other pair of earrings belong to Elizabeth. I don't know about the gold watch and the other ladies ring. My signet ring I haven't worn because of my damaged hand." The Staff Captain said he now wanted the steward's cabin searched to see if there was anything else that had been stolen on the outward voyage from any of the cabins he had been responsible for and that he was to be kept under lock and key until the ship reached Southampton when he would be handed over to the police. His hands and shoe laces were untied and he was led away by Fred and another Master at Arms. Fred had used James's phone again to ask for another Master at Arms to assist him to take the steward and put him under ships arrest under lock and key. The Chief Steward and the Staff Captain then left James's cabin to go and search the steward's cabin and locker. The jewellery was collected up and James was asked to let the ladies know that they could reclaim that what belonged to them from the purser's office because they would have to sign for the articles they reclaimed. James of course had been given his ring back there and then.

James knew that Fred would be letting him know tonight what went on after they left his cabin and what they had found in the steward's cabin and locker. James knocked on the ladies' cabin door but had no reply, which James was not surprised at for he guessed they would be having afternoon tea somewhere. He went back to his cabin and took the pain killers he had intended to take before he entered his cabin and found the steward. He didn't know what to do, whether to go and look for Amy and Elizabeth or slip a note under their cabin door. With his hand hurting him quite badly now after all the tying up and the exertion, he decided on the note and a snooze. He took a sheet of writing paper from the folder on his desk come dressing table and wrote a short note addressing it to the two ladies by name, asking them to ring him on his cabin number directly they came in, as he had something important to tell them. He put the note into an envelope and went and slipped it under their cabin door before returning to his cabin, kicking his shoes off and stretching out on his bed. He must have gone into a deep sleep maybe due to the pain killers, of which he had taken three instead of two, because he woke with a start when his telephone started ringing. He came to his senses, got up and picked up the receiver. A sweet voice said that it was Elizabeth and that she had read the note and what was it James wanted to talk to them about. James asked if Amy was there too and when he found out she was he said if they did not mind he would go along and see them. Elizabeth said it was alright to go along now before they started getting dressed for dinner. James rinsed his face round and combed his hair, got into his slippers and went along to see the ladies. He knocked on the door and was let in by Elizabeth who invited him to sit down and asked if he would like a glass of sherry, for they always had a glass before dinner. James accepted and said that would be very nice. She poured out quite liberal amounts of what turned out to be very dry sherry. "This should give you an appetite for dinner," she said. James took the glass thanking her and began to tell them about what had happened just after lunch, but before going too far asked them where they kept their jewellery. Amy answered first saying they kept their bits of jewellery in the cabin safe, why was he asking? James went on to ask them to check if anything was missing. Amy went over to the wardrobe where the safe was housed and opened it. James hadn't even looked at his in his cabin. She was a little while sorting things out when she said, "There are two of my rings missing and a pair of earrings, as it happens the three most valuable pieces of jewellery I own and all given to me by my late husband." She beckoned Elizabeth over and asked her if there was anything of hers missing. At first she said she did not think so, but after doing a second check said there was a pair of her earrings missing, the most valuable pair she had. James was not aware that the steward was able to open the safes in the cabins and thought he was only an opportunist thief but he was obviously a professional. He would certainly have a lot to discuss with Fred that night when they got together. James went on to explain to Amy and Elizabeth exactly what happened, how, after catching him red handed, the steward had tried to beat him up at least throwing a punch that would have led to a probable beating but how he had managed to throw him hard enough to knock him out. He told them both that they had to go to the purser's office to reclaim their items of jewellery and sign for them. They asked what would happen to the steward and what they would do for the rest of the voyage. James told them something would be quickly sorted as the Chief Steward knew all about it and would organise a replacement bedroom steward.

"What about the stewardess, will she be changed as well?" Elizabeth asked. Having not seen her, James could not give her an answer other than she would have to wait and see, but didn't think so.

James left the ladies after having had another glass of sherry and went back to his cabin to get himself bathed and dressed for dinner. After the bath, he got his clothes out of the wardrobe and drawers and chose the best tie he owned, the one he would wear again on gala night, when most of the first class men wore their dinner suits and white tuxedos. He thought he would try and put his cuff links in as his thumb and little finger were beginning to work. He thought to himself that you do not realise how much you rely on your hands functioning properly until something goes wrong with them. Tying his tie he found easier but his shirt buttons, cuff links and tying his shoe laces he still found much more difficult than normal. He was dressed and ready to eat by half past seven, so decided to take a stroll around the promenade deck for half an hour prior to going in to dinner. However, before leaving his cabin, he rang the bell to call the bedroom steward, for surely by now a replacement would have been provided. He didn't have to wait long before there was a knock on his door, James called, "Come in," and a small fresh-faced young man with curly black hair and a slight colour, showing mixed race, entered the cabin.

"Good evening, sir," he said, "My name is Michael and I am your replacement day steward, is there anything I can do for you before I go off duty at eight o'clock?" James said he was pleased to meet him and could he arrange to have four bottles of beer and two appropriate glasses put in his cabin. Michael said, "Consider it done, sir, and I will see to your bed when I get back." James said he was just going to dinner so would he have the beer put on his bill and be kind enough to do the same every night until getting to Southampton. The new steward was so much better than the last one and James was sure all the other passengers he was looking after would see the difference. James assumed the night steward was the same one as before, although up until then he had only seen him once.

They left the cabin together, the steward going for the beer and James for his stroll. Journeying to the prom deck James found people scurrying around up and down the stairs between decks, some dressed for the evening and others still in their casual gear. He found the differences in styles fascinating; the way the Americans dressed, some of the men looked quite hideous in shorts that were too long and baseball caps that had the most ridiculous logos on them, not to mention the socks they wore with their sneakers. Was it the style or was it trying to make themselves appear and feel young, he could not make up his mind, but what he was certain of was that the American woman must spend a fortune on makeup and beauty treatment, far in excess of the British and most other nationalities he suspected. He supposed that if you have plenty of money, you can spend it as you see fit, so who was he to criticise? If he ever became rich, perhaps he would do the same. Reading about the Americans and seeing the movies, the men with their big Havana cigars, gold watches, gold chains and nougat-sized gold and diamond rings, and the women dripping with diamond jewellery always seemed farfetched, but seeing it with your own eyes, is believing!

He took a leisurely walk around the prom deck passing the time of day with those that nodded or said hello but always trying to remember their faces, in case he bumped into them another time. There were not too many young first class passengers on this trip, so looking for the bloke he was trying to find was going to be in cabin class, which is where he was going to concentrate tonight. He would of course start off in first class round the bars and in the lounges but mainly in the cabin class, as that is where the action seemed to be, or at least that would be the most likely place to start looking seriously. He looked at his watch and, seeing it was already eight o'clock, he started making his way down to dinner. He was reluctant to take the lifts at any time, thinking the exercise would do him good. As he got to the dining room entrance, a bell boy hurried past him and went over to the head waiter who was welcoming in the diners. The head waiter, being tall, had to stoop a little to listen to what the bell boy had to tell him. James heard him say to the bell boy, "Tell Mr. Renton an extra setting can be arranged at his table but give me fifteen minutes to get it organised." The bell boy hurried away and the head waiter called over one of the table waiters on the actor's table and told him to move the table settings around a little closer so that an extra place could be set and another chair found. The waiter got on with it right away before the other guests at the table arrived. That could have been a bit embarrassing, especially if they had already started eating, but the head waiter must have weighed that up before agreeing to the actor's request. The Head Waiter nodded to James as he began heading for his table where all his fellow diners were already seated with their drinks. "Come on, James," Henry said, "we've been waiting for you before we start ordering." James apologised for keeping them waiting and said how kind and polite it was of them to do so. Henry asked James if he would join them in having a glass of wine. James said yes and Henry poured.

Amy looked up and said, "It should really be champagne you know, for what James has done today, in fact we will have some," and calling the wine waiter over ordered a bottle from the wine list.

"What is this all about then?" Henry enquired with a somewhat excited manner. Amy explained to the family with the occasional interjection from Elizabeth what James had done and being only two cabins down from him how it had affected them. Helen enquired how James had managed to knock the steward out with his damaged hand, to which he had to admit he had a black belt in Judo. "Had the steward's punch landed I am sure the outcome would have been much different, but it didn't, so I was able to do what judo teaches you and that is to use your opponent's aggression to your advantage, for that is what judo is, a means of self-defence rather than aggression. I suppose in some ways I am lucky he hit his head on what he did, for had he hit me I might be in hospital. As it is, he is under lock and key, and I am here! I do not know more than that other than, he will be taken from the ship under escort to the nearest police station when we dock in Southampton." Amy's champagne arrived in an ice bucket together with the appropriate number of champagne glasses – the wine waiter asked if he should pour now, but Amy asked him to wait until a little later, after they had finished what they were drinking at present. David and Victor were ready to take their orders. James now having more use of his left hand albeit still hurting decided he would try to eat a more substantial main course rather than some of the stodgy stuff he had managed with one hand. He asked Victor, if he ordered a steak medium to rare, would he cut it up for him if he could not manage it himself. Victor said it would be no problem to do that or anything else he wanted regarding his meal. They all decided they would think about a sweet when the time came, but ordered their starters and main courses. The two waiters went away and the conversation returned to the burglaries, questions like how did he get into the cabin safe, who the gold watch and the other ring belonged to and how he only picked out the most valuable items? James said he might be able to answer some of the questions tomorrow, but to have this sort of thing happening was not good for Cunard's reputation. Elizabeth piped up and said she was only glad James had done what he had and where was this champagne? Amy drew the attention of the wine waiter and when he came over she asked him if he would like to pour now please.

The two ladies toasted James and thanked him for what he had done being backed up by Henry, Rachel and Helen. The starters finished and the plates removed, it was a little while before the main course arrived. It was whilst they were waiting for their main meals that voices started to be raised once again on actor Steve Renton's table. There was a general feeling of contented eating and conversation around the whole room but directly the voices were raised it seemed everyone in the room stopped eating and talking to look over to where the row was coming from. Raised voices went to shouting, shouting went to very bad language then a punch was thrown. It was now the turn of the Staff Captain to intervene. He got up from his table, excusing himself from his guests who were always invited to the Captain, Staff Captain, Chief Engineer and Staff Chief Engineer's Tables. He got to the table just before the Chief Steward, who, seeing the Staff Captain getting there first, backed off. The Staff Captain addressed himself to the actor in a very calm and gentlemanly way but was met by a hail of drunken abuse. Being in his evening dress uniform with his four gold stripes on his epaulets seemed to have no influence on Steve Renton what so ever, he just carried on cursing and swearing. The Staff Captain asked what the situation was regarding the other diners on the table, were they friends and acquaintances. He of course knew Renton's wife, but this was the second night on the trot that he had caused a commotion and what for? He said that if Steve did not quieten down he would have to leave the dining room or be escorted out by the Master at Arms, who he would call if it became necessary, and he would be banned from all the public rooms and bars and would be refused passage on any of Cunard's vessels in the future. To this Steve Renton raved he didn't want to be on the F-----g ship any way, he wanted to fly, but wasn't allowed to by his contract. The Staff Captain once again warned him that if he did not quieten down, he would have him forcibly removed from the restaurant. Judy Mendise was now in floods of tears and not being able to stand the embarrassment any more ran from the room with all eyes focusing on her. The men on the table tried in vain to get Steve to sit down and behave, but it became clear if the rest of the diners were to enjoy their meal, this man would have to go. This being the case, it was obvious that he was not going to leave voluntarily so the Staff Captain called the Chief Steward over and asked him to call for two of the biggest Master's at Arms to come and remove this man. By now the remaining diners had resumed eating their meals, but with one eye on the disruptive table. The Chief Steward went away to do as the Staff Captain had asked and the Staff Captain asked one of the table waiters if he would kindly go over to the Captain's table and with his complements ask the Captain if he would come over to join him. The waiter hurried across the dining room where he could be seen talking to Captain Baron, but of course, not being able to hear what was being said as the Captain's table was just about the furthest from where James and his company were sitting. Captain Baron could be seen excusing himself from the table and walking the most direct route past the other tables between his and where the problem was. The Staff Captain introduced the Captain to the table members, Steve Renton in particular, and asked the Captain if he would have any influence on this passenger that was causing so much unpleasantness and disruption. Captain Baron spoke to Renton in a most dignified and commanding way, although quietly, not loud enough to be clearly audible but obviously effective enough to get the actor to get up and walk out of the dining room, just as the Masters at Arms were coming in.

As the actor left the table, he said to the men at the table, "There you are, guys, you all owe me one hundred dollars each," and left the room walking as straight as a die. The other members sat at Steve Renton's table were now laughing and one of them, who it turned out to be the actor's manager, said to the Captain loud enough for everybody to hear, "He bet us all one hundred dollars that he could get you over to his table during dinner. He tried last night and failed but tonight, what a performance from both him and his wife, that's what you call acting. Don't worry, Captain, Steve will apologise to everybody tomorrow night and the table wine will be on him!" Captain Baron was not in any way amused and made this plain, he asked everybody in the room to excuse the antics of Mr. Steve Renton and his wife Judy Mendise who are Hollywood actors that had caused such an interruption to their dinner. He was sorry for any embarrassment it might have caused and promised it would not be happening again, of that they could be assured. He thanked Captain Mathews his staff Captain and the Chief

Steward, Mr. Martin, for the part they played in this charade and to the Masters at Arms for attending the scene so promptly. He thanked everybody for their understanding and hoped they would enjoy the rest of their meal. He, the Staff Captain, and the Chief Steward returned to their respective tables to resume their meals which would by now be cold. By the time the Captain had returned to his table and sat down the restaurant was alive with conversation, including James's table. It was Rachel that made the first comment by saying she wondered what the repercussions would be, if any, but did admit it had brought some element of entertainment, though there would be those stuffed shirts that would take great exception to such goings on. Whatever one thought about it, the acting was good, for the way Steve Renton left the dining room it was obvious he was as sober as a judge and not drunk at all, and it must be agreed those others on the table played their part.

The champagne and the meal finished, Henry asked if anyone would like a liqueur or a brandy. "Not you though, darling," he said to Helen, "but if you would like anything else just say."

Helen took it as a bit of a put down for she responded by saying to her father, "I am seventeen, I am on a ship not in a public house or hotel so would it really be too much to ask if I could have a Tia-Maria?" Henry said he was sorry, but of course she could and called the wine waiter over. The ladies said they would get them the next night but could not guarantee the entertainment. When they had finished their drinks the family and the ladies agreed to meet up in the main lounge later, but being invited to join them, James declined saying he had a prior engagement so could not make it. On leaving the restaurant together, the family went their way, the ladies towards their cabin and James headed for the boat deck.

Getting to the boat deck, it was almost dark, and James started taking a slow stroll. It was a very bright night, chilly but not too cold and with the sound of the spray and ripples produced by the bow wave that could be seen by the illumination of ship side lights, James's thoughts went back to Susan. How they had got on so well and the kiss, oh yes, the kiss! The smell of her perfume came back to him and he felt sad that she was not with him at that moment, but what it did to him was bring back the determination to try and catch the sod that had tried it on with Carol.

CHAPTER 5

After the excitement of the day so far, James thought he may have some success tonight, even to get a lead on his quarry would be something. He lit a cigarette and carried on walking until he had finished it, stubbing it out and wrongly throwing the butt end over the side. He had a quick look in the lounge as he went by and saw it was mainly the older passengers already playing bingo. He then went to the Veranda Grill where things were a bit livelier. He thought he might hang around a bit to observe some of the comings and goings. There were some slightly younger passengers that he was sure never went into dinner as they were not dressed for it to start with and he could not remember seeing them. He had been standing around trying to look inconspicuous when Joyce came up to him and asked how his hand was today. He said it was making good progress and not giving him quite as much pain and that by changing the dressing it was making it easier to manage. She had a drink in her hand and he was sure she hadn't been in to dinner. He asked her if she had eaten that evening, to which she said that she had stuffed herself at lunch time and could not face dinner, although she was sure she would start feeling hungry by about ten o'clock and would find somewhere to eat then. James asked her how she had occupied herself during the day and she said she had lain in until nearly eleven o'clock due to a very late night, or to be more accurate early hours of the morning. "Doing anything interesting?" James enquired, without being seen to pry.

"As a matter of fact, I met up with quite a nice young man who plied me with drinks and we went back to my cabin for a night cap - if you know what I mean!" James knew what she meant and asked who the young man was and would she be seeing him again. Joyce said she didn't know what his name was but gave a rough description of him. James wanted to know if any arrangements had been made to meet tonight to which she said, "No." She said she was not a normal pick up, but this guy really knew how to charm the pants off a girl and had in fact done just that. Smiling, she said she didn't know why but she really got to fancy him in that sort of way. "Where did you meet him?" James asked.

"What are all these questions about?" Joyce asked, getting a bit up tight with the probing James was doing. "What I do is none of your business, or who I meet or where I meet them." James apologised for being nosey and reassured her he meant no offence. She said as a matter of fact she was down in a cabin class bar, the one amidships; she didn't know what the room or bar was called, but someone she knew had a key they could use to go through a gate leading to the cabin class. There seemed to be a lot more life down there than up here in the first class so I thought I might give it a try. It was there that this chap came and spoke to me and asked me if I would like a drink, I never look a gift horse in the mouth, so said yes, I would love one."

"When did you decide you fancied him?"

"After about three cocktails," she said.

"Did you happen to go to the toilet at all while you were with him or leave him for any other reason?" James went on.

"Well, yes, I left him twice, once when I bought a packet of fags from the bar and again when I went back to my cabin to get some photographs I wanted to show him."

"Did you still keep drinking the cocktails or did you change your drink?" Joyce assured him she did not change her drink because he had a jug full of the cocktail made up for her. "Did it taste any different after you came back with the photos?" James wanted to know. She said no, but it was

117

after that when she started feeling sexy and wanted to take him to bed. "You would obviously know him again," James went on, "seeing you slept with him." She replied that sure she would. "Could we have a walk around the bars in the Cabin Class together to see if we might see him again?" James wanted to know.

"Yes, of course we can," Joyce replied, "as long as you buy the drinks. Even if I can't remember the face, I will remember the shoes."

"What is it about the shoes?" James ventured, "What makes you remember his shoes?"

"They looked different to normal shoes, it was the leather, they looked more like hide, they looked handmade and would have cost a lot of money."

James, once again being very careful, had a good look around before opening the first to second class segregation gate. Joyce was very curious now regarding what all the questions were for and asked James what he was up to. He said he wanted to meet the man she had been with because he had a problem; if as they went from bar to bar perhaps she would point him out. They first of all went to the cabin class lounge where there was plenty going on with a group playing some trendy music and quite a few on the dance floor jigging about. No ball room dancing in this class, by all accounts neither were any of them dressed for it. James asked Joyce to have a good look at the men while he got her a drink. What would she like? She said she would like a bloody Mary please with one piece of ice and James thought this would be on the Captain's bar bill - in fact, if he bought her any more drinks they would go on it as well. James got to the bar and asked the barman for a bloody Mary and a gin and tonic with a lemon slice and one piece of ice in each. While he was waiting for the drinks to come, he turned round to look away from the bar but accidentally bumped a chap as he turned, spilling his drink, not very much, but enough for the guy to complain. James said sorry but that was obviously not good enough for him. He got quite aggressive about it, and when

James explained it was a pure accident and that he did not mean to spill his drink he would not accept it. James offered to buy him a refill but the chap told him to stick it up his arse which now made James angry, but he wanted no fuss, for he was here on a mission. When the man asked James who he thought he was, James just ignored him. The barman brought the drinks he had ordered to him and told him how much it would be, James passed over the card the Captain had given him and said, "Will you please put it on this account?" The barman looked at it and raised his eyebrows but did what James had asked and handed it back to him. As James went to leave the bar with the drinks the man he had bumped into went to trip him up, but only managed to make him stagger and although he lost his balance, he did not fall, neither did he spill the drinks he was carrying. He turned to the man and said, "Unlike what I did to you, that was not accidental, but I won't make the same fuss about it as you."

This time the man said, "What do you want to do about it then?" To which James, pointing with his eyes to his hand said, "With this, not a lot, but without this, quite a lot but not in here." With that, he just turned his back on the guy and went back to Joyce. Giving her the Bloody Mary, he sat beside her on the seats she had found. "Have you seen anyone looking anything like your nameless man from last night?" Joyce, with bewilderment in her voice, said. "I know it sounds silly, but how could I have slept with a man I had only met two hours before and not known what his name was?"

James replied "When you've been drugged!"

"What do you mean, when I had been drugged?" James asked her if on her travels she had ever heard of 'Spanish Fly' and went on to explain to Joyce what had happened on the way out to New York and why he was so keen to identify the man. He explained that he didn't know his name, if he was a passenger that went ashore in New York, whether it was a member of the crew or anything else, is all he had to go on was a sketchy description. "It is now apparent he is a member of the crew or a man doing a return trip without a stop over, which is unlikely to the point of being out of the question. If this man approaches you again, will you please report it to the Master at Arms, the phone number of which you can get from the purser's office. I can assure you it will get back to me. The other thing I would like you to do is keep this matter entirely to yourself, it must not be discussed with anybody and certainly not your newspaper, only me - can you understand why?" Joyce promised she would not tell a soul because, if nothing else, she had in fact been raped, albeit with her consent, and would not want it broadcast or it might put her job in jeopardy. All this now explained and their drinks finished, she and James started their tour of all the other places they could find that served drinks. "Where were you when this guy first asked you if you wanted a drink?" James asked, and Joyce told him in the lounge bar which is on the same deck as the cinema, but didn't know what it was called. "What time was it?"

"About nine thirty, I think, it must have been about then as it closed at ten o'clock and we went to the Veranda Grill. It was from there that I went to get the photos I told you about so it could have only been then that he drugged the cocktail." James asked her what he was drinking to which she replied, "Whisky and water, I think?"

"Do I assume you finished the cocktail and went back through the segregation gate with this bloke?"

"Yes," she said.

Looking at his watch, James realised he only had another half an hour before he had to get to his cabin for eleven o'clock to meet up with Fred. He told Joyce they just had time to visit one more bar before he had to leave her for about half an hour, but would be back with her if she didn't mind staying up late. The next bar they visited was closed from ten o'clock, or at least that was what it said on the notice that had been left on the bar shutters, with the recommendation that anyone wanting a drink try another bar saying where it was. Joyce suggested to James that they go up to the Veranda Grill, where she knew some people and would be more comfortable waiting for him there. Once again, when they got to the segregation gate James was very careful that there was no one around. He opened the gate, ushered Joyce through and then closed and locked it behind him. They made their way to the Veranda Grill where they found a seat which Joyce said she would keep for his return. She told him not to worry about her for she would get herself a drink and, if she could get one at this time of night, a cheese and ham toasty. He reminded her to be alert to any approach or if she saw the man again, to try an act in a way that did not compromise her. She said she would be careful and would see him in a little while. He left her lighting a cigarette and settling herself down after calling a waiter over.

He got back to his cabin at ten minutes to eleven and found a note under his door telling him that Fred would be fifteen minutes late as he had to do some following up on an engine room greaser that would take him about fifteen minutes to undertake. The beer and glasses were on the coffee table and the bed was pulled down and his pyjamas neatly put out over his pillow. That's better, James thought, I will have to give this steward a tip at the end of the trip. While he waited for Fred, he sat and thought what else they could do to make their search more effective. He opened one of the bottles of beer and just sat and thought. If he was hunting for a leg over every night, how would he go about it, especially if he had a sex-inducing drug at his disposal but did not want to get caught? He was still thinking about it when Fred arrived. James got up from his chair and went across and opened the door. Fred, dressed in civvies, came in and at James's invitation sat down. He said he hoped James had got his note and started to explain why he was late. He nodded at the offer of a beer, which James opened and poured, and carried on with the reason for the delay in meeting. He said he had been following up on an engine room greaser because he sort of fitted the description Carol had given him, but when he got showered and went straight to bed in a six birth cabin he knew he had the wrong man.

James then went on to explain about Joyce and what had happened to her and so was sure it wasn't the greaser Fred had suspected. Before he went on, James floated the idea that if the Captain agreed the next morning, would it not be better if they now searched as a team together rather than operate independently? Fred said he had checked as thoroughly as he could the crew's movements and thought he had something when he came across the greaser. "But what," pressed James, "made you suspect him?"

"It was one of the stewards that I spoke to who said this greaser was doing funny things at funny times."

"Like what?" James asked, "What sort of things?" Fred said, apparently, according to the steward, he comes off watch at twelve noon, has a wash and some lunch and then no one sees him again until seven o'clock in the evening when he goes in for his dinner and then at eight o'clock back on watch again until midnight when he has a shower and sometimes goes off again or turns in - tonight he turned in. One of the other greasers said whenever he comes back from wherever he's been, he is carrying something with him, but he didn't know what it was, he is very secretive." James said he intended following up his lead with Joyce and invited Fred to go with him. They were so busy talking that they only drank one bottle of beer each before James said he had promised Joyce he would not be long so thought they ought to get going back up to the Veranda Grill.

When they got back up to the bar, James looked over to where Joyce had been sitting but saw a middle aged couple sitting in the chairs Joyce said she would keep for herself and him when he came back from where he was going. James looked at Fred with a degree of alarm on his face and said, "I left her over there." He looked around to see if she was anywhere else in the room; he even went out onto the balcony to see if she had gone out for a smoke and a breath of air. It was no good Fred looking as he had never met her so would not know who he was looking for anyway. Not finding her inside or outside of the Veranda Grill, James started to get worried. He was sure she was a woman of her word and if she said she would wait for him that is exactly what she would have done. He went over to the couple sitting in the seats they would have been occupying and excused himself for interrupting, but asked how long they had been sitting there and had they seen the lady that had been sitting there before they took the seats. They said they had been there for about fifteen to twenty minutes and no, they had not seen a lady fitting the description James gave them. "Please excuse me asking, but is that your handbag under your chair?" James asked the lady.

"What handbag?" she said, looking under her chair, obviously not knowing it was there. "I only have a little evening bag that I have here," she said, lifting up her arm, "I don't carry a big handbag like that around with me at night." James was only checking for he was sure it was Joyce's but had to be certain.

"If you don't mind, I'll take it, for she was supposed to be waiting here for me, and I will give it to her when I find her, unless you would like to put it behind the bar for the barman to take care of until she comes back?"

"I'm sure you can be trusted, young man, so it might be better if you take it to her." James bent down and picked it up and together with Fred went over to the barman and asked him if he had seen the lady sitting over there, pointing in the direction she had been sitting.

"You mean the well preserved lady that is older than she looks, the one with short blond hair and the large earrings and very high heeled shoes? Yes, as a matter of fact I saw her leave about half an hour ago."

"Was she with anyone or on her own?" James asked to which the barman replied that she was with a man, who was being a bit pushy with her. "I was busy at the time but seem to remember him more than just persuading her to go with him." James thanked the barman and, with the handbag, left the Veranda Grill with Fred in tow.

"What do we do now?" Fred asked.

James said, "Let's dump this hand bag in my cabin, I don't want to walk into bars with a hand bag over my arm, and then we'll visit every bar on the ship that is open and if we don't find her we will go to her cabin. I know the number, and if she's not there I'll get the night cabin steward to open the door. I have a strong suspicion our man has got her." They dropped Joyce's bag off in his cabin and went all over the ship looking in all the bars that were still open. They went into every state room and lounge in all three classes. The segregation gate key was red hot when they had finished. The library was closed and the cinema was locked up for the night. There was nowhere else they could think of looking other than searching every passenger, officer and crew cabin. Could she have gone overboard, Fred suggested, but James said if she had, the distance they had gone since she went missing, even if the ship was turned round they would never find her. So, what were they to do? There must be hundreds of places someone could be stowed on a ship the size of the Queen Mary, but where to start?

James thought to himself, I'm only twenty-three years old albeit nearly twenty-four, I've hurt myself quite badly, I don't know the ship but am having to learn fast and have now become a detective. With these thoughts in mind, James said to Fred, "We have to tell the Captain what has happened, but first I am going back up to the Veranda Grill to talk again to the barman. I think there must have been a bar waiter because Joyce called somebody over to serve her just as I was leaving to go down to meet you." Before making their way to the Veranda Grill, James said, much as he felt guilty, he thought he ought to go through Joyce's handbag to see if anything in it would give them any clues, so they went back to his cabin.

He took everything out of her bag and went through all the items it contained to see if there was anything at all that might be helpful in finding her. Her purse was the first thing he inspected but found only a few dollar bills and some change, together with a couple of pound notes, other items such as sun glasses and what appeared to be reading glasses, lipstick, lace hanky, comb and nail file were all of no help, but the small bottle of pills was. "I wonder what these are for," James said turning to Fred who he hoped, would know, which as it so happened he did.

"They are pills you take when you have diabetes, I know those tablets because my wife used to take them." James said he thought diabetics had to inject themselves with insulin. "Not necessarily," Fred corrected. The rest of the contents of the handbag were just things that all women carry around in their bags. "But, hey!" Fred thought out loud, "Where is her cabin key? She would have surely had that in her handbag." James looked again and in a compartment he had missed was her cabin key and a couple of introductory cards telling anyone she presented them to that she worked for The Times newspaper with a Fleet Street address and telephone number.

Putting all the contents back in the handbag, James said the next stop had to be her cabin before they went to the Veranda Grill to talk again to the barman. Joyce was either well off or her newspaper were footing the bill as her cabin was a large one on main deck. James used her key to open the door and when inside realised what a neat and tidy person this lady was. He asked Fred if he would look in the drawers and cupboards because his hand was now giving him a great deal of discomfort and he could not be bothered to get pain killers now. Fred did as he was asked and found in the drawer in her dressing table not one but three passports, they supposed required for entering different countries, together with other papers that were of a private nature and which they thought not needed to be looked at. James asked if all the passports contained the same name and photograph, to which Fred replied two have Joyce Sheen and one in the name of Joyce Harding with a different photograph of the same person in each. The rest of the drawers and the cupboards contained clothes for all weathers and climates until Fred came to the drawer that was full of her underwear. Not wanting to rummage through this one, he went to shut it when something made a noise when he pushed it shut. Reopening it, it made a slight noise again that he had not heard on the original opening. He pushed down on the silky underwear and felt a lump which when he lifted the clothes he exposed a small pistol. Fred said, seeing that everything about this lady was so in order, he was surprised her passports, private papers and this pistol where not in her cabin safe. Her bed was pulled down so the stewardess had been in, but they could not see any point in talking to her, or at least not at this moment in time.

Not finding anything else and being careful when they left the cabin that nobody saw them, they went to the Veranda Grill and were surprised to see so many people still drinking. James went up to the bar to speak to the barman who was still on duty serving and said he was sorry to trouble him again but could he describe the man who had left with the lady they had spoken of earlier. The barman was getting a bit frustrated because it was now getting very late and he was almost on his own due to two waiters having been called away after food being served finished, leaving only one and him and not being able to shut the bar, even though the numbers of passengers drinking had reduced considerably from what had been there earlier. Fred asked him if there wasn't an official closing time for the Veranda Grill, the same as all the other bars on the ship. The barman said if there was, he had not heard of it. James asked where the waiter was, to which the barman said he didn't know just at that moment, he was on his own and struggling. James thanked him and turning to Fred said quietly, if that were the case, who was it that Joyce called over for it was after ten o'clock that we came up here because the other bar we went to shut at ten. Turning back to the barman, apologising, James asked him again if he could describe the man. The barman said he had only seen them at a glance as they were heading across the bar on their way out, that the guy was about five feet ten tall with dark hair and was casually dressed; he was sorry but could not help any further. Armed with this information, James and Fred went up to see the Captain who when they got there, they learnt from the Tiger, had gone to bed. The Tiger recognised Fred and asked what he was doing in civvies, to which he told him not to worry about that but could he wake the Captain and tell him Mr. Royston and Mr. Baker had to speak to him urgently.

The captain was not very happy about being wakened from his sleep, which was quite understandable. James and Fred were shown into the Captain's day cabin by his Tiger and told that the Captain would be with them shortly. Captain Baron came into his day cabin still in his pyjamas with a dressing gown over them. "This had better be very important, gentlemen", he said, "for I need my sleep." James said he realised that, but what they had to report was an emergency and that they had come direct to him before going to see or talk to anybody else, including the Staff Captain. Captain Baron was now fully awake and eager to hear what the two of them had to say. "Please sit down and tell me what it is that is so important." James went on to explain exactly what had happened since coming out from dinner and about meeting Joyce the night before. The Captain immediately took in the emergency of the situation and apologised for being so sharp at being woken up, saying they had done the right thing by going straight to him. "Will you please go over it again, but more slowly, all the places you have looked for Ms. Sheen. I know the lady you are referring to, she is a foreign correspondent for The Times newspaper. I have had her at my table on several trips in the past, and I'm surprised if she has allowed herself to be kidnapped, if that is what has happened."

"What about if she has fallen or been thrown overboard?" Fred suggested to the Captain, but like James had said, had that happened, it would be impossible to find her by going back and it would have been more than likely that she would have been drawn into the ships propellers and that was not worth thinking about. The Captain sat for several minutes just thinking of what his and their next move must be. He got up from his chair and started pacing his day room floor. How long could he wait before making a search of all the cabins, and should he make an announcement over the ships tannoy system, telling everyone on board what had happened? Captain Baron turned to the two of them and said, "I know you have been awake and about all day, but do you think you can stay awake for a few more hours, say, until daybreak, and continue looking in places like store rooms, machinery spaces, anywhere a person could be gagged, tied up and hidden. I think the life boats are out of the question as it would be virtually impossible to lift someone up into any of those alone and I would doubt if there is an accomplice involved in this. If you can do this until day break, then report back to me, we will go from there. We will continue thinking this is a kidnap, and by the way, I do thank you both very much for what you are doing and for what you have done so far. I take it you are now working together and I think you had better forget about your Master at Arms duties now, Mr. Baker, and just concentrate on what you are doing with Mr. Royston here, for we must try and find this lady before anything serious happens."

"There are just two things I should mention, sir," James said, "I found Ms. Sheen's hand bag where we were supposed to meet in the Veranda Grill, and in it I found her cabin key. I looked because it might help find her. I also found some tablets which indicate she is a diabetic and ongoing into her cabin we found three passports and a small pistol. We have left them where they were and hope it is only the bedroom stewardess that has her cabin master key and that there are no others, other than the one I have and the one which should be held in the purser's office." The Captain told him not to worry about that but to get searching the ship for time was being lost talking and that he would see them again at daybreak, and not to forget the clocks go back an hour at midnight.

Leaving the Captain's day cabin, they had to decide how they were going to carry out the search, for there was a lot of ship to cover and not a lot of time to do it. James said that although it was his first trip, he knew the sort of machinery spaces to search and Fred, having been on the ship a great deal longer, might know other parts of the ship that would be worth looking at. They agreed they would meet up every hour to compare notes and agreed it would be wasting time to look together, but where to start? James suggested they start from the lowest deck and work upwards and that way they would not have far to go to meet up in the main deck foyer every hour. They checked that their watches showed the same time and off they went. James did not think for one minute she would be in any of the main machinery spaces, so decided to work up from the working alleyway. He assumed that wherever she was, if on board, she would be incapacitated and that whatever compartment she was in would not be locked because, where would the kidnapper get the compartment key? He looked in fan flats, workshops, paint and rope stores, refrigeration and air conditioning machinery spaces, anywhere that did not have a locked door, and tried doors that he didn't know whether they were locked or not or what was behind them. He knew it was possible, she could be anywhere, but just kept looking as he worked his way up through each deck in turn.

It took him an hour to cover three decks and found absolutely no sign of anything untoward. He met up with Fred on the hour and both raised their shoulders - nothing. They carried on, James with anything electrical or mechanical that was behind a closed door or a space someone could be possibly hidden. Once again, on the hour they met up and still nothing. "I cannot get into this bloke's head," James said, "I've been trying to think where I would put somebody if I kidnapped them, it would have to be somewhere nobody visits, or only very rarely. We only have two more hours before daybreak but we should cover what is left to search in that time."

The next hour seemed to pass even quicker than those previous, for the Queen Mary was only the second biggest liner in the world and there were so many places to look. Once again, the two of them met up in the main deck foyer to discuss what they had found, if anything. James had wished he had been able to wear overalls, but this was out of the question being too suspicious to anyone seeing them; it would be difficult enough as it was to explain what they were doing at that time of the day. Towards the end of the last hour they intended searching before going back to the captain, James had a brain wave. Where was one place he had not looked or even thought of looking up to then? – The funnels. He was sure there was enough space to hide a body and, although there was machinery including the soot washers inside each funnel, it was worth a look. He climbed up to the base of the funnels and managed to get the door of each one open; it was the first time he had been inside and soon realised that had Joyce been left in any one of them she would by now be dead, for the escaping funnel gases would have choked her. Holding his hankie over his mouth and nose, he had a quick look around with the aid of the only light illuminating the funnel space but found nothing other than soot, dust and the fumes within the funnel casings. It was when he got back to the main deck foyer that he realised just how dirty he had got in a very short time. "Where the hell have you been?" was Fred's first question when they met up. James explained he had had a brain wave and followed it up, but realised as soon as he entered the first funnel casing that this was not the place, but still undertook the search of the other two as they were possibly dealing with a mad man, so nothing could be left to chance. To start with, what was the point of kidnapping Joyce in the first place? If it was for money, who did he think was going to pay any ransom and what would he do with her when they got to Southampton? Because he was so dirty, James suggested Fred go to his cabin with him so he could have a wash and change of clothes before going to see the Captain together.

It did not take James long to wash and change into other clothes and while he was doing so, Fred went through all the places he had visited, hoping to at least get a lead on where Joyce could possibly have been hidden. It was just getting light when they got up to the Captain's cabin, where they found him already in his day uniform eating his breakfast. "Please come in, both of you," the Captain invited. "And would you like a cup of tea or coffee? You both look like it would not go amiss." They both asked for coffee – not too strong. The captain asked if they had got anything to report after being up all night and didn't seem too surprised when they said they had found absolutely nothing.

"So," Captain Baron said, "where do we go from here?" James went through all the places he had looked followed by Fred. The captain sat very thoughtfully for what seemed an age before saying, "Well, gentlemen, I do appreciate what you have both done so far but do you have any suggestions as to what I should do next?" James was the first to speak up, saying, was he correct in assuming the ship was not at capacity and that could they find out from the purser's office what cabins in all classes were not occupied? It would then be a case of checking each of them for the signs of occupation. He appreciated this was not going to be an easy job because of curiosity of the cabin staff, but if it was left to them, the word of what was being done would flash round the ship in no time at all. To check all the occupied cabins was really out of the question, for apart from causing alarm among the passengers, it was also questioning their integrity. The captain suggested that they leave the problem with him and that they should get some breakfast and some sleep before reporting back to him at two o'clock when they could decide the way ahead. James said he had to report to the hospital to get his dressing changed that was currently filthy, plus his hand was giving him a great deal of pain. With that, both Fred and James finished their coffee and left the captain to run his ship.

James wondered if he would ask the steward to bring him some breakfast to the cabin but then thought better of it and decided to go into breakfast in the dining room and from there straight down to the hospital to get his hand sorted. He was very surprised when he got to the dining room to see so many early birds and even more so when he got to his table and found Helen and Elizabeth already starting on their breakfast. James sat down rather wearily and said good morning to both and enquired why they were so early. Helen said she had mentioned that she intended going to the gym this morning before leaving the lounge last night and Elizabeth asked if she could join her. The gym gets a bit crowded by nine o'clock so they thought they would get an early start and get into it early, directly it opened. James asked if they had enjoyed their evening and did they spend it together, to which they said they had, apart from that actor and his crowd who became very noisy. Helen said she found him very strange and would not trust him an inch, but thought perhaps that is how famous people behave when they are not acting. Elizabeth asked James if his hand was giving him a lot of pain as he looked very drawn and tired, and that if she didn't know better she would have said he had been up all night. James just shrugged her remark off but said he was going to the hospital after breakfast so the doctor could take a look at it. The waiter, who had obviously seen James arrive, came over to the table and, after saying good morning, asked James what he wanted for his breakfast. Having been up all night and on the go, James was ravenous. He ordered a large breakfast and said yes he would like coffee and toast to accompany it. While he was waiting, he took a good look around the other tables that could be viewed with ease and that were occupied, to see if there was anything he could pick up on, but there was not. He was in conversation with Helen, asking her how much longer she had to spend at school when suddenly he thought of something. When she said she was seventeen and in her final year but when dressed up as she was last night she could get away with passing for being in her twenties easily, an idea started to take shape in James's mind. When his breakfast arrived, he, Helen and Elizabeth continued the small talk until he finished. He said he would have to leave them and get to the hospital, and didn't think he would see them at lunch time but would certainly see them for dinner. He hoped they would have a good day and got up to leave the table. It was as he got up that Helen asked why James's dressing was so dirty, for although while getting washed and changed he had tried to clean it up, it was still very grubby. He had to think on his feet and quickly, so said before going to bed he went to adjust the Louvre in his cabin and a lot of sooty like dust came out all over his hand. Helen wasn't satisfied with that and asked why he had used his damaged hand to do it. James said it was because he had a glass in his good hand and didn't think about it. She then asked if it had hurt, to which he said no it moved easily but had obviously not been adjusted for a long time. He told Helen and Elizabeth that he was now off to see the doctor and would let them know what he had to say at dinner that evening. It was while he was on his way to the hospital that the thought suddenly occurred to him that tomorrow night was formal dress when every man travelling first class was expected to wear a dinner suit or white tuxedo, and of course he had nothing like that. Yet another problem to overcome, he thought! When he got to the hospital, Dr. Maiden was seeing to another patient, but had told Jean to get the dressing off and make sure the wound was clean directly he came in so he could examine the hand. Jean's first question, of course, was why it was so dirty and how long had it been like it. James, having told Helen how it had happened told Jean the same thing. Jean's look told James she did not believe him, but got on with cutting the dressing off to clean the now exposed wound. His whole hand was not quite so swollen now, but was all colours of the rainbow. The nails on the middle three fingers were black and whatever the stuff was that Jean used to clean his hand stung a bit. While waiting for the doctor to finish with the other patient, he got into small talk with Jean as she was getting rid of the old dressing and swabs. What did she do to get into nursing on ships and how long had she been doing it? She told James she had to be fully qualified and twenty six before she could even apply for sea going nursing. She said she had thought of going into the army or RAF and had finished up going to sea in the Merchant Navy. Asking how long she had been sea going, she said she had been on the Queen Mary for two and a half years thus evading the full question. James was still not able to work out her age, which was obviously why he asked the question in the first place, but guessed she was into her mid-thirties, not that it mattered one jot. When Dr. Maiden got to James he was very pleased with the healing process and, after telling Jean to put a light dressing on, told James to be careful what he was doing with it. James asked him if it would be possible to supply a protective glove of some kind and Dr. Maiden said they could supply a modified glove and that he wanted to see him again the day after next. He said James was looking very tired and suggested he not burn the midnight oil and get more sleep.

James left the hospital saying, "Thank you," and "Cheerio," both to Dr. Maiden and Jean and to Barbara as he passed her on his way out. He was now very tired indeed and could not wait to get to his bed, knowing he was to report back to the Captain at two o'clock. He was lucky, for when he got back to his cabin the bedroom steward had made his bed and put the cabin to rights, not that it was in too much of a mess, seeing he had spent very little time in it. He put the 'Do Not Disturb' notice on the outside of the cabin door and went to bed directly he had shut it. He must have gone to sleep within minutes as he could not remember a thing after getting undressed and getting into bed. It was one o'clock when he woke with a bit of a start and wondered for a moment where he was but soon got onto an even keel. He felt like having a cigarette but then thought better of it because he would have to come back later to a cabin that would smell like an un-emptied ashtray. He wiped around his face with a wet flannel before getting dressed. He made his way to the Captain's quarters and got there five minutes early, where the Captain's Tiger told him to go straight in. He knocked the door and on the command, "Come in," entered the cabin. Fred was not yet there which was convenient for the Captain, who said he wanted to speak to James alone. He instructed his Tiger to tell Fred to wait when he arrived and that he would not keep him waiting long. He invited James to take a seat and after asking if he had had a good sleep and how his hand was, asked if he had any thoughts on the way ahead, as they were well on their way and that Ms Sheen had been missing for over twelve hours. Before James gave the captain an answer, he had to ask him about clothing. He said that not to blow his cover, so to speak, he would have to get hold of a dinner suit for tonight's formal dinner and probably some other clothes as he could only wear the same gear into the restaurant with nothing other than a second pair of trousers, and a change of tie. He only had a few going ashore cloths with him because he thought he would be in uniform all the time, apart from a run ashore, so thought it unnecessary to bring any more than he had.

The Captain said he was quite correct and that he would contact the ship's shop and arrange a loan if it was possible.

He thanked the Captain and proceeded to put his thoughts to him. Firstly, to search all the cabins that were not officially occupied, then, all the life boats, just in case there had been more than one kidnapper, and after having searched the funnels, thought of one other place that could be a possibility and that was the ship's cargo holds. The Captain's eyes opened up when James suggested the cargo holds, saying that they were secured on leaving New York and would not be opened again until they were ready to unload on arrival in Southampton. "What has made you think of the holds, James?" the captain asked.

"Well, there must be passengers' cars among the cargo, and what better place to hide somebody than in a Rolls

Royce or one of those huge American Limousines? Food and drink could be supplied and blankets for warmth and, being tied up, whoever was being imprisoned would not be able to escape. If the holds are not guarded, which they would not be if they had been secured, no one would see the comings and goings of any one likely to be doing such a thing as kidnapping." The Captain went very quiet, and when he spoke, he said to James, "Are you sure you are an engineer or have you been reading too many detective stories? How could anybody get access to the holds when they are locked up?" This James could not answer but just thought it was a possibility, the same as the life boats.

Although he was tired, James was so focussed on trying to find who it was that had tried it on with Fred's niece, and if it was the same man that has now got hold of Joyce. He said he, together with Fred, had searched in every place they could think of without even a trace of anything to follow up on.

The Tiger knocked on the Captain's door and on getting a, "Yes," went in and said that the Master at Arms had been waiting for ten minutes, was it all right to now show him in? Captain Baron indicated that he show him in and invited Fred to sit down, which he did. He asked Fred questions on the same lines as he had asked James, and he, like James, came up with only negatives. He was asked if he had any new ideas as to how to proceed, for although he was the Captain and responsible for the safety of his ship and the welfare of the passengers on it, he had to tread very carefully with regard to his next set of actions. He had to prevent causing alarm and panic among the passengers and at the same time not give any clues to the person they were looking for that they were on his case. Fred, like James before him, suggested they search the unoccupied cabins but had no idea how to go about it without there being rumours spreading into the Pig and Whistle where the crew members socialise, and then through to the passengers.

The cargo holds were the easiest option to start with because the captain could arrange for some sort of exercise to be carried out that would enable the vehicles stowed there being checked for security and safe stowage. The watertight doors could be opened and access given to the holds without suspicion being created that it was anything but that – just an exercise. But who to get involved was a question that had to be asked and answered. Before this idea was adopted however, once again James interjected and suggested that perhaps it could be made an emergency fire drill. Captain Baron asked why make it a fire drill rather than just an exercise to which James said, "By making it a fire drill it could be a way of killing three birds with one stone. By making it a fire drill, the holds could be searched as part of it with perhaps the first officer being the officer overseeing the search where he could organise a thorough search of the vehicles and any other space where someone could be hidden and incorporated in the fire drill, employ officers and Masters at Arms on each passenger accommodation deck to supervise the searching of all unoccupied cabins by the bedroom stewards and stewardesses on each deck. The engineer officers and ratings will automatically go to their fire stations and will carry out their routines as on all occasions when there is a fire drill, including the running of the emergency generator. If it is announced over the passenger address system that there was to be a fire drill which is for exercise only, and that passengers are required to proceed to their emergency stations the officers allocated to each deck can organise the search of all the cabins not being occupied". James appreciated that it would take time to set up such an exercise as it would have to be done differently to what he understood was the norm. Names of passengers would have to be taken, and the search of the cabins would have to be controlled with the cabins searched thoroughly and monitored, but although it would be time taken to organise, it could all be incorporated into one exercise and the three birds killed with one stone. A fire drill that is maritime law had to be carried out, that could include the search of the holds and the unoccupied cabins. If a late afternoon time was given for the drill to be carried out, it would allow time for the Staff Captain to organise it all, for there would have to be orders given to comply with what was needed to get a result. If the names of the passengers not attending the drill were known, it could maybe give a lead to who might be covering their tracks.

The Captain listened to what James had to say with an expression of, 'who is this guy!?' However, knowing how hard it was going to be to carry out the necessary searches, it was a proposal worth consideration. Who was to do what was going to be the captain's biggest problem without creating suspicion, especially as James could not take part other than as a passenger, although Fred in uniform could be a great asset to the procedure in his capacity as a Senior Master at Arms. "The problem I have with your idea, James, is the time it will take to carry out the search of the cabins and state rooms, as a fire drill only takes about half an hour from sounding the alarm to completion, bearing in mind it is only an exercise and not the real thing." James went on to suggest that perhaps it could be as a result of the roll call at each fire station when a passenger is found to be missing, which of course is the case and an effort has to be made to locate them.

If Ms Joyce Sheen is not accounted for when a visit is made to her cabin, then that is the reason that a search of the ship can be made with no suspicion at all involved and it could take as long as it takes by whoever is delegated to carry out the search. The fire drill, after the fire in the hold has been extinguished and the search completed, can be ended over the passenger address system and the passengers and crew stood down, except for the searchers.

The fire drill and missing passengers from the fire station attendance list appealed to Captain Baron and he said that it made sense if it was organised properly. He said he would call his heads of departments together and, through them getting their people detailed off for the parts they had to take, get the fire drill organised for five o'clock. This would not interfere with passenger's afternoon tea or dinner as this timing would be after one and before the other. He would not have to name the passenger they were looking for, but of course a check would have to be made on all passengers that were also not at their emergency station. As he was saying this, he picked up his telephone and asked the operator to connect him to the Chief Purser and called his Tiger and told him to get the Staff Captain and Chief Officer to come along to his cabin right away. He thanked and dismissed James and Fred and told them to carry on searching the ship in any way they could without it being obvious what they were doing. James suggested to Fred that he get out of his uniform and put some casual clothes on so that they could wander freely and mingle with the passengers all over the ship before redressing in uniform for the forthcoming fire drill. James said he was going back to his cabin and would meet Fred there when he had changed.

James got back to his cabin but not before bumping into Amy and Elizabeth, who were, according to them, going for a bit of fresh air before going for afternoon tea. They said that James was now not looking quite so tired and seeing the clean new dressing on his hand asked how it was. James bent his hand up a bit almost making a fist and said that now the dressing was that much smaller it was becoming more like a hand rather than a lump on the end of his arm and was not quite so painful.

After excusing himself, he opened his cabin door and thought he could smell a scent he recognised, but could not think from where or when he had smelt it. After having spoken to the Captain about getting some more clothes, including a dinner suit and all that goes with it, he had forgotten about it with all that was being discussed, but he had to go and see about it as soon as he could. He waited for Fred to come before leaving the cabin to go to the ship's tailoring shop. When Fred came, he asked him to do what ever investigating he thought could help their cause. They left James's cabin and went to the lift, which was only a short distance along the passage way. Fred said he was going up to see what was going on on the upper decks and that he would meet James outside of the tailor's shop in about half an hour, which should give him enough time to arrange what he had to acquire. James got out of the lift after asking the bell boy to stop it at the promenade deck where the shops were and as there were no other passengers in the lift, he shut the doors and took Fred straight to the highest deck the lift went to at Fred's request.

James had a bit of trouble in the shop and had to insist on calling the manager. The manager, when he arrived, said it was possible for James to borrow some clothes but that it was highly irregular. He was reluctant to lend them, but would much prefer to hire or sell them. James explained that some of his baggage had been lost or at the least mislaid and that he had been invited to the Captain's table that night and was due to go to a lunch time cocktail party tomorrow when smart casual dress would be required. The shop manager started to get agitated and explained to James that he might get the sack, to which James muttered under his breath, "If only you did but know it you might get the sack if you don't let me have some clothes." It became a difficult situation whereby the shop manager did not want to step down from his stand point but James had to get some clothes that looked reasonably smart for that night's formal dress without letting on why. "What would I have to do to persuade you how important it is for me to be properly dressed tonight and tomorrow?" James asked.

"It would take the Captain himself to persuade me," replied the manager thinking that would end the matter and get rid of this rather tiresome young man.

"If that is all I have to do, I will arrange for him to come and see you as soon as he is free."

The manager, thinking he had the upper hand, said smugly, "I await his visit."

James asked him if he had the clothes to fit him on board, to which he replied, "This is the Queen Mary of Bond Street, London, young man, of course we have clothes that will fit you!"

Knowing the Captain was up to his eyes in arranging his fire drill, James began to feel less confident as to whether he could get the Captain to come down to the shop. All he could do was ask the Captain directly the fire drill was over and hope for the best. "I will see you later," James said, leaving the shop and the manager who by then had a look that said 'get out of my shop, you scruffy little urchin.' Fred was waiting outside and just a look at James's face told him there had been a problem. As they walked away together James started to explain what had gone on, to which Fred said he was not in the least surprised because he had had trouble with this man, who had some time ago tried to get him the sack. It was while they were trying to decide what to do next in way of being constructive that they encountered Judy Mendise and a few of what appeared to be hangers on rather than friends. They were obviously shopping as she and a couple of the women had got carrier bags on their arms. As they passed the group, the smell of perfume hit both men that brought forth the comment from Fred, that he wondered how some of these American ladies looked and smelled when they woke up in the mornings. James said he hadn't seen many American woman before coming to sea, but realised they really knew how to slap on the makeup, and some of the jewellery was a bit flash too. Whether it was real or not was of course another matter, but having said that, some of the ladies looked a bit special, even those that were getting on a bit in age looked well preserved. James explained to Fred who Mrs. Renton was and what had gone on in the dining room. "Is that the actor Steve Renton you are talking about?" Fred asked. "If it is, he did a trip on the Queen Elizabeth last year and caused a lot of trouble. Who he thinks he is I don't know. He is only a bit part actor that has never hit the big time and been in any major films."

"Whatever he is, he has a few hangers on the same as his wife and one thing is for sure, our Captain has his card marked for the way he tried to show him up at the first night's dinner," said James.

They walked together from the shops up the stairways to the upper decks, where they went outside into quite a nice bright day. There were a lot of passengers sitting around in deckchairs, some in the sun, what there was of it, and others in the shade with blankets over their knees, while the more active ones were playing deck quoits and shuffle board. There were a few reading and others enjoying drinks and tabnabs, which the deck stewards had provided. James and Fred walked among them, with Fred getting told off for just knocking into a table where two ladies and a gentleman were playing dominos and unfortunately the dominos were knocked over. Fred apologised profusely but was only partly forgiven by the man, who said they would have to start that game again as their hands had now been exposed. After covering all the open decks with not a clue as to what they were looking for, they decided to await the fire drill that was not far off now. Fred said he was going back down below to get into his uniform again and would see James after dinner at a quarter to nine in the main deck foyer.

At a quarter to five, the ships tannoy system came alive, announcing that it was the Staff Captain speaking and that to meet with Board of Trade regulations there was going to be a fire drill in fifteen minutes time. It was for exercise only, but that all crew not on duty and passengers would be required to report to their emergency stations, where their names would be checked off and they would be given instructions as to what to do in the event of a real fire.

At five o'clock precisely, the ships alarm was sounded and all the passengers that were on the open deck left what they were doing and started making their way to their emergency stations. It was just before leaving the boat deck that James noticed a passenger that was sitting alone with a blanket over his knees and a newspaper covering his face. Thinking that the passenger, who was a man, was perhaps deaf or in a very deep sleep, and had not heard the alarm, went over to wake him to tell him he should go to his emergency station as the ships alarm had sounded. When he got to the side of the deckchair, James spoke to him quite loudly telling him the fire drill was about to start but got no response. Without touching the man, he gently lifted the newspaper away from his face thinking that would wake him, but to James's surprise and shock, he realised by the face under the paper with blood having dribbled from his mouth and down onto his shirt and jacket that the man who he recognised was dead. Rather than shout for help, James thought before going to his emergency station he would go to the bridge and report what he had found. He put the newspaper back over the man's face and hurried without running, up to the bridge. When he got there, he found the Captain and the Officer of the Watch together with the crew members that were on duty. Having just hurried from the boat deck up to the bridge, he was a bit out of breath, but was able to quickly explain to the captain what he had found. Captain Baron asked him what had he done when he found him and on explaining to the Captain that all the other passengers that had been on deck had left to go to their emergency stations, he was alone. Captain Baron calmly picked up the bridge telephone and dialled the hospital number and asked to speak to one of the doctors. It must have been Dr. Cummings that came to the phone because it was his name that was mentioned. The Captain told him to meet him on the boat deck immediately and to bring a nurse with him and that he would meet them where James had explained the passenger was. He then told the Officer of the Watch to contact the Second Mate and get him up on the bridge. He told James to lead the way and so they returned to the boat deck where they found the passenger still as James had left him. While they waited for the doctor and nurse to arrive, which was not very long, James explained to the Captain that he recognised who the passenger was, but did not know his name, but that Captain Baron would recognise him as well, and it was one of the actor Steve Renton's sidekicks.

When the doctor arrived accompanied by the nurse that happened to be Jean, he quickly realised what all the urgency was about. The Captain asked the doctor to examine the passenger quickly and get him down to the hospital as soon as possible, hopefully before the fire drill was over. Doctor Cummings quickly removed the paper from the man's face and instantly declared him dead. He removed the blanket from his legs and asked Jean to help get him out of the chair and lay him face down on the blanket on the deck. It was as they were doing this that a knife could be seen sticking out from his back which had obviously been driven into him through the bars of the chair from behind. There was very little blood, which was a good thing, for what little there was could have been from anyone that had even had a nose bleed. Doctor Cummings, whilst wrapping the body in the blanket, instructed Jean to go as quickly as she could back to the hospital and get the two orderlies and a stretcher to pick up the corpse as soon as possible. James said he would accompany her in case he could be of any help. As they were about to leave the scene, James heard the Captain tell the doctor to make sure that under no circumstances was anybody to touch the knife with bare hands so that finger prints could be retained. The doctor said he would remove the knife himself and put it in a plastic bag. James and Jean hurried off to the hospital where Jean got Barbara to fetch the two orderlies from their emergency station immediately. While she was away, Jean collected together everything she could think of that would be needed to get the dead man's body back to the hospital which of course included the stretcher. Barbara could not have been gone five minutes before she was back with the two orderlies, to whom Jean gave precise instructions and a reminder that what they were going to do was not to be talked about. When they arrived back on deck, the doctor had got everything ready for the transfer of the body back to the hospital where it would be dealt with.

All except the Captain and James went back to the hospital; the Captain told James to follow him back to the bridge. Captain Baron was, to say the least, furious, and asked James what on earth would be likely to happen next. It was bad enough having what they thought was a kidnapping but now to having a murder as well all on the same voyage was going too far. Some people think captains have an easy time, entertaining and being the main man on the ship. They also realised the responsibility was his for the safety of the ship and getting it from port to port, but he had a crew to look after everything. If only they knew what a captain's responsibilities covered, they might think differently.

When they got back to the bridge, the Captain asked how much longer the fire drill was going to last. The Officer of the Watch quickly brought the captain up to speed with regard to the current situation and asked what the captain wanted to do next. "Get this bloody fire drill finished and then get the ship back to normal as soon as possible," was his reply.

With that, the Staff Captain came onto the bridge and went straight over to the captain. They spoke very urgently for about five minutes, a conversation James tried but failed to get the gist of. The Captain himself went over to the microphone and announced that it was the Captain speaking, that the fire drill was now complete and thanked the passengers and crew for being so attentive and attending the compulsory exercise.

Getting things back to normal took a little while. Passengers began returning to their cabins, some to their books and papers on the deck and those who fancied an aperitif or cup of tea before getting ready for dinner made their way to cocktail bars and public rooms, wherever their fancy took them.

Captain Baron asked James if he knew where Fred's cabin was and could he go and get him, to which James pointed out that it would not be the norm for a passenger to go into the crew's quarters. "Oh, Christ, I forgot for a minute, what I am doing?" He turned to the Officer of the Watch and asked him to get the bridge seaman to go and get Mr. Baker the Master at Arms and bring him to the bridge. "When he arrives, send him into my bridge cabin," he instructed, and invited the Staff Captain and James to follow him into the small cabin that was situated at the back of the bridge, behind the chart table.

CHAPTER 6

When they got into the small cabin that was hardly used, as its purpose was only ever for when the weather was really bad and the Captain needed to be at immediate notice, he asked the Staff Captain to sit in one chair as he sat in the other and invited James to sit on the side of the bunk. "Now, gentlemen, we will start off with a fire drill shakedown and then see where we stand as regard to the rest of what has gone on during this voyage, which is turning out to be a nightmare."

"Starting off with the fire drill, what have we learnt from that, was anything found in the cargo holds and what has the search of the empty cabins brought us?" The Staff Captain said they would have to wait until the first officer reported back to him and the search of the cabins was not yet completed and so there would be a slight delay with that too. Fred was still not with them yet so James thought this an appropriate time to bring up the problem he had had trying to get some clothes for tonight's gala dinner and some more suitable clothes to those he had with him. When James quickly relayed what had gone on at the tailor's shop to Captain Baron, he vented some of the tension he was under by blowing his top. "He wants me to go to him? ... Not bloody likely, I will send for him directly this meeting is over and you will be notified when you can go and pick up your gear after being fitted for it, if he says they have it available. I will also tell him this is his last chance. I have had to warn him before about his attitude towards passengers and their complaints. It's surprising what you learn from passengers when they are at your dinner table. It's probably why he is employed at sea. If he was in the Bond Street store in London, I am sure he would have had the sack long ago. But never fear, James, you will be appropriately dressed for dinner tonight."

At this, James made sure he would be on his normal table because he had another idea to try and catch the rapist come kidnapper. Captain Baron pressed him on this, but James said he would have to get some parental permission before he could put the idea to the Captain, which would be as soon as possible after dinner tonight. It was at that point that there was a knock on the door and when told to come in, Fred appeared. "Sit down next to Mr. Royston," the Captain invited and immediately he had perched himself on the edge of the bunk next to James, the Captain asked him what he had to report. Fred said while the fire drill was being undertaken, after getting his own name ticked off at the emergency station, he found out the cabin and locker of the steward that was under lock and key for stealing, as well as other crew member cabins that were unoccupied due to the fire drill. "And what did you discover?" Captain Baron wanted to know. Fred went on to explain what he had discovered; in the locker that he had to force open, a copious amount of jewellery and a letter that was obviously from the person who was handling the stuff he was stealing. The Captain told Fred he had done well and asked what he had done with what he had found. Fred said he had put it all in an envelope, which he then produced for the Captain to inspect and said he intended having it put in the purser's safe. Captain Baron opened the envelope out onto his desk and, in front of them all as witnesses, went through the items of jewellery and carefully removing the letter from its envelope, using his handkerchief as Fred had done, read it out to those assembled. "This is a problem we can now forget until we get back to Southampton, gentlemen, and if you leave the envelope and jewellery with me, Mr. Baker, I will put it in my cabin safe from where it will be handed over to the Police when they come aboard, which they will do because they have already been notified of what has gone on. Was there anything else you found Fred?" the Captain asked.

"Yes, sir," Fred continued, "I looked at every pair of shoes I could find but found none that matched the description we have of whoever it is we are looking for regarding the attack on my niece and Ms. Sheen the newspaper lady.

As they sat there waiting for reports to come back, Captain Baron went to the cabin door and asked a seaman to go and see his Tiger and get him to bring four cups of tea and some biscuits or cake to his bridge cabin. The tea arrived together with biscuits and cake that was handed round by the Captain's Steward before leaving. The four men were half way through their refreshments when there was another knock on the door, this time it brought the First Officer into the little cabin. Captain Baron, now realising this cabin was not nearly large enough, said, "Drink up and we will go to my day cabin where we will have more room."

On getting to the Captain's day cabin and all finding a seat, Captain Baron sat at his desk, after first putting the envelope Fred had given him into his safe, and asked the First Officer what he had to report. Mr. John Roberts, the First Officer, said that a thorough search had been made in the cargo holds and that nothing untoward had been discovered. That all the cars had been locked but looked into and unless anyone had been stowed in the boot of any of them, which was unlikely, there was nothing found, and in any case, had that happened, whoever it was would have been suffocated by now. The Captain agreed and asked if there was anything else to report. The First Officer said the lists of the passengers and crew attending the fire drill were now available; did the Captain want them sent to him direct or should the pursers deal with them? Captain Baron said he wanted them sent straight to him and as soon as possible, please. While they waited for the lists to be brought to them, the Captain picked up his phone and asked the operator to telephone the Manager of the Tailor shop and tell him to report to the Captain immediately. Captain Baron summoned his Tiger and asked him to let him know when the tailor shop manager arrived and show him into his night cabin, as he was presently occupied with important business. It was only ten minutes later that the Tiger knocked on the door adjoining the day cabin and informed the Captain the shop manager had arrived. Captain Baron asked to be excused for a few minutes while he sorted out a small domestic problem and asked his steward to get the officers assembled whatever they would like to drink while they waited. Getting up, he went to his night cabin door, closing it behind him.

Those left in the day cabin could not hear exactly what was being said, but with voices raised knew things must be becoming very uncomfortable for the manager of the ship's tailors shop. Captain Baron first posed the question to the shop manager, who the hell did he think he was, expecting the Captain of the most famous liner in the world to go to him? To which the manager said he had only been joking, being the first thing that came into his head. This was not accepted and he was then read the riot act by the Captain, who on completion notified him that this was the third and last time he would be reprimanding him and that he intended writing to his head office in London with a copy to the Cunard head office requesting his removal from his ship due to this being the third time he had had to warn him of his behaviour regarding passengers. He concluded that he was to meet Mr. Royston's request regarding the clothes he needed for tonight's gala dinner and the other items he would need and if he did not, he could expect the sack soon after the ship docked in Southampton. He then dismissed him and returned to his day cabin where the officers waiting stood up until he sat down again at his desk. "Right, gentlemen, please be seated, where were we, and by the way, Mr. Royston, if you go to the tailor's shop after you leave this meeting I am sure you will be served with what you require for tonight and until you get to Southampton on a loan basis. If you have any more problems, report them to the Staff Captain here who will deal with it, but I am sure you will have no further trouble."

It was soon after the meeting resumed that the Chief Purser came to the Captain's day room door with the lists of the passengers and crew attending the fire drill. When he asked if there was anything that he could do to assist the Captain, Captain Baron said yes, could he now bring him a copy of all the passengers and all the crew aboard on this current voyage. The chief purser saw no difficulty in providing these and again asked if there was anything else he or any of his staff could assist with, to which the Captain said he would let him know, but thanked him for what he was doing already. The Chief Purser left and went back to his office and within about fifteen minutes a junior purser brought the lists requested back to the Captain. On receiving the second lot of passenger and crew details, the Captain immediately gave all the paperwork to James and directed him and Fred to take them away somewhere quiet and go through them with a fine tooth comb and by comparing the two lists, see what they could come up with. It was then that Captain Baron declared his thoughts that perhaps there could be a stow-a-way on board and perhaps by holding the fire drill this could expose him, even though the ship had been searched from top to bottom looking for Joyce. "Off you both go and report back to me as soon as you can with anything that you discover." James asked if that could be later that night as there was the gala dinner, after he had sorted out something to wear with the tailor shop manager and he also had to seek permission to do what he had in mind that he had spoken about earlier. Before leaving, Fred asked the Captain what was going to happen about the murder, to which the Captain replied that he would wait until he heard something back from the doctor and at the moment they should just concentrate on the job in hand.

James and Fred had to decide where they could be quiet and private so asked the Chief Purser if it would be possible to go to the biggest passenger cabin available, one that had been thoroughly searched but that would have enough room and table space to spread out all the papers that had been given to them. The Chief Purser complained a little when this request was made, saying he had offered some of his staff to undertake what James and Fred had been told to do, but when James explained that as few people as possible were to know what was being done, the Chief Purser backed off and said the most expensive suite on the ship had not been purchased, so they could use that, and went and fetched the key himself and gave it to James.

They went to the cabin, or rather the suite, that had been allocated and on opening the door both stood wide eyed, taking in the luxury and resplendent furnishings of the accommodation in which they had to work. "Shows what money can buy," Fred exclaimed, and James had to agree, for neither of them had seen anything like it. It was fit enough for the Queen and Prince Phillip to occupy, if they ever made a trip on the Queen Mary, which was unlikely seeing they had the Royal Yacht. They entered the cabin and within a very short time had organised the tables and chairs in such a way as to accommodate the task they were set to do. Directly everything was laid out, James asked Fred if he could make a start and that he would be back from the tailor's shop as soon as he could, otherwise it would close and that would make a situation worse than maybe it already was. When James left the cabin taking the key with him and asking Fred to lock the door behind him, he made straight for the tailor's shop. When he entered, the man serving said the manager was not available but that he had been told that Mr. Royston would be coming in and that he was to accommodate him in every way and to make sure everything he was supplied with was checked for damage or defects and signed for in triplicate, giving the top copy to Mr. Royston before leaving the shop.

It took James nearly an hour to try on and acquire all the items of clothing he thought he would need for that night and until he got back to Southampton. This accomplished, he asked the young man that had dealt with him what he had to do to return them. The young tailor said he just had to bring it all back before the shop shut for the last time before docking and it would be dealt with, and if there was no damage he would hear no more about it. James thanked him but could not resist asking what his boss was like when he came down from seeing the Captain. He said he didn't know he had been up to see the Captain, but that wherever he had been, when he got back he was in a mood whereby he could commit murder, and after giving orders regarding Mr. Royston had stormed out of the shop and he hadn't seen him since. Having put most of the clothes and shoes into bags and the suits and jackets into dust covers, James managed to carry them back to his cabin.

Once again, he bumped into Amy and Elizabeth, who were just returning to their cabin for their glass of sherry and to get ready for dinner. He walked from the lift to the cabin with each lady carrying a part of his load. On reaching their cabin door, Amy gave Elizabeth what she was carrying and opening their cabin door and went in, while Elizabeth walked on the few paces to James's cabin. James had to put some of his bags on the deck so that he could retrieve his cabin key from his pocket before opening his door. The two of them stepped inside, where James asked Elizabeth to put what she had onto the bed, while he dropped what he was still holding into one of his chairs before retrieving what he had put down outside of the cabin. "I am assuming you are coming to the gala dinner tonight seeing you have just spent a small fortune on clothes," Elizabeth said, to which James replied that he was, albeit perhaps a bit late. He enquired what time she and Amy would be going in for dinner, to which Elizabeth said probably not too early and if he was going to be a bit later than usual, would see him then; that is, if he didn't want to join them in a glass of sherry. James said he had something very important to attend to and would she excuse him on this occasion. They left the cabin together with James locking the door behind him and walking with Elizabeth the few strides to her cabin door that had been left ajar. She pushed it open and went through with James calling out cheerio to Amy before she closed it. He then high-tailed it back up to the suite they had been allocated where he found Fred up to his eyes in paper. There were little piles all over the cabin, on tables, chairs and even one pile on the floor. "You have been busy while I was gone," James commented. "Have you got anywhere yet?" Fred said he had separated all the fire drill lists of passengers and crew together with the same for the ships current complement. If they could now each take a list they could compare and note the differences and perhaps discover something that they could follow up. James said that it sounded a good idea and set about doing just that, but not before saying that he could not stay long as he had to get ready to go to the gala dinner. Fred said he would stay on until he had to go for his meal and would come straight back directly he had finished. James said he didn't know when he would be back, as he wanted to try and get Helen to help him do something but had to get her father's permission before he could do anything about it, but when he did get back, if Fred hadn't finished, they would have to work on through the night. To this it was agreed and so they made a start. The details on the lists were quite comprehensive and proved to be a great help with the crews lists and the passengers. James remained with Fred for about three quarters of an hour before he said he would now have to go and get himself spruced up for dinner and that he would get back to Fred as soon as he possibly could, warning him it would not be for a few hours. Fred said he would carry on and might even be finished before James returned.

It was with this last remark ringing in his ears that James left Fred to it and went back to his cabin. Once again, as he entered the cabin he could smell the slightest hint of a familiar odour but could not put his finger on what it was and so thought it was his imagination as other than the bedroom stewards and Fred, no one else had been in the cabin. He knew it wasn't Fred, so perhaps it was the after shave of one of the stewards. Whatever it was, he just dismissed it and got on with having a shower, shave and getting dressed. With his hand as it was, he still had some difficulty getting dressed and in trying to do his cufflinks up and fixing his bow tie he had to admit defeat, and decided to knock on the ladies' door to see if they had left to go to dinner. His knock brought a, "hello who is there?" from inside the cabin and when James said who it was, the door opened very gently and not by very much. It was Amy, and on seeing James standing there said, "Hello, James, have you come for a glass of sherry?" She seemed quite disappointed when James said he had come to ask a favour. Elizabeth was sitting reading a magazine when James entered the cabin and putting the magazine and her sherry glass down, got up from her chair when James said what the favour was. She said that Amy suffered with arthritis in her hands and so it would be easier if she did up the top button of his shirt, insert the cufflinks and tie up his shoes. When she had finished, James thanked her and said that when they were ready to go to dinner he would accompany them if they rung his cabin number. He went back to his cabin and within only ten minutes got the call. He combed his hair before leaving the cabin then locked it behind him and met up with the ladies as they were locking theirs.

Both ladies were dressed in long dresses which oozed quality and class and with very tasteful jewellery both looked a million dollars. James complemented them both and jokingly asked if they would mind his company for the night. They said how smart James looked and they would be glad to accompany him to dinner. They took the lift where the bell boy wished them an enjoyable dinner and evening as the lift doors opened for them to alight. They took the short walk to the restaurant where the ship's photographer was taking photographs of couples and groups with the captain as they entered the dining room. James suggested that Elizabeth and Amy had their picture taken with the Captain without him in it as it would be one to savour in years to come. After the flash of the camera taking the ladies standing either side of the Captain, he made small talk and as they moved away, the Captain quietly asked James how he had got on and how smart he looked. James told the Captain quickly that he had had no trouble at the tailor's shop and that Fred was carrying on alone until he re-joined him and that he would be doing just that as soon as he could; but he could not see them finishing until the early hours at the earliest, and would see the Captain at nine o'clock in the morning as usual with anything they had to report. He caught up with Amy and Elizabeth just as they got to the dining table where Henry, Rachel and Helen were already seated and perusing the menu. They greeted each other as though they had known one another for years rather than only a couple of days. Henry was wearing a couple of miniature medals on his dinner jacket left lapel, while Rachel was wearing a very stylish silk dress with a heavy gold necklace about her neck and Helen looked gorgeous with her blond hair having been, James presumed, professionally fashioned. The table waiters stood behind the chairs of the ladies, Victor behind Amy and David behind Elizabeth, putting their table napkins into their laps when they had sat comfortably. They gave them and James their menus and asked if they wanted the wine waiter to attend the table. James, hoping the Captain wasn't going to mind too much, offered to purchase the wine, which he did when the wine waiter got to the table. He chose, with the wine waiter's assistance, a bottle of red and a bottle of white; it was a bit pricey but he hoped it was going to be worth it. The wine waiter went away leaving the two table waiters to take their passengers' orders.

After Victor and David took the orders, the wine waiter returned and asked James to taste the wines before pouring whatever each of them preferred and putting what was left of the white wine into an ice bucket. It was Henry who started the conversation by asking what they had been doing all day apart from going to the fire drill. They each had comments to make about the fire drill and said was it really necessary to have a fire drill so late in the afternoon when it would surely have been better mid-morning? After all, it was only an exercise. James tried to explain what he thought might have been the thinking behind it, although of course he knew differently, but suggested that if a real fire happened it could be in the middle of the night and he supposed the Captain would not be very popular if he called for an exercise at two o'clock in the morning. They supposed James was right but still found it a pain all the same. With Rachel sitting next to Henry and Helen sitting next to her mother, James had the opportunity to sit the other side of Henry, which turned out very convenient. James asked him if he was going to the main lounge after dinner and that if he was he would like to have a word with him. Henry, with a look of curiosity, asked James, if it was nothing they could discuss at the table. James explained he would like it to be in private rather than with the assembled company. Henry agreed and said it could be arranged when they got to the lounge. It was when they were about half way through their meal that Helen noticed there was not one person sitting at Steve Renton's table and wondered aloud – "Why?" Amy looked up from her dinner and remarked it was probably because he had promised to put a bottle of wine on every table for his behaviour the night before and if he wasn't there he wouldn't have to. "Oh, Amy, you are such a cynical soul sometimes," Elizabeth said, "you really are." So it became obvious, the word had not got around that the actor's manager had been stabbed to death that afternoon.

They had finished their meal and the two bottles of wine that James had ordered when Henry suggested that they take coffee in the lounge with a liqueur or brandy; they thought this to be a good idea and all got up from the table, thanking the waiters for the service they had provided and made their way to the main lounge. When they had made themselves comfortable in chairs that were quite away from where the band was going to be and not too close to the dance floor, Elizabeth insisted on paying for the ladies' liqueurs and James's and Henry's brandy. While they waited for the drinks to come, Henry asked James if he could explain something to him that was the other side of the lounge. James said that he would if he could and followed Henry across the lounge where it was quiet and they could talk. "What do you want to talk to me about?" Henry asked. James didn't know how to start, but eventually said he was seeking Henry's permission to take Helen on a tour of the ship, if she wanted to see how it was in Cabin Class for instance. "Why would she want to do that?" Henry asked, and it was then that James had to blow his cover on the understanding of complete confidence and secrecy as far as Henry was concerned. That he was not to mention a word of what James was about to tell him even to Rachel. James explained about Carol on the way out to New York and then about Joyce who they still had not found and asked Henry if he would, to put it in plain language, allow Helen to be used as bait, but assured him that she would be completely safe at all times. Henry's first and natural reaction was to immediately say no, that it was out of the question, but when James explained that they only had three more days to catch this man and the reason for the fire drill was to get information associated with Joyce's disappearance, he thought again and gave his permission but only if when explained to Helen, she agreed to go along with it together with the assurance that she would be safe.

Having been away from the group for nearly fifteen minutes, Henry looked at his watch and said they should get back, otherwise questions would be being asked that might be difficult to answer. They strolled back to where the ladies were sitting with their coffee and liqueurs and deep in conversation. Rachel looked up and said, "Has James been able to help you with what you wanted to know, darling?" Henry, picking up his nearly cold coffee, assured his wife that he was satisfied with what James had explained to him. It was Henry who asked James if he would be kind enough to show Helen other parts of the ship rather than her sitting with them all the evening and getting bored out of her mind. James said he would be delighted to if Helen thought it was a good idea. Helen was obviously not really looking forward to spending another night sitting with her parents and jumped at the chance to do something different. When she and James had finished their drinks and the bingo was about to start, the two of them went off together. It must be said that they looked fine together, for Helen, dressed as she was, looked as old as James. "Where shall we start?" James asked.

"Wherever you like," was Helens reply, "you can take me on a mystery tour, but please get me back to my parents by eleven o'clock or they will become worried about me." James promised that he would but he had to have a talk with her before they started off.

They stopped and had a drink in one of the cosy lounge bars looking out into the darkness of the night and James filled Helen in to what he was doing and what part he wanted her to take. He, of course, had to swear her to secrecy but she was up for it and thought it would be exciting if anything came out of it. James told her he would not let her out of his sight, but from a distance. She was to go into everywhere he took her on her own in first and cabin class. Knowing there must be a difference between the classes, she pointed out to James that maybe they might be overdressed for other passenger classes. James had not thought of that, and of course there was something in what she said, if he took her into cabin or second class accommodation which was aft of the ship and tourist or third class that was forward, more him than her, they would be totally out of place and stick out like sore thumbs. Speaking of which, his hand was beginning to hurt so it was time to take another couple of pain killers. James suggested they go to the Veranda Grill, where things had occurred where Joyce had been concerned, and not to forget that he would be watching out for her every minute and that if anybody approached her she was not to have a drink if it was offered to her or even more so if it was given to her. They agreed on half an hour before they moved on to somewhere else. Helen complained that James had offered to show her around and here she would be sitting on her own for half an hour with no one to talk to. James said that he thought she was good at conversation and would be able to find another young lady or woman to talk with during that time; he promised it would be the only time he would leave her without his company for that long. She agreed to go along with his request just to see what happened, if anything. She went in first and when James saw her find a table at which a young woman was sitting, he went to the bar where he could keep a close eye on her. She had only been there a few minutes when a bar steward went over to the table with a drink for the lady Helen was sitting with; James was too far away to hear the conversation that was started up, but it was the other woman that spoke to Helen first. Whatever it was, Helen shook her head and the woman shrugged her shoulders so James assumed she had asked if Helen wanted a drink while the waiter was there. He didn't know what the waiter said to her but took a good look at his shoes. James thought for a minute and seeing the barman serving the drinks was the same one he had spoken to late last night, called him over. "Is that one of the waiters that was on duty last night?" he asked him, "And how many are there on duty tonight?" The barman said he wasn't sure as being a gala night there were more on than usual but there were probably ten at that moment but the numbers would reduce as the time got late and some of the older passengers, and, with a small smile, some of the young couples would go to their beds. James watched Helen get into quite heavy conversation and wondered what they were talking about; he guessed he would find out in due course. As the waiters moved about the grill, delivering drinks, taking orders or collecting glasses, James took note of their footwear. It was after about fifteen minutes he went over to the table and asked the ladies if they would like a drink. Helen making no sign of recognition said she would like a cocktail and the other lady said no she already had a drink. James said he would order it from the bar and would be back a little later on and sit with them, if that would be alright. He didn't stop and wait for an answer but went back to the bar and ordered Helen a cocktail, telling the barman who it was for. He thought that perhaps if who he was looking for saw someone chatting up these two young ladies he might try it on himself. He watched the waiter take Helen's drink over to her. In the next quarter of an hour, two men headed in the direction of the table but did not stop or even acknowledge the girls. After finishing the tonic water with ice and lemon that he had ordered for himself, he thought the bait hadn't worked and so went over, keeping his promise, and sat with the pair of them. He had not been there for more than a couple of minutes before the other lady finished her drink, said cheerio to Helen and left the table and the Veranda Grill without even acknowledging James. The pair of them remained at the table while Helen told James what the conversation had been between her and Gina. It appeared Gina had met a man the night before who said he would meet her at ten o'clock tonight in the Veranda Grill but had obviously not turned up. She said he had tried plying her with drinks but because she was on some special tablets she could not drink very much and refused when he kept asking if she wanted another. He also asked her to go with him to another bar but she told him she was waiting for someone who had promised to meet her but had obviously been delayed. "What else did she say?" James probed, "Did she describe the man, did she say anything more about him, why he talked to her or where he intended taking her and why did she want to meet him again?" Helen said it was only in light conversation that she mentioned him and it was the reason she was sitting at the table. James asked if she had told her what part of the ship her cabin was or what she had been doing so far since leaving New York. Helen was getting fed up with all these questions and said she understood why he was asking them, but could not tell him any more than what she had, and could they now go somewhere else.

James apologised and said he would not leave her any more on her own and that he would now take her around the ship to see what they could find of interest. In the next couple of hours they visited just about every place they had entertainment except the cinema, where the film being shown was nearly over. They had only a couple of drinks but not too many, in order that James would not be in trouble from Henry when he got Helen back. In one of the bars they visited, a close up magician came to their table and both of them were amazed at his sleight of hand. They danced a little and it was then that James realised how mature Helen was for a seventeen year old, apart from dancing she wanted to really snuggle up. James didn't mind too much, but was wary of anybody seeing them that could tell her father. They even went out on deck together and all the time James was alert for anything he might see that could give him a lead. All in all, James was satisfied with the evening and when the time came to return Helen to the main lounge and her father, he said how much he had enjoyed being in her company. Helen said would it be possible to go into cabin class to see what went on there if they dressed casual? James said yes, but it would have to be tomorrow and they could sort something out at breakfast in the morning. When they got back to the main lounge, the band was playing a quick-step to which Henry and Elizabeth were dancing; Amy and Rachel were sitting it out and were just chatting. On reaching Rachel and Amy, Rachel asked her daughter if she had had fun, to which Helen replied that she had and would like to do it again tomorrow. Helen asked James if he would like to have one more dance before he went off, but just as she said it, the dance came to an end and Henry and Elizabeth returned to the table. Elizabeth thanked Henry and said she was getting too old for the faster dances and much preferred the slower ones. James thanked Henry for allowing him to escort his daughter and would tell him more in the morning at breakfast but that he had to go now as there was someone he had to meet at eleven o'clock.

As he moved away from the table to leave, his gaze fell onto a pair of black shoes being worn by a man leaving the room. He could not be sure, but they were not ordinary shoes. He could only see the back of the man and in his hurry to catch him up, bumped into a waiter that was carrying a full tray of drinks. The waiter did his level best to avoid dropping the whole tray but still could not help spilling some of the drink onto a couple of the passengers that sat nearby. James was very embarrassed and apologised to the waiter and the passengers that had drink spilt on them saying it was his fault and not the waiter's. The couple wiping themselves down with the napkins the waiter had provided for the purpose said accidents happen and that was clearly what it had been. By this time, the man wearing the shoes James had seen was out of sight so there was no point in trying to follow him, so James made his way back up to the cabin where Fred was still working.

Most of the papers were now in just two piles with further, what looked to James like notes, on a separate table. "I'm sorry to be so late," he apologised, "but I thought I had a good idea that has not materialised and you have been so busy." James went on to explain what he had been up to and what the outcome had been and Fred showed James what he had been doing. He explained exactly how he had gone about comparing the two lists of the passengers and the crew members and, going over to the table, picked his notes up and asked James to sit down. The first thing he explained was that there were two crew members on board extra to the list for the crew. One of them gave the name of the steward that was under ship's arrest and could not possibly have been at the fire drill and the other one gave a name that is not on the list of crew members. He had checked on who should have been on duty and those excused fire drill and they were the only two anomalies. Turning then to the passenger lists, those too had a name on the fire drill check list that was not on the passenger manifest list. "So what conclusions have you come to?" James asked.

Fred continued, "So far, this is what I have come up with, now that you're back, can we go over everything we can think of that will give us a lead as to who these people are, and where they are being accommodated, in fact anything we can find out about them." James's first thought, especially where the extra passenger was concerned, was that there must be a stowaway on board, but this had been checked out by the purser's office. Then he had a thought; was the murdered man's name on the fire drill list?

"What murdered man?" Fred demanded to know.

"I am so sorry, Fred, but being so absorbed in trying to find the rapist I completely overlooked telling you that I found a dead man on the boat deck just before the boat drill commenced."

"Who was it, do you know and where is he now and how did you move him without anybody seeing?" James explained exactly what he had done, and that it was the actor Steve Renton's manager.

"As far as I know he's in the hospital where Dr. Cummings will be trying to determine the time of death. It is known how he was killed because there was a knife still stuck in his back. The Captain is dealing with it and liaising with the doctors. I don't know what they are going to do with the body, but being so near to England they would not be allowed to do a burial at sea, plus the fact the death is not due to natural causes. I suppose they must have somewhere cold to put him until he can be taken from the ship by an undertaker after the police have released the body. I would think no one will be allowed ashore when we dock until the police give permission!"

"Right then, to get back to the subject in hand," James suggested, "for it is getting very late and I have told the Captain we will report to him at nine o'clock." James mentioned the smell of scent he had noticed when he went into his cabin and how it reminded him of a perfume he had smelt before but couldn't remember on whom or where he had smelt it, but realised he was once again getting off the matter in hand and so did not mention anything more about it. Fred spread his notes out so they could both study them and began by suggesting they deal with the crew first. "You say you think there are two men more on the ships staff than there should be?" James asked to be shown how he had worked this out.

Fred said, "It was impossible for the steward under lock and key to attend the boat drill, so who had got his name ticked off?" James asked Fred if the steward would be allowed visitors, to which he said no, he was in solitary confinement.

"Let's go through that steward's details in depth", James suggested, which they did. His full name, his address, his age, his mother and father's name and what his previous employment was." Let's quickly scan the lists and see if any other crew member has anything to do with him, as he was one of those that were transferred from the Lizzy at the end of her last trip." They first went down the list of those who had been transferred from other Cunard ships to the Queen Mary for this trip and it was whilst doing this that they discovered that the steward who was under lock and key was the half-brother of another steward, whose mother was the same with different fathers. One had come from the Lizzy, whilst the other had come from a passenger cargo ship sailing out of Liverpool. What they had to do was find out who the other steward was and where he was working, as this wasn't listed. This did not, however, account for two extra men that were not on the company books - or were they? They went carefully through all the sheets they had been given, but could not identify who the extra men were, unless there had been a mistake made.

The steward that had been put under ship's arrest was Michael Banes, his half-brother was John Leaver and their mother's maiden name was Daphne Watts. Michael, was two years older than John, they were unmarried and had the same home address. They knew where Michael was, he was under lock and key so they now had to find out where John Leaver was working. They spent the next hour going through all the lists they had with a fine tooth comb, checking every detail of every member of the crew. Names, locations, dates, and everything that was listed about them, and then checked the ships departments, Bell Boys, Trimmers, Firemen, Greasers, all of the catering department, Medical Orderlies, Seamen, shop men and women, hairdressers. Fred even checked all the other Masters at Arms. They checked every bit of paperwork they had been given but could find nothing else apart from the occasional DR (Decline to Report), which was disciplinary. When crew members and officers have this stamped in their discharge books, it indicates to any future employer that they had broken company rules and been hauled up before the ship's captain for punishment or reprimand serious enough to make this necessary. Neither of the two half-brothers had a DR, so how long Michael had been stealing and not getting caught would only be known if the police charged him with theft when they returned to Southampton. When taken to court, he might ask for other offences to be taken into consideration before being sentenced. If he was sent to prison, his chances of being employed by a British company would be very bleak, although he might get employment from a foreign country if he sought it.

Over the next two hours, Fred and James went through the whole of the passenger lists comparing the names and details of everyone that was on the lists to those attending the fire drill. It was then that it was discovered that not only was Joyce Sheen's name not on the fire drill check list, as would be expected due to her disappearance that the whole thing had been arranged, but she was also not on the list of passengers. Although both James and Fred by now, at nearly four o'clock in the morning, were very tired, and James's hand was giving him a lot of pain, they checked and double checked to try to cross match every passenger but could not find anything on a Miss, Mrs or Ms. J Sheen. They looked to see if she was down anywhere as a last minute booking but found nothing. "We will have to check with the purser's office later today," James said, "in order to see if she handed in her passport." Now Fred brought up the man that had been murdered. Did they know his name from the passenger list? James said, other than Steve Renton and his wife Judy Mendise who had booked under those names and not Mr. and Mrs. Renton, they would have to check what was on their passports if Renton and Mendise were stage names. They thought their passports would have to contain their real names, but this could be easily checked through the passport numbers listed against their stage names. As for the dead man and the rest of the actor's party, they did not have a clue, but could find out by going through the purser's office. So having been as thorough as they could and with a little success, they decided they must get some sleep. They agreed to meet at the Captain's day room at nine o'clock and, collecting up all the papers and putting them in their respective envelopes, left the cabin, switching the lights out as they went and locking the door behind them. They decided to walk down the stairs rather than call the lift, James carrying the envelopes and saying goodnight when he got to his deck. They shook hands and James said he was sorry Fred never got his beer, but perhaps they would be able to make up for it tomorrow night.

James, opening his cabin door, and was immediately aware of that smell, only faintly but it was not his imagination. His bed was turned down and there was a note on his coffee table telling him the four bottles of beer were in the fridge and signed just, "The Steward." James wondered if he would have one of the beers and take a couple of pain killers with it, but decided he would stick with the cool water in his thermos jug. Getting undressed was not easy, but taking the bow tie off was easier than trying to put it on. He also had a job with the top shirt button. He didn't bother to undo his shoe laces but just got them off with the laces still tied up. He was now so tired he got into bed in just his underpants and must have gone into a deep sleep, for when he woke up, it was twenty minutes to nine and he had forgotten to put his alarm on. Bugger it, he thought, I'm going to either have a late breakfast or not have one at all. He splashed some water on his face directly he got up and got ready for the day as quickly as his hand would let him, picking up the envelopes as he left the cabin and went quickly to the Captain's day room. By the time he got there, he was running ten minutes late. He was ushered into the Captain's day room by his Tiger, who asked him if he would like a cup of tea or coffee, to which James said, "Coffee, please." Fred was already seated with his beverage and so, after apologising to the Captain for being late, James sat down next to Fred. Captain Baron was, from the look on his face, a very worried man. He looked as tired as James felt and Fred did not look the picture of health either. "What time did you two get to bed last night?" was the Captain's opening statement. When told nearly five o'clock, the Captain wanted to know why that late. Before James could answer, the steward brought his coffee to him, the Captain asked him to get him another cup and Fred, when asked, said he would like another cup too, please. Captain Baron told James he had learned some of what they had achieved and that he understood there was an element of success. James explained in detail what they had uncovered and what they wanted from the pursers. He asked the captain if the doctors had come back to him yet regarding the murdered manager of Steve Renton and if they knew what his name was. The Captain, sipping his coffee which had just been brought to him, replied that the doctors had reported their findings and strictly speaking it had not been murder. He explained that as James had observed, there was very little blood near or on the clothing of the body, there was obviously some but not as much as what might be expected. The knife must have pierced the heart, although this will be ascertained by a post mortem that the doctors are not allowed to carry out on the ship; that will have to be done ashore under the police jurisdiction by a qualified pathologist. The reason for the lack of blood seems to be due to the fact that the man was already dead when he was stabbed and had been for at least two or more hours, from either a heart attack or a stroke. "Now this is surely a mystery," James could not help saying, for what point was there in anyone wanting to kill a person that was already dead? The Captain was wondering about the same thing. "But that is what will have to be established by the police when they come on board, which will be by boat before the ship docks. I have been in touch by radio telephone and if we have not been able to solve anything, then not one person will be allowed to leave the ship or until at least everyone on board has been interviewed, and that includes me. This could take hours or even days before everyone is allowed ashore, it could even delay sailing on the next trip. The whole situation is a bloody mess. So it would seem that we now have two detectives detecting two crimes and one that hopefully is done and dusted."

"I, as the Captain of this ship, without official permission from the company, can and do install you both as ship's detectives. You will be able to undertake tasks the same as private detectives ashore. You can interview who you like, about what you like, as long as it is kept as private as possible, using me as your manager, for want of a better title. You are, I know, totally untrained, but with what you have managed to uncover and the suggestions you have so far put forward, and the hours you have put into trying to find a rapist and now the reason and culprit of an intended murder, I think it only fair to release you from your duties as Master at Arms, Mr. Baker, and in your case, Mr. Royston, carry on as a passenger but in a slightly different capacity. I still don't want the passengers or ship's company to know what is going on, other than those who know what they know already. I will keep the Staff Captain informed as I see fit, but I insist you keep me up to speed with the morning and evening meetings and, of course, any other time if something comes to light that I should know about or can take action on." James and Fred looked at one another, not knowing what to say, but accepting the challenge the Captain had set them.

They gave the Captain an outline or at least James did, of what their next line of enquiries would be, taking one thing at a time unless they found that there might be a connection in any way as with, for instance, the two half-brothers. The Captain said he would instruct the Senior Purser to give them every support they needed and also that of the Chief Steward and wished them luck as they left.

CHAPTER 7

After having asked the captain if they could retain the suite they had been allocated to do the crew and passenger paper work, he readily agreed and told Fred he could move into it if he wished. Fred thought about it but declined as he felt it would be more beneficial to still be in crew quarters, where he could stay in touch with whatever was going on below decks.

They left the Captain's day cabin, thanking his Tiger for the coffee as they passed the little pantry that he used. He said it was a pleasure and after-all it was his job, adding, could he have a quiet word with them? James said yes, of course he could, but could it wait a couple of hours so that he could snatch a bit of breakfast and go and visit the hospital. They agreed where they would meet and both went down to James's cabin. When they arrived, the day bedroom steward was in the cabin making the bed and cleaning it up. He had changed the bed linen and when James went into the bathroom saw that the towels had also been replaced. He asked the steward his name and was told it was John Leaver. "Well, John, I know you are busy but would it be possible to get me some breakfast?" The steward said he would try, but it might be a bit late now. James said he didn't necessarily want a cooked breakfast, but had had to see the Captain and that he had got up too late to get his breakfast first, so a continental would do if he could manage it. He was only gone ten minutes before he returned with a tray on which was food enough for three people let alone one. He said he would leave him to eat his breakfast and come back later to finish the cabin off.

James asked Fred to join him if he was hungry and, to be polite more than being hungry, he did. Although they had had a cup of coffee with the Captain, they still enjoyed what the steward had brought. "What do you think of what Captain Baron has done?" James enquired. Fred replied it was unbelievable to even think such a thing could have happened. James said, "Well, where do we start?" Fred said he was going to go and get out of his uniform and would for the rest of the trip dress in civilian clothes the same as him. James said while he was doing that he would go and see the doctor to let him have a look at the progress his hand was making and get it redressed and would meet him back there in about half an hour's time. James rang the bell and when the steward came to see what was wanted, James said he was leaving the cabin, thanked him for the food and told him he could now finish what he still had to do in the cabin whenever he was ready to do so. As the steward left, taking the tray with him, Fred asked, "What are we going to do first when you get back from the hospital?"

"I have said we will go and see the Captain's Tiger in a couple of hours, but before we do that, I think now we know who my bedroom steward is, it might be a good thing to talk to him. If you get back down here and I haven't got back perhaps you could get hold of him and see what he has got to say about anything to do with his half-brother or anything else. If I am back, we can do it together." This was agreed and they left the cabin together.

When James got down to the hospital it was after ten o'clock and very busy, so busy in fact there were a couple of people waiting outside. He was making up his mind whether to wait or go back later when Sister Jane came out to see what the couple waiting outside wanted. She saw James and indicated to him to wait there and she would see to him as quickly as she could. She spoke briefly to the waiting passengers and after looking at their watches they moved off, obviously agreeing to come back later. As soon as they had moved away, she went over to James, who asked her what she was doing on duty at that time after being up all though the night. She said they were at full stretch and so when she should have gone off to bed, she was asked by the other sisters to stay on to help cope with the numbers coming into the hospital. James wanted to know what had brought this on, for surely it wasn't normal. Jane said there had been a lot of tummy upsets among the second class passengers which the doctors had thought was a mild dose of food poisoning. Both doctors had been up most of the night visiting passengers who said they could not get down to the hospital. None of the nursing staff had had much sleep since about two o'clock in the morning. Jean and Barbara had been called out to assist Mary and her and they had not stopped. James asked if he should go back later if there was so much going on. "No, I think Dr. Maiden wants a word with you anyway. Come in with me and I will get that dressing off and then get the doctor to look at it and he can tell you what he wanted you for." Before she started removing the plasters that were acting as outer covers, she asked him if his hand was still very painful and was he still taking the pain killers regularly. He said he was managing to do most things with his damaged hand but by not resting it as much as perhaps he should, when the painkillers worked off it hurt and throbbed quite a lot. She took the dressings off as gently as she could before going to see Dr. Maiden to let him know James was ready to be seen.

When Dr. Maiden finally got to James he looked very tired. He examined James's fingers and asked him to move them this way and that as much as he could. After telling him the healing was still progressing satisfactorily and that the movement seemed to be as good as it should be in the time since the operation, he wanted to know about the dead man that was now being kept in a cold room. Was it James that had discovered the body, he checked, and was it partially covered in a blanket with a paper or magazine over its face? James assured the doctor that was the case and ventured to ask why he was asking. The doctor explained that he told the Captain his findings and was not sure of the facts that he had given him. "I should not be talking to you like this because it is unethical but I am not sure he was stabbed where he was found. I am assuming you know from the Captain that it was not the stabbing that killed him but the question is, did the person who did the stabbing know that the man was already dead? This will have to be officially established by a pathologist, but I think I might be right. Anyway, it is now in the hands of the Captain and I suppose I will have no more input into the matter until I'm called to give my opinion if there is an enquiry or a court case. Thank you for confirming that it was you that discovered the body and I believe you know who the man is." Dr. Maiden said he wanted to see him again the next morning and that Jane would redress the fingers. With that he went into the ward and Jane came over to apply the new dressing. When she had finished, James thanked her and hoped she had a good sleep when she did finally get to her bed and hoped to see her around. She said she hoped so too, but she could not be sure.

James made his way back to his cabin, well over the half hour he estimated he would be gone, and found Fred in his cabin with John Leaver, who had let him in with his master key. They stopped talking when James entered, but carried on with what they were talking about when James sat down on his bed. He listened as Fred asked how he had got the job of bedroom steward and what ship he was on sailing out of Liverpool. He told him he was a bedroom steward on the Media a passenger cargo ship, but wanted to get on the big liners. He said he was surprised he was put on the Queen Mary seeing his half-brother had just been transferred from the Queen Elizabeth. Fred then asked him how he got on with Michael and was thrown a bit when he said not very well. Asked why, he said they didn't have very much in common and while they were growing up he didn't like the company Michael kept. They went to different schools, and on leaving, Michael entered the merchant navy while he started an apprenticeship as an electrician. However, after only nine months the firm went bust and so he had to give that up and found it difficult to find other employment. His father had died after an accident and Michael's father had been in prison for a long time and so contributed nothing towards the upkeep or wellbeing of his wife and son, before or after the divorce. His father, on marrying Michael's mother, looked after them all until he got killed. Fred then asked John if he had tried to see Michael and did he know why he had been put under ship's arrest. To this John said he did know why Michael was under ship's arrest but he had not seen him or even asked to see him. As far as he knew, he got into trouble on the Queen Elizabeth. He didn't know what for but they hadn't sacked him, so he thought it could not have been anything too bad, but they had transferred him. Fred then asked if Michael ever got into trouble when he was on leave to which John said yes, he gets drunk a lot and gets into fights. James, who up to that point had not said a word, asked John if he knew Bill Carter. John had no hesitation in saying that he had not heard his name mentioned and that he certainly had never met him as he never went out with Michael and that nobody with that name had ever come to the house. James then asked how his mother treated the two boys and what made John go to sea rather than pursue an electrical career? John said when they were young their mother tried to treat them alike, but Michael was always rebellious and even more so after his father went to prison. Because he was a dunce at school, his classmates used to ridicule him which made him rebel even more and he was always fighting. It got to a stage when he was about fifteen that their mother was frightened of him and could not manage him at all. Because he, John, was clever and went to the grammar school, this drove a wedge between them. Michael was very jealous because he thought that being the eldest he had to be top dog, but because he was the way he was, their mother always seemed to treat John better.

Regarding joining the merchant navy, he joined up because of the money Michael was earning, and wasting, and not giving any of it to his mother, because he said she was already getting the allotment he was making to her, which was a pittance. So he wrote to Cunard and asked if they had any vacancies and they said they did, in the catering department, and so when he first went to sea, he washed dishes in the galley of a passenger cargo vessel. He had never been on the same ship with Michael before and it was, he felt sure, a mistake that they were together now. James then asked him why was it that he had replaced his half-brother when he was caught stealing? To this, John just shrugged his shoulders and said he didn't have the faintest idea, and furthermore didn't know what Michael's job was; he was just taken from the second class cabins he had been allocated and was told he had been promoted to first class, which of course was very good news as he would get a higher wage and hopefully better tips, all of which would allow him to give his mother more at the end of the trip.

James complemented John on his attitude towards his mother and hoped that his promotion would be successful with perhaps more to come. He asked him if he had socialised with Michael since they left Southampton, to which John said no and that they were not billeted in the same cabin which was good for him because it meant he did not have to speak to him. "What about at meal times?" interjected Fred.

"Certainly not then," replied John, "I sit with those I've made friends with and whenever Michael comes in or is already in our mess we never speak. You see, I don't like him." Fred went on to ask who Michael sat with before being put into solitary confinement. John said he usually sat with three blokes he thinks were another steward, a seaman and a fireman, and if not with them he sat on his own; it would appear there were not very many that liked him either. James asked if he could find out the names of the three men he used to sit with and let him know what they were as soon as he could.

With the time now getting on, they thought they ought to get back up to see what the Captain's Tiger wanted to tell them. They thanked John for answering their questions and said that if he found out who the three were they wanted to know about, would he write their names down and leave them in the cabin on the coffee table. John asked if James wanted his four beers left tonight, for he had noticed that the four he had put in the fridge yesterday were still there. James said, "Yes, please, they might come in useful."

James and Fred went back up to see the Captain's Tiger, who was just coming out of the Captain's day cabin with a tray of empty cups and plates. This time they asked his name and where they could talk in private. He said his name was Arthur Phelps and that they could converse in his little pantry if they didn't mind standing up while they talked. They agreed, and so as the Tiger was washing and drying the cups and plates, he explained that he was able to hear some of the conversations that went on in the Captain's quarters, and so had some idea of what was going on. He explained that he was not aware of everything but thought they might like to check up on a first class table steward who hung out with the steward that had been put under lock and key. Fred asked him in what respect; what should they check on, and for what reason? Arthur said he was in a six berth cabin, now only occupied by five with Michael Banes being locked up, and that he seemed to cause trouble whenever he was among the other stewards he shared with. James asked if he knew how or why he causes trouble, to which Arthur replied, "Because their cabin is next to mine and there has been a lot of shouting and very bad language this trip."

"Have you got any idea what is causing it and what the arguments are about?" James wanted to know. Arthur seemed to think it was mainly because of the hours he keeps and that he either keeps them awake late at night or wakes them up in the early hours of the morning. "But why should we know about this?" was Fred's response, to which Arthur said he thought they were looking for a person who had tried to rape a passenger on the voyage out to New York. "If you know that, Arthur, what else do you know and who else have you spoken to?"

"Nobody," Arthur replied, "I know how to keep my mouth shut and am very loyal to Captain Baron who treats me well. I know, again from what I have heard, that as little number of people as possible are to know about what is going on, that's why I've asked to speak to both of you in private." James and Fred thanked Arthur and said they would follow up on what he had told them. "And by the way, what is this table waiter's name?"

"I am pretty sure it is Dennis Waye, but perhaps you ought to check to make absolutely sure before talking to him," he warned.

Getting near to lunch time, they knew that Dennis Waye would be serving at table or at least be getting ready to do so, plus the fact James was feeling peckish and Fred said he could do with a bit of lunch. They agreed to meet by the shops on the prom deck at half past one and Fred said he would do his best to see if he could find out the names of the other members of the catering staff that were sharing the cabin with Dennis from the crew list.

James popped into his cabin before he went to lunch and found the note left by John on the coffee table. The three names he had written down were: The Seaman, Ted Richmond, Fireman, Andy Good and Steward, Dennis Waye. Armed with this information, James went for lunch. Being early, only Amy and Elizabeth were there. They looked up when James arrived and both said hello to him.

"Well," Elizabeth asked, "Where were you at breakfast time? We missed you." He said he had had a late night and that he had overslept. Elizabeth with a twinkle in her eye said, "I hope you didn't keep Helen up half the night, for she missed swimming this morning and nearly missed her breakfast." James blushed a little, before telling both the ladies that he had returned Helen to her parents by eleven o'clock, but had been waylaid before he got back to his cabin which made him very late to bed. Elizabeth gave a little smile and admitted she was only teasing. When they were half way through their starters, Henry, Rachel and Helen joined them. They greeted each other as they sat down, Henry and Rachel next to Amy and Helen next to James. Victor came to the table, as did the wine waiter to take their orders from the family. They went to Helen first and after ordering she turned to James with a bit of a gleam in her eye. "You know who we were looking for last night?" she said, "Well I think I saw him in the lounge before Daddy and I left to go to our cabins."

"What makes you think that?" James was quickly on the case.

"I don't know what it was about him, but he looked me over almost to the point of mentally undressing me. He was smartly dressed in his dinner suit but had some rather different shoes on. They were black and polished, but were made of a different type of leather than usual. I remembered you mentioning something about shoes, so I just wondered if it was your man."

"Did he speak to you?" James asked, and, "Was he with anyone?"

She said, "He did not speak, probably because I was with daddy, but he sort of nodded in my direction and no, I think he was on his own."

"What time was it?" James then asked, to which Helen replied it was well after midnight as the band had packed up and daddy had finished his last drink after talking to a man who works in New York near to his office but had never met before. "It was definitely after twelve. I remember looking at my watch when I got back to my cabin and by then it was just after one o'clock."

"Did she see where he went?" Helen said that her dad was saying good night to the man he had met and invited her to say good night too, so she didn't see where he went or in fact if he left the lounge at all. "What sort of build was he and was there anything you noticed about him? Would you recognise him again if you saw him?" Helen by now was becoming confused as James's questioning was becoming quite heavy. "One thing I remember is that a few seconds after he passed by, I smelt a rather nice aroma of after-shave or body lotion. Whatever it was, it was a rather unusual smell but very nice." James apologised for questioning her so heavily, but was getting excited because it would appear that Helen had in fact clapped eyes on the man they were after. This, now the third time, just after midnight it would seem, that this man had been at bay. Having to get Helen back to her dad by eleven o'clock foiled the attempt to catch this man, whoever he was. James wondered if he could try again that night, if Helen's father would let him keep her longer. If the main lounge was the rapist's first port of call, then perhaps if they waited until after midnight they could be lucky. James thanked Helen and apologised profusely for spoiling her lunch, which had arrived and was getting cold after she had answered all James's questions. Helen said she was sorry she did not point the man out to her dad, but seeing he was talking to the man he worked near it would have been rude to interrupt him. Excusing himself, James said he had a lot to do and on getting up from the table said he would see them all at dinner.

James noticed as he weaved his way through the tables that there were five people sitting at Steve Renton's table, but neither Steve or his wife were there. As he left the dining room to go up to meet Fred, he was aware of that smell again, like in his cabin, very faint but nevertheless the smell was the same. There was nobody near him, so once again he could not follow anything up. He met Fred outside of the tailor's shop where James had had so much trouble. He was smiling when James arrived. What was he smiling about, James wanted to know.

"It seems that your shop manager friend is having some trouble with that actor bloke, what's his name, Steve Rent money or something?"

James said, "You mean Renton, what sort of trouble?" Fred said he could not hear what was being said but that there was a lot of arm swinging and finger pointing going on. It was as they were talking that the actor punched the shop manager and knocked him down and by the appearance of it, out cold. Fred could not hold himself back at this juncture and entered the shop with James following close behind. Addressing the actor, Fred said he was sorry but what he had just witnessed could not be allowed on a Cunard ship and therefore he was going to have to report him. Steve Renton was angered to such an extent that Fred had a job to calm him down. He said he was not used to being spoken to like it and wasn't going to let a two bit bum like that, pointing to the man he had just knocked down and was still lying motionless at his feet, get away with it. The fact that he was still out cold made James take an active part in what was going on and going over to the phone on the counter, asked the operator to connect him to the hospital. The phone was answered by Barbara, who said she would be right up and would let one of the doctors know what had happened. In the meantime, Fred was still trying to get out of Steve Renton what had made him angry enough to hit the shop manager.

He was saying how he had gone into the shop and asked to see some suits. "The manager had asked the size colour and style I wanted, which was fair enough, but it was when he pushed his luck and tried to sell me shirts and ties and all the things that I did not want or ask for that I started to get annoyed, especially when he said being a famous actor, I could afford all these things. I tried to keep my temper but when he said 'What about some new shoes to replace those that you must have thrown over the side because they would have had your manager's blood on them.' That was when I hit him, which I will do again if he wakes up before I leave here." It was then that he realised he was answering questions being put to him by a total stranger, someone he had never seen before in his life. "Who the bloody hell are you and why am I answering your questions?" Fred told him in no uncertain terms that he was a senior Master at Arms or, in other words, a ship's policeman and that this incident would be reported to the Captain who would have to deal with it as he saw fit, but he assured Mr. Renton that the Captain did not approve of fighting by his crew or passengers or any other disturbance if it came to that. As the tailor started coming round, Steve Renton went to keep his threat, but Fred held him off. The disturbance had been noticed by several other passengers who started to gather outside the shop, making it necessary for the nurse and doctor to have to push their way through when they arrived. Fred asked James if he would keep his eye on Mr. Renton while he got rid of the audience. He moved outside and explained that nothing was wrong that there had been a little accident and that there was nothing for them to see or worry about. The group dispersed, some of them having a little grumble, but went on their way. "What I want to know," Steve Renton raved on, "is how the hell he knew my Manager was dead? It's been hushed up, and why should he say that I would have blood on my shoes and have thrown them over the side." This was something Fred and James would be asking the manager when he came properly round. Dr. Cummings had examined him for signs of concussion and Barbara had stopped his nose from bleeding, which it had started to do as he came round. The doctor said he wanted him to go down to the hospital but he refused, saying his assistant was not available and he did not want to shut the shop, so he would manage. With that, Fred took Steve Renton back to his state room door and told him to stay in the cabin and that he would be seen later, the doctor and nurse went back to work and James and Fred left and went up to the cabin/suite they were using to work from.

When they got to the cabin, James asked Fred if he had had any luck with his enquiries regarding the three friends of Michael Banes. He said he had, in as much as he had contacted the fireman and the seaman. "What about the steward Dennis Waye?" Fred said he hadn't seen him but had arranged to see the other two at different times, convenient to them, in their cabins. "Were they curious you wanted to talk to them and did they want to know what about?" James asked. Fred said they were a bit, but agreed to talk. They made their way down to the crew's quarters, which in his new role James could now do, and went to the cabin of Andy Good the fireman. When they knocked the door, Andy opened it and invited them in. He recognised James and wanted to know why he was not in uniform and what he was doing in the crew's quarters? He also asked how his hand was, as he had heard he had damaged it. He told them to sit wherever they might feel comfortable and wanted to know what they wanted to talk to him about. James started by asking how he got on with Michael Banes. "Oh! It's going to be about him is it?" James asked why he was immediately taking that attitude before a question had been asked, to which Andy replied that if it was about Michael it might be problematical, as trouble seemed to follow him around. Fred interjected saying it was only because he was always seen with him whenever they were socialising or in the dining room. Andy went on to explain that he knew Michael from school and been a friend ever since and although he was like a loose cannon, he was not a bad bloke really. He knew he had been caught stealing and that it was James that got him locked up and that he didn't like him. He did not actually say he was going to get James back, but from the way Andy said it, he was sure he would have to look out for retribution at some time. James asked if he knew a Bill Carter, to which Andy replied that he did, that he had been another school pal. Asked if he knew what he did for a living, Andy said he and Bill went on the buildings as bricklayers mates, but Bill got fed up with it because the work was so hard and they had to work from dawn to dusk. He said there must be easier ways of earning a living and decided to go abroad to try his luck. "Is he back in England now?" was the next question.

Andy answered, "No, Bill is, as far as I know, still in Spain." Fred then asked what he did for a living out there, and was he still in contact with him. Andy said he didn't hear from him much now, other than a Christmas card, but he knew Michael was still in contact with him. Fred asked again, "What does he do for a living? What is his job now?" Andy said he didn't know, but believed he was pretty well off because he understood that whenever Michael goes over to Spain to visit, Bill always pays the fare. Fred went on, "How often does he go over to Spain?" Andy thought it was almost every time he went on leave depending on the time of year more than anything. Andy was quite amiable but wanted to know why they were asking all these questions about Michael. They said they had to make some enquiries and that could he help them on another matter? Did he know of any rumours about anyone in the engineering department at the moment? Andy replied that the only one that he knew of was a Greaser that ran a card school and was winning a lot of money as the banker with Black Jack and Crown and Anchor, but other than that, no, but he was sure the day would come when they would be talking about how much he had lost. He said he did not mix much with the rest of the crew, as him and the other three, including Michael before he was locked up, just kept to themselves. James thanked him for answering their questions but before they left the cabin, he asked if he had an address in Spain for Bill Carter if they exchanged Christmas cards? Andy said yes, but it was at home, he didn't have it with him on board. He did remember though that he lived in or near one of the Costas but could not remember which one. As they left the cabin, James took a quick glimpse at the shoes that were scattered about the cabin, but none of them fitted the description he was looking for.

So what now? James suggested that they have a look and see if there was anyone in the cabin where the steward was causing trouble. Fred led the way. When they got there, Fred suggested they check to make sure there was no one still sleeping, as the stewards on night duty might not have got up yet, so he quietly cracked open the cabin door to see. Although he had been as quiet as he could, someone from the darkened room asked, "Who's there?" Fred said it was only him, giving his name, and would it be possible to talk to him. The voice said to give him ten minutes to get washed and dressed. Having to wait, Fred invited James into his cabin, which was not far away and was absolutely spotless and very tidy. He explained that the other Masters at Arms he shared with were all ex-policemen or service men and were very clean and tidy. Fred asked if James had time for a quick bottle of beer, seeing they had an opportunity. Fred got down a couple of glasses and two bottles of beer out of a fridge. "How do you manage to have a fridge in your cabin?" James remarked. "The engineers don't have them in theirs!" At this Fred smiled, "This was not supplied by the company, it was bought second hand ashore from the Sally Army in New York, but was a bit of a job getting a suitable 220 volt motor to work it. One of our blokes is good at electrics and he rigged it up for us." Fred poured the beer and whilst doing so discussed what they wanted to know from the chap they were going to see. They drank their beer and decided roughly what they wanted to know from the steward. James didn't like drinking beer quickly, especially larger which always seemed to be more gassy than bitter, but seeing it was only a small bottle he was able to finish it comfortably before they went back to the steward's cabin.

The steward was now up and dressed in running trousers, tee-shirt and slippers and welcomed them in when they knocked the door. Now that the lights were on, James could see the cabin layout, with two lots of double bunks sited on one side and one on the other. It was a big cabin with an element of comfort with four small armchairs and a table and lockers on the outboard bulkhead. They were invited to sit down, which they did, before asking which steward he was. He said his name was Harry Mills and gave the names of the other occupants, putting emphasis on the last name as the one giving them all the grief, his name being Reginald West. They quickly went through what the other cabin members did and what it was about Reginald West that made him so troublesome. Harry, who James guessed was in his mid-forties, went through all their jobs, which turned out to be him as a night bedroom steward, two as bar waiters, one first class and one in second, two table waiters both first class, and the pest, as he called Reg West, who he said was a relief first class steward used as and when the Chief Steward saw fit.

Fred took the lead on this one, asking Harry to explain why it was that he and his fellow cabin mates could not get on with this chap and what it was they really had to complain about. Harry explained that on this trip so far, Reg had been employed in the Veranda Grille as a bar waiter which was fine during the day, but he would come in at all sorts of times during the early hours, wake up those who were sleeping and generally make a bloody nuisance of himself, and that aftershave he uses is bloody awful. "He comes in some nights absolutely stinking, making it necessary for us to spray the cabin with air freshener. It's not too bad at the moment as one of the others must have had a spray round before they left the cabin this morning. Another thing is, there are occasions when he doesn't sleep in the cabin. God knows where he sleeps then, but surely he has to sleep somewhere, not that we are complaining, it is better when he's not here." James asked if he had not slept in the cabin any night since leaving New York, to which Harry replied, "Yes, the first two nights out, but he had a couple of nights when he wasn't in the cabin on the way out."

Fred went on, "What sort of bloke is he? Does he ever get angry, temperamental, agitated or moody? Is he a friendly man?"

Harry thought for a minute before saying, that he thinks himself to be a real lady killer. "He is often boasting about what women he has had and doesn't mince words as to how he has had them. If I was to have a guess, I would say he is even up to being a pervert or rapist. He seems to be obsessed with sex and whenever he reads anything it's either a sex book or porn magazines. I certainly would not let him in the company of my daughter, if I had one. I've got two sons so never have that worry."

"Do you have any idea what he keeps in his locker, or do you ever see him get dressed in anything other than his uniform?" James enquired, to which Harry replied, "He is very secretive, or to put it nearer the truth, a sly sod who doesn't let anybody see anything much. Even when he has his locker open it's done in such a way that nobody sees what's inside." James went on and asked how this man dressed to go ashore. Once again, Harry said he did not know, as he had never seen him go ashore.

"What about when he's in Southampton?" James pressed.

"Let me tell you straight if it makes any sense," Harry went on. James got the impression he was pushing this man too far as did Fred, who so to take the heat out of the situation, said to Harry, "How long have you known Reg and how many trips have you had to share a cabin with him?" This was a better question because Harry could answer it without any trouble. He said he had known of him and seen him on the Queen Elizabeth in particular for nearly a year and on one trip, when he was suffering from appendicitis, he was relieved by him, but he had never had to share a cabin with him before. Harry went back to what he was going to say which was, as unlikely and even perhaps farfetched as it may seem, in his opinion, Reginald West was two different people with a different name for each of them.

"What on earth makes you think that?" Fred asked and was surprised at what Harry had to say. How it has all been done he could not say or even have a guess at, but he had a thought that perhaps Reginald West was known as something else on the passenger list. He said the reason he thought this was because of the little time he spent in the cabin even though when he was there he was a pest, he never had a shower or bath and yet he was never dirty and he was sure he should have had more cloths in his locker; even though no one knew exactly what was in it, he just felt there was something about him that wasn't right. Fred looked at his watch and seeing that they had been with Harry for nearly half an hour realised they were going to be late getting to the seaman's cabin. They thanked Harry for being so helpful and departed.

When they got to Ted Richmond's cabin, Fred apologised for being late and explained that they had been held up. Ted wanted to know if what they wanted to talk to him about was very important or could it not wait until he finished work, which would be at about five o'clock. James said it was quite important, and would be better then than later and would not take very long. After being invited to sit down, James opened the conversation by asking, how was it that he was so friendly with Michael Banes. Ted said it was because he'd sailed with him before and because he seemed a bit of a loner who didn't seem to mix with others much, he just befriended him. Did he know he was a thief was the next question, to which Ted said he didn't and that it was a surprise to him that he had been put under ship's arrest. He knew he had been in bother on the Queen Elizabeth, but that it was not serious. He also knew he was a bit rowdy when they went ashore but that he didn't find him that bad that he couldn't be a pal. James asked if he knew much about Dennis Waye. Ted again said, no, they just all seemed to get along as a little group and kept themselves to themselves. The next question was did he know of a Bill Carter, to which Ted said no. Did he know how Michael knew Dennis? Again there was a 'no', but he did add they didn't see much of him, especially this trip.

Fred then asked several other questions that Ted answered, especially about Michael looking in Jeweller's windows while in New York on their runs ashore. Fred pushed it by asking if he ever went into any of them, to which Ted said, "Yes, and always on his own. Whenever we went to go in he would tell us to bugger off and would meet us, usually in the Seaman's Mission for a last drink before getting back to the ship."

"Did he always appear to have plenty of money?" Fred then asked and was told he was never ever short of money. It had become obvious that they were not going to learn any more than what Andy Good had told them. They thanked Ted and hoped that he didn't mind answering the questions they had put to him, but that he had been very helpful. Before leaving the cabin Ted asked why they were asking about Michael and what it had to do with him. James said he was unable to answer that, other than to say it was necessary.

It was as they were going back up to the cabin/suite that James had yet another brain wave. Directly he got to the cabin, he went in and immediately picked up the phone and got the operator to put him through to the hospital. He asked whoever it was that answered if Sister Jane was on duty. After a few seconds she came to the phone. James said who was calling and asked her if she would be on duty tonight and on learning that she was night off, asked her if he could come down to the hospital to see her. She wanted to know if it was for any specific reason, to which James told her he would tell her in a minute and that he would be right down. After putting the phone down, he turned to Fred, and asked him to stay there until he got back and that he should not be very long. He left the cabin and made for the lift where the bell boy was just about to close the doors. He didn't see who had just got out but someone must have, because why else would the doors have been opened? When James got in he told the bell boy to go down to the lowest deck he went to, which he did without stopping. He got out thanking the young lad and made his way to the hospital.

When he arrived, Jane was waiting for him. He asked her where they could talk in private and was led to a little office just off the working alleyway. She opened the door with a key she had on a little bunch and said, "Will this do?" James said it was ideal. She wanted to know why he wanted to

189

speak to her so urgently. "You did say it was your night off tonight, didn't you?" James asked, to which she nodded, so he went on, would she do him a real big favour? She said of course she would if she could. "I don't want to seem facetious or to embarrass you, Jane, but you are a very attractive young lady and, out of uniform I bet you look stunning and so can be of great assistance to me." Jane looked very coy and tried hard not to blush for she was of course very flattered. "How can I help you?" she said. James now had to explain to her what had happened and what the Captain had asked him and Fred to do and a little of what was going on. She knew about the killing as that could not be kept away from someone who worked in the hospital, but she was unaware of the other things. He asked her if she would be a passenger just for tonight and act as bait, in an attempt to catch the man they were after. She said she would if she was allowed to do such a thing. James assured her he now had the authority to ask it of her, but would get it confirmed by the Captain. Jane was still very cautious and asked if she would be recognised as she was, after all, seen by a lot of the passengers and crew when they visited the hospital. James was sure she would not because she had only just joined the ship and was mostly on night duty. Anyway, it was agreed she would do it and James said he would brief her properly when they met tonight but for now he had to get back to Fred who would be waiting for him. Before he dashed off, Jane asked him where and when they would meet, which made him think for a minute before saying in the cabin/suite. He gave her the cabin number and said he would see her there at ten o'clock.

By the time James got back he was quite excited about what he had organised and asked Fred to take part. He explained what he had in mind and Fred would be a second pair of eyes watching Jane. He didn't want her to come to any harm if boyo was on the prowl.

By now it was nearly three o'clock and James suggested to Fred that they go to one of the bars to see if they could get a cup of tea and some tab-nabs. They found one on the sun deck and sat for half an hour drinking tea and eating fancy cakes. They went over what they had achieved since first thing that morning and started to plan what they were going to do after dinner and probably what they would be doing well into the early hours of tomorrow morning. Fred asked if James intended following up on the attempted murder, to which James said they were. He said they would concentrate on trying to locate Joyce Sheen, if only they could catch the man they were looking for and James said he intended following Steve Renton tomorrow. In his new role, he wondered if he would be able to question any of the actor's party and would ask the captain tonight if he could. This settled, they decided that there was no need to question any of the other members of Harry Mills' cabin as Harry had been pretty forthright and what they had to do now was find out if their Mr. Reginald West was a passenger under another name and what that name was. He was obviously the extra passenger that could not be accounted for. They got out the passenger lists again, but from it could glean no idea of who the extra passenger was and what cabin they were occupying. James now had another thought, what passengers had cabin keys allocated to them? There were at least two keys per cabin and a spare which was located in the purser's office. That is where they would go now before James would have to start getting ready for dinner.

They went to the purser's office and asked to see the Chief Purser. The purser in the office asked if it was important and couldn't he help them? James said, "No". The purser pushed a button and said he hoped the Chief was in his personnel office. Within seconds a phone rang. When the purser put the phone down, he directed them to the Chief Purser's office. They were there in seconds and put it to him what they wanted to do and asked him if he could think of any way they could identify a passenger cabin that could be being used without them knowing about it? He said the Queen Mary was a very big ship and even with the amount of passengers on board, which was a long way from being at capacity, it could be possible that a cabin be occupied by a non-paying passenger, but he did not know how this could come about. After the search of listed unoccupied cabins had been carried out as part of the fire drill, as far as he was concerned that was all that could be checked. The thing was, after James had put his theory to the Chief Purser, how would they know who was in what cabin under a false name? If the man they were looking for was a crew member and a passenger, he would have to have a passport and a discharge book in the same or different names. The steward they were beginning to suspect was one name with a discharge book in that name, and the other, a passenger they did not know, with a passport. Was there any way that a check could be made, for a search of that cabin was critical. James said he had up to two hours to go through all his and Fred's notes and all the passenger lists again, together with the passports they had been given, to see if they could cross match everything to see if they could find a discrepancy that would indicate that there was such a passenger. It would be worth a try and the Chief Purser said he would give them a hand personally.

The Chief Purser went back with James to the main purser's office leaving Fred, and without asking any of his staff on duty, got all the crew discharge books, together with his copy of the crew list out of the safe they were kept in. He asked James to help him carry it all back to his office. After they had sat down, the Chief Purser introduced himself as Jarvis Mathews, and between them started going through all the documents they had. They started at A and went through all they had alphabetically. More than anything it was the photographs that James was interested in. He asked Jarvis if he could kindly get the passport of Reginald West who is a steward and maybe a passenger. Jarvis got up and went to the main office to look for and get the passport for Reginald

West, but came back with nothing, saying he could not find a passport under that name. It was Fred who suggested that they look again through the steward's roster under reliefs, if there was such a heading. There were three names listed but none of them were Reginald West, so they now had a problem, for they would have to identify him before they could do anything else. Again it was Fred who said it was no good trying to find him now, for if he was working he would be getting ready for dinner if he was waiting at table, and could be anywhere in the ship if he was needed as a relief. James thought for a minute and asked if he could use the Chief Purser's telephone. When told yes, he picked it up and when answered, asked the operator to put him through to the Chief Steward's office. This she did and after five or six rings it was answered, but not by the Chief Steward himself; whoever it was said his boss was not available. James asked if it was known where the Chief Steward was likely to be, but there was a negative response. James started getting cross due to the offhand manner in which he was being answered, so asked the person who he was speaking to who he was. When told 'the second assistant catering officer', James told him that what he wanted the Chief Steward for was urgent, who it was that was calling and could he please contact Gavin Martin and ask him to come to the Chief Purser's office as soon as possible. After about ten minutes Jarvis Mathews' phone rang, and when answered, the caller said the chief steward had been contacted and would be with them within the next five minutes or so. The Chief Steward arrived and looked as if he had been hurrying and asked what the urgency was. James explained what they had discovered and wanted to know if he knew all his staff well enough to give them the information they wanted.

The Chief Steward was totally mystified at what James told him, saying he would have to look into the matter because he did not make out the work rosters personally so would have to get the information they required, but felt sure there would be a simple explanation to the queries James and

Fred had. He would, when he had finished his tea, get straight onto it and would let them know as soon as he could what he had found out. James told him what table he was sitting at in the First Class Restaurant and that if he could get the information to him before he finished dinner he would be much obliged, for the sooner he could have it the better. It was decided that they could go no further at that time and so would start getting ready for dinner. Both James and Fred thanked Gavin and Jarvis for their help and left the office, with Gavin looking quite bemused and worried. He said he would get back to James as soon as he could and would of course, as requested by the Captain, keep it all low key. As he moved off in the direction of his office, James and Fred went back up to their cabin/suite.

They sat in the armchairs opposite one another and just relaxed. It was James who spoke first and said if he had not hurt his hand, he would still be on watch in a sweaty engine room or boiler room or be working down a smelly propeller shaft tunnel. Whatever he was doing it would be hard and hot work, but not nearly as mind taxing as what they were doing now. Fred agreed that he too would be more comfortable doing his job as a Master at Arms than what he was doing now, but said he was finding James good company and knew he was as passionate and focussed on finding who the man was that had tried it on with his niece as he was. They agreed that they had now laid the foundations to catch this man and were hoping that if he tried it on tonight they would catch him.

James said apart from Carol, he was worried about what had happened to Joyce Sheen or Harding the Newspaper Correspondent. She was either being kept captive on the ship or had gone overboard and he didn't think the latter applied in the least, which meant that if they caught their man they would find her.

They set out what they would each do that evening, meeting place, times and how they would use Jane as their decoy and at the same time try and keep their eyes on Helen who might well be the target, seeing what she said about the way the guy looked at her last night.

Fred said he would still do some sniffing around down in the crew's quarters before he had a meal and would see James in the prearranged place at the time they had agreed or soon after. James reminded him that they had to report to the captain at nine o'clock before all that started and hoped they got approval for what they intended doing. He said for now though, he was going down to take some pain killers as his hand was throbbing and would then get himself ready for dinner and see if he could get the ladies in the cabin near him to have a drink with him before dinner. After locking the door behind them, they shook hands and thanked one another for what each of them had done, and that they would meet in the Captain's day room at nine o'clock.

James knocked on the cabin door of Elizabeth and Amy before going to his own and on being answered by Amy, was delighted when they accepted his invite for a drink before dinner. He said he would knock again at seven o'clock so that they could go in for dinner at eight after their drink.

Getting to his own cabin, he took two more pain killers because he was doing more and more with his damaged hand each day, including accidentally knocking it when it really gave him a great deal of pain. On one occasion when he lost his balance, he had put that hand out to save himself from falling and with all his weight on it he nearly passed out with the pain. He had a bath after a few minutes, sat down and relaxed under the warm soothing water. He shampooed his hair with his undamaged hand and after drying himself, put on his underwear and dressing gown. He wondered whether he should partake in a beer seeing he had a half hour to spare before he had to get dressed, then thought better of it as he would probably have wine with his meal, after having a couple of drinks with Elizabeth and Amy, not to mention another couple during the evening when entertaining Jane or at least watching out for her. So he just read the ship's daily bulletin. It was while he was sitting there quietly he realised the ship was beginning to roll a bit, only gently, but enough to warrant putting the stabilizers out. This would mean the ship would not roll so much but if the sea state got over about five or six they would have to be withdrawn, for if such a heavy vessel had them come out of the water, they would bend up and would not be able to be brought inboard. There were two sets controlled from each generator room and had been fitted long after the Queen Mary was built. It did not stop the roll but reduced it considerably.

James got dressed, still of course with some difficulty, but with little ways he had adopted he was able to manage his buttons and laces. Just before he was finished, a knock on the door brought John Lever his bedroom steward into the cabin to refresh the water in his thermos jug, change his towels and turn down his bed. John was as always very polite, and mentioned how elegant the ladies just along the passage were when they were dressed up in their finery. He said he had seen to the ladies' cabin before coming along to his. He told John that those were two of the people his half-brother had stolen from and that they did not know that he was that steward's relative. James asked John how many cabins he had to look after, to which he replied between him and the bedroom stewardess Ruby, he had eight and that there were twenty four cabins in that deck section making three stewards and three stewardesses on the port and starboard sides. "How many bedroom stewards does the ship carry?" James asked, but he didn't know and just said, "A lot." John was such a nice young man that it did not seem possible he and the guy under lock and key could have the same mother.

James left John still doing what he had to do and went along to his ladies, as he was now calling them, to escort them to the observation lounge. When he tapped lightly on the door, it was opened immediately by Amy who was, as John had described her, extremely elegant, as was Elizabeth when she came to the door to join her sister. They were both wearing long dresses, were tastefully made up, their hair nicely done in their individual styles and with similar patent leather shoes. They looked much younger than they actually were, although James did not know their actual ages, but guessed they were into their sixties. They wore tasteful jewellery and both carried small purses to complement their dresses. Elizabeth carried a stole for her shoulders and Amy a very fancy light weight cardigan. They said what a pleasure it was for both of them to be taken out by such a good looking young man and hoped he would have no regrets at taking out two old ladies that were old enough to be his mother. His response to that was that he was as proud to be taking them out, as he would be his mother. They looked at one another, and then at James, and they all had to laugh. He asked them if the observation lounge was a choice they would make to have a quiet drink, as he had only been in there twice before, but it seemed to be such an appropriate place for what they were doing.

They sat comfortably with a good view out to sea and didn't have to wait very long before a waiter came over to serve them. James pointed to the ladies, who had studied the wine list. Elizabeth asked if it would be alright to change from their usual dry sherry and have a cocktail instead. "Of course you can, choose anything on the wine list or if it is not on there, I am sure the waiter here can get the barman to make it up for you." The waiter nodded, but both Elizabeth and Amy said the cocktails listed were so comprehensive they would choose one from the wine list. They both made their choice and James said he would have a small beer. While they made small talk, the ship was still gently rolling and Amy wondered aloud if the weather was going to deteriorate and the sea become rougher. James had not noticed when he had read the ship's newspaper, the Ocean Times, what the weather forecast for the next twenty-four hours was supposed to be and so could not give any assurance one way or the other; Amy hoped not, for she was enjoying things just as they were. Their drinks arrived and James asked that they be put on his bill, giving his cabin number. It was Elizabeth who said they had a secret and would James like to know what it was? Being intrigued, he said he would, so Amy told him they were trying to have a different cocktail every day, and tasting the one she had just received said how nice it was and that she might have another. She said the thing she liked so much about cocktails was all the fancy things that came with them, apart from the fruit and ice she just loved cocktail cherries, but it was the swizzle sticks and little umbrellas that went with them. She said she was collecting some of them that were different, and getting them from different ships she was building up quite a little collection. Amy, who had chosen a drink of her liking also said how nice hers was and likewise would have another.

While they sipped their drinks, they talked about the trip so far and how lucky they were to be on the table they were on and what nice people they had met. They thought the family were great and how well they had all got on. They asked James what he did with himself all day as they never saw much of him other than at meal times, and not for very long then. James wondered how much he dare tell them of what he was, what he had done and what he had got involved in, starting with the outward voyage. He decided he could confide in them and so told them most of what had gone on from meeting Fred's nieces, hurting his hand and going to the New York hospital. He told them what he was saying was very confidential and that it was to go no further. They asked what would be happening to the steward that stole their jewellery, and what was going on with the actor whose manager had died or been killed? James told them about

Joyce after what had happened to Carol, and that they were looking for someone who was still on the ship. He did not, however, let on that he had asked Jane, one of the nursing sisters to help him or what they were going to do tonight.

They called the waiter over and ordered the same round of drinks again, this time the ladies insisted on paying; it didn't matter how much James protested by arguing that he had invited them for a pre-dinner drink. They said they appreciated what James had done and it was a pleasure being in his company, but that they felt they had to stand their ground and that after all, they could probably afford it more than him. It was while they were waiting for the waiter to come back that Steve Renton and his wife came into the lounge and found a couple of seats at the bar. They were both dressed for dinner but not accompanied by any of their table friends. The ladies started to whisper and James had to ask what they were whispering about. They said they wondered why they were on their own and not with the crowd of hangers on. It was then that James thought he might try and talk to them and would ask Captain Baron at nine o'clock if he could, for he really felt there was more to this guy and his wife than met the eye.

When the second round of drinks arrived, the waiter remembered who had what, and handed them out before placing a few very tiny cut sandwiches and some olives on the small table that was by them. Amy thanked him and slipped him a dollar. He thanked her and asked if there was anything else he could get them. Amy said they would like a finger bowl and a napkin which he went to get straight away. James had not really taken his eyes off Steve Renton and his wife since they had sat up at the bar; he could only see them side on from where he and the ladies were sat, but could see they were deep in conversation. Steve, not being a big man, was perched up on the bar stool with his trouser leg having gone above his black sock showing a bit of bare skin on which was a tattoo half covered with the sock and half exposed. What the tattoo was James could not determine from a distance, it could have been a small dragon, or maybe a rampant lion, but being half covered and too far away he could not make it out. It was only when Elizabeth said that she thought it most unladylike for women to have tattoos, and was looking in Judy Mendise's direction when she said it, that James noticed she had a small tattoo on the same leg as her husband that could be seen under the fold of her long dress as she was sitting. It was very delicate and just above her ankle. Even though it was under her stocking, it could be seen very plainly, together with the gold chain that also adorned the same ankle. Why they do it, she didn't know but in her opinion if they had been born like it they would have wanted them removed.

Getting back to what James had told them and their apparent dislike of the two actors, the ladies asked James if it would be of any help if they kept an eye on that pair, as they called them. "How would you be able to do that?" James wanted to know.

"Well," said Elizabeth, "follow them, see where they go and what they do."

"We cannot go to their cabin, of course, unless invited," interjected Amy, "but we could see and even listen, if we got the opportunity, to what they and their cronies are all about."

James said, "But you are on board this ship to enjoy your journey home, not to help me find a criminal, for that is what the person I am trying to find is."

"We know that," went on Elizabeth, "but it will give us something more to do than just sitting around reading, sitting in the sun, what there is of it and eating and drinking, plus, it will be fun being nosey." At this, the three of them had to laugh but Elizabeth was serious and Amy was with her all the way; they would be James's secret agents. James said if they thought they could get into the actor's company at any time, not to join their gang of course, but get in conversation with them, it could come to something and it would be time that he and Fred could not afford to spend. So it was agreed, starting from after dinner tonight they would be on the case. They finished their drinks and started to leave the observation lounge when two more of the Renton's party came in and headed straight to the bar to join them. The ladies were now so eager, they were already wondering what the little group were going to talk about. But for now, for them it was dinner and they made their way to the restaurant. The Head Waiter greeted them as they entered and on confirming that James was James Royston, handed him an envelope containing a note from the Chief Steward. He thanked the head waiter and was escorted to their table by Victor. He sat down after the ladies were seated and opened the envelope with the butter knife. He excused himself to the rest of the table guests, for Henry, Rachel and Helen were already at the table when they arrived, but said the note was important and that he had to read it there and then. It read: Have not got a Reginald West listed or recorded on my staff list, what do you want me to do? I will be with the Captain at nine o'clock.

James stuffed the note into his jacket pocket and once again apologised, before saying good evening to the family. Rachel said it was her turn to buy the wine and picked out a red and a white that she thought everyone would enjoy and without asking any of them, gave her order to the wine waiter to bring a bottle of each. James, now being able to eat anything he wanted, chose artichoke as his starter with a medium sirloin steak to follow. The wine duly arrived and after tasting both, Rachel asked the wine waiter to pour that which each preferred. James took a red and on tasting it, complemented Rachel on her choice and said it was just right to go with his steak. As they all settled down awaiting their first courses to arrive, Helen asked James if there had been any further developments. He said they still hadn't found who they were looking for, but that the noose was tightening and that he expected something to come to light by tomorrow afternoon at the latest. She assured him she was still alert to what she knew of the situation, but that she didn't think she could help or get involved any more than she had. Amy gave Helen a little nudge and cast her eyes to the Renton's table as they trooped in. There were still eight of them sat down so there was a new hanger on who was replacing Steve's manager. Their starters arrived and so the conversation reduced, especially with James who having ordered an artichoke, had to concentrate on eating it, as he scooped the flesh from the leaves. It was only the second one he had ever eaten and was unsure whether he really liked it, but what he did know was it was something his mother would never have been able to afford.

Once again as the meal went on, there seemed to be quite a lot of loud discussion coming from the actor's table, mostly, it would seem, good humoured; that is not to say that most of the tables near to them were not steeped in conversation. Looking across the room, James took note that the Captain was not at his table yet and being the time was already well after eight o'clock and because the other passengers at his table were eating, he must have sent word that he was not going to be there that evening, for they would not have started without him. It was nearly nine o'clock when James wished his table companions a very pleasant evening and hoped he might see them later and, thanking Rachel for the wine, left the table heading for the Captain's day cabin. He got there right on the dot of nine o'clock and on knocking the cabin door was invited in.

The Captain was on his own, with none of the others expected having turned up yet, so inviting James to sit down, offered him a drink. James said he had noticed he had not gone in for dinner tonight to which Captain Baron explained was due to a radio telephone call he had received from the Cunard Office in New York. There had apparently been a query over passenger numbers, and he had been asked if he was carrying two passengers by the name of Sheen and Harding? "I am so sorry, Captain, but did I forget to mention that when Fred and I searched Joyce Sheen's cabin the day after she went missing, we found three passports and a pistol. Two of the passports were in the name of Sheen and one, an older one, was under the name of Harding."

"Oh yes, now I recall, you did tell me but with everything else that has been going on I had forgotten, not that I would have connected it to the New York office communication. What did you do with them?" James said they had left them where they were in the cabin, should he go and get them? The captain said, "Yes, go now and hopefully there will be somebody around to let you in." There was no way he was going to ask anyone to let him in to the cabin when he had a key and so went to his own cabin first to get the key from Joyce's handbag, which he had put in his safe. He retrieved the bag from his safe and took the key from the zipped up compartment before putting the bag back and locking it up again.

He took the key to Joyce's cabin, and making sure there was no one around, opened the cabin door and went in quickly. He breathed a small sigh of relief when he found the passports were still where they had been left, and while he was at it he decided it might be wise to remove the pistol as well. This too was still where Fred had previously found it, and carefully removing it from among the underwear with his hankie, he wrapped it in the handkerchief and put it in his trouser pocket. He took a quick glance around the cabin and was sure no one had been in since he and Fred had left it. He opened the cabin door very slowly just enough to get his head out and looked down the passage way to see if it was all clear. A stewardess was going into a cabin about seven or eight down from him but went in without looking right or left. As she went in, James came out and quickly locking the door behind him moved away from where the stewardess might come out and made his way back to the Captain's day cabin. When he got back, Fred and the chief steward were with the captain waiting for him. Captain Baron asked James if he had managed to get the passports without any bother and James explained what he had done. He asked the

Captain if he had a large envelope that he could use to put the pistol in that he had not touched with his bare hands. He was handed one and James carefully transferred the pistol from his hankie into the envelope, which he then handed to the Captain to put in his safe along with the hoard of jewellery that Fred had given him earlier. The Chief Steward could not help himself, looking up, he said to the Captain, "When I first encountered this young man I thought what a bumptious little upstart he was but after seeing what he is doing and the way he is going about it, ably assisted by Mr. Baker here, I must say I have completely changed my mind." The Captain nodded and winked at James, who thanked Mr. Martin and said that perhaps they had got off on the wrong foot, and it was left at that.

They now turned to the passports and examined them, this time in great detail. Captain Baron got out his copy of the passenger list and went down the names. When he came to J. Harding he put a pencil mark by it and continued down to Sheen, that he found was also there and put a pencil mark by that too. It appeared that this same person was listed twice. James commented that the discrepancy that he and Fred had highlighted was now evident. There was one passenger down as two on paper and one crew member down as a passenger and as a crew member, which is where the difficulty came in.

"We have the photos and slightly differing details of one, the passenger Joyce Sheen/Harding, but we are more in the dark regarding Reginald West, if he is the passenger crew member we are looking for."

James said "We hope that after getting your note, Gavin, for which I thank you by the way, you can shed some light on Mr. West."

"Yes, I can," the chief steward replied, "and it isn't good. We have a man who is being employed that we know nothing about whatsoever. We do not even know if he has a passport or a discharge book, so other than knowing he is sharing a cabin with five others, as far as I am concerned he does not exist. I know I am responsible for all the catering staff but cannot blame myself for this situation and cannot put any blame on the pursers or any of my senior officers. I have not done anything about this man, because if he knew that we are investigating him he would go under cover, which will make it really hard for you to locate him."

James said the trouble was that they did not know what passenger cabin he was occupying or what name he was going under as a passenger. "As far as the pursers are concerned, the passenger numbers are correct, which they would be if one is two and the other is nothing, it sounds complicated, but is in fact the situation."

Fred said he would try to contact Harry Miles again, the steward they had spoken to earlier, in an effort to identify Reginald West and not just go on a description that could apply to half a dozen others. James explained what he and Fred were going to attempt tonight and sought the permission of the Captain to involve nursing sister Jane as he had planned. He was comprehensive about it, but when assured she would be safe, that either Fred or he would have her in view for the whole time she was being used as a decoy, the captain agreed, on the understanding that Jane knew exactly what she was being asked to do. James said he had briefed her thoroughly and that she was up for it. That being the case, it was agreed that the trap would be set at ten o'clock, in fifteen minutes time. One other thing he had to mention was that the two ladies in the cabin along from his who just happen to sit at his dining table had volunteered, without any prompting, to keep a watch on the actor Steve Renton and his wife. Captain Baron asked James if he thought it wise to have told his table members what was going on but James assured him security was tight and he felt sure there would be no breaches. The Captain wished them good luck and James thanked Gavin Martin for his assistance before he and Fred left the cabin to go to their cabin/suite.

CHAPTER 8

They got back to their cabin/suite at five minutes to ten and dead on ten o'clock there was a knock at the door. James went to the door and standing there in front of him was a most beautiful young woman. Jane said good evening and asked if she would do. James was almost speechless as he invited her in. He introduced her to Fred, who said he had met somebody just like her at the hospital on the outward bound trip and smiled. He joked with her by asking if she had a date tonight and Jane, having a sense of humour, said she hoped so. They sat and agreed on their plan of action and reassured her she would be safe. She said she was glad to hear it and asked if there had been any problem with the Captain regarding her undertaking this task. James told her what the Captain had said and referred her to Fred, who backed him up. Jane said that she did not have a lot of money to pay for drinks and to tip waiters, but James assured her she would not need a lot of money as he would pay for the drinks for her. Although she was dressed nicely, it was much the same as Carol and Susan had been, in fact, seeing her made James think of Susan. He had to quickly but only temporarily discard any memory of her because there was work to do and Jane, as nice as she was, was in no way going to be a replacement for Susan.

By the time they had got up to the main lounge, the bingo had finished and the dancing was well under way. The fact that it was not a gala night, the men were in lounge suits, as were James and Fred. This was a new experience for Fred, who had only ever gone to the main lounge once before and that was as a Master at Arms to help out when a fight started and one participant had to be taken away. "Should we have a drink here?" Fred asked, and got a flat answer, no, they would just sit for a while, then, James and Jane would have a dance while Fred kept a look out, particularly for the waiters that were on duty. Fred said he was going to have a small beer so he could mingle with a drink in his hand rather than just sit or walk around with nothing. They sat for ten minutes or so before the band started playing a waltz to a piece of music that Jane said she loved and would James do this dance with her? This seemed natural enough, so James gave Fred the wink and taking Jane by the hand, took her onto the dance floor. James whispered to Jane that they would keep to the outer edge of the main dancers, because he wanted her seen and so they began to dance, firstly at a distance but as the dance went on, Jane got closer, she was obviously enjoying herself.

As they moved to the dance floor, Fred called a waiter over and ordered a small beer. When the waiter came back he asked him if Reg West was on duty tonight and was told no, he didn't think so; if he was, he certainly wasn't in the main lounge. While his cohorts were dancing, Fred covered just about the whole of the main lounge. The waiter that had served him must have been right, for Fred didn't see any of those on duty who were anything like what Harry Miles description had been of Reginald West, plus all the waiters he saw had regulation polished leather shoes. So, was he looking for Reginald West the passenger, this was the question. The waltz turned into a foxtrot which James was struggling with, but that Jane could do well. It had now been fifteen minutes since they took to the floor and Jane was most disappointed when James said he thought that they should call it a day when the dance ended. They left the floor holding hands and went back to where they had been sitting. Fred came over to them when they had sat down and the music was finishing. He said straight away, "Nothing in here, James, let's try the Grille." And so they made their way to the Veranda Grille. This time they left Jane to go in on her own and find a table. James went to the bar and Fred took up position where he could see her clearly without being conspicuous and having only just having had a beer, didn't want another one. James, however, ordered a drink for himself and seeing the barman knew him, asked if Reg West was on duty tonight. "Doing what?" the barman wanted to know, and when told waiting at tables, he said he didn't know a waiter by that name and was certain there had not been one on this trip, or at least not in the Veranda Grille.

Jane had chosen a table where a couple had just got up, leaving the used glasses and crumbs of whatever they had been nibbling still there. However, it was only seconds before a waiter came over to remove the glasses and wipe down the table. As he finished he asked Jane if she was drinking and if she wasn't, could he get her one. She was just about to say she would have a sweet sherry, when a gentleman came to the table and said, "Whatever the lady would like to drink, and get me a double whisky and water, please." Jane said she would like a port and lemon. The man asked if he could join her and before Jane could reply, he sat down. He introduced himself as Trevor and went on to tell her he was from London and that he had been to New York on business and was on his way home. He went on to ask her if she was alone and when she said, "Yes, at the moment," he must have thought he was in. When the waiter came back with the drinks, he made a big thing of getting his wallet out and giving the waiter a five dollar tip from a large wad of dollar bills. He moved his chair round to be nearer to Jane, that meant Fred had to change position, for his view was now being blocked by the man sitting with her. As it happened, it would not have mattered as James had a better view. After finishing her port and lemon, Trevor invited her to have a cocktail which she accepted, and as planned, before she even sipped it, said she had to go and powder her nose. He stood up as she left the table, sitting down again to await her return. Fred picked up a nearly empty beer glass on a table near him and although having not seen him go to his pocket or make any attempt to touch the cocktail, went across and clumsily managed to kick the table leg of the table Trevor was sitting at as he staggered by. With Jane's cocktail knocked over and the glass smashed on the deck, he apologised profusely to Trevor for being so clumsy and offered to pay for the drink, but Trevor wanted to be big time and said not to worry he would get another one. Fred did his best to slur his way into conversation with the guy but he was having none of it. Realising his ploy wasn't going to work, Fred gave him a very smart pat on the back and apologised again before slightly unsteadily making his way to the bar in the direction of James. It was only a short time after he got to the bar that he got into conversation with him, as though he had never met him in his life before. James asked quietly if he thought he was their man and got a no, but they would have to leave it to Jane to deal with. They watched Trevor order Jane another cocktail which she tasted, but indicated that she did not like it and pushed it away. Seeing she was doing so well and thinking he could bail her out, James went over to the table and introduced himself as Jane's boyfriend. Jane introduced him to Trevor and said she had been waiting for him. Trevor said, "But you said you were on your own." Jane contradicted him by saying he had asked if she was alone and she had said yes and he had not given her time to explain that she was waiting for someone. James said he was sorry if there had been a misunderstanding but he and Jane had some friends to meet and would have to leave. With that, Jane stood up said goodbye and accompanied James out of the Veranda Grille.

James and Jane waited outside until Fred came out and agreed to try the observation lounge. Looking at his watch and seeing it was still relatively early, James suggested they hang around and have a drink before moving on. He said he thought if anything was going to happen, it wouldn't be before midnight. Once again it was quite busy and with a piano playing, it was quite a relaxing atmosphere. They once again split up, with Jane finding a table with only one other person sitting at it. She was a bit older than Jane and not so well dressed and smoking a cigarette she looked a bit tarty. However, as Jane approached the table she welcomed her company. Fred once again went to one side of the room and James to the bar, where he ordered two small beers. He asked the barman if Reg West was on duty tonight and once again the barman had no idea who Reginald West was, he had never heard of him. James caught Fred's eye and motioned that there was a drink for him at the bar. Seeing there was a good view from where James was standing there was no harm in Fred joining him, which he did.

Jane was already in conversation with the woman she had joined, who had called a waiter over. She asked Jane if she would join her in a drink and Jane said that was very kind of her and yes she would like a gin and tonic. The lady ordered what Jane had asked for and a double whiskey and soda on the rocks. It was then that Jane realised her new found friend was well on the way to being drunk. She was an American who had just been recently divorced and was on her way to England to look for a new life. She said she had been in the main lounge and the Veranda Grille and now here looking for a pick up, but with not a sniff of luck. She said one bloke had approached her, she thought his name was Trevor, but he turned out to be a big time show off and she didn't fancy him. Jane asked if she had been approached by anybody since leaving New York and was very interested in her reply. She said a rather nice smelling chap had asked her to dance in the main lounge the second night out, but it was just before the band finished playing and so they only danced once. She said he suggested that they go to the Veranda Grille where they could get a drink until well after midnight and so they went. She said he ordered a cocktail in a jug, she supposed like a Tom Collins or something like that, whatever it was it had loads of fruit and bits and pieces in it. Whatever it was she got a bit high and had no hesitation in agreeing to sex, in fact she felt very keen. She said it was only after having the cocktail drink that she started feeling so sexy but she remembered it quite distinctly. "Can you tell me the name of the chap you were with?" Jane asked and got a very embarrassed, "No," from her companion. "I told him my name, which is Margaret Yates by the way, but he never told me his." Jane introduced herself and went on to ask if she knew what her man did for a living, or where his cabin was or where he was heading when he left the ship in Southampton? She said he did most of the talking, and what he talked about was nothing to do with himself. "I really do feel cheap and ashamed that I had full sex with a man that I knew nothing about, or even his name. What I do know though is that he is good in bed. He tried allsorts and I do not recall having had any resistance to his demands, and I have never done anything like it in my life before." Jane's next question was did he stay all night in her cabin? To this she said no, and she didn't know when he left as she must have passed out, but when she woke up she was still naked but in her bed and covered up, but with the most splitting head ache and her mouth was as dry as blotting paper. "Is there anything particular that you can remember about this man and would you recognise him again if you saw him?"

"You bet I would," she said, "and I would not let him near me again and there is one thing..."

"What's that?" Jane encouraged.

"It was his shoes, they were so unusual, he seemed to treasure them, not that I blame him for they were really classy. They were made of hide I think, were very stylish and I would say cost a fortune. It was when he took them off and when he got undressed he put them so carefully on top of his clothes."

"I assume you got undressed as well," Jane prompted, and got a wicked look when she replied, "I didn't have to, he did it for me. The only other thing is, as I think I said before, he smelt nice, whether it was body lotion or aftershave I don't know, but it was a pleasant but unusual smell."

"Did you tell anybody what happened that night?" Jane then asked.

"I was too ashamed until now, and I don't know why I'm telling you, perhaps it's the drink, for I think I've had too much." Jane had finished her drink while she had been listening, unlike Margaret who had been doing all the talking, so when Jane asked if she would like another she declined and said she would drink what she had left and then go to bed. She finished her drink in one gulp and said that it was nice talking to Jane and that she might bump into her again tomorrow. She got up from her chair very unsteadily, but as she walked away she seemed to gain her composure and would be safe enough getting back to her cabin.

James and Fred had witnessed this and could not get over to Jane quickly enough, and it was when she saw them approaching that she spotted Margaret's little shoulder bag hanging at the side of her chair. She turned to call her, but she was gone. When they got to her, James started to scold Jane, asking why the hell she had spent so much time talking to the woman that had just left. Jane was quick to respond, saying, "You just wait until you know." She went on to say it was just as well he had told her as much as he had about the man they were after, because she was able to get from that lady just about everything they wanted to know about him except his name and cabin number. She said the steward you questioned was quite right, he seems to be a cool calm and depraved pervert, who uses some form of sexual accelerant to get sex from a woman. "James, we must catch this man!" She went on to explain to both of them what Margaret Yates told her and said there was no point in trying to get any more sense out of her now because at a guess she would say she is already fast asleep. "Do you know what cabin she is in?" James asked. "If she has left her bag behind, she may have got her cabin key in it and so would not be able to get into her cabin, unless there is a night steward still awake on her deck that could let her in with his master key." Jane took the liberty of looking in her little evening shoulder bag and in it she found a hankie, lipstick, cigarettes, lighter, a few dollar bills, some American coins, a condom and her cabin key. Jane asked if she should go to the cabin to see if Margaret was alright and they decided that Fred should go with Jane to check, while James carried on going round the bars. He said he would meet them in fifteen minutes in the Veranda Grille and he would be at the bar. They left the observation lounge together, with James going one way and Fred and Jane going the other. James went to two bars he knew would be open, one of which was the most popular in second class, using his segregation gate key to get to it. It was getting late but not yet midnight and there were still quite a few passengers around, more so in second class than first. It was the waiters he was looking at, just to see if any of them looked to be the one he was after.

When he got back to the Grille, Fred and Jane were already there waiting at the bar, by the look on their faces, there was something wrong. "What's up?" James asked.

"We couldn't find her," they said in unison.

"Where did you look?" he asked. They had looked in her cabin, in the passenger ladies toilet in the passageway and had walked back to the observation lounge separately, one on the port side and one on the starboard, but could not find her. Fred took a guess that maybe she had gone out onto the open deck to get some fresh air. It was worth a try, so they went out to the boat deck near her cabin and ongoing onto the open deck nearly fell over her. The side of her face was covered in blood and was still bleeding from a gash over her left temple. Jane said she was unconscious but that her pulse was strong and that she wasn't going to die but that they had to get her to hospital to have the wound stitched. James thought to himself, "What the bloody hell is going to happen next, as we try to solve one thing something else happens." Jane tried there and then to bring Margaret round, but with no success. What now was the question, for something had to be done. Jane said the hospital would have to be informed and if the two of them could handle the situation, Jane would be obliged, because if hospital staff saw her out of uniform they would start asking awkward questions. Fred said he could handle it if James could telephone the hospital to get someone there while he stayed with her. James said he would do it now. As he got up from kneeling down, he saw a movement along the deck. He called out "Who is there?" but whoever it was started running. James gave chase after telling Jane she would have to ring the hospital. Whoever it was ran like the wind and disappeared round the front of the boat deck under the cover of darkness, by the time James got to the other side of the ship there was no sign of him. He tried each deck door as he got to them but knew he wasn't going to find anyone and so went back to where he found Jane still with Fred. Jane had just managed to bring Margaret round and had her sat up holding Fred's handkerchief over the cut on her head. Jane asked if she remembered her and could she stand up. She said she knew who Jane was and that she thought she could stand up and walk. Fred said he would take her down to the hospital and would meet them in the main lounge as soon as he could.

James and Jane made their way to the main lounge discussing what had just happened. The bar was still open when they got there and James ordered a brandy for each of them, saying he thought they deserved it. They had just sat down in an armchair each to wait for Fred, when low and behold Elizabeth and Amy appeared. James asked them if they would like a nightcap and they both said they would like a brandy too. He called a waiter over and asked for two brandies. They moved to where there were four chairs together and waited for the waiter to come back. Elizabeth was particularly excited saying they had kept their eyes on Steve and Judy Renton all the evening and had even managed to get into conversation with them. She explained what they had done and how they had managed to get an invitation to join them for a drink the next night had come about. James had to apologise to Jane for not introducing her to his two ladies and telling her that they were two of his table companions and what they had volunteered to do. He told them that Jane was a nursing sister and what had just happened and that they were waiting for Fred to come back from the hospital before going back to the Veranda Grille. The ladies said they would like to go too, if that would be alright, as four pairs of eyes would be better than two if Jane was still going to be the decoy. So when Fred arrived and they had finished their drinks, the five of them moved off to go to the Veranda Grille again. As they were leaving, they could see that the main lounge bar was closing and anyone that still wanted to drink on would be joining them shortly, so by going now they would get a better seat.

Jane once again went and sat on her own at a small table suitable for two, while Fred went to the bar to keep Jane in his sight, with James, Amy and Elizabeth finding four chairs and a table adjacent to Jane. This worked out perfectly as Fred could observe the whole room as well as Jane, and James had the added advantage of being able to talk to his ladies with regards to what they had done and witnessed. He asked them what they would like to drink and both said almost in unison, "Another brandy, please," but that was to be their lot or they would make themselves unwell. So calling a waiter over he ordered the brandies, a gin and tonic for that young lady over there and a small beer for himself, hoping Fred had ordered independently. Because the Grille was still not too busy, the drinks came very quickly. The waiter put theirs in front of them and took Jane's to her table. She gave James a little nod of acknowledgement and a smile. It was Elizabeth being the more excited of the two ladies that started off. She said they waited at the dinner table until the Rentons had ended their meal together with their guests, which was, by the way, long after Henry, Rachel and Helen had gone, and followed them to the main lounge. They had waited until the group had all sat down after shifting chairs about, before they sat in chairs as near to them as they could. It was while they were stretching and moving the furniture about that Elizabeth noticed that two of the men had a tattoo just above their left ankle; she could not distinguish what it was but they definitely had a tattoo. She said the drinks Steve ordered were varied, and by the way, it was always him doing the ordering, they did not see any of the other four order a thing. She said one of the group with a tattoo on his leg left them at about eleven o'clock and never returned; others, they thought, from time to time had just left to go to the bathroom. James asked if the one that left the group had fancy shoes on, but they both said they had not noticed. Amy said that as they followed the group, at least one of them smelt extra nice, but could not say which one as they left all together. When they got their drinks they just talked together, and a couple of times voices were raised a little, but there was nothing else untoward except that Judy, being the only woman, seemed to be being put down quite a bit, and it was not going down well. It was not leg pulling but serious, or so it seemed, until that one man left and then the whole atmosphere seemed to change. It was at that moment that James had the idea.

He went over and asked Fred to go and sit with the ladies, still keeping his eyes on Jane, and if no one had come near her by one o'clock, he was to call it off and escort Jane back to her quarters, adding that Amy and Elizabeth would see themselves back to their cabin together. Fred asked where he was going and James said he was going up to check from his lists what accommodation the Renton's were occupying and said he was going to see if the night bedroom steward was around to speak to and also find out who the day time steward and stewardess were. After that he was going down to the hospital to see what had happened to Margaret Yates, who he wanted to ask something. He left Fred, who had got himself a drink, some of which he had left in his glass that he carried over to the ladies. Jane was still at that time sitting on her own, but not for long when passengers started coming in from the main lounge. It was Trevor, who once again asked her if he could sit with her and buy her a drink. This time she said he could, and she would like a brandy as a night cap as her boyfriend had been called away and had said he would pick her up there directly he had finished his business but if he was not back by one o'clock to carry on to bed. She said it was up to him if he wanted to stay and chat, but that is what she would be doing and she would rather have someone to talk to than just sit on her own. It was now after half past midnight so it would not be for long. Trevor excused himself and went to the bar to get the brandy which gave Jane time to let Fred know what she was doing. She was sure Trevor was not their man and it would help her kill time for half an hour. She felt sure the man that James had chased and lost wouldn't be trying anything else on tonight, plus, with them there and James coming back within half an hour there was nothing to worry about. Trevor brought back the brandies and they just sat and chatted.

Meanwhile, James had gone up to the cabin/suite and looked up the passenger list. The Rentons were in a suite on main deck, that he found out later had been occupied in the past by some famous people; Victor Mature, Tony Curtis and Janet Leigh for a start, not that it was of any interest to him right then. He went to see if anyone was around and was lucky to find the night steward. James introduced himself and asked the steward when he comes on in the evening and could he tell him the names of the steward and stewardess that are on duty during the day? He asked him if he had been serving these cabins all trip and was told he had been doing those cabins for the last two years. James then asked if he had to bring meals to the cabin in the evening or at night. He said he did, but usually only one which he finds strange as Mr. and Mrs. Renton usually eat in the restaurant, but he is only a steward and who is he to question if they have meals in their cabin. "They tip well, so I just do what they ask without question."

"That's fine," James assured him, "you carry on doing what you do, but can you tell me if those who form a group with the Rentons have cabins anywhere near here?" The steward said there were two cabins either side of this theirs, which is a suite. "The two either side are twin cabins and are occupied by his friends, I say his friends because they are all men. One of them now only has one in it, because I believe the gentleman is in hospital, or at least that is what I've been told." The next question James had was, did any of the occupants use unusual but nice smelling aftershave lotion? The steward said that two of the cabins did smell rather nice and pointed out which two they were. James noted the numbers and went on to ask if he knew all the passengers by sight? He said that he did, and really found them a strange lot. James asked, "What's strange about them?"

"Well, most passengers leave a 'my room is available to clean' or 'do not disturb' tag on the door, but at all of their cabins you have to knock loudly and wait until they open it, and if they do not open the door you do not go in. I did that on the first night out and got really told off."

"So you only do anything in their cabins while they are in occupancy?"

The steward said, "Yes," and when asked if that included Mr. and Mrs. Renton's suite, he said "yes" again, especially theirs as it was that one he went into without knocking first. James thanked him for the information and asked him not to divulge to anyone what had been said between them, it was very important that he keep tight-lipped.

After speaking to the bedroom steward, he went to the telephone exchange and going in, found only one man on duty. He explained to the man who he was and what he was doing and being quiet at night time, the operator said that it only needed one body to man the exchange and that the ladies that were on duty during the day were stood down. James, after saying it was a good time, asked about cabin telephones. He asked the operator if it was possible to put a stop to one cabin phoning another. The operator explained that it was possible by making the cabin phone only connect to the exchange and that any calls required would have to be redirected from there, that way no calls could be made direct.

James asked him there and then if this could be undertaken with the phones in the cabins on main deck that he gave him the numbers for. The operator looking at the cabin numbers James had given him immediately pointed out that one of the cabin numbers was the suite the film star Steve Renton was occupying. "Yes, that is quite correct," James confirmed, "and the other cabin numbers are adjacent to it. I want any calls they make directed through the exchange and that in no circumstances are those cabins to be connected to each other. I will get a list of contacts they cannot make to you, signed by the Captain, and if any of those number cabins telephone, they can only be connected to the people I give you. I want you to make sure this is adhered to by all of your operators. These cabins are under ship's arrest and are ex-communicated other than the contacts on the list I will supply you with." James made the operator say that he understood what he wanted done and if there was anything he did not understand before he left the exchange.

He then moved on to the hospital where he found Jean on duty. He asked her if Margaret Yates was being retained and if she was awake, would it be possible to speak to her as it was very important. Jean asked if James wanted to get her the sack, but when he told her that he was trying to catch the man that attacked Margaret, that it wasn't an accident that she had had, she said she would see if she was awake. She came back to James and told him she was, but that she was in shock so he would not be able to stay long and that she would have to be there when he asked her questions. James was actually pleased that Jean would be present as she would be a very reliable witness if one was ever required. Jean showed him into the ward where Margaret was the only patient. She recognised him straight away, and said she would answer any questions she could. He asked her first if she knew who it was that attacked her. She answered immediately that it was the bloke that had nearly shagged her to death the night before. She said when she had left his friend Jane, she had gone back to her cabin and when she got

219

there he was waiting for her. He asked if he could come in, and when she said no, he grabbed her. She said when she left Jane she had had enough to drink, in fact felt quite tipsy. However, when this man got hold of her she soon sobered up, kneed him in the groin and ran out of the nearest door leading to the open deck where she would hopefully meet other passengers. He managed to catch up with her and as she struggled with him he must have hit her in the face with something for she didn't remember any more until she saw Jane looking down on her. He thanked her and Jean for letting him talk to her and hoped she would be able to leave hospital in the morning.

He looked at his watch and seeing it was very nearly one o'clock almost ran all the way back to the Veranda Grille, where he found them all still there including Trevor, who by then Jane realised was a very nice fellow, all be it that he was a bit flash. Amy asked if there was anything else that her and her sister could do and James said, "No, not tonight," and thanked them for what they had done that evening. As they went off, James heard Trevor ask Jane if he would be able to meet her again tomorrow, she said it was impossible tomorrow night, but if he gave her his cabin number she would contact him when she could. He gave it to her, they shook hands and he gave her a little peck on the cheek, before thanking her for her company and leaving her with Fred and James.

James suggested he and Fred escort Jane to her quarters before they went back to his cabin for a chat about what he had done after leaving them earlier. Jane said she would be alright on her own, but James insisted on an escort. It was surprising how many passengers were still about but it became much quieter when they got to the crews area. They saw Jane to her cabin door where both James and Fred thanked her for what she had done and both gave her a peck on the cheek. She whispered how it had been an interesting evening and how lucky she was to have three men kiss her in one night. She quietly opened the door to her cabin as they left.

They got back to James's cabin at twenty past one and both looked a little worse for wear. James put the beer on his table into the fridge assuming, like him, Fred didn't want any more to drink. They sat opposite each other and James explained what he had done and said all there was to do later was to speak to the Renton's day steward and stewardess, before springing the trap. He thought they were just about there but not quite, for they still hadn't found Joyce and still didn't know the name of the man they were after. So they still had a little way to go. By the time they had finished talking, it was almost two o'clock in the morning and they had to have breakfast and be at the Captain's day cabin at nine o'clock. Fred said he would see James there and wished him sweet dreams.

It was just before eight when James was woken by violent movement and realised they were in some bad weather. He got up and looked out of one of his two portholes and could see why he had been woken, the surface of the sea was boiling. The waves must be thirty feet high and the Mary was not only rolling, for James presumed they must have retracted the stabilizers but she was pitching and tossing heavily as well. He decided that although the weather was bad, it might play into his hands. He got himself washed and dressed as quickly as he could, put his overalls on and his cap and went down to see if he could find Gordon Caligan the Electrical Officer he had made friends with on the train before joining the ship together. He was lucky because Gordon was getting ready to start his day's work. He was very surprised to see James and very curious why he had come to see him. James asked if he would do him a big favour by lending him his tool bag for about an hour. Gordon asked him what the bloody hell he wanted his tool bag for and James said he would tell him later. Gordon went and got the bag from the electrical workshop and asked James to get it back to him as soon as he could. Taking the tool bag, and foregoing breakfast, he went along to Fred's cabin before he went to his and asked him to get dressed in his Master at Arms uniform and come with him directly he was ready, they had a job to do. "What are you doing in overalls?" Fred wanted to know while he was changing into his uniform. "I am hoping to get into the Renton's suite and their friends' cabins, that's what," James said. "And I want your assistance. I will explain as we go." Fred commented how bad the weather was and was surprised when James said it was because it was that bad he could do what he intended doing. "And what is that?" Fred wanted to know.

James explained as they went up to the main deck, that in this weather all porthole deadlights should be closed and that due to the inclement weather, a serious electrical fault had occurred and had to be located and fixed as soon as possible and to do both things they had to get entry into the cabins. "Christ," Fred said, "what the hell will you think of next, you should never have been an engineer, you are a born sloth." They got to the Renton's suite and found both the day steward and stewardess. They asked if any of the passengers had come out of their cabins yet, giving them the cabin numbers and got a negative answer, so James put his plan into action. He knocked on the Renton's door and got no reply, so he knocked again, this time very loudly. On still not getting a reply, after a little wait he asked the steward to open the door with his pass key. The steward became very nervous saying that if he opened the cabin door he could get the sack as he had been told in no uncertain terms that in no circumstances should he open any of those particular cabin doors without it being opened by the occupant first. Fred said to the steward that if he did not do what he was told he would definitely get the sack. The steward unlocked the door but did not go in; instead, he let Fred enter the suite past him. The cabin was dark but soon became illuminated when Fred put the light switch down. He heard a grunt come from the room next door, which is where he found the occupants sleeping, two in the double bed and one in a single bed. He put the light on in that room also. While Fred woke up the sleepers, James went to the curtains covering the portholes and drew them back. The deadlights were not closed, so he started to close and secure them with the deadlight key. While James was completing this, an unholy argument started in the bedroom. Fred started to explain the reason for their entry into the cabin, but Steve Renton was having none of it, he was sitting bolt upright in the bed with his wife next to him trying to cover her modesty with the sheet. Renton was shouting that it was an invasion of their privacy and who let them in? By the time James got to him, Fred was holding back his temper, for just because this man was a famous actor he wasn't going to speak to him the way he was. He told him to shut his mouth and listen. Whoever was in the single bed was rather agitated and that is obviously where the grunts were coming from. While Fred dealt with the Rentons, James went over to the single bed and on pulling the bed covers back found a very, very distressed Joyce on her back, hands tied to each side of the bed and a tape of some sort over her mouth. Her hair was a mess and where she had cried so much her face was streaked and dirty. When James went to the bedside and undid her hands, she threw her arms around his neck almost to the point of throttling him. He had to push her away, to be able to pull the gag away from her mouth. "Thank God you have found me," she sobbed, "I thought these people were going to dispose of me. They threatened me so many times with throwing me over the side if I shouted out for help and have prevented me from moving other than go to the toilet and even then only with her," looking over to Judy Mendise. "What did they do with you when the stewardess and steward came to clean the room?" James wanted to know. She pointed over to a large almost walk in wardrobe on the adjacent bulkhead and said, they used to put me in there and shut the door, gagged and bound, hands and feet. While all this was going on, the ship was bucking about like a bronco on heat, so James used the deadlight key on the other ports in the bedroom. For the sea to be hitting at the porthole glass as it was gave an indication of just how rough the sea had become. Joyce now got out of bed dressed only in her underwear and petticoat and went towards Steve Renton. Fred held his arm out realising if she got to him she would do her best to kill him. James held her arm and ushered her into the day room of the suite, leaving Fred to deal with the Rentons. He closed the bedroom to day room segregation door and told Joyce to get a wash or shower and if she could find her cloths to get dressed.

James picked up the telephone and asked the operator to put him through to Captain Baron as soon as she could. It was only seconds before Captain Baron came on and asked who was speaking. James said it was him and that he had found Joyce Sheen and would he kindly spare the time to come to the main deck suite the Rentons occupied. He gave the Captain the suite number, who said he would come down as soon as he could get there. As he put the phone down, Joyce came out of the bathroom looking much better than she did when James had first uncovered her. He said directly the Captain came down they would sort something out, but he wanted her to go to the hospital to get checked over. It was while they were sitting waiting for the Captain to arrive that the bedroom door came flying open and Steve Renton came out with Fred being almost dragged behind him. Fred Baker was a big powerful man and for Steve Renton to overpower him took some doing, but even though James had the injury to his hand he was still able to assist Fred in gaining control over the raging fury of the actor. Fred called the stewardess into the cabin and asked her to go and assist Mrs. Renton who was still in the bed and had remained there because she was apparently naked. They eventually had to bring Steve Renton to his knees and asked Joyce to pass them two of the curtain tiebacks, which she did. They managed between them to tie the actor's hands behind his back before telling him to sit in a chair and not to move and if he did he would see to it that he did not try it again. Renton then gave up and calmed down. Fred went to the phone and asked the operator to contact the Master at Arms office. When the phone was answered, Fred told the recipient of the call to send two Masters at Arms to the main deck accommodation mid ships port side, giving the cabin number, where they were required urgently.

Captain Baron and Staff Captain Mathews arrived and immediately took charge of proceedings. The Captain went straight over to Joyce and asked her how she was, and wasn't surprised when she told him, "Very shaken up." He said he wanted her to talk to Mr. Royston and that he would speak to her in length at a later time. He suggested that they go to the cabin/suite they used before going down to the hospital for a check-up. He told James that he now wanted to see him and Fred in his day room at ten o'clock and not nine, and if she felt up to it to bring Ms. Sheen along as well. James asked the Captain if he could speak to him in private and so they went to the corner of the day room. James asked if he could respectfully make a suggestion. He told the Captain how he had found Joyce but of course until he spoke to her, had no details of the kidnapping but he would know all that by ten o'clock. His suggestion was that he put the Rentons under ship's arrest and put a Master at Arms outside of the cabin door until they had got to the bottom of what went on and reasons why it all came about. He said Fred had sent for two Masters at Arms to come and make sure no one left the two cabins either side of the Renton's suit, because he was sure the rapist was in one of them. Captain Baron thought for a moment and then said it was probably the best thing to do and that food and drink could be served to them and that there was no possible reason for them to leave the cabin.

CHAPTER 9

When they arrived at the cabin/suite, James unlocked the door and invited Joyce in and told her to make herself comfortable. He rang the bell to call for a steward, something he had not done before, and took his overalls and cap off. When the steward arrived, he asked him if he could bring them some breakfast. He asked Joyce if she would like some and if so what she wanted, before ordering what he wanted for himself. He asked Joyce if she needed any pills for her diabetes to which she replied that they were not essential at that time. He also asked the steward, that seeing he was going to the Galley, could he take a tool bag to the electrical workshop, telling him where it was. He thanked the steward who then went off to carry out the requests that had been made of him.

Turning to Joyce, he first asked if she was up to answering a lot of questions. She said that she was and so James asked her to go through, in detail, what happened after he left her in the Veranda Grille up to when he found her in the Rentons' bedroom. Before she went into all of that, she asked if anyone had found her handbag. James assured her he had and that it was safe in his cabin and that is how he knew she suffered with diabetes, because he had had to go through it to find her cabin key. "Oh, bloody hell," she said, "so you have been through my cabin as well I suppose?"

"Well, yes, I had to in order to see if we could find anything to trace you."

"Well, what did you find?" she demanded, in not a very happy tone of voice.

"We found three passports and a pistol," James confessed. "So will you now please tell me what you are all about and what has happened? But before you do that, let me tell you that those passports being in two different names for the one person has not only caused me, or should I say us on the ship problems, but also the Cunard Office in New York." She said she was sorry about that, but it was necessary to carry them at all times, and it was her business. Had he not gone through her things, he would have been none the wiser. She then asked him if he had read the papers that were with the passports and when James said no, she gave a small sigh of relief and said that that was at least something, for those are very private and are not for public consumption.

The steward brought the food and drink they had ordered on what James could only describe as a tea-trolley. Although the toast was cold, the rest of their breakfast, being covered, was still hot, as was the coffee they had ordered. James thanked the steward when he said he had delivered the tool bag back to one of the electrical officers who wasn't surprised to see it. He left the cabin/suite and while they ate their breakfast Joyce was able to relay to James exactly what had happened to her two nights ago.

"Well, I am a foreign correspondent working for the Times Newspaper," Joyce declared. "I have to go all over the world at the drop of a hat and so have three passports to cover that."

"But why in two different names?" James asked.

"Harding was my married name and Sheen is my maiden name," she explained, "and I have had cause to use both even within the last six months. The reason I am going back to England by ship and not flying is not because of what I told you but because I was sent to follow up on some news that had got to my editor regarding some mischief the actor

Steve Renton was getting up to and was sent to America to follow it up."

"What sort of mischief?" James wanted to know.

"Well, if I tell you, will you promise me you will not let it come out when we meet the Captain in less than an hour?" James promised and so she told him that he was heavily involved with the mafia, and that all the guys that kept his company were not necessarily friends but also members of the mafia that were making sure he did not step out of line. Unbeknown to Joyce, this had rung alarm bells for James who now associated it to the killing of Steve Renton's Manager, but he could follow up on that later. Being on a higher level than main deck, Joyce said, "Can't this bloody ship keep still? I know we are in the Bay of Biscay but there is a limit. Anyway, somehow Renton, or one of his group, must have found out that I was on board and that I was going to expose them in one of the biggest and most famous newspapers in the world, let alone Britain, so in a way I suppose I'm lucky I haven't been thrown overboard, but perhaps they wanted to find out what I know. I was waiting for you in the Veranda Grille and this chap came up to me and said that there was a very important radio telephone call for me and that he had been sent down from the radio office on main deck to take me to pick up the call for it had to be answered personally and not relayed to me by messenger. This of course was so feasible that I went with him immediately without question. He made me hurry so much that I forgot to pick up my handbag, hence why you found it under my chair. I assume that's where you found it. We rushed up to the main deck, bearing in mind I had never seen and certainly not met this man before in my life, and didn't know where the radio office was, it was when we got to what I realised was accommodation that I started becoming nervous and it was when we got near to the Renton's suite that I started getting man-handled by the man. He knocked at the door and when it opened, pushed me in so hard that I went sprawling onto the cabin floor. On getting to my feet, I was told if I screamed or shouted they would kill me. They questioned me, asking why I was doing the trip and if I was the woman who worked for the Times Newspaper. At first I tried to deny it, but soon realised that to take that route was going to get me into even more trouble than I was already in. There were five men and Mrs. Renton, or Judy Mendise as she prefers to be called, in the cabin, and they looked ugly, not physically I don't mean but menacingly. They asked me how much I knew and what had I already passed on to my newspaper. I still refused to answer and so they tied my hands and feet in the beginning and taped my mouth. There was no way I could get away and certainly not contact anybody." She said they uncovered her mouth only when they fed her food morning and evening. She said they untied her legs and hands when she had to go to the toilet and was always escorted by Judy but always rebound when she was finished and when they put her back on or into bed, as James had found her, with her hands tied to the side of the bed. James asked how the steward or stewardess did not see her and she said they used to bundle her into the large bedroom wardrobe and threatened her that if she made a noise and made it known that she was being kept captive, they would dump her over the side, which would be a pure accident, so whenever the room was being serviced she kept quiet. She knew it was not just a threat that they were making but something they would carry out. "What about your diabetes?" James prompted. She said she had tried that one but one of the men, she didn't know which one, also suffered from it and took the same medication and so was able to keep her going.

"Do you know that all of the group have a tattoo on their left leg just above the ankle, even Judy?" James said that they did know, but had yet not been able to work out what it was a tattoo of. Joyce said it was of a lion encircled by a snake, but had no idea what it was supposed to symbolize.

By the time they had finished their breakfast and Joyce had covered all she had to tell James, it was getting on for ten o'clock. They left the cabin, and seeing the steward on the way told him he could clear away the breakfast things and thanked him yet again. They got to the Captain's day cabin just a couple of minutes after ten and on getting there were shown in by the Captain's Tiger. The Staff Captain and Fred, who were already with him, stood up as Joyce entered.

"Please sit down, Ms. Sheen, and you, Mr. Royston," making it formal for Joyce's benefit. While James went over to sit with Fred, Joyce sat next to the Staff Captain. "Right then, lady and gentlemen," the Captain began when they were all comfortable. "I must apologise for the weather," but assured them it was due to abate in the next few hours. "Well," the Captain said, "I must congratulate you, Mr Royston and Mr. Baker, on locating and freeing Ms. Sheen, but I am sure not as pleased as she is." Joyce nodded in agreement. "So, can we first of all go through what Joyce has to say, and see where we go from there?"

She went through all that she had told James, only leaving out any mention of the mafia, which she was able to do, and ending up by saying how well James in particular had done in order to find her. It was now with the Captain's approval that James put to the group what he wanted to do next.

The first thing he wanted was to get the assurance from Fred that there would be no way that any of the men in the adjacent cabins to the Rentons' could go anywhere. Fred gave that assurance and said all his men had been given their instructions and that they could be relied on to be efficient and dependable. "Right then, if it is with the approval of the Captain I would like to do the following to try and get the so called rapist. The fact that we don't know either his name as a steward or a passenger, we can only go by identification, so I propose we get the steward we spoke to in the cabin he occupies on the odd occasion to identify him. Next, we will have to question the man he identifies and find out how and why he has been able to undertake this double identity. When we have established this, we will have to find out when he first came on board, seeing there is no record of him being a member of the crew. This is because, although I think he is a member of Steve Renton's group, he must have been on board on the outward trip if he is the man we are after, otherwise he would not have been able to do what he did to Fred's niece Carol. What we do then, if Harry Miles does identify him as Reginald West, is find out from him what his real name is and also see if he owns a pair of rather expensive leather shoes and uses a nice but unusual smelling aftershave or cologne. I would like Joyce and Margaret Yates also to identify him, if they will be prepared to, in order to double check and also to put pressure on him to spill the beans, for want of a better expression. We then, with threats of the police and almost certain conviction and imprisonment, find out what his connection is with Steve Renton. When that is done, if we are successful, I would like, with Joyce's help, to try and find out why, and I think I have a good idea why, Steve Renton's manager was murdered. Although we know he probably died of a heart attack or stroke, he was still stabbed and we want to find out who did it. The police will find out I'm sure who is responsible when we give them the facts and information that we have, but the ship could be impounded by them for hours, if not days, as a crime scene and that is not what anybody wants, particularly the Captain and even more so Cunard."

The Captain and the others just sat and listened to James without interruption and when he had finished just looked at each other, before Captain Baron said, "James, how much sleep have you had since leaving New York, because to work out what you have so far, and what you now intend doing, you cannot have had much, and seeing you are only twenty-three years old and being on your first trip on this ship as an engineer, I am amazed as to how you have managed it."

James was embarrassed and said that if any of them had a hand that hurt like his did sometimes, they wouldn't get much sleep either, which reminded him he had not been down to see the doctor about it this morning. He said it had been more by fate due to an accident that had drawn him into all of this and that what he had done seemed to come naturally to him.

The Captain then said that he was leaving everything they had talked about to James and Fred and that if he was required for anything to just let him know, otherwise he would see them as soon as they had anything to report. James, having not yet done so, told the Captain what he had arranged at the telephone exchange and requested that the Captain rubber stamp it with the Chief Telephonist, which he said he would do.

As James got up, he asked Fred to meet him in the cabin/suite in about half an hour after he had seen the doctor and they would work out their plan of action and would contact Joyce as soon as she was required, if that was still alright with her. As he left the Captain's day cabin, he saw Arthur Phelps, the Tiger, and thanked him for the information he had given them and said how helpful it had been. He then made his way down to the hospital where he saw Jean straight away. She said she wondered where he had got to, seeing he always kept such good time in meeting his appointments. James apologised if his lateness had put anybody out, but that he had been detained by the Captain. He also thanked her again for letting him speak to Margaret Yates last night and explained quickly how helpful it had been and asked if she had been released from hospital yet. Jean said she had, and that the only reason she was kept there overnight was due to the possibility of concussion, but directly Dr. Cummings had seen her this morning, before handing over to Dr. Maiden, he gave her the OK to leave the hospital and go back to enjoying the rest of the trip, if she could.

"Now then, young man," Jean said, "let's have a look at that hand," and asked how it had been. James said he still had to take painkillers now and again, but that he could move the three middle fingers more each day and that would it be possible now that most of the swelling had gone down if she could possibly dress the fingers singly. She said she would see what Dr. Maiden had to say when she had got the dressing off and she would act on his advice. She said the doctor would not be long, but that he had had to go to a passenger that was suffering with awful sea sickness and, having lots of money, could afford to get the doctor to go to her. As it happened, he got back within five minutes of Jean telling him this and directly he got back, he put his medical bag down, washed his hands and looked at James's fingers. He said being as young and fit as he was, James's healing powers were just about at their prime and that his fingers were getting better so quickly he would probably be able to take the stitches out before he left the ship in Southampton. He told Jean she could dress the fingers individually and to keep them bending as much as he could. Jean did the dressing as she had been advised and James left her giving her a small kiss on the cheek as he did so. As he got to the door, he turned and asked if Jane was on duty and was told yes, but that she was very busy. That said, James went back up to the cabin/suite where he found Fred waiting for him.

Fred said how good he felt about what they had achieved between them and how complimentary the Captain had been and that with only just about thirty-six hours to go before they docked in Southampton how they might be able to get a final result from all that they had done. James said he hoped so and also to solve the murder, or attempted murder.

"Right," James said, "let's go and find Harry Miles. He will be on duty at this time so it's a matter of finding him." Fred suggested that the Chief Steward's office would know exactly where he was being employed, so that is where they headed. They were told where they would find Harry and when they found him they asked if he would go with them and said they would only keep him away from his work for about twenty minutes, if that. Harry stopped what he was doing and went with them. They took him to the main deck cabins where they found two Master at Arms sitting either side of the five adjacent cabins. Fred asked if there had been any problems and was told that the bloke in the after one of the five had tried to get out but had been persuasively detained in the cabin, and that it had taken two of them to persuade him, if Fred knew what he meant. He was the only one however, although the others had opened their doors, but when told they would have to stay where they were until they were advised they could leave their cabins, they had accepted it. The one that wouldn't gave a lot of trouble and has probably had a fall sometime this morning and hit his face. They got hold of the steward and asked him to open the cabin where the troublesome man was, but not to go in. This he did with his pass key and stood back while Fred went in first followed by James and Harry. The man was sprawled out on his settee when they entered, but got up immediately. Looking at Harry he said, "What the fuck do you want?" They didn't really have to ask Harry if this was the man, but he nodded when James asked him if it was the man known to him as Reginald West. They thanked Harry and said he was free to go back to his work. Directly the cabin door closed behind him, so Reginald started trying to throw his weight around and it was Fred who persuaded him to calm down and sit down because they wanted some questions answered and that if he did not answer them, it would be worse for him if he had to answer to the police when they docked in Southampton.

He did calm down a bit but protested vainly at being wrongly accused of doing anything wrong. James asked Fred if he could smell anything to which Fred nodded. "Right, while you watch him," James said, "I will search the cabin," and, looking at Reginald, said, "and don't even think of getting away, as there are two big Masters at Arms still outside."

"Yes, I know," Reg said, "one of the bastards hit me, look at my face." Fred said he could not see the lump he was referring to, and that if he was a good boy he would not have another fall. James started going through his cabin with a fine tooth comb, he was of course looking for a certain pair of shoes. Those he found in a linen bag in the bottom of a wardrobe drawer, and a fine pair of shoes they were, it was no wonder that they stood out when compared with an ordinary pair. They were obviously handmade and were of a real quality black hide. Then going into the bathroom he found the toiletries and it was the aftershave that had the quite distinctive exotic odour. On giving the container a little spray, he found it strange how he smelt the slightest smell of it in his cabin just the twice. Now to try and find this man's real name and what he was about. He asked Reginald what he had in his cabin safe, to which he replied, "Nothing." James, not believing him, asked for the combination so that he could prove it. Very reluctantly, looking at Fred who was clenching a fist, Reg gave it to him. James tried it twice before saying if he didn't give him the correct number Fred might have to make him have an accident, and he didn't want that, did he? He then gave the number again and this time the safe opened. In it he found more porn magazines, photographs and other filth, more than he had ever seen in his life before, not that he had ever been that way inclined, together with his passport and quite a lot of money, both Sterling and American Dollars. His real name was Peter Evans, he was twenty eight years old and came from Bath. "Well, Mr. Peter Evans, it would seem that you are in really big trouble, so you better have something to say for yourself."

"If I tell you what I know about the Rentons and their group, could that help me with the police?" he wanted to know. Fred, being an ex-policeman, said he thought it might but it depended on what it was he had to tell them. James said he would go into all of that after he had answered some more questions.

The first question was, did he do the outward trip and was it as a steward? He answered, "Yes." Did he dress up and chat up women for sex in the evenings? Again, he said, "Yes." How did he get involved with the Rentons? He met them about two years ago while in America and was so infatuated with Judy that he would do anything for her. He lived with them for most of each year and only went home to England on holiday twice.

"Who chose to sail on the Queen Mary?"

"Judy Mendise."

"What was the reason for it?"

"Because they were coming to England for Steve to make a picture and they wanted someone to be a crew member."

James asked, "Why?" That question Peter couldn't answer and James was sure he didn't know by the way he said it, but as he had already said, he was so besotted by Judy that he would have done anything she asked without question. The next question was the one that James wanted the answer to most. What name did he go under going to New York, and what name was he using now as a passenger?

"As a steward I was a stowaway, so to speak, that just came aboard and went into a steward's cabin and when the other occupants asked me my name I just said Reginald West, which was my Grandfather's name."

Fred butted in, "But your Grandfather and Father's name must be Evans."

"But my mother's name was West."

"So it was your Grandfather's name on your Mother's side you took?"

"Yes."

James then asked, "And what about the passenger name?"

"I go under my real name, but the Rentons did the bookings and I don't know under what name."

"Was it Judy who made you have a tattoo on your leg, just above the left ankle?"

Again, Peter said, "Yes," but he had made a mistake and had his on the right leg above the right ankle because he did not think it mattered but then found out it should have been on the other leg, the same as all the other mafia members. James wanted to know what the tattoo was all about and was told that all the Rentons' friends have one.

"Why do you want sex so much with young women and why are you so depraved that you have to have all this pornographic material? And what is it you put into the ladies' drinks you go with? We know that is what you do, because you overdid it with Mr. Baker's niece, which is the reason we've been after you." He said he didn't know a Mr. Baker but did when Fred told him who he was.

"I only know it as Spanish Fly," Peter said, "I haven't got a clue what it actually is, I got it in Egypt on a trip but what I do know is that it works quite well on older woman as well as young ones." He said he was sorry about Fred's niece and that he did use too much, but she was very nice and he really fancied her. James had to step in to stop Fred beating him to a pulp, but he managed to control himself.

James told him he would have to stay under ship's arrest but that the Captain would want to talk to him before he handed him over to the police, and once again he warned him that it would be to his advantage to tell the Captain everything he wanted to know. Before they left Peter to remonstrate with himself, James asked him where the Spanish Fly was. Peter, realising he now had nothing to lose, got the little bottle and gave it to James who took it, together with the passport, shoes, porn material and aftershave.

Armed with the items he had collected form Peter Evans' cabin, James, together with Fred, headed for the Captain's day cabin, but when they got there the Captain's Tiger said he was entertaining some VIP passengers who would have normally been on his dining table tonight, but that he had cancelled so was giving them drinks now in way of an apology, prior to lunch. However, he would go in and discretely see when the Captain would see them. This he did, and said that the Captain was sorry he could not see them now, but would see them at one thirty. They decided that they would have an early lunch and James invited Fred down to his cabin for a beer and to be able to put all he had collected into his own safe. When they got to the cabin, James found everything spick and span and saw that the steward had left him a note. James invited Fred to sit down while he went to his fridge to get the beers and the cold glasses. He poured the beers and when sat down himself, asked Fred if he would like to join him for lunch in the main restaurant so that he could show him off and meet again his fellow table members. Fred said he would like that very much as it would probably be the only time he would ever be able to eat with first class passengers in the main restaurant. So it was decided, and James telephoned the restaurant there and then and asked if it would be possible to speak to the Head Waiter. When he came to the phone, James asked him if he could arrange another setting at his table for lunch. Being such a large table for six, the Head Waiter said it would just be possible to squeeze another place, albeit a bit tight, and that he would be pleased to welcome his guest. This now settled, the two of them were able to relax and enjoy their beer.

The Captain had been quite right about the weather. The ship was not moving nearly as violently as it had been and James felt that it would not be long before they would be able to put the stabilizers out again, which would make it much more comfortable for everyone. Fred asked James why he had asked Peter Evans if he had a tattoo on his left leg. Seeing that Fred was his partner, James thought it only right in this instance to break a confidence; the promise he had made to Joyce. But before he went into that, he read the note that the steward had left him. It was from Margaret Yates who said she would like to meet James in the observation lounge at three o'clock. James told Fred what the note said and then went on to explain about the Rentons and the mafia. He said he wanted to interview the Rentons because he thought he could solve the attempted murder if he could get them to talk, but would have to question them separately. He conveyed as near as he could, word for word, what Joyce had told him and said if he asked the right questions to each of them, he was sure he could find out who stabbed Steve Renton's manager. He had his own ideas about the stabbing, the reason for it and who it was that carried it out, but of course he could be completely wrong.

They finished their beers and went up to the restaurant where, as he had said he would, the Head Waiter welcomed Fred. Even though he recognised who he was, he made no comment or indeed had no objection on this occasion to a crew member eating with the first class passengers. James thought he must have had some knowledge of what he and Fred were doing.

Victor, who was waiting nearby, when given the nod by the Head Waiter, came over and escorted them to their table. He said, "Hello, Fred, and what are you doing eating in here?"

Fred just said, "I've been invited and have had permission from on high." They got to the table before anyone else and Victor did his duty, as if Fred was a bona fide first class passenger. He asked James if he would be requiring a lunch time drink and when James said he would be having water, he then had the courtesy to also ask Fred, who also said water would be fine, and so he poured it for them. He gave them their menus and then excused himself saying he had to go back and bring in the other guests as David was off this lunch time. Having put an extra chair at the table to accommodate another diner, the chairs where just a little closer to each other than normal, but in no way making it uncomfortable to eat. Fred said he had had to go into the dining rooms of all classes on many occasions doing his job, but never thought he would be able to eat first class himself and knew he would never be able to afford to travel first class on a train let alone the most famous liner in the world. James explained that the engineer officers ate from the same menu, with just a few exceptions, but in their own dining room because there were so many of them, being eighty-three, albeit not all eating at the same time. "For the same reason, or so they say, the engineers are not encouraged to mix with the passengers and why you lot are told to report us if we do, if you know what I mean," thinking of Susan. Fred smiled and said he knew it went on but he always thought it unfair that the deck and radio officers could rub shoulders with the passengers but only the Chief and Staff Chief Engineers could. Before James could get on his soap box, Victor came over to the table with Elizabeth, Amy and Helen. Both James and Fred stood up when they got there and wished them good afternoon. James heard Helen tell Victor that her mum and dad would not be long, but would be in for lunch.

Having been in the company of all three ladies whilst undertaking their detective work, Fred felt very relaxed and so found it easy to converse with all of them. It was Helen, having volunteered to be a decoy, who asked if they had had any success with catching their man, and when James said that they had caught him just a few hours ago, all three of the ladies wanted to know how they had managed it. James said it was very complicated and because of police involvement when they docked at Southampton, it was not possible to tell them anything. He said he knew they had been so helpful in their quest in catching this man, but could not divulge any of the details and certainly not his name. The only thing he did say was that they had also located the lady that had been kidnapped and freed her. It was why they were still digesting the news that James had just given them that Henry and Rachel arrived at the table. Before they sat down, James introduced Fred, who stood up and shook hands with both of them while James explained who he was and why he had invited him to lunch, hoping they did not mind. Victor, who was now being overworked, did the necessary before taking the orders from the whole table. He must have spoken to the

Head Waiter before Henry and Rachel arrived, for within ten minutes of them sitting down, David, the other waiter arrived, said hello and when told that Victor had taken their orders immediately went to the galley.

James asked if all of them had had a good morning and if they enjoyed the entertainment last night. They said the comedian was hilarious and had his audience literally crying with laughter, the singer was very good too. They said they were glad the weather was improving as it was quite uncomfortable even sitting down, with the ship being tossed about so violently, but with such good entertainment and the band managing to play, it made for a good night, not for dancing though; even the few that tried had to give it up as a bad job. Victor and David came back with what had been ordered for starters before busying themselves with other things. Helen once again, seeing she was facing towards the Rentons' table, noticed that there was nobody sitting at it. "They seem to be a weird lot," she said, "but that is perhaps what happens when you become famous, not that they're that famous." James thought to himself, 'If only you knew.'

Fred was hitting it off famously with Amy and Elizabeth and sitting between Henry and Rachel, James was able to talk mainly about Helen and what her possible future might be. Henry said she had it in her to be a doctor, but Helen wanted her to take up law, but of course it would be up to her in the end. Whatever it was she decided on, they assured James they would be giving her their full support, for being an only child she was the most important person in their lives.

It was Henry who first noticed James's hand and that his fingers appeared to be so much better. James told him what they had done and that he could now use them a lot more and that any exercise he could give them was all to the good. He said they were still very painful at times and that he still had to take painkillers, but not so often now. Rachel wanted to know what he intended or would be allowed to do when he got back to Southampton, but of course James could not give her an answer. He knew what he would like to do, but it depended on a number of unknowns. Having finished their starters, Victor and David cleared their plates away and went for the next course, which in Fred and James's case would be their last, for they still had quite a lot to do. It was while they were waiting for the main meals to come that the Head Waiter brought a note to the table and gave it to James, who opened it there and then and just said that was fine and thanked him. He looked over to Fred and said, "The Captain will now see us at two o'clock and not one thirty."

They finished their meal and, knowing that they had to leave before the rest, Fred thanked them for their company and making him feel so welcome and that he might see them again before they docked in Southampton, or at least he hoped so.

Seeing they now had an extra half hour to kill before having to see the Captain, James suggested that they go and talk to at least a couple of the men in the cabins next to the Rentons'. They made their way to the main deck cabins and found that the Masters at Arms had done a lunch relief, and had been told that meals had been taken in to all the cabins. James knocked on the most forward of the five cabins and was answered very quickly by a man dressed as though he was just going out to run around the decks or play some form of sport. He was not very happy looking, although James would have been surprised if he had been. The man at the door asked what James wanted and when told he and his colleague just wanted to talk to him regarding his release from ship's arrest, he opened the door and let them in. As they entered the cabin, the other occupant came out of the bathroom, still in his bath robe. James asked what their names were so he could check them against his passenger list, when told what they were he asked if he and Fred could sit down.

The first thing the men asked was when was this bloody stupid ship's arrest thing going to end, for they had not the slightest idea what it was all about, and that when they got to Southampton they were going to go to the Cunard offices and complain and seek compensation or, if necessary, sue the company for the imposition they had been subjected to and perhaps even for deformation of character. To all of this, James just said they could do what they liked, but all the time they were on this ship they were under the Captain's command and it was him they had to answer to and that they, himself and Fred, were carrying out the Captain's orders.

"All we want to do is to ask you some simple questions and if the answers or the information you give us is satisfactory, you will be able to carry on as if nothing has happened."

The big man in the bathrobe said, "But nothing has." James ignored the last remark and just asked the first of the questions he wanted answers to.

Did they both work for Mr. Renton? They both answered, "Yes." What were their jobs? They were both employed as bodyguards.

"Why did the Rentons want bodyguards, for they are not that famous, or is it because they belonged to the mafia?"

"It's because they are famous."

"Why do they have a tattoo on their left leg just above the ankle and what does a lion encircled by a snake represent?" The man in the bathrobe looked down at his left ankle, what for James didn't know for he knew it was there. James then asked them if the other members of the Renton group belonged to the mafia and to this there was no answer.

"Well then, if you are bodyguards, how did you let Steve Renton's manager get stabbed to death?" The one that let them in said they were nowhere near the boat deck, which led James to ask how did they know he was stabbed on the boat deck? Again there was silence. "Why was Joyce Sheen kidnapped?" No answer. James was getting quite annoyed now because they were not giving anything away. What then were they smuggling, or if not them, then the Rentons? The answer to that was that they were not smugglers. What do the others in the other cabins do for the Rentons? And it was then that they both chimed in saying they were all just friends who were taking a trip to England while Steve made a movie. James said that was not the story Peter Evans was telling.

"Who the hell is Peter Evans?" they said, looking at each other.

James said quite quietly, "He is a rapist who uses drugs to get women into bed. He has told us a lot about you two and the Rentons, and what you are all up to in order to get off lightly with the police."

The man in the bathrobe said, "No, he hasn't, he would not dare, for it would be more than his life is worth to tell you anything." James then asked if that was why Steve Renton's manager was stabbed to death, because he had said he was going to tell somebody what was going on. Also that is why Joyce had been kidnapped because she had found out about the mafia and was going to write about it in her column in The Times newspaper.

James was taking a stab in the dark when he said, "It was you two who actually did the kidnapping by luring her away from the Veranda Grille telling her that she had an urgent phone call and then bundling her into the Rentons' suite. There is no way you can deny the fact, and you will be charged with kidnapping. The Rentons will only be charged with aiding and abetting a kidnap which is a much lesser charge. If you don't believe us, we will bring Joyce Sheen down here to identify you with the Captain of the ship as a witness and it will then be put in the hands of the police when we dock in Southampton." James, knowing the half hour they had to kill was up, just said, "Think about it, gentlemen. We will be back later to see if you have anything else to tell us, or perhaps you want to do a long prison sentence." And with that, both he and Fred got up to leave.

The two men were worried, so James thought it best to let them stew a bit and see what happened. As they came out from the cabin, Fred said to the Master at Arms, be careful and make sure that pair don't try and get the jump on you to get out of the cabin and get away, not that he could imagine where they would go.

They headed to the Captain's day cabin and on reaching it, the Tiger said that the Captain was waiting for them and that they were to go straight in. James knocked the door and was told immediately to go in. The Captain was most apologetic for not being able to see them at the planned time but he had to rearrange some entertaining. He explained that the passengers that had been allocated to his table for that night's dinner had been told that the invite had been cancelled and so had in place of it, been his guests for drinks at lunch time. "Now, gentlemen, the reason I have made this cancellation is because being the last dinner of this voyage I have some people I have to thank for what they have done for me. I therefore want you and Fred to dine with me tonight, along with Sister Jane Freeman, your cabin neighbours Elizabeth and Amy and I believe Helen who shares your dining table, and Ms. Joyce Sheen. The Staff Captain will be inviting Helen's mother and father together with Margaret Yates, if she feels up to it, to come, as well as both doctors and sister Jean. Invitations are already made and sent out, including yours to your cabin/suite as you call it.

Now then, what have we got to discuss to bring me up to speed?" James said that since this morning they had located and put under ship's arrest the rapist who has a passport in the name of Peter Evans, together with the name of Reginald West that he is known as by the stewards and a name that they did not know which Steve Renton booked his trip with as a passenger. They had got him to admit he was the man they had been hunting for.

"We have also put the Rentons under ship's arrest, together with the rest of the members of the Renton party. We want to get Joyce and Margaret Yates to identify the rapist and the men who actually kidnapped Joyce, and we have yet to interview the last two that we have not had time to speak to. We have them and the Rentons to question, which we are doing in such a way as to get one lot to implicate the others."

The Captain wanted to know how this was going to be accomplished, to which James explained that they had already started on the two kidnappers by telling them that they will be in far more trouble than the Rentons, and have given them time to think about it. He told the Captain that he had items in his cabin safe that he had meant to bring up to him that were taken from the rapist's cabin, explaining what the items were, and that he would bring them up to go in the Captain's safe with the other items they had acquired. He then went on to say what help he wanted from the Captain to try and find out who carried out the stabbing and why.

Captain Baron called his Tiger and asked him to find Staff Captain Mathews and ask him to come to his cabin as soon as he could please. He then asked James what time he wanted him to go with him. James said he had had a note from Margaret Yates who wanted to meet him in the observation lounge at three o'clock, but had no idea what for, so if the Captain could be ready for four o'clock he thought it would be possible to go to the main deck cabins and the Rentons' suite and do the questioning he wanted to do with Fred and the Captain in attendance. Captain Baron said he would be available and asked James to come for him whenever he was ready. James and Fred left the cabin meeting the Staff Captain as they did so. He nodded acknowledgement but did not speak.

James asked Fred if he would go and find Joyce and bring her to the observation lounge. Fred said if he could not locate her by going to her cabin or looking in places she might likely be, should he have her paged over the ship's tannoy system? James said no, if he could not find her by three o'clock, then never mind they would see her at dinner, but it would be better if he could find her and bring her to the observation lounge. Fred went off and James made his way to meet Margaret. It was quarter to three when he got to the observation lounge and obviously too early, as Margaret was not there yet. He went over to the ship's side and took an armchair near to the windows and lit a cigarette. The sea was quite calm now and seeing the weather forecast was for fine weather for the next couple of days, it was going to be pleasant for the rest of the trip. He had only been sitting there for a few minutes, going over in his mind how he was going to go about getting to the bottom of the Renton situation, and not yet finished his cigarette, when he was tapped on the shoulder. It was Margaret. She was still very badly marked around the face, but gave him a little smile when she said, "Hello." He said hello in return and asked her to have a seat and if she would like a drink. She said she would like some coffee, black and very strong. James called a waiter over and ordered what she had requested and a white coffee for himself. While they waited for their drinks to come, James asked her how she was feeling after such an ordeal and why she wanted to speak to him. She started off by thanking him for saving her life, for she was sure if he had not come along when he did to give chase to the man who was attacking her, she would have been thrown overboard. But he said she had already thanked him. She said she knew that, but wanted to thank him properly and that was not by just saying thank you. The waiter brought their coffee and poured it for them before leaving. Sipping her very hot coffee, Margaret told James that she was an extremely rich American who owned a multimillion dollar business. "I don't want you to argue with me, but I want to reward you financially if you will give me the information I require." James said he was embarrassed because what he did anybody would have done. She supposed that could be true, but it was him who was mainly responsible for catching the man that raped her and then tried to kill her. James gave her the information that she wanted which included bank details, and then asked her if she would go with him to identify the rapist, if it was indeed him. As she said yes, Fred appeared accompanied by Joyce, who he had found playing bridge. James introduced Joyce to Margaret and gave Joyce a quick run-down of what had happened to her. Joyce was shocked to see how damaged her face looked and said that might have been her fate or worse, except that she had to be either kidnapped as she was, or got rid of all together, which Margaret was quick to point out nearly happened to her.

After the initial introductions, James put it to Joyce that he wanted her to accompany him and Fred, together with Margaret and Captain Baron, to the cabins that were occupied by the people responsible for their respective situations. He explained how he and Fred had worked hard to catch up with these people, and if they, Joyce and Margaret, could positively identify them then it would be much easier for the Captain to hand them over to the police when they docked in Southampton. They both agreed wholeheartedly and said they could not wait.

James went over to the telephone that was on the bar and asked the barman if he could use it. He dialled the Captain's cabin direct and not through the operator, just in case she might listen in, and was answered almost immediately by the Captain himself. When James said he wanted his help now, a bit earlier than four o'clock, Captain Baron said he would come to the observation lounge immediately. By the time he reached them, Margaret had finished her coffee, lit a cigarette and was talking to Fred. This gave Joyce the opportunity to whisper to James that she could not find her pistol, to which James reminded her that he had given it to the Captain and that it was in his safe. "Why do you want it now?" he enquired, to which she said, "To protect myself." James assured her she would be quite safe and that she would be well guarded by those with her. He also said, while he had the chance, that he wanted to have a talk with her sometime before the end of the day in private. It was as she was agreeing to this that Captain Baron came into the observation lounge and headed over to them. He said good afternoon to the ladies and James explained to him how now was the ideal time to accompany him, Fred and the two ladies to the Rentons' group of cabins to establish and confirm who the rapist was, to positively identify him, determine his double or maybe treble name and to find out who killed Steve Renton's manager and for what reason.

So the five of them went to the main deck accommodation where they found the Masters at Arms on duty and the day steward and stewardess. Fred asked one of the Masters at Arms to go and round up the rest of his colleagues and report back here as quickly as possible, in case they would be needed, and to bring some handcuffs. James asked the remaining Master at Arms if there had been any problems, and got a negative as an answer, and then asked the stewards how many times they had been called upon and for what. They said they had had to get meals, clean linen and towels, refill thermos jugs with ice water, but nothing other than just routine things. James asked the stewardess if there was anywhere Margaret Yates could sit while the rest of them went into the first cabin. The stewardess said she would see to it, that she could sit in the little pantry they used just a little further down the passageway. So with Fred remaining outside until the other Masters at Arms arrived, James, the Captain and Joyce went to the first cabin, occupied by the two so-called bodyguards. When James knocked on the door, it was opened by the man that had been previously dressed in the bath robe, now tidily dressed in open necked shirt and flannel trousers. James told him the Captain wanted to speak to them and asked if they could come in. Knowing he had no choice, he invited them in and immediately he saw Joyce he started to panic, which James was delighted about, it was putting them on the back foot before questioning them again. The Captain remained standing, giving him a position of authority. He asked both men occupying the cabin to sit down, which they did without question.

"Right, gentlemen, if that is what I have to call you," the captain said, "I want you to tell me if you have ever seen this lady before?" The two of them nodded, and one of them said she was the woman they had been told to get, using whatever method they saw fit. The Captain asked them how they had lured Ms. Sheen to the Rentons' suite and how they had treated her. It was the man who had worn the bath robe that explained how they had told her there was a very important phone call for her and that they would show her where she could take it. "Being Mr. Renton's bodyguards, you obviously knew the reason she was wanted," followed up the Captain, and put on a look of shock when they said they did not know what for, but always did what they were told. "But surely you do not do everything Mr. or Mrs. Renton tell you, do you?" asked the Captain. "Especially when it is breaking the law, not only in England but in America too." They said between them that they didn't know they were kidnapping, but were just told to go and find Ms. Sheen and bring her back to the Rentons' suite, forcibly if necessary. Joyce now spoke up saying forcibly meant rough, for they did not treat her gently in any way shape or form. "What happened when you got her to the cabin?" the Captain asked. Directly they got her to the cabin, Steve told them to get out and not to come back until he called for them. Captain Baron then turned to Joyce and asked if that was the truth. Joyce said that it was and that directly the men had gone, Steve threatened that if she screamed or shouted he would shut her up and showed her a hypodermic syringe. She said she knew he was not bluffing and was frightened as to what the syringe contained. Turning back to the two men, the Captain asked if they had ever had to do this sort of thing before for the Rentons and was told that on several occasions they had been ordered to undertake the same sort of task but not on a ship. "Is it to do with the mafia?" the Captain pressed. "Due to your tattoos, we know you are low grade mafia members."

The pair clammed up. "What's the matter?" butted in James. "Will you be in trouble if it is found out that you have grassed on your bosses?" Again there was silence from the two of them. Having established that the two men were the ones that had kidnapped Joyce and that they were going to tell them nothing else, the Captain said that he had no alternative but to continue to keep them under ship's arrest until the police took over when they docked, but if there was anything they wanted to tell him before they docked tomorrow afternoon they could contact him through one of the Masters at Arms outside their cabin. Captain Baron then asked Fred and James if they had any further questions and being told, "No," went to leave the cabin.

It was then that Joyce took a hand; the glass ashtray that was on the coffee table was a heavy one but with not the slightest effort she picked it up from the table and smashed it into the face of the one she said had hurt her. "Take that, you cowardly bastard," she said and was about to do the same to the other man but for Fred's intervention. He caught her arm as she was about to swing it again, much to her disgust. "For what you two caused me, if I had a gun I would shoot both of you and would suffer the consequences gladly, and I haven't got to those two next door yet." Apart from her anger which had appeared to increase her strength, she was a fit woman and had done considerable damage to her victim's face. It was pouring with blood and obviously had to be dealt with immediately. James asked the other man to get him to the bathroom and try and stop the bleeding while they arranged for a doctor to come and attend to him. He went to the door and asked one of the Masters at Arms to get a doctor here as soon as possible, that it was an emergency. There was nothing any of them could do, so they left the cabin having to deal with Joyce as they went, for she was still wild with anger.

Having got her out of the cabin they had to calm her down, which they did after a few minutes by saying how wrong she had been taking the action she had, and that she must keep her temper under control or it would jeopardize what they were trying to achieve. She apologised profusely and said she realised she could be in trouble herself for what she had done, but that they did not know what she had gone through during the last nearly three days. They got to the little pantry where Margaret was and went straight to the cabin where Peter Evans, or whatever his name was, was located. They once again asked the Master at Arms if there had been any problems and on being told, "No," knocked on the door. There was no answer, so they knocked again, this time much louder and waited; still no answer. James called on the stewardess who had been sitting with Margaret and asked if she would use her master key to open that cabin door, but not to go in. She did what she was asked and let James push past her into the cabin. The pleasant but strong smell of perfume that was now quite familiar hit James as he entered, followed by the Captain, Fred and the two women. Although James tried to usher both Joyce and Margaret back, it was already too late for they had already seen the body on the bed.

It was Fred who went over to the bed and put his hand against the man's neck, then his face down almost touching his mouth before shaking his head indicating the man was dead. He had had to do this on several occasions while in the police force and knew what he was doing. James asked Margaret first if this had been the man that had raped her and then Joyce if it was the man that she had met. Both confirming it was him, the Captain asked them to leave and that he would see them at his table tonight at dinner. Both women turned away and left the cabin leaving the three men to deal with the problem they had encountered.

The Captain now took over and asked James and Fred to search the cabin to see if there was a suicide note. They found three letters on the chest of draws, one addressed to his mother, one to the Captain, and the other to Judy

Mendise, Steve Renton's wife. In the bathroom they found the wet towels Peter had used to wipe himself down after showering, with the empty bottle of aftershave in the bin together with an empty brown bottle unlabelled . He had donned his towelling bathrobe and laid himself out on his bed after taking whatever it was that had killed him. James asked the Captain if he could get the doctor to come into this cabin after he had seen to Joyce's victim and when told that was a good idea, he went and spoke to the Master at Arms telling him to ask the doctor when he arrived to come to the cabin they were in as soon as he had dealt with the injured man. When he was told the doctor was already seeing to the injured man, James went in to see the doctor himself. He was in the bathroom when James entered the cabin already attending to his patient. The man's face was now cleaned of blood exposing the injury that had been done to it. Turning to James, Dr. Maiden said he would have to deal with it in hospital because not only was the gash in his cheek needing stitches, but also he thought the cheek bone and the nose were both broken and he was lucky he was not going to lose an eye. James asked if he would need any assistance getting his patient to the hospital and was told no, he would be able to walk, but could a Master at Arms accompany them? He would send Dr. Cummings up to see them when he got back to the hospital. James left the doctor telling the Master at Arms to make sure the patient was handcuffed and that he was escorted until he was returned to his cabin after the doctor released him. The patient was to be guarded at all times.

Returning, James found the Captain deep in thought. He had read the letter addressed to him and also the one addressed to Judy Mendise. Passing them to James, he said he was not going to open the one addressed to the mother but what did James think of what was in the two he had opened? Before reading the letters, James told the Captain exactly what he had arranged with Dr. Maiden and that if Dr. Cummings was available he could be expected soon. James read the letter addressed to Captain Baron first, it was a complete confession that he was the man who raped Margaret and admitted he had tried to rape Fred's niece on the trip to New York. He said he was sorry, but that his constant urge for sex was beyond his control. It was not enough just keeping Judy Mendise satisfied, because Steve Renton was hopeless in bed, but he just loved the challenge of getting a woman to submit to his desires. He went on to say that although he had the tattoo, he was not really a member of the mafia, but that all the others in the Rentons' group were in some way or other. His main purpose was to try to keep Mrs. Renton satisfied because she was a nymphomaniac and that he was not the only member of the group keeping her happy.

He said he could not face a long prison sentence and therefore he was going to drink a massive amount of what he knew as Spanish Fly, all he had left, and hoped it would be enough to put him to sleep for ever. He asked for the letter to his mother to be delivered to her at the address on the envelope and that he hoped she would forgive him for what he had done. James was shocked at reading what he had used to kill himself, for he had taken the Spanish Fly away as evidence, so it could only have been that Peter had another lot that they hadn't found.

He then turned to the second letter, having passed the one he had just read to Fred. The second letter started off telling Judy that her husband knew what he was doing but not the others. He told her how good she was and how generous she had been for his services. He said all the stuff he used to put in her drink was gone and that he was sorry for leaving her. He thanked her for being his friend as he did not have many and hoped she would not think too badly of him. He also said he hoped she would be treated alright in prison, as he was certain that is where she would end up, either in England or in America if she was to be deported. He said, or certainly implied, that if they got Steve for all the things he had been up to over the last couple of years he would be getting a long prison sentence too, that is if the mafia didn't kill him first. He signed the letter off with, "Love for ever, your true friend, Pete."

After reading it, James again passed it to Fred and turning to the Captain said, "We got the right man but too late." It was as he was saying this and Fred was handing the letters back to Captain Baron that Dr. Cummings appeared at the door that had been opened by the steward. "What have we got here then?" he said addressing Captain Baron, as he moved towards the bed and the body. The way you are going on Captain I will have more bodies in the cold room than you will have at dinner. Captain Baron agreed that this trip had been a little different to any he had done before, and it was not over yet. Dr. Cummings examined the body, but not disturbing it more than he had to, said he was not a pathologist but he would have a guess at saying the man died within the last couple of hours, but cause unknown. Captain Baron said he had left a suicide note and that he had taken a form of poison. The doctor suggested that the cabin be locked up and left exactly as it was, because being so near to England, if the temperature of the cabin was turned down as low as possible, the body should not deteriorate and the police would be able to see things exactly as they are and it would be a lot easier for all concerned if the police were able to deal with everything from scratch, including organising an ambulance to take the body for autopsy. Captain Baron ordered the cabin to be completely sealed and the room temperature reduced to its minimum setting. He put the two letters in his pocket and asked Fred to oversee the cabin's security and left with James to go to the two cabins they had not yet visited, leaving the Rentons till last.

James knocked the first cabin door and the occupant, a large man that James had only seen sitting with the Rentons opened it and, seeing the Captain, invited them in. The Captain once again took the initiative by inviting the passenger to sit down, while he and James remained standing. This cabin was exactly the same as Peter's but more untidy and could be classed as a steward's nightmare.

"Right then," Captain Baron said, "who do I have the pleasure of talking to?"

"My name is Hargraves, Geoffrey Hargraves, and I might say it is no pleasure talking to you, even if you are the Captain." He went on to complain about being confined to his cabin and wanted to know what it was all about. Ignoring the complaint, the Captain went on to ask, what was Mr. Hargraves association with the Rentons? It transpired he was their legal guru and was at that moment working on how he could make a case to sue Cunard as well as bringing cases for other members of the Renton group who he understood were being kept under ship's arrest. James asked him, quite flippantly, if he was also the senior lawyer for the mafia group of which he was a member. Hargraves asked, "What mafia?" and who the hell was James to ask such a question?

"I ask the question because of the tattoo above your left ankle," which he could just see from where he was standing, with Hargraves sitting down and his trouser leg drawn up slightly.

"Mr. Royston is this ship's detective," the Captain explained, "and has been investigating Mr. Renton and his group." James took another gamble when he accused the lawyer of sleeping with Judy Mendise.

"You would have to prove such a statement or I will have you up in court", he threatened, but James went on.

"Not when we have Mr. Peter Evans telling the court he was sharing her with you and others." Having said that, Hargraves knew he was skating on thin ice because he was sure Steve did not know of his antics with his wife. He may have guessed it with Peter, but not him.

"So, Mr. Hargraves, what is Mr. Renton up to, and what is he coming to England for, is it really to make a movie or is it on mafia business? The police have been contacted and will be on board before we dock so being a lawyer you must know that in England if you assist the police you can get at least some consideration, if you get the message." It was now that both James and Captain Baron could see how worried he had become, but they did not know what he was worrying about most, Steve Renton learning that he had been bedding his wife, or the police arresting him for working for the mafia.

He tried to bluff his way out of trouble but James fired another broadside when he said, "So, you knew nothing about why and how Jim Kennedy was killed?" Being under pressure, he blurted out that Kennedy wanted out and threatened to go to the police and so had to be shut up. Steve said he would make sure he never said anything to anyone to expose what they were doing.

It was then that the Captain asked in a very superior way, what were they doing? It was now the moment that the lawyer had to make up his mind what he was most scared of, the Rentons, the mafia or a stretch in prison. He said he was refusing to answer any more questions other than to say he was not a murderer. James spoke again, this time telling Hargrave that that was not what the bodyguards had said.

"Those two lying bastards would tell you anything to get themselves out of trouble, especially one of them."

"Which one?" James asked.

"The bigger one of the two, Ivor Bocock, not only does he tell lies but he is a real thug."

"What about the other one?"

"Oh! He is so bloody thick he doesn't know a lie from the truth. He just does what Ivor tells him."

James, now in full flow then, asked, "Even to commit murder?" It was then that he decided to come clean and tell all he knew about the killing of Jim Kennedy, so he could clear himself from any blame being laid at his door.

"Jim Kennedy has been a member of the New York Mafia for years and when Judy Mendise, whose father is one of the elders of the group, married Steve Renton, who as you know is an actor, albeit at that time only a bit part actor, and still in my opinion a bloody hopeless one, he was appointed his manager to keep an eye out for them. Steve, of late, has been getting too big for his boots and Judy has, to a point, gone the same way. It is as though they want to form a breakaway group in England. This is going against what Judy's father and the other elders in America want and it was Jim's intention to blow the whistle on them to Judy's father." James asked what the Rentons were up to that would not be tolerated in The States, to which Hargraves answered, "Forged paintings and jewellery theft, the New York group are more into extortion, blackmail and drugs and don't want to be exposed, which is what Judy and Steve could cause if they are caught, which they are now going to be." James went on to ask if he knew what the tattoo was all about and was told that it was a sign of allegiance to the group and represented the strength of the group, hence the lion, encircled by the snake that kept them together.

It was now the Captain's turn to interrogate the lawyer by asking if he knew where the murder took place and how the body got up to the boat deck. He said it was done in the Rentons' suite after they were all called together without anyone knowing what for. He said drinks were passed round before Steve told them that there was a traitor amongst them. He did not say who it was at first and until Judy went behind Jim and jabbed him in the back with a hypodermic needle, they had no idea who it was Steve was referring to.

"So what happened then?"

"Well, it took only about thirty seconds before Jim collapsed on the floor. Judy got me and Ivor, as the two nearest to where he fell, to lift him into the bathroom and put him face down in the bath, where she stabbed him in the back again, this time with a dagger. Where the dagger came from no one knows or why she stabbed him when he was already dead. It seemed that whatever the injection Judy had used, it more or less stopped blood flow, for there was very little blood, and what there was soon cleaned away down the plughole."

"How did they get him to the boat deck?" James asked, and was told that the Rentons had acquired a wheel chair from somewhere and bundled him into it and with a blanket put over him, wheeled him to where he was found. "Did they meet anyone on the way?" was the next question.

"Yes," was the answer, "and one old gentleman actually said how poorly Jim looked as he passed." Asked who took him, Geoffrey said they all did, as Judy thought if they all went as a group it would look more normal. They had sat him in a deckchair covered his legs with the blanket put a hat on him and a magazine over his face.

"When did this all take place?" James then asked, and was told about five minutes before the fire alarm was sounded. "So after leaving him, you all went to your emergency station?"

"Yes, that is correct," was the reply.

Having asked all the questions they could think of between them, they left the lawyer to reflect on his situation, with the Captain telling him he had to remain in the cabin under ship's arrest until the police put him under police arrest when they would take him ashore into police custody. They left the cabin and joined up with Fred who said he accompanied the doctor and Ivor Bocock down to the hospital himself and after treatment had just brought him back up to his cabin. They asked Fred what the visit to the hospital had resulted in, to which he said Doctor Maiden was sure his cheekbone and nose were fractured but had stitched the wound to his face. Fred had to smile when he said he hoped he was never on the end of Joyce's temper, for she had certainly left her mark on her victim's face. Captain Baron, looking at his watch, said he wanted to see the Rentons and try and wrap this up before dinner. The time by then was getting on for five o'clock and they all had to get ready for dinner for eight. Before they went to the Rentons' suite, James asked Fred if he would do him a favour and go down and visit Michael Banes and see if he had a tattoo just above his left ankle and bring the answer back up to the Rentons' suite. Fred went off as requested as James and the Captain knocked on the Rentons' cabin door. It was opened by Judy Mendise, who on seeing who it was went to shut it again, and would have done had James not put his foot in the way. He pushed the door against her resistance and in doing so pushed her back into the cabin, but also hurt his hand in the process. However, he entered the suite with Captain Baron behind him.

The Rentons were taken by surprise, for it seemed as though they were not prepared for any sort of visit. Steve Renton was at the writing desk with a pile of papers in front of him. James wondered if it was the film script he was learning, but of course had really no idea what it was. Judy, after gaining her composure, went and sat in an armchair and picked up the drink from the coffee table she was obviously drinking before answering the door. Steve Renton got up from the desk dressed in his shirt, trousers complete with red braces and rather nice carpet slippers. He made no attempt to greet the Captain with a hand shake, in fact just the opposite, the aggression he was feeling showed on his face when saying, "What the bloody hell do you want? It is bad enough being confined to our cabin without having you coming in interrupting our peace and quiet." The Captain introduced James as the ship's detective and explained that they were there to get some answers to some very important questions that if they did not answer them it would probably be worse when the police started their investigations. Judy jumped in and said they had nothing to say about anything and why didn't they go away and pester somebody else. It was while all this aggravation was going on that there was a knock at the door and on opening it James found Fred standing there. What had he found out James wanted to know, before Fred had got into the cabin? "I don't know what makes you think of these things, James," he said, "but yes, Michael Banes has a tattoo on his left leg." James thanked him and took Fred into the cabin and introduced him. "Oh no, not you again," was Steve Renton's immediate reaction to Fred, "the sod that gave me so much trouble in the tailor's shop."

Getting the nod from the Captain, James started by asking Judy Mendise why she had killed Jim Kennedy. "I don't know what you are talking about," was her immediate reply. James went on to tell her exactly what she had done without divulging where he had got the information. She flatly denied any knowledge of his death. Fred asked if he should get one of his colleagues outside in to help him search the suite. The Captain said, "Yes," and so Fred moved back to the door. Steve, totally enraged, said the Captain had no right to search their living quarters, to which the Captain answered as he had done before, that it was his ship and that because he had evidence that criminal activity had taken place he had every right and intended pursuing it. Fred came back into the cabin with another Master at Arms and they started to search. James continued his questioning by asking what the Rentons' connection was with the New York Mafia. Once again it was a question they tried between them to bluff and lie their way out of. By now Captain Baron was getting fed up and, looking at his watch, said he was going to give them five more minutes to give some answers or he would be handing them over to the police complete with the witnesses they had. It was then that he gave Judy the letter that Peter Evans had written to her. The Captain explained that he had had a copy taken of it which was part of the evidence they were holding against them as well as statements from their bodyguards and their lawyer Geoffrey Hargraves. He said they still had one more cabin to visit, that of the Rentons' accountant, but that was currently on hold for the police to deal with. Judy Mendise, having read the letter, burst into floods of tears. She went over to Steve and said that Pete was dead, having committed suicide. While her head was buried into his shoulder Steve read the letter and realised the game was up. He asked the Captain and James what Geoffrey had told them and when told, decided to come clean and tell them what had gone on from start to finish. It was just as he was about to start that Fred came into the cabin from the bedroom and bathroom with a collection of hypodermic syringes, needles and several bottles suitable for injection fluid with some left in them. He had them in a hand towel so they retained the finger prints of the user. They had also found a dagger similar to the one found in Jim Kennedy's back, so there was now no doubt the truth had to come out. This took nearly an hour, for nothing, as far as James was concerned, had been left out.

When the inquisition ended, the Captain, with the towel, James and Fred, together with the Master at Arms, left the cabin. The time was well after half past six and they had all to get ready for dinner. James said he had to go to the hospital because when he pushed into the Rentons' cabin door he had hurt his injured hand and it was giving him pain so he wanted to get it checked out. So although they left the cabin together, leaving the Masters at Arms on guard, when they got to the lift they parted company, saying they would meet the Captain, as invited, at eight o'clock in the restaurant.

James went down to the hospital where he saw Jean, who undid the dressing and said she did not think his hand was damaged any more than what it already was, but gave him a painkilling injection after redressing his fingers, saying he could drink with it and it should take the pain away for at least six hours. He thanked her and made his way back to his cabin where he sat quietly with a cigarette and a bottle of beer from the fridge. He felt absolutely exhausted but knew he must not doze off to sleep.

He finished his cigarette, but before drinking the last of his beer, he started thinking about Susan. He wondered how she was enjoying her holiday and hoped he would be able to see her when she arrived back home, if he was signed off on sick leave. His thoughts were broken by a knock at the door.

He swallowed the last drop of his beer and got up and answered it. It was John Leaver the day steward and the half-brother of Michael Banes. He said he had come to turn James's bed down for the night and asked if he could have a private word with him, because he would be too busy tomorrow as it was docking day and he would have to get cabins sorted out ready for the new passengers for the next trip. James said he could as long as he made it quick as he had to get showered and dressed for dinner with the Captain.

John went about his duties and said he would come back and change James's towels after he had showered but he would like to know what would be happening to Mike so he could let his mother know when he got home. James said it was out of his hands and that he didn't know what action would be taken by the police as it had come to light that he was in trouble for something else other than just stealing. It was at this time that James asked John if he knew Michael had a tattoo on his leg and did he know how long he had had it? John said he did because Michael had come out of the shower about six months ago and he had it then. As a matter of fact, he had liked it and had had one done the same on the top of his arm.

"Do you have tattoos then?" James asked.

"Yes," replied John, "I have three, would you like to see them?" James said he would if he was quick. John took his shirt off and there was one on the top of each arm, and he had his mother's name across a heart on his chest just above his own heart. The one on his left upper arm was of a tiger encircled by a serpent and on the opposite arm in the same place, was the one like Michael's.

"Do you know if Michael has any others?" James enquired.

"I don't think so," he replied. John wanted to know why James had mentioned tattoos and could he tell him why he asked as he put his shirt back on.

"It's just something that was noticed on Michael and I wondered how long he had had it, that is all," James replied, wishing John all the best for the future in case he did not see him before he had to leave the ship.

With the steward gone, James had a quick shave and shower and, still with an element of difficulty, got himself dressed in his loaned dinner suit and was so glad he had a clip on bow tie, a tie up one would, he thought, have been an impossibility to manage. He was just able to manage his cufflinks and tie his shoelaces. Looking in the mirror, he felt like a first class passenger but then remembered what he had joined the ship as and had he not hurt himself, what he would still be doing now. As the novice that he was, he could not comprehend what he had done and how he had managed to do it. He wondered what would have happened if the Captain had flown him home and also how the conversation would go at the dining table tonight. It was at a quarter to eight that the gentle tap on the door brought James back to reality. He opened it to be confronted by two beautifully dressed ladies who wondered if he would like an escort to the Captain's dinner table.

CHAPTER 10

James, on shutting the cabin door, took the arms of Amy and Elizabeth as they made their way to the main restaurant. It was while they were waiting at the table with their glasses of sherry that had been offered to them by the waiter as they entered the dining room, that Elizabeth just happened to mention that they had not seen anyone at the Rentons' dining table for nearly two days and wondered why. Before James could offer any explanation, Sister Jane, accompanied by Helen, who she had met getting their sherry, came over to join them together. Again there was no time for James to say anything about the Rentons' empty table before Fred arrived suitably dressed in the dinner suit he had borrowed, albeit a bit tight but certainly good enough to make him respectable, in fact making him look a million dollars. Joyce joined them very soon after, looking resplendent in her evening gown and looked very feminine seeing what she had done to Ivor Bocock with the ash tray. They finished their drinks and had their glasses collected by the wine waiter, who politely asked them if they would stand behind their chairs as Captain Baron arrived, which was imminent. They did as they were asked, each of the ladies so elegant in what they had chosen to wear, all in long dresses, excluding Jane who had on a very beautiful cocktail frock. The Captain, as was his habit, arrived right on eight o'clock and invited the ladies to be seated, assisted by the table waiters, before gesturing to James and Fred to be seated as he sat down himself. He called the wine waiter over and ordered champagne as well as red and white wine of his choice. He asked if they were all acquainted, which they were to a degree, with the exception of Joyce, who the Captain introduced to those who had not met her.

When the champagne arrived, suitably chilled, the wine waiter poured eight glasses, leaving what was left of the second bottle in the ice bucket. The Captain got up from his chair and gave them a toast, "For the efforts of two of you in particular, and to the rest of you that helped bring justice to criminal activities on this ship, I give you my sincere thanks." Raising his glass to all his table guests he went on to say, "I have been at sea for many years and the Captain of this ship, one of, if not the most famous and well-loved in the world for three years and never in all that time have I had to deal with such instances as have occurred during this voyage. Not only has a Ship's Master never, as far as I can recall, had to undergo such goings on as has befallen me this trip, and never has he had to get so personally involved as I have, but I have all of you to thank in some way or another for getting me through the ordeal. Due to a very unfortunate injury to Mr. Royston, an Engineer Officer, and a Master at Arms who should have been on leave, we have been fortunate to solve not one crime, but four. There will be a lot of police activity when we arrive in Southampton, but due to the detective work carried out by these two gentlemen the police will not be holding disembarkation up for too long. I am a proud man tonight and I thank you all." He said what he had to say quietly enough for those at his table to hear, without making it a speech for the whole dining room. Those at the table drank a toast to each other, which is what the Captain wanted, and on sitting down ordered his meal. The four waiters, with two diners each to deal with, soon got things underway, as did the conversations between them. Captain Baron sat between James and Fred and said he was getting everything organised ready for the police to board as they approached the Isle of Wight; they would be coming out on the pilot boat earlier than the pilot would normally come on board. He said he wanted James and Fred to be there with him when the police boarded and would be leaving the Staff Captain to berth the ship.

After each course, at the Captain's suggestion, they changed table places, except for him who stayed put. Being only two men, James and Fred moved among the ladies and a different pair of ladies sat each side of the Captain and by so doing and taking their drinks and table napkins with them, they were able to get to know the whole of what had gone on for the last five days. James wanted to get to speak to Joyce more than anyone to find out more about her and what she intended doing through her newspaper regarding the Rentons. He sat next to her but before he could broach the subject she said, "Could we talk together in private tomorrow morning when I will tell you all I have learned about the Rentons, why I was sent out to The States to investigate them and what I now intend writing about them. I think you might find it interesting, but of course you must not say anything to anybody until it has appeared in 'The Times', because it will be an exclusive. I will tell you in strict confidence because I think you deserve to know. I've done a tremendous amount of research and to have it leaked would waste all the time and effort I have put into it. I'm sure they have somehow found out about me and what I was doing and have gone about trying to shut me up. Had it not been for you, I am sure they would have succeeded. I'm sure when I report back to the office and talk with my editor you will be well rewarded financially as well as in type for what you have done. So now, you give me a bit about you."

James was quite taken aback and just said, "What do you want to know?" Before he answered her, he turned to Jane, who was sitting the other side of him and apologised for not speaking to her while he had been engaged in conversation with Joyce. Jane said not to worry she was being well entertained by Helen who, it appeared, had quite a lot in common with her that she would probably tell him about if they ever got the chance. So turning back to Joyce, James went through more or less what he had done since leaving the grammar school, what his background was and what he had in mind to do for the future. He really didn't like talking about himself, for to him it seemed a bit like boasting and he hated boasters, but up until then he thought he had done quite well for himself and not let his parents down so why should he not be proud? At the end of his little resume, Joyce asked, "But are you going to stick with engineering?" Why did she want to know that James wanted to know, it seemed an odd question to him. "Because as a detective, you are a natural, I know being on a ship is a confined area where people you are investigating cannot go anywhere but you are only twenty-three years old, and look what you have achieved. As a junior engineer, albeit an officer, what contact would you have had with the Captain on any ship let alone this one and one where the Captain was dependant on you to solve crimes that were occurring on his ship? I know you have been well supported by Mr. Baker, but the main driving force has been you. It's amazing that this has come about, but maybe you could use the opportunity to start up a private investigation or detective agency with Fred as a partner. You could be employed by shipping lines, big companies experiencing fraud and more to the point, which I am suggesting as a journalist, contract out your services to newspapers. If Cunard, for instance, would not give you employment as a ship's detective, or if you like a Security Officer, then what I have just recently been doing could benefit from what you can achieve and have done. It might have reduced my workload considerably and kept me out of some of the somewhat dangerous situations I have found myself in, thus benefitting my employers. You should give it some thought, it could be very worthwhile for both of you."

James had to admit it was worth thinking about and he would put it to Fred later, but a lot would depend on what the outcome of the foreseeable police case would uncover. If what they had done between them transpired to be successful then it could be something to consider for the future and could prove to be a very lucrative business. Their main course finished and their plates removed by the waiters, it was time to change seats. He had noticed that while he was talking to Joyce, Fred had been in very heavy conversation with Elizabeth and Amy, especially Amy. The change round now brought James between Helen and Jane, with the Captain having Elizabeth and Amy either side of him and Fred now between Helen and Joyce. More wine was poured before their sweets arrived and so the conversations continued. It was at this time that they heard Staff Captain Mathews give a toast to those on his table, they were too far away to hear exactly what he was saying, but it must have been good for his guests clapped loudly as he finished. They could see the glasses being raised and like them it was champagne that was in them. James asked what the two young ladies beside him had found they had in common, after telling both of them how lovely they looked and how grateful he was for what they had done for him and the danger they had put themselves in, albeit under strict protection. Jane said her education had been somewhat aligned to Helen's, both being at boarding school and having had similar interest in horse riding and athletics. However, they were different in that Jane's mother and father struggled to keep her at university, but it would appear that was not the case with Helen. Jane said to James how honoured she felt being invited and sitting at the Captain of the Queen Mary's table and that she was sure the other nursing sisters would be envious of her. James said he felt exactly the same and knew for sure Fred was. It is something that never happens, but it had to them.

On completion of the meal, the Captain invited them to smoke if they so wished and offered cigars to the two men before calling the wine waiter over to take orders for any liqueurs or brandies that were required. Captain Baron had been the perfect host and it was James that stood up and thanked him on behalf of all the other guests at his table and hoped that the small amount of help they had all given him would be recognised on arrival in Southampton. The Captain acknowledged the thanks and went on to request the pleasure of their company in the main lounge on completion of the meal.

It was as they were leaving the restaurant that Fred was approached by a very agitated Master at Arms. James, excusing himself to the ladies and the Captain, went over to where Fred had ushered his colleague. "What's the matter?" James enquired and was told by Fred that their Mr. Bocock had tried to get out of the cabin and had to be restrained by two Masters at Arms, but in the process of containing him, Dave Ingles had managed to get away and they didn't know where he had gone. "Bloody hell," said James, "and I thought it was all over." Fred asked his colleague what they had to do to restrain Bocock and how did Ingles get past the passageway sentries?

He said they had to knock Bocock about a bit to get handcuffs onto him and they also tied his legs together and left him in the cabin. Ingles was able to overpower the passageway sentry with brute strength and a very lucky punch that knocked the sentry cold and although the sentry the other end of the passageway gave chase he was gone, and could now be anywhere. James told Fred to go and see for himself what was happening and he would go and inform the Captain. He went into the main lounge and, apologising, took the Captain away from his guests just briefly to put him in the picture as to what had occurred. Captain Baron was beside himself, saying that after all they had achieved, they now had a loose cannon to deal with. James was not so worried, for as he said, Ingles could or would do nothing without Bocock leading him by the nose.

"So what do you intend doing, James?" the captain asked.

"Nothing too much other than to make sure the Masters at Arms stay alert and go looking for him ourselves, with Joyce if she will accompany us."

"What if you don't find him?" he suggested.

"Then he will return to the cabin where Bocock is, and seeing we are down there, we will go in to see the Rentons' accountant as he is the only member of the Renton group that we haven't visited or even spoken to, and you never know we might learn something else about the illustrious couple."

James got to the main deck cabins just in time to see Fred and another one of his colleagues pushing Steve Renton back into his suite with the threat that if he tried to get out again he would be handcuffed together with his wife. James said to Fred that they should go in to the accountant just to see what he had to say. They asked the steward to unlock the cabin door which he did, and on entering the cabin found a very un-sober individual slumped in an armchair completely out of the game. Fred asked what they should do about the situation to which James replied, "Give me a hand to get him into the shower." Fred went to remove some of the accountant's clothing but James persuaded him not to bother and just picked him up and laid him on his back half in the shower tray with his face directly under the shower head. Turning the shower full on with the setting set to cold, it didn't take long for him to start spluttering.

Although not sober, the man was able to shout out to "Shut the bloody water off." They let it run until he managed to get to his feet and shut the water off himself. "What the bloody hell are you two silly bastards playing at and what are you doing in my cabin?" When James told him who they were and what they were doing in his cabin, he was not impressed and told them to fuck off. They dragged him out of the shower after throwing a bath towel at him with which to dry himself.

"Right then," James said, "are you the Rentons' accountant or the New York Mafia groups?" Although slurred in his speech, with his American accent he said he was the Rentons' book keeper and what did it have to do with them? "So why have you got the mafia tattoo on your leg?"

"Because the Rentons made me have it," was his reply.

"Where are your books?" Fred demanded.

"In the bloody safe, of course, where else would you expect them to be?" he answered.

"So open it," Fred said, "and quick about it for we have not got a lot of time to waste." The man said no, that what is in the safe is private and confidential. Fred now took full charge of the situation. He picked the man up from the chair he had slumped in by his very wet shirt front, popping a couple of buttons off in the process, and punched him so hard in the solar plexus that his fist almost touched his spine. "Open the bloody safe or there is plenty more where that came from." The accountant almost doubled up, could hardly answer "No" again, but when Fred went to hit him a second time changed his mind. He may not have been sober but he knew what pain was and didn't want any more of it. He went over to the wardrobe with Fred's not too gentle assistance and managed to work the combination lock. Inside they found all the evidence they wanted to convict the Rentons and also help the police with mafia matters. They left the cabin armed with what the safe contained and the accountant sat back in the chair Fred had lifted him out of with a fresh bottle of whiskey they found and a glass, hoping he would drink himself back to sleep.

On leaving the cabin, they made their way up to their cabin/suite/office, where they put the books and documents they had removed from the accountant's cabin into the safe. They decided they would have a look around as many of the first class state rooms and bars as they could to maybe spot Dave Ingles, although they thought it more likely that he would make his way back to the cabin he had escaped from, purely because he would be out of his depth being alone. It was unlikely he would be able to work out a plan to hide until the ship docked and then try to get off the ship undetected. However, they could not bank on it and therefore via the Captain, would have to have all means of escape from the ship covered when the ropes went out.

They spent over half an hour searching before going back to the main lounge where the dancing had started. The Captain's guests were seated and had now been joined by those sitting at the Staff Captain's table which included Helen's parents, one of the doctors and of course Margaret Yates. Although her face was still showing the signs of her beating, she was dressed to kill and but for her injuries would have looked very attractive. She said she was feeling much better now when James asked how she was and said she was so pleased she had decided to join the Staff Captain's table for dinner. When they arrived, there was a dance in progress and the Captain was dancing with Amy while Henry danced with Elizabeth and, being no suitable or available men around at the time, Jane and Helen were dancing together. James called a waiter over and ordered a large gin and tonic for himself and a large whiskey for Fred at his request. They found themselves a seat and sat to wait for the dance to finish so they could let the Captain know what had happened.

The band ended the dance and they all returned from the dance floor to their drinks. There were a lot of people in the main lounge, being the last night on board before tomorrow's arrival in Southampton. The Captain came over to James and Fred and asked them what had happened and was quite satisfied with what they told him. He said he was going to say good night to his guests because he had a lot to do before he would be able to turn in and advised James and Fred to get an early night for they would be having a very long and busy day tomorrow.

James promised they would not be too late and asked what time the Captain wanted them in the morning.

The captain said eight o'clock would be fine and reminded them to complete their customs manifest forms.

James asked Jane if she had seen her man of last night at all and when she said no, he wondered if it was a disappointment, but he would never know. He asked if she was ready to end her evening and when she said she was ready to go back to her quarters, he offered to escort her. She said that it would be kind of him and went round saying goodnight to those she had been entertained with. Fred said it was getting late and that he would be leaving, but not before he asked Amy and Elizabeth if they needed an escort too. They agreed that it was getting late and accepted the offer Fred made. They said goodnight to Henry, Rachel and Helen, who were staying on for a little while longer and Joyce and Margaret, who were discussing their respective encounters with Peter Evans and how he, if he could have got some help, might still be alive.

Before leaving the lounge with their respective companions, James asked Fred if he would meet him up in their cabin/suite when he had delivered his ladies back to their cabin. James took Jane down to the nurse's quarters and once again thanked her for what she had done for him and hoped she had had an enjoyable evening before kissing her good night. It was not the same sort of kiss he was keeping for Susan, but enjoyable all the same. There was no feeling of rejection on Jane's part and she said goodnight and that she might see him again before they docked or, if not, when he returned to the ship after his sick leave.

On leaving Jane, James headed straight up to their cabin/suite office where he unlocked the door and on entering went over to the wardrobe safe and took out all the papers they had taken from Steve Renton's accountant. He had just started laying them out, when Fred arrived carrying two small bottles of beer. James smiled and got two glasses from the bathroom. They poured the beers and set about trying to decipher pages of figures in ledgers and to understand correspondence, receipts and invoices which were beyond them. What James decided was that they take the suppliers names and what they were supplying that had gone through the books rather than try to work out figures.

They soon realised that it was not all Renton but some of it was Mafia, and they also listed all the names that had mention within the paperwork, one of which was familiar, a Mr. William Carter, the man receiving the jewellery Michael Banes stole. "This is good," James remarked, "this connects Michael Banes to the mafia without a doubt. I wonder if some of these other names are also stolen good suppliers. I think we had better put this lot away and give it all to the Captain in the morning for him to put with everything else that has got to be handed over to the police." They re-bundled it all up, putting their notes and names on the top and put it back in the safe, deciding that at after one o'clock in the morning, they would turn in and meet up again in the Captain's day room at eight o'clock. James said he was going to get a last bit of fresh air before he went to his cabin and Fred said he would join him. When they got to the boat deck they both went out into the cold night air and decided once round would be enough. While they walked together, the evening's events were discussed and James's ladies were brought up, how nice they were etc. and how attractive Amy was in particular. James said he had noticed Fred giving her some attention, to which Fred said he had taken a fancy to her and had arranged to meet her next time he was on leave and had exchanged names and addresses.

"Aren't you married?" James asked, thinking he was a happily married man.

"No", Fred said, "my wife died two years ago at fifty with a brain tumour and I've been living with my son and his wife since then, so you never know, we are both free agents." It was just before they completed their circuit that James put it to Fred, how would he like to go into the private detective business? Fred's initial reaction was, are you pulling my leg or what, but when he realised James was serious he said, "What, sort of bloody question is that to ask somebody at this time in the morning?"

"Just give it some thought, it is an idea I have had put into my head that we can speak about later, but think about it, I'm going to." With that, they opened the door into the accommodation and as they did so bumped straight into David Ingles who was coming out. On seeing who it was, Ingles turned and started to run but was not quick enough for Fred, who was after him in a flash and, with the neatest rugby tackle James had ever seen, brought him down before he got to any of the passageways. Pulling his hands behind his back, Fred, getting up, pulled him to his feet saying, "And where do you think you are going my lad?" James thought straight away, if that is not a policeman or ex-policeman, what is? Still keeping hold of him with his hands behind his back, Fred marched him, complaining bitterly that Fred was hurting him, back to his cabin on main deck, with James following on behind. They did not use a lift, they just walked down the stairs between decks. A couple of times Ingles tried to break away from Fred but he had no chance; Fred had him in an iron grip and was not going to release him from it until he got him back to where he wanted him. When they got back to his cabin, they knocked the door and waited what seemed like an age for the door to be opened, and when it was Fred just pushed him in knocking the pair of them over. "We have brought your mate back," he said to Bocock who was in the process of getting to his feet, "he got lost" and slammed the door shut. Turning to the Master at Arms on duty he said, "If any of these people break out from their cabins, I guarantee you will get the sack, so be particularly careful when the stewards have to go in. In fact, as a precaution, do not let any of the stewards in any of the cabins, in case they try taking them as hostage. If they want anything, it can all be done at the cabin door with one of you guarding them. James was very impressed with what Fred had arranged and admitted to himself it was good thinking on his part as he had not thought of hostage taking, which would have been very difficult to deal with. Leaving the main deck together, James mentioned very quietly as they went to their respective cabins -- "What a team."

James got back to his cabin and on starting to get undressed, realised how tired he was. He decided he would not bother to put his clothes away but would see to it all when he got up. He set his alarm for six o'clock which would give him time to get up put his clothes away, shower, dress and get some breakfast before going up to the Captain's day cabin. His hand was not feeling too sore at that moment so he thought he would give the painkillers a miss in case they put him into too deep a sleep, keeping in mind he was only going to get four hours maximum. He set his alarm clock before he got into bed, turned the light out and didn't know another thing until the alarm went off.

CHAPTER 11

James woke and just lay there for a while getting his thoughts together, knowing today was going to be, to say the least, very interesting. He reached for his cigarettes, but then thought better of it and got out of bed. He went over to his bathroom and went to the toilet before having a shave and shower. When he had cleaned his teeth, he came out with the bath towel wrapped around him and put his clothes of the night before back where they should be and got dressed. Although he had not taken pain killers before going to bed, he was not feeling much discomfort from his hand. He wondered if Dr. Maiden would allow the nurse to take out the stitches today or whether he would have to wait and get them removed later at his GP's surgery; he would have to wait and see. It was seven fifteen by the time he was ready to go for breakfast, but in that time he had got the clothes he had borrowed from the tailor's shop packed up and already to be returned.

He went to the dining room where he found Victor on duty. He told him he could not hang about waiting for any of the others to arrive as he had some important work to do before eight o'clock. He ordered the usual cereal, fruit juice, coffee and asked if he could have scrambled eggs, stewed tomatoes and crispy bacon with toast to follow. Victor went away to get what he had ordered and was soon back. While he was starting his breakfast, Victor asked if he had enjoyed his meal with the Captain. James said he had, as had all the rest of the table guests and then realised Victor and David would have been redundant. Victor smiled when James suggested that they had been given the night off and said they had had to replace the two extra table waiters that had been put on the Captain's table. When he was nearly finished his cereal, Victor went and got his scrambled eggs so there was no delay between courses. When James had finished he thanked Victor and said he would see him at lunch time. When he left the table, the dining room was hardly occupied other than for the real early birds who took early morning exercise, which did not include any of his table colleagues on that morning.

He went firstly to main deck and checked that everything had been quiet during the night and that Fred's instructions were being carried out regarding the bedroom stewards. When told everything was under control he went on up to their cabin/suite/office to collect the accountant's papers from the safe. It was just before eight o'clock when he got to the Captain's day cabin, where his Tiger asked if he would like tea or coffee. James said he had just had breakfast and so would not be requiring either, but thanked him for asking. He knocked the Captain's door and was told to enter. Captain Baron sitting at his desk looking as tired as James felt. He asked James how he had slept and what time he got to bed. When James told him, he wanted to know what he had been doing after he left the lounge. James handed him the books and bundle of papers he had brought with him and told him that he thought he would find it interesting reading and that he had made some notes on some of the contents that he understood. He added that he could now definitely connect Michael Banes and his fence to the New York Mafia. "The other thing you might be pleased about, Captain, is that the escaped bodyguard David Ingles is back in his cabin under our Masters at Arms security." When Captain Baron asked how they had caught him, James just said they had run into him by accident or at least Fred had.

"So," said the Captain, "one way and another, the two of you had a very successful day."

"Yes, sir, we did and if the accountant drank what we left with him, he should be no trouble, although saying that, he might have a hangover and a painful tummy." The knock at the door brought Fred in who, unlike James, had accepted Arthur Phelps' offer of a cup of coffee.

Captain Baron untied the pack that James had given him and read the notes he had made, but, like them, he thought that to try to digest what the papers contained would be a waste of valuable time; he would just hand them over to the police together with all the other evidence they had collected. Before the Captain could go on, Fred said how he had enjoyed last evening, and told the Captain how honoured and proud he was to sit at his table and that it was an occasion he would never forget.

Captain Baron said he was grateful for what they had all done and it was a way of thanking them collectively. He said he wanted to go over everything that had occurred during the last four days so he could give the best brief he could to the police when they came on board. James asked if he could be allowed an hour to talk to Joyce Sheen before they did that, because he felt sure he would have the last bit of the puzzle at hand then. Fred asked if he was needed to accompany him, to which James said no he would do this himself if Fred didn't mind, but that he could do him a very big favour by taking all the clothes he had borrowed back to the tailor's shop. He could get John the bedroom steward to let him in to his cabin where he would find all that had to be returned on his couch. Fred said of course he would, and with a smile asked the Captain and James if he should give the manager their regards if he saw him. This remark went down like a lead balloon. As Fred left to go to James's cabin, so did James to go to see if Joyce was in her cabin. She was and, letting him in, said she was packing but could spare half an hour to have their little private chat. She said she had quite a lot to do before they docked this afternoon, but yes she would find half an hour to talk with him.

She stopped what she was doing and rang for the stewardess, who when she arrived was asked to fetch two coffees and some biscuits.

"Right, young man, what do you want to talk about and why?"

James just said, "The Rentons." Why had she been sent to America in the first place and what had she learnt about them that she was going to write about in 'The Times'? Joyce was very cagy as what she was going to write was an exclusive. Once again, she made James promise that not a word of what she was about to tell him was to be repeated to anyone and she meant anyone. "Not even the police?" James said gingerly.

"Especially not them," she said. The bedroom stewardess brought the coffee and asked if she should pour it for them? Joyce said no she would do it herself, which she did directly the stewardess had closed the door behind her.

As they sat drinking it, Joyce started to tell James why her editor had sent her to New York. "It was because he was aware of rumours that the New York Mafia was up to no good and that it could indirectly affect Great Britain. It was all to do with making money illegally which was being spent on the supply of arms to Ireland." She said that by taking her life in her hands she had managed to acquire information that, if it could be proved, would expose what was going on. She found out that Judy Mendise was the daughter of one of the mafia elders and was up to her neck in what was going on. Being an actress, although of no great fame, and being married to an actor was quite a good disguise to hide behind. She and Steve Renton, her husband, another not so famous actor, although neither of them would admit to this, were attempting, or at least Steve was, to try to diversify and rip the mafia off. He was, in fact, trying to set up his own cell in England. He was using extortion, blackmail, stolen jewellery and horse racing to make illegal money. "I have enough on them, much more than they realise, to either have the FBI involved in America or the metropolitan police in this country, in any case, my newspaper will print what is going on before any other as an exclusive. When I said I took my life in my hands, it was dangerous enough for me to acquire a gun, hence why you found it. Purely for self-defence, you understand, but I don't have a licence for it in England yet." James asked when she would give the police the information she possessed. "When they read it in 'The Times,'" she said. He was not satisfied with that and said surely she would have to tell the police all she knew when they questioned her, which they were bound to do, and seeing she was the person kidnapped, they would question her in depth, so she would have to tell them the truth or perjure herself, which is a criminal offence warranting a custodial sentence. She said she realised that and hoped they would not ask the right questions so she would not have to divulge anything that would make tasty reading in a newspaper. She emphasised to James that after what had happened to her and the way she had been treated, she intended getting her own back on the Rentons big time.

Her aim, and she was sure her editors would agree, was to expose what the American Mafia were doing and to perhaps have enough evidence to get something done about it. She did not know why Steve Renton was trying to form his own cell in England but guessed it was purely for greed and what in his and his wife's eyes was power, but fear of exposure had led to the killing of Steve's manager James Kennedy. If by what James had told her the injection had been enough, she wondered why it had been necessary to stab him after he was already dead, there surely had to be a reason, but what was it? James could not offer an explanation and wondered if in fact the police would be able to find out when they questioned them. They could do no more and would only ever be told what the police would be prepared to tell them, which would be very little he supposed, especially if the FBI got involved. And so it was left. James said he had to go back to see the Captain to do a final wash up with Fred and was looking forward to getting home. Joyce thanked him again, this time accompanied with a kiss and a reminder to think about what she had suggested regarding being a private detective instead of an engineer. She gave him her card and suggested that any time she could be of use to him, he only had to pick up a telephone and if she was not in her office she would always leave word how he could contact her. She said she might see him again before they left the ship, but if she didn't to please stay in contact.

This James promised to do and on saying goodbye wished her luck and looked forward to reading her articles in 'The Times,' which from then on would be his newspaper of choice. He left her cabin with a slight wave, not knowing whether he would ever see her again.

CHAPTER 12

James made his way back to the Captain's day cabin wondering what their respective futures held, but on arriving and bumping into Fred just before he got there, any more thoughts of his future were dismissed to be replaced with what was going to happen in the next few hours. Captain Baron's Tiger, as usual, asked if he could get anything for them. They both said no but thanked him and also for the help that Arthur had given them during the trip back to England.

On knocking the door of the Captain's day cabin and getting a positive response, the two of them entered to find Captain Baron and Staff Captain Mathews together with the Chief Steward Martin and Senior Purser already seated with coffee. Captain Baron welcomed them in and offered them the same. He went to the tray that his Tiger had obviously provided for the purpose and poured them each a coffee. Sitting back down in his chair, he started to sum up the previous four days. He explained that he had got them together because they would all be likely to be questioned by the police and he wanted any anomalies they might have, cleared up so they would all be singing from the same hymn sheet. The Captain, with the help of James and Fred, then went through the events that had occurred starting with catching Michael Banes stealing jewellery to the present time. How Banes had been put under lock and key, Joyce Sheen had been kidnapped and found, Margaret Yates who had been assaulted and raped, Peter Evans who had committed suicide, the Rentons, their bodyguards, accountant and lawyer, who were all under ships arrest and confined to their cabins without being able to communicate, and Steve Renton's manager who was on ice after being killed, awaiting an autopsy.

Captain Baron asked each of those present if they had anything to say or was there anything they did not understand regarding what he had just gone through. Fred said that he was satisfied that the person that had tried to interfere with his niece was in fact the man that had committed suicide and that he appreciated what James had done and that he was a natural detective and how much he had enjoyed working with him, especially as he had worked under the handicap of a badly damaged hand. The Staff Captain complimented both of them and said he wondered what sort of damage it would have done to the Cunard Company. The Chief Steward said a lesson had been learnt by the exposure of not one but two of his department being law breakers, especially where Peter Evans was concerned, for he was, in fact, an undiscovered stowaway and that in future a far more stringent vetting of his staff would be undertaken, even though it should be done by those who employed them prior to any voyage. The Senior Purser, much like the Chief Steward, said he would make it his business in future to double check crew and passenger numbers and credentials.

When it came to James's turn, he thanked them all for their kind words regarding what he and Fred had done but gave them all a word of warning, that not too much was to be made of the Joyce Sheen's kidnapping if or when asked by the police about her. He explained that he had spent half an hour with her prior to coming to this wash-up meeting and that she had made him promise not to divulge any more than was absolutely necessary to the police, as she had an exclusive that would do her career a lot of good and did not want anything to rob her of the reward she would get from not only months of hard but also dangerous work. That anything the police wanted to know, she would tell them herself and that way she would know exactly where she stood. It was after he had finished, he turned to the Captain and thanked him for the way he had gone out of his way to support the efforts of Fred and himself, and although being only twenty-three years old, had grown up during what had all been due to an accident. He explained what a friend he had made of Fred, and that maybe in the future they could become distant relatives. He had met some very nice and charming people, namely his dining table members who in their own ways had helped him do what he had done. With a wink to the Captain, he also suggested that maybe Fred had gained from the experience too and that perhaps something could come of it. To this Fred gave a little smile, knowing exactly what James was referring to, although of course none of the others assembled had a clue what he was talking about.

As the Captain was ending the discussion, there was a knock at the door, which was opened by the Staff Captain, who was nearest to it. A radio operator was standing there and said a signal had been received addressed to Captain Baron, marked urgent, which he handed to the Staff Captain. He waited in the doorway until the Captain had read the message, and left when he said there would be no reply. Captain Baron said the message was from the metropolitan police headquarters at White Hall in London and read as follows: "Will be boarding your vessel with a party of approximately eight persons, including a pathologist and request accommodation and suitable facilities to be made available to undertake investigations as soon as possible after boarding." The message was from Commander Bryden of Special Branch stating the position for pick up and time. Captain Baron turned to his Staff Captain, giving him the signal, saying would he arrange everything and would he make sure the navigating officer got them to the pick-up location at three o'clock as advised. Staff Captain Mathews left the cabin to do as instructed and asked the Chief Purser to accompany him. The Captain asked James if he had to attend the hospital any more and could he find time to write him a full report on his activities during the last five days before docking. James replied that he did and that he would make sure the Captain had his report before the police boarded. He said he would also alert the doctors that there would be a pathologist coming on board and would they make sure everything was done to cooperate with him on his arrival. The Captain said, "The better we make the arrangements, the sooner the investigation can be concluded and that can only be good for everybody concerned."

James left the Captain's cabin with Fred and the Chief Steward, who said he had some organising of his own to do. James asked Fred what he was going to do and was not surprised when he said he was going to go and find Amy before he went back into uniform ready for the boarding party to come aboard.

It was only going to be a few hours before they were due to pick up the police, so on arriving at the hospital and meeting Jean, he asked if he could see Dr. Maiden straight away as he had an urgent message for him. Jean said he was not available right then but Dr. Cummings was and that she would get him. It took only a few minutes for Dr. Cummings to arrive and for James to pass on the Captain's request. He then asked if the stitches could be taken out of his fingers. Dr. Cummings said he would prefer it if Dr. Maiden dealt with it, seeing James had been under him and if he didn't mind he would have to get things organised for the pathologist's visit. Jean said Dr. Maiden should not be long, so would he like to hang on for just a little while? James asked if it would be alright if he sat in the little office while he waited, to which Jean said yes that would be fine, but please not to hamper Jane who was in there writing up a report. As the little office door was closed, James knocked gently before opening it, to see Jane concentrating so hard on what she was writing she never heard him enter. He just sat on the chair that was available and watched her. There was no doubt how attractive she was in uniform but he remembered her from a few nights ago and last night when she looked absolutely stunning. He had been sitting there for nearly five minutes before she realised she was not alone and was startled when she looked up from what she was doing and saw James. "What are you doing here?" she asked, putting her pen down.

"I'm waiting for Dr. Maiden to see if I can have my stitches removed before we dock," he replied, "and didn't want to sit in the hospital. Jean knows where I am and will come and get me when he arrives and she told me not to disturb you as you were writing a report, which I have to do for the Captain when I leave here."

"Well, as it so happens, I have just finished mine – it's an end of first trip report which we all apparently have to submit to the company's head office. Would you like to read it? It makes for good reading and I doubt if they get too many like it, for I have left nothing out." James said he didn't think it right as surely it was private, to which she said he could if he wanted to. But he declined. A knock at the door and Jean said Dr. Maiden was back and would see James right away.

Dr. Maiden got Jean to remove the dressings and after a little wipe round he examined his hand. "You are a very lucky, young man," he said, "or have I told you that before?" James said yes he had, but could the stitches come out? The doctor had a very thorough look at the fingers and got a magnifying glass to look at the middle one. "I'm sorry, James, but it really is too early to remove these stitches without taking a risk of hampering the healing process. With what I have heard you have been doing since you had your accident, I am surprised the healing has progressed so well. However, by using it as you have, I think apart from the knock you gave it, it is coming on fine. I would think you will be able to have them out safely in about five days' time, and I hope your GP, who you must go and see, appreciates the skill that Dr. Shooter has. It really is amazing what he has achieved, for you could quite easily have lost your fingers, if not your hand."

He turned to Jean and asked her to redress the fingers with as light a dressing as she could while he sat and wrote a note which he asked James to give to his doctor when he got to see him. He asked him if he would be coming back to the Queen Mary when his sick leave was over and that if he was, he would like to join him for a drink, and that if he didn't, he wished him the very best of luck for the future. James thanked Dr. Maiden and Jean and said how much he appreciated what they had done for him and would have to see what the future brought to whether he would see them again; he hoped so, but only time would tell. As he was leaving, Jane came into the ward and handing Dr. Maiden her report said what interesting reading it should make and, pointing to James, said, "And what a part this man has played in my first trip at sea." With that, once again thanking them, he left to go and write his report.

It was as he was making his way back to his cabin that he happened to bump into the manager of the tailor's shop. He looked at James with so much hate in his eyes that James thought he was going to hit him, but instead he just said, "You little bastard, you've got me the sack," to which James replied with nothing to lose, "You got yourself the sack, and from what I see and hear of you, not soon enough. I hope you get the sack altogether and not just from this ship for you are an obnoxious man who thinks too much of himself," and strode on towards his cabin. He was waiting to hear footsteps behind him and was prepared, but none came.

When he got there, who was just coming out of Amy and Elizabeth's cabin, but Fred? He shook his finger at him and said, "I have a mind to call a Master at Arms to get you reported for being in a passenger's cabin." They both fell about laughing and inviting Fred in for a last bottle of beer before getting on with his report before berthing in

Southampton, they entered James's cabin. He went to his fridge and took out two of what were now eight bottles of beer and said, "Do you realise, Fred, we've not had time to drink these because we have been so busy, although we have managed a few better tipples as we have gone along. In my case, I hope the Captain isn't going to be too upset when he gets his bar bill, although I did not take advantage of the privilege the access to it gave me."

Once again, they both laughed and this time Fred said, "Can we drink a toast?"

"Certainly," James replied, "To what?"

Fred lifted his glass and said, "To us," and added, "Will you be my best man, James?"

"Christ," he managed to stammer out, nearly choking himself in the process, "you don't hang about do you? I fancied there was something between you and Amy, but to get to asking me if I will be your best man is fast work if ever there was, but of course I will, I'll be honoured - when?"

"Oh, not for a while, there is a lot to sort out, but I have popped the question and she has said yes." They finished their beer and James went back to the fridge and took out two more bottles, saying with news like that, they could not let it go at just one. Fred asked what the doctor had said about his hand and had the stitches been removed now. James said the doctor had advised another five days and that his own GP could make the decision.

By the time they had finished the second bottle of beer it was lunch time and Fred said he was going back to his cabin to change into his uniform and pack a few bits and pieces before he had his lunch, ready to go ashore as soon as he could after the police had finished with him. James said he would also pack but his would have to be all he had with him due to not knowing what he would be doing when his sick leave finished, but he had to get the report done first. Fred once again shook hands and said he would see him later when he supposed the police would be calling for them and, opening the cabin door, was gone. James got his suitcase out from where he had stowed it and put it on the bed ready to start packing. He had just opened the drawers to start when he had to break off to answer the knock at his door. On opening it he found Amy standing there with a smile on her face that said it all. "Will you be coming to lunch?" she asked. "I would like you to come and help me celebrate."

"Of course I will," he replied, "and I know what for, and I'm so pleased for both of you. I have a report to write first but it should not take long."

"Will it be allowed for Fred to join me do you think? That's what I have also come to ask?" James thought it would be allowed, and assured Amy he would see to it and what time did she intend going to the dining room. She said at one o'clock, if that would be convenient. He said it would and he would go and arrange it right away. So when she had gone with her thanks ringing in his ears, he shut the drawers he had opened and left his cabin to contact Fred and arrange with the Head Waiter to again make room for an extra place at the table. He knew the Captain would be busy and so did not seek his permission but assumed he would give his approval. By the time he had done this, time was getting on, but still just enough time to get his report done and at least some of his clothes packed. He had just started packing when he heard a cabin door being shut so thought it was time for him to join his ladies. He was satisfied with his report, although it could have been in a little more detail if he had had more time.

He got to the restaurant and his table where he found all his table companions already seated, but Fred had not yet arrived. He had just taken his seat when Fred came in apologising for being late, but that he had had a little problem to sort out. He was sporting a large bruise on his cheek and a split lip.

Before Amy could ask, James asked him what had caused his injuries, to which Fred explained that he had had a run in with the fireman friend of Michael Banes. He said he had not gone on watch, had got terribly drunk and had gone for him for getting Michael into trouble.

"Where is he now?" James wanted to know.

"In hospital," Fred said, "in a lot worse state than me. My intention was to just quieten him down but when he hit out I had to use forceful means, especially after the lucky punch had landed in my face." He said under normal circumstances, a Master at Arms would have dealt with him long before he got down to his cabin, but seeing there were so many of them being used to keep the Renton crowd under ships arrest, there weren't any to keep order in other places. He apologised to Amy for coming to lunch as he was, but better that than let her down. He assured her he was not a violent man and took his seat next to her that had been purposely left for him. Henry called the wine waiter over to pour the champagne he had ordered for the toast he intended giving. When the drinks were poured, Henry got to his feet and made a little speech. He wished the couple well, adding he thought what a lucky chap Fred was and wished both him and Amy a very happy future together. They all got up barring Fred and Amy, raised their glasses, and wished the pair of them good health and happiness in the future. Elizabeth said she was thrilled for Amy, but hoped she would not move too far away and that that was not the last cruise or holiday they would be having together. Amy quickly squashed that idea and, looking at Fred, said they were sure they could not let that happen.

With the niceties over and their lunches ordered, Henry wanted to know what was happening on board. James said he could not tell him anything other than what he already had, but that the police would be coming onto the ship before she was due to berth. He said the Queen Mary would be slowing right down at about three o'clock to pick them up and that directly they could start their investigations, they would. Henry wanted to know if any of them would be called to give statements or anything, to which James said he did not know, but was sure he and Fred would be needed.

By the time they had finished their lunch it was nearly two o'clock and not very long for James to complete his packing. He said what he was going to do and asked to be excused. Henry said that that was probably the last they would see of each other and so gave James a piece of paper and told him that he could always get them at one or the other of the addresses and phone numbers and that would he please keep in touch.

James promised he would and shook hands and kissed each of the ladies before leaving the dining room, leaving Fred to escort his fiancé back to her cabin with Elizabeth. Directly he opened his cabin door, he found the envelope that had been slipped under it. He opened it and read the note from the Captain requesting his presence at three pm, on the dot in the second class lounge. James looked at his watch and, seeing he had only about three quarters of an hour to complete his packing, reopened all his cabin drawers and his wardrobe and got all his washing gear from the bathroom. Although it seemed a lot, it did not take him long to stuff it all into his case and get the lid shut. It really didn't feel like twelve days since he had left Southampton and what he had done in that time seemed unreal. He thought so much had happened he could write a book about it.

After checking that he had not forgotten to pack anything, and was making his way to the second class lounge, it came over the ship's intercom from the Chief Officer, that the ship was slowing down to a virtual stop, but there was nothing for passengers to worry about, they were just picking up the pilot. On arriving at the second class lounge, James found a notice outside telling passengers that this stateroom was out of bounds from three o'clock with three brass stands supporting a red rope across the door. Stepping over the rope, he found over twenty chairs and a few coffee tables to accommodate the police and people they were likely to be interviewing. At five to three with the ship slowing down, the Captain came in and said he had to go and welcome the police on board so when all the others that he had sent notes to arrive, would he get them seated in the chairs over there, pointing to half a dozen armchairs separate from the main cluster. Within the next five minutes, all those that the Captain had written to had arrived and on James's direction had taken their seats. Fred was one of those, now dressed in his Master at Arms uniform, and on arriving whispered to James that he had just left the hospital to check on the fireman Andy Good to see how he was and what damage he had done. "Well," James said, "what did you find?" Fred said he had been lucky enough to see Jane and she told him that Good had got a suspected broken jaw and the doctor thought some broken ribs, but of that he could not be sure, but he would have to go to hospital directly they docked. When Fred told her he had caused the injuries and why, she just said it must have been a very heavy fall that he had sustained but assured Fred he would be all right in a few weeks.

By quarter past three, the police were in the seats provided and the ship was underway again.

Captain Baron and Commander Bryden were the last to arrive and introductions were made. As the officer in charge, the Captain asked Commander Bryden if he would say a few words regarding how he intended conducting the investigation into everything that had gone on over the last five days and on the voyage out to New York. Commander Bryden firstly introduced his officers: One superintendent, two inspectors, three sergeants and four constables, all detectives in civvies, and four constables who were in uniform, together with a pathologist and his assistant. He said arrests would be made after questioning and he would deal with each incident as individual cases, led by the Superintendent and the two inspectors. He said he would like to see the Captain on his own first while the Superintendent organised the inspectors and talked to Mr. Royston and Mr. Baker, who he had been made to understand were the main people to talk to. He then went off with the Captain, who had suggested they go to his cabin.

Having been told who the officers were in the armchairs, the Superintendent assigned the inspectors to start interviewing them and took James and Fred himself to the far side of the lounge where they found three more comfortable chairs. Before he started asking questions, Fred asked if it would be possible now that the investigation was in the hands of the police, if the uniformed constables could relieve his Masters at Arms, who had been on guard duty for over thirty-six hours making sure the Rentons' cabins were keeping their occupants under ship's arrest. The Superintendent, who said his name was John Beavis, motioned over to one of the sergeants who came across to them. "This is Sergeant Mark Devon," the super told them, to which Fred immediately asked if he had a father who is or was a Chief Inspector, Graham Devon. On replying, "Yes," Fred said he had been his boss when he was in the police force and what a coincidence. The Superintendent asked what deck and number the cabins were that were being guarded, and when told, instructed the sergeant to take three of the constables to relieve the Masters at Arms that were currently on duty and to tell them to report to the second class lounge. As he went off to carry out the orders he had just been given, John Beavis got down to business. He asked James first to give him a full account of what was to be investigated from leaving Southampton to the present time. James said how complicated it had all become but went through every phase of what had happened, what they had found out and what they had done about it, with the understanding that it had all been with the authority of Captain Baron. He left nothing out and told the superintendent what the Captain had in his safe. He then turned to Fred, who likewise gave a full account of his part in it all, but excluded the recent injury he had sustained. John Beavis said that he would probably not want to see either of them again, but that they were not to leave the ship until the investigation was completed. He shook hands with them both and left them to go over to where his two inspectors were just finishing their interviews.

James and Fred were just discussing what they would do now when the Captain's Tiger Arthur Phelps came into the lounge obviously looking for them. On seeing them, he went over to tell them the Captain wanted to see them right away and accompanied them as they made their way to the Captain's cabin. He said he knew the police had only been on board less than an hour, but did they know what was happening yet? James said it was far too early to even hazard a guess at what actions they would be taking. When they got to the Captain's cabin, Arthur knocked the door and on the command, "Come in," said he had found Mr. Royston and Mr. Baker and that they were here.

Captain Baron said, "Show them in and can you please bring in some more coffee, also will you arrange for beverages and sandwiches to be sent down to the second class lounge?" They went in and were told to sit down. James immediately noticed the Captain's desk was covered with the contents of his safe and that the folder containing all the papers he had removed from the Renton's accountant had been gone through. Commander Bryden addressed them both, saying from what the Captain had told him they had done such good detective work they should be in the police force and not ship's staff. Fred said he had been a policeman, but when his wife died he decided to change his career. The commander went on to ask more or less what the Superintendent had asked, but having spoken to the Captain asked them for more detail. They went over again what they had told the Super, answering everything they could including as much detail as they could. The only bits they had no answers to were those concerning the Rentons, what they were up to and why they had killed Jim Kennedy. They knew how but could only guess the reason for it. The other thing James said that remained a mystery was why they kidnapped Joyce Sheen and did not throw her over the side, like he was sure would have happened to Margaret Yates if he had not got to the scene when she was being beaten up by Peter Evans, rest his soul. He had made certain connections but could not learn anything about the Mafia but was sure the FBI would be interested. It was then that the commander divulged that the FBI had in fact been on to them and would be taking over when their investigations were over. The coffee came and after pouring it out and distributing it, the Tiger left.

While they were drinking the coffee, Captain Baron said he was sure both James and Fred would be summoned to the Cunard Head Office, but did not know when, as it would depend on when his report was received, which would be being posted as soon as they were alongside with gangways out. Fred ventured to ask Commander Bryden who would have to be retained for questioning. He said he had got a list of all those that had been in anyway involved in all the incidents, so the Captain would be contacting the purser's office to get word to all those on his list notifying them that they could not leave the ship until they had been questioned and would appreciate it if they could congregate in the main lounge. "The only gangway that will be put from the jetty to the ship will be the one used for getting stores and luggage on and off, with rollers rather than with a walkway; the passenger and crew's gangways would be kept ashore until the police were ready to let those passengers not required for questioning ashore, that goes for the crew as well. The cargo holds will start to be unloaded, cars etc. and everything possible will be done to make the disembarkation as swift as possible. At this moment in time, it is envisaged that the Rentons and their associates will, after questioning on the ship, be transferred to New Scotland Yard in London for further questioning and possible deportation to America if the FBI request it." He checked again with James and Fred who they would consider to be the main players, as he put it, that should be interviewed first.

Before James could reply, Captain Baron said to the commander he had a ship to berth and would he excuse him while he went and did it, saying he would give this list of the passengers and crew the police wanted to question to the Chief Purser and leave it to him to get them into the main lounge. Commander Bryden thanked him and went over to the Captain's desk and asked James if he would come and check that everything he and Fred had given to the Captain for safe keeping was there. James went over it all without touching it and assured the policeman that it was all there and emphasized it had not been handled by them with bare hands. The commander put gloves on and put it all in a canvas bag that he had either acquired from the Captain or had brought with him. He threaded a piece of wire through the top of the bag when it was closed up and then through a lead seal before squashing it with a pair of special pliers. "Right then, young man, I am very impressed by you and your colleague here, so now we are alone, go through those you think can help us most with our enquiries."

James started going through all those he thought could help the police the most and in order of priority in his opinion, with Fred adding to the list as he started going through them. Joyce was the first person he mentioned and added that it was really important that they let her leave the ship as soon as possible and that if they wanted to interview her again she would be in Fleet Street so would be easy to contact. He put Margaret Yates next, then Michael Banes who he said would be able to expand the link to the Mafia through his fence Bill Carter. He then went through all those he thought could add something to the investigation. His ladies, the crew members, one of which was in hospital but should be fine to interview, Helen, Sister Jane, the Rentons' day and night stewards and of course very importantly both doctors, Maiden and Cummings. He suggested, "If you interview all of them, you will form a picture that you can complete when you interview the Rentons. I would leave them until last, for although I am sure they will deny everything, you will have enough on them to arrest them on the spot. I would respectfully suggest," he went on, "and I'm sure Fred will back me up, that if you interview the bodyguards first and then the accountant, they will sing their heads off, especially if you threaten them with long prison sentences. The lawyer is your speciality for they can twist anything if they are good enough and I can't imagine the Mafia employing a duff one. It will depend how much you can frighten him, we did a bit, but I am sure you can get a lot out of him before you hand him over to the FBI."

Commander Bryden sat and listened intently, before suggesting that James was doing his job for him. James apologised but explained this was due to the last five days focussing on all that had gone on. The policeman patted James lightly on the back and said, "Don't worry, James, I am only pulling your leg. I'm very grateful for what the pair of you have done, and like the Captain, am astonished that being so young you have managed to do what you have and with an injury such as you have sustained."

To this Fred said, "Here here, he is a natural." The commander said there was nothing more James or Fred could do now, but that on completion of the investigation, he would call the pair of them to his London office and tell them what he could of the outcome. He wished them both well and added that he hoped James's hand would make a full recovery and said they could leave the ship as soon as the passengers not required for questioning where free to go.

CHAPTER 13

As the Queen Mary edged her way up Southampton Water, James decided he would like to go on the bridge and witness the berthing of the great liner if the Captain would give him permission. Fred said he was going to continue to carry out his duties until the ship got alongside as he usually did, but told James he wanted to see him before he left the ship. They agreed that it would be sensible to meet up in James's cabin after he had been down to see if he could say cheerio to a few engineers; they agreed on six o'clock.

James went up to the bridge deck and was stopped by a seaman who said the bridge was out of bounds, and why did he think the rope with the notice 'Private keep out' on it was for? He asked the seaman if he would ask the Captain if Mr. Royston could come on the bridge. The seaman said he had told him the bridge was out of bounds and that no, he would not go and ask the Captain anything. It was then that coincidentally Captain Baron came out onto the wing of the bridge and looking aft saw James with the seaman. He was within earshot of James and so he called for the Captain's attention and asked if he could come onto the bridge? The Captain nodded to the seaman who reluctantly let James pass. On entering the bridge, he saw the pilot and asked Captain Baron if he kept out of every body's way could he watch the ship being berthed? The Captain, of course, said, "Yes," and went back to concentrating on the job in hand. The pilot asked for the ship to be slowed down even more as the tide was incoming and also it would be easier for the tugs that were now waiting just ahead of them to take their stations alongside the great ship. As they approached the tugs that were waiting for the great lady of the sea, James went out onto the flying wing bridge deck to see them put their ropes up ready to push and pull as instructed by the pilot. Looking down on the tugs they looked so small against the great hull that they were going to help manoeuvre into her berth. Being steam tugs, they were all making a little smoke from their funnels, but not enough to smoke out the ship or the passengers that were now gathered in great numbers on both sides, some to see if they could see anyone that might be waiting for them and those that, like James, wanted to watch the tugs.

Movements started being given to the engine rooms via the respective telegraphs and James felt a little bit sad that he was not on the end of one of them, opening and closing the manoeuvring wheels. As they approached the jetty, a starboard turn had to be made and as she turned sideways onto the tide the tugs had their work cut out pushing against the great vessel. James was amazed at the skill it took to berth a Queen, for it must have been the same procedure to berth the Queen Elizabeth or in fact any large liner. The pilot gave the orders push and pull and by how much to the tugs by name as well as giving the helmsman and the engine movements he required. Watching and listening to him made James realise there was more to berthing a liner than he realised and was so pleased he had been given the opportunity to experience it.

James was in a bit of a dilemma now, for he wanted to see them ring off – finished with engines from the bridge, but did not want to miss saying cheerio to any of the engineers he had become friendly with. He decided to stay. The captain said he thought James had done enough for one trip and it being his first, he was sure he wanted to get home. He said he would be seeing the pilot off and then would go back to his cabin to read James's report that he hadn't had time to do yet and see what police commander Bryden wanted of him, and he was sure his working day had many more hours to run yet. He shook hands with James and once again thanked him for all he had done, wished him luck and left the bridge, followed by everybody else but one seaman who was left on duty watch.

James went down to the engineers' accommodation to see if he could find Bob James, who he had not managed to see although intending to. He got to what had been his cabin before the accident and Bob was just getting out of his overalls. "Hello, Bob," he said "sorry I haven't been down to see you or the others, but I have been a little bit occupied." Bob asked after his hand and supposed he had been occupied enjoying his bloody self, he knew if it had been him he would have. James said as it so happened it had been a very eventful five days that he would tell him about when he got back from sick leave. He said he would go round and see if he could find Gordon and would call back and see Bob before he went ashore. When he got to Gordon's cabin, he was likewise getting ready to go ashore. He said hello to James and much like Bob asked after his hand and implied he had not seen him because he was enjoying the passenger bit. He asked him how many times he had got his leg over and was quite disappointed when James told him he had not had time for any of that. Gordon then asked him what had he been doing with himself then, and James just said he had been busy. By not going home this time he might be interested to get 'The Times' newspaper for the couple of days before they left again for New York. When Gordon wanted to know why, James just said he might learn something. The article would be written by Joyce Sheen and it might answer a few questions he had asked. After saying cheerio to Gordon and hoping he would see him again when he came off sick leave, he went back to say cheerio to Bob, but not before getting his phone number so he could ring him whenever he might be on leave, to be able to go out for a beer if it was possible. Not really wanting to spend any more time saying hello and cheerio to engineers, he went back to his cabin. When he got there the door was open and John his steward was clearing the sheets off his bed and getting rid of the used towels and generally getting the cabin ready for the next occupant. James went to his fridge where there were four beers still remaining. He asked John if he liked a beer and when he said yes he did, he gave them to him and wished him good health. Although explaining that it was not a lot, he also gave him a five pound note, explaining that he did not have a lot of money and in fact had not been paid yet. John said he understood and thanked him. He asked if he could manage his case with only one hand for if he could not, he would take it for him. James thanked him for his thoughtfulness but said he wasn't going ashore just yet as there was a delay in getting the gangways from shore into the ship, or so he had been told. He asked if he stayed until six o'clock, would it interfere with what John had to do. John said he would be around until eight tonight and he could leave his cabin until last.

At six o'clock, as planned, Fred arrived with his suitcase and said the gangways were being put out in half an hour's time, so they had that amount of time to make arrangements to meet again. They swapped names and addresses, telephone numbers and promised to stay in close contact. They didn't know if they would be called to head office in Liverpool, if it would be separate or together, but agreed if they were and it was the same day, they could meet up and travel together. James asked if Fred had given any more thought to working together in the future and he said it depended on a lot of things but he had not forgotten. He asked what he was going to do as far as Amy was concerned, to which Fred said he would know more about that when his leave ended, for he was going to take the leave he was owed by being called off the leave he was on. He had changed into his shore clothes and had been with Amy for the last half hour and had made arrangements to go and stay with her and Elizabeth for a few days to thrash out what would be best for the three of them. He said how ironic it was that fate had thrown them together coming home from New York and James and Susan together on the way out, in each case over only five days. Fred asked if James was really serious about Susan. He said he was and that he would be seeing her as soon as he could when she got home from her holiday with Carol. "If in a couple of years' time," he said, "we decide to marry, will you return the favour and be my best man?" Fred said he would be proud to and they would then be family, albeit in-laws so to speak.

He told Fred that Joyce had just left and was desperate to get to Fleet Street. "It was just before six o'clock that she came to see me and said she thought she would just try and see if I was still here, so she could say how she got on with the police. She said she was given an inquisition that you cannot believe, but has been given permission to print what she likes as long as she can prove all that she reports. She has got her passports back and the pistol, as long as she promised to get a UK licence for it. She has asked for and got my address and phone number, for although she told us she can be contacted through the paper, she would like to be able to send a Christmas card." She had thanked him, telling him she would be in contact and hoped they would both be interested in what she had to write in tomorrow's paper. "She said that by the time she got to her office, she would be working all through the night getting it into tomorrow's edition but it would be worth it. She said she will be surprised if any film maker in this country ever employs either of the Rentons again, but Judy Mendise, she rather thinks, will be in prison either here or in the States for murder, and I doubt whether he will have much of a life when he comes out of prison, for the Mafia will not like what he has been doing, and so he could have some sort of fatal accident; only time will tell, but it is her intention to make it as bad as she can for both of them. She asked me to pass her good wishes on to you and with a smile and a peck on the cheek for both of us, she was gone."

It was well after six o'clock when the pair of them picked up their cases and headed for the deck the gangways would be located, leaving the cabin door ajar as he could not see John. James asked Fred to keep an eye on his case while he returned the key to the purser's office and on returning, continued to the gangways that had now been put in place. They agreed to get a taxi together, to drop James off at Southampton Central railway station and Fred to go onto his sister's house in Southampton. On getting to the end of the gangway, both said cheerio to the Masters at Arms that were on duty.

They got a taxi without too much delay and on arrival at the station, Fred said not to worry about the fare, that he would pay and James could square up with him next time they met up, which he hoped would not be very long. They shook hands as James got out and the taxi drove off. It was an overcast day and James hoped it was not going to rain as he had quite a walk from Portchester station to his parents' house. He purchased his ticket, a single to Portchester and only had to wait ten minutes for it to leave from platform two.

He got off the train and on walking from the station home thought what a trip he had just had. He wondered what his mother and father would have to say. It managed not to rain and in twenty minutes he was putting the key in the front door lock. "Hi mum," he shouted out, "what have we got for tea?" His mum came out from the kitchen and after flinging her arms round his neck asked him how his trip went. "Christ, mum, let me get in the door, I've only been away twelve days." He put his case down in the hallway and as he did so she noticed his damaged hand. "What have you done to yourself?" she said. "How bad is it?"

"Oh that," he said, looking down at his hand, "it's only a scratch mum and nothing to worry about", he said, hoping she wouldn't keep on about it. "Where is dad?" he asked.

"Where he normally is at this time of the day," she said, "in the lounge watching the news."

James went in and said, "Hello," to his dad, who nodded and carried on watching the television as though he had only been away a day. He went back to the kitchen and asked his mother if it would be alright if he had a bath before she got his meal which of course it was and so he went upstairs, unpacked his case and had a nice warm bath.

As the time was getting on after his long relaxing soak, he got himself dressed in his pyjamas, dressing gown and slippers before going down stairs. His mother asked him what he would like to eat and when he told her she went into the kitchen to get it. He sat down with his dad who this time asked him if he would like a glass of home brewed beer. After pouring the beer, his dad asked him how the trip went and then realised he had hurt his hand. James had to tell him how he had done it, but said he wasn't going to say anything to his mum. When she had prepared his meal, she asked if he wanted to sit at the dining table or have his meal on a tray like they always liked to when it was that sort of meal. He went for the tray and so all three of them sat comfortably without the television on while James related his trip. He said at the end that he had to make an appointment to see the doctor tomorrow if he could get one and it would depend on him when he could go back to work. They sat up quite late talking until his dad said he had to go to bed because he had a busy day ahead of him tomorrow. James said he wanted to get a good night's sleep too and so they all went off to bed.

It was nearly ten o'clock when James woke up. He had had the best night's sleep for ages and after a wash and shave felt in great shape. He was half way through his breakfast when he suddenly remembered the doctors. He asked his mother if it was too late to ring for an appointment. She said it was, but she had made one for him; he was to see Dr. Jordan at five thirty that evening. He thanked his mother, who asked how bad the injury really was, as watching him trying to do things it must have been pretty bad. He went into how bad it had been, but how good the surgeon was that had done the operation and that he had saved his fingers if not his hand. He said it had caused him so much pain at times that he didn't know what to do with it, but was only taking pain killers on the odd occasion now. He hoped the doctor was going to be sympathetic towards him as he wanted some time off to see a young lady before he had to go back to sea, if he decided that was what he wanted to carry on with. After breakfast he walked down to the paper shop and bought 'The Times'. On getting it home, it didn't take long to find the article he was looking for. Joyce had made the front page. "CRIME ON A QUEEN" the headline read and the article went onto pages two and three. She said she would be up all night writing it which she must have been and probably held up publication for it certainly was a 'Times' scoop. She left nothing out and slated the Rentons terribly, but would never be able to be taken to court because every word that had gone into print was true and she could prove it. After reading it himself, James gave the paper to his mother to read and said, "That is what my first trip to sea turned into and, as you will see, I am well mentioned."

His visit to the doctor turned out to be another one of admiration for Doctor Shooter the New York surgeon. Dr. Jordon read the letter James had given him from Doctor Maiden, and when he removed the dressings could not believe what had been done to James's fingers. He said what a lucky chap he had been getting the surgeon he had, for he had undoubtedly saved his hand. The doctor told him he was not going to remove the stitches for at least three more days, but that he was going to remove the blackened fingernails. This he did in his treatment room with the help of his nurse and between them they removed the nails of his middle three fingers. It was not unbearably painful, but the nurse said it would be better that they were removed to give the new nails an opportunity to grow back properly, which they would in a few months. After the nurse had redressed the fingers and

Dr. Jordon had seen two or three other patients, he called James back in and told him he wanted to see him again in three days' time to have the stitches removed and that he was giving him a sick certificate for three weeks. He said it might be longer but he was saying only three weeks at the moment; he would see how the new nails were in three weeks' time. James thanked the doctor and made an appointment with the receptionist for three days' time on his way out.

CHAPTER 14

James started counting the days, working out exactly when Susan was going to get home. She had two weeks holiday, five days of which had been taken up on the Queen Mary, leaving nine, one of which would be taken flying home. Of those eight, two had been while the Mary was in New York, and five more coming home so she should be home tomorrow. He would leave one more day for her to get a good night's sleep and get rid of some jet lag, before he went down to see her. He decided he would telephone the number she had given him and double check her day of arrival. He rested up at home just reading and watching the television during the day and in any case his fingers were very painful having had the nails removed and he had had to take two lots of painkillers. He telephoned at six o'clock before his mum dished up his dinner and got Susan's sister. After saying who he was, he asked when Susan was due to get back from her holiday in New York. Her sister told him her mum and dad had gone to the airport to pick her up that night. He thanked her and said he would ring tomorrow at about seven o'clock.

Once again he got up late. He laid in bed reading until after nine, and after breakfast again went down to the paper shop and got 'The Times'. This time an article written by Joyce Sheen, gave the account of the Queen Mary rapist. The article in no way blackened the Queen Mary's name; in fact, Joyce had gone out of her way to protect Cunard's reputation. Names were mentioned including both his and Fred's. James guessed the other newspapers were pulling their hair out knowing nothing about what Joyce was writing about. It was about two o'clock when the phone rang and James answered it. The caller asked if that was James Royston who was on the Queen Mary, and on being told yes, the phone went dead. James immediately thought that it was a reporter checking down the Roystons in the phone books of Southampton and Portsmouth hoping he would get a lucky break, which he had. When his mum came in from shopping, he told her about the phone call and who he thought it might be and advised her that if the doorbell rings in the next couple of hours, tell whoever it is at the door that you don't know any James Royston. She had only been indoors less than an hour when the doorbell rang. She did not answer it straight away, so it rang again this time for longer. When she did go to the door, James heard her giving whoever it was a right mouthful about being patient when someone is on the toilet. James heard the caller ask if James Royston lived there and his tone of voice when his mother said her husband's name was Norman and that she did not know a James, she only had two daughters. He heard her ask what he wanted this James for and he said it did not matter. Not prepared to let it go at that, she said, "By the way you rang my door bell, you must have wanted something important, so why say it doesn't matter?" Looking out of the door past him, she could see Daily Express on the car door. "You are a newspaper man, aren't you?" she said and when he said, "No," she called him a liar. "It says Daily Express on your car door?"

When he left with a flea in his ear, and his mother had shut the front door, James went out into the hall and gave her a big hug. "What's that for?" she asked enjoying her son's affection.

"I now know where I am coming from" he said.

"What on earth do you mean?" his mother said.

"Well, it's like this, mum. I've been told by several people that I'm a natural detective, and being only twenty-three years old, albeit nearly twenty-four, I seem to find it easy to come across something that doesn't seem right and instinctively know what to do about it. Listening to you just now getting rid of that newspaper man made me realise where the gift, if that is what it is that I have, has come from, it's you. I only guessed who it was, but the way you got rid of him short shift was worth listening to, and the thing about it was, he was convinced you were telling the truth, I am sure of that because Joyce told me journalists are not easily put off when they are seeking a story."

His mum smiled and just said, "Come and have a cup of coffee."

James was just wishing the time away so that he could speak to Susan and thought to help pass the time he would see if Fred had got back to his own house and if he too had had the papers after him. He picked his mum and dad's phone up and dialled the number Fred had given him and didn't have to wait long before it was answered by Fred saying, "Hello, Fred Baker speaking." James wished him good day and asked how things were his end. Fred said he had read 'The Times' and what Joyce had written and had had a call from a bloke from the Daily Express.

"What did he have to say?" James enquired.

"Well,", Fred said, "this morning I had a phone call and directly I answered it, like I just have you, it went dead, but within an hour I had this bloke knock at my front door and ask if he could come in? When he was told no, he could not, he started the old routine. At first I thought he was a salesman, but directly he mentioned the Queen Mary I knew what he was and told him in no uncertain terms to get back in his car and push off, or words to that effect. Being a big man and him only small, he didn't argue, but I'm sure I haven't heard the last of him or someone like him. If I get too much of it though, I will go back to my sister's place, but I will let you know if I do." James asked him if he knew if Carol was home and if she was now well. He said, "Yes she is. She telephoned this morning to tell me that she was home safely and that their holiday was wonderful."

"Did she ask anything about our trip home?" James wanted to know, to which Fred said, "Yes, she did and I told her that I would tell her all about it sometime in the future, but that she could learn something about it if she could manage to get the last two editions of 'The 'Times'." James said he was waiting until seven o'clock until he rang Susan, and would go down to see her if he could that evening. He told Fred that if he did not hear anything from him regarding going back to his sister's, he would ring again in a few days and they could arrange to meet somewhere for a drink or a meal. Directly he had said cheerio and put the phone down, it rang. James called his mum and asked her to answer it. She picked it up and said, "Hello," and after listening for a few seconds said, "I think you must have the wrong number for my name isn't Royston, and I do not know anyone around here with that name, I am sorry," and put the phone down. She said, "It was a woman this time asking for you and mentioned the Queen Mary."

James thought to kill some more time before seven o'clock he would go down the pub for a drink. When he walked in, there were only a couple of people in there so it was very quiet, he got himself a pint from the landlord who, knowing James quite well, asked how he was and had he had a good trip, for he had been reading 'The Times'. James said he had, but that he could not say anything about it due to the police involvement. The landlord said he understood and just let James go over to a table in the corner, hoping there would be no one else come in that knew him. The landlord had been replaced by his wife when James went up for a second pint and she said he had had to go to the cellar to change a barrel and have a sort out down there. James thought no more of it until when nearly finishing the second pint and thinking it was time he made his way back home, a chap came in and looking round the bar came over to James and said hello, did he remember him from school and could he buy him a drink? James said he didn't remember him from school and was it the local newspaper he worked for? Once again, it was just instinct that told him what the chap was and giving him short change, left the pub, but not before telling the landlady she should not tell lies and that they would not be seeing him in their pub again. He made sure the chap in the pub did not follow him, or anyone else if it came to that, if he had someone outside watching for him. He started off in the opposite direction to where he lived and after turning into several roads going in different directions was certain that no one was following him before making his way back home. When he got home, he told his mum what had happened and that if he was going to be hassled like this he would have to move out both for his sake and for theirs.

When it got to seven o'clock, James telephoned Susan and once again got her sister. He asked if he could speak to Susan and was told she was in the bath and that could he ring again in half an hour or so. He said he would and put the phone down. The next half hour seemed like a lifetime, but when he rang again the phone was answered by Susan. "What has taken you so long to ring?" she said, "I got home last night." He said he knew but hoped she would sleep in and get over a bit of jet lag. She said she had tried to get him that morning but the number she rang got a miserable woman who said she had got the wrong number and that there was no James Royston living there, so she had waited for him to ring her, and then she was in the bath. James said he would explain all when he saw her and could that be tonight? She said yes, of course it could, but she had work in the morning so would not want to be too late to bed. He asked what time and she said eight thirty would be fine if that was ok for him.

He rang her door bell right on eight thirty and she opened the door. On seeing him she flung her arms round his neck and their embrace nearly took James's breath away. She said she had been thinking of him all through the holiday and could not wait to see him again. She asked him in to meet her mum and dad and her sister before they went out, so he would at least know who they were. James went in and was introduced to them and found them very nice people. They said they had heard all about him and were glad he had come at last, for Susan had been like a cat on hot bricks since she had been home. Susan said that they were now going out but would not be late as she had work in the morning and didn't want to be late the first morning back. She slipped her coat on and off they went. James had borrowed his dad's car and asked if there was anywhere Susan would like to go? She said, "Somewhere quiet, so that we can talk. I want to know about what happened during your homeward voyage." James had no trouble driving as his hand had now stopped giving him the pain it had after the finger nails were removed, plus the fact he had taken a couple of painkillers before he left home.

He drove the car to the top of Ports downhill and found a spot as far away from the other two cars that were parked there as he could. After putting the hand break on and turning the lights out, he switched the engine off. "How is your hand now?" Susan asked. "And have you got to go to hospital anymore?" James gave her an account of everything that had been done to his hand, told her when the stitches were going to be removed and that he was officially off sick for at least three weeks. They embraced, with the smell of Susan's perfume once again bringing back their meetings on the ship. They talked nonstop for nearly two hours. They discussed just about everything there was about themselves, Susan's holiday, how Carol was and what they would do for the next three weeks. James said he would probably have to go to London to see the police and perhaps the Cunard Offices in Liverpool and also intended them both having a night out with Fred and Amy if it could be arranged. Susan said how pleased she was to hear about her Uncle Fred and hoped he would be as happy with her as he had been with her aunt. At ten thirty James started the car, but not before they had kissed again. He drove her home, but would not go in when they arrived. "If I come in, and we get talking with your mum and dad, God knows what time you will get to bed." So kissing her once again, he said good night and arranged to meet her at seven o'clock the next night when he would take her to the pictures.

They met and went out for the next three nights up to the weekend, when James asked Susan to come and meet his parents. They made a good couple, with both sets of parents pleased with their children's choices which drew them even closer together.

It was the following Monday that James received a phone call from the Cunard Offices asking him to report to Mr. Mathew Braden's Office at ten thirty on Wednesday. James asked what the summons was for and was told he would be told when he got there. He waited until the afternoon and then telephoned Fred to ask if he had been invited to report to a Mr. Braden in Liverpool. Fred confirmed that he had, with time and date that were the same. Fred asked if James would be going by train. James said he would, but because the meeting was at ten thirty he intended going to a hotel the day before and would claim the cost back from the company, as well as the train fare. They agreed to meet at Waterloo station under the clock the next day and would cross London to get the same train for Liverpool to book into the same hotel. While they were there they could have a meal, a drink and discuss when they could have a get together with Amy, Elizabeth, Susan and Carol, who James was sure would like to join them.

James had checked to see if the Queen Mary had sailed on time and was told it had, so knew that the police had transferred their enquiries to New Scotland Yard. He was convinced they had not been concluded, but wondered how long it would take.

On Tuesday morning, James got the train to Waterloo, where he met Fred at the time arranged and they travelled together to Lime Street Railway Station where they alighted and got a taxi to the hotel they had been advised to choose. It was not too far from Lime Street and about the same distance from the Cunard offices, so on booking in, settled down for the evening. They had dinner in the hotel restaurant and coffee and brandy in the lounge area. They discussed what each of them had done since getting home and were both pleased for each other how their romances were going. James asked Fred if he had seen Amy, and what had they decided between them? He said he had spent a couple of nights with her and Elizabeth, and that they had set a date to get married in six months' time on board the Queen Mary with the Captain marrying them. They both thought it romantic to get married on the ship they met on and Elizabeth was thrilled because she was going to do the trip free, being the Maid of Honour, Amy was going to pay her fare. Had they decided where they were going to live was James's next question, and would Elizabeth live with them? Yes, Elizabeth would live with them, that was a certainty, and if they did move away from either of their homes, Elizabeth would be sharing the cost of whatever property they purchased. It all sounded brilliant to James and he was reminded he was required to be the best man, his fare also being paid. They decided that as it was now ten o'clock, they would have one last nightcap brandy and then turn in.

It was seven when James got his call and 'The Times' slipped under his door. He got up and telephoned Fred's room number and arranged to meet him for breakfast at eight. They had a substantial breakfast and after sitting reading their papers, looking for any article Joyce might have written, decided to get dressed in their suits and leave the hotel at ten o'clock to be at the Cunard offices a little early. They got a taxi that dropped them right outside and James gave the driver four shillings for the fare and one shilling for himself.

They went in and at the reception desk said who they were, showing their passes, and who they had come to see.

The young lady checked a list she had and on reaching Braden said, "Oh yes, you have an appointment at ten thirty. You are just a little early, but if you go up to the third floor, you will find his office when you get out of the lift and turn right, about four offices along. When you go into his office, you will find his secretary and she will tell you what you will want to know." The pair of them thanked her and followed her directions. On reaching Mr. Braden's office as the receptionist had directed, they found his secretary who said he was engaged at the minute but would not be keeping them waiting very long, and offering them a chair they sat down and waited.

After ten minutes Mr. Braden's door opened and whoever it was that he had been interviewing left, and within five minutes the secretary got a buzz on her intercom asking her to show the gentlemen in.

They both went in, James first followed by Fred. Mr. Braden stepped out from behind his desk and introduced himself and, shaking hands, asked them to sit down. He had two files on his desk, one quite thick and the other with only a couple of sheets of paper in it. "Right, gentlemen," he said "you will want to know what I have called you up here for. It is due to the tremendous work you did on the voyage back to Southampton from New York. I have been asked by the senior management to offer you jobs as Senior Security Officers. You can be sent to any of the Cunard vessels either together or separately to undertake detective type work similar to what you performed on the Mary coming home. It is a newly created position and will carry the salary level of first officer, or in your case, Mr. Royston, senior second engineer officer. Would you like to take up the posts?" James asked if they could have some time to think about it and Mr. Braden said of course and he would see them again at three o'clock. They left the office and went back to their hotel where they ordered coffee and sat and talked over the proposition that had been put to them.

"What do you think, Fred?" James put the ball straight into Fred's court. Fred had given things some thought on the way back to the hotel and said there were several points he wanted to discuss.

"First and foremost, we are a team and therefore will not be separated and put on different ships. What authority will we be given and who will we be ultimately responsible to? I think if we form a company, Royston Baker Private Detective Agency or something similar we can hire our services to whoever we like and ask our own price."

James was cautious about Fred's proposal, as he had gone into the merchant navy to get out of National Service, which, if they were employed by Cunard, he would still be in. To operate a detective agency he wouldn't, and would therefore be eligible for call up. Fred asked if he had had call up papers issued to him and if so what did he do about it? He said he had and that he had returned them stating he was going in the merchant navy and was not contacted again. Fred suggested that if that was what he had done and had not told a lie, he would probably not be contacted again and if he was he could always put on a green coat and say he did join the merchant navy.

He said, "Life is a chance, so why not take one now?"

James asked what they would do for money to start up their own business, for he did not have any. Fred said he had some savings and it would not cost much to set it up; they would not have to even have an office to start with. He could afford to get headed paper and other stationary they would need and he could get another telephone line put into his house under the company name. They could arrange fliers advertising their service and in time get themselves known in many other ways. But what would they do for wages, James wanted to know. Fred said they could take up the Cunard offer, but as self-employed instead of as employees.

It was so convincing what Fred had proposed and would be a great adventure to take up, and being young as he was, what had he to lose? By half past two they had agreed to go for it and so when they got back to Mr. Braden they were able to put to him that yes they would like to take up his offer, but on their terms and as a detective agency and not as employees. Mr. Braden said the company would have to have first call on their services if he agreed to it and would have to agree to the fees they were charging. They would have to pay all their own expenses and the accommodation would be at a reduced rate without any special facilities made available to them. It was Fred who brought up that as long as they had the support of the Captain of whatever vessel they were on, they would agree to the terms under which they accepted the contract. James asked before they left if their expenses would be paid by the company for their visit and was told yes as long as they produced receipts. It was agreed and so they went away to get themselves registered as a Private Detective Agency, with the promise that they would contact Mr. Braden directly they were up and running, taking the card he offered them.

And so it was that the two men that had met by chance and had worked so well together were now partners in a private detective agency. James said as well as Cunard, he still had Joyce to contact and was sure they could get work through her. They travelled home full of what they were going to do, and how they were going to plan the future. They would have to insure themselves well for what they were going to undertake for it could, they were sure, be very dangerous at times. When they got to Waterloo, they went to get their respective trains and said they would contact each other soon. They had sorted out what tasks each would be doing to set up the business and would remain in constant contact.

When James arrived home, his mother said she had signed for a letter the postman had delivered so thought it might be important. She gave it to James who opened it in front of her and on doing so thought he was going to pass out. The letter was from Margaret Yates and contained a

319

cheque for five thousand pounds. The letter told him that she was now fully recovered from her ordeal on the ship and that this was the thanks she was giving him for saving her life and hoped that perhaps Fred could be given a little something from it for the part he played in the whole affair. She gave her address and telephone number where she was staying but said this could change but she should be there for at least the next three months. James said he had to phone Fred and tell him there would be enough money to start their new enterprise without going into his savings and that what they had arranged could be paid for by cash if necessary. His mother asked what enterprise? James told her what he had decided to do and she thought he was mad and said she thought his father would say the same. However, he said he was going to go ahead with his plan and take a chance on the outcome.

Another week passed, enough time for everyone who got to know of James's intention to digest it and stop telling him he was mad. Susan thought it was a great idea and backed him all the way. They discussed what it might be like if they got married in a few years' time and Susan's argument was that they would be established by then if the business took off and should be able to afford to get married, but also warned that wasn't it premature to be talking of marriage yet?

It was Monday morning and only a few days before James had to go back to see the doctor. His hand was now in almost full use and with the scarring minimal, he wondered if he would be signed off for any longer. The post arrived soon after breakfast as usual and among the mail was a letter from the police addressed from New Scotland Yard. James opened it and it was signed by Detective Commander Bryden himself. It contained an invitation to go and see him and said that the same letter had been sent to Mr. Baker. In it he said the Queen Mary crimes had been investigated thoroughly and that if he wanted to know the outcomes, he would see them at three o'clock on Wednesday, the day he was due to visit his doctor. James telephoned Fred and asked him if he had received his letter and would he be able to go, he said yes and once again agreed to meet under the clock at Waterloo Railway Station this time at twelve o'clock or as soon after as possible. They could have a spot of lunch and could then go on to New Scotland Yard. James suggested that while they were up there, he would like to drop into Fleet Street and see if they could see if Joyce was in her office, without making an appointment. Fred agreed.

James telephoned his doctor's surgery and asked if his appointment with the doctor could be transferred to the next day, Thursday, and agreed on the time he was offered.

He saw Susan on Tuesday evening and they went to her local pub with her mum and dad.

James explained that he was going to the police in London in the morning to learn what had been done regarding the happenings on the voyage home that he was so involved in and that he hoped to see the lady that had been kidnapped. It was after ten o'clock when they got home. Susan's mum and dad went in after asking if James wanted a cup of coffee or cocoa. He said he must get home and proceeded to say goodnight to Susan. As time went on, their embraces got more and more intimate and this night was no exception. Susan asked how much James loved her and was told all the way. "Do you mean what I think you mean?" she asked pushing her body right into his, and when told yes, she just said – "Soon." She opened the front door and after giving James a last kiss, went in, leaving him to go and get in his dad's car and drive home.

He caught the ten thirty-two fast train from the Portsmouth Town station the next morning that arrived at Waterloo at eleven fifty-eight. On arriving, he went straight to the clock and found Fred already there. They decided they would go to a little café they had found just outside of the station and had a fish and chip lunch. It did not take long for

Fred to ask about the money to finance their new enterprise but said he appreciated James making the whole lot available to the business. He said it would even pay their wages until the contract payments started coming in. Getting off that subject, they had a little wager as to what had happened to all those attached to the Rentons. They would not have long to wait and they would find out for certain. They agreed that they thought by now the FBI would be involved, if not in control, and that would be kept secret.

They got to New Scotland Yard in good time and registered at reception before making their way up to the second floor and Commander Bryden's office. When they arrived, his secretary told them the meeting was going to be held in a small conference room down the hall and escorted them to it.

She knocked the door and ushered them in and before leaving was asked by her boss to get the coffee and biscuits now, please. The Commander rose from his chair and shook their hands and re-introduced them to the other officers in attendance, together with Captain Baron, which came as a surprise for he had obviously not sailed on the last voyage. After sitting on the chairs indicated, the coffee arrived and was served by the secretary. On completion of that and offering the biscuits to everyone, she left the room. James was sat next to Detective Superintendent Beavis, who said how busy they had been since they last met. He asked him how his hand was now and when told it was coming on fine, said he was pleased to hear it.

Commander Bryden opened the meeting by thanking all in attendance for their unstinting efforts in bringing what had been some most unpleasant happenings to a conclusion as far as the Metropolitan Police were concerned. As he explained on the ship, he and his men had dealt with all the criminal incidents as individual cases, and had had great success doing it that way, so he would go through them in order, leaving the murder and Mafia until last as these matters were now in the hands of the FBI and that the whole of the Renton clan were going to be deported back to the States.

He started off with Michael Banes. "He was officially arrested for theft and GBH and asked for twelve other cases of theft to be taken into consideration. He has been tried in court and sent to prison for two years and with no remission clause. He will serve the full two year term. His fence was traced and picked up in Spain and deported back to London for questioning when he sang like a bird, leading to further arrests aligned to the Mafia in New York. He has also been to court and will be serving three years with no remission and has been put under the scrutiny of the FBI. A great deal of jewellery and other stolen property has been recovered, but it will be difficult to trace the owners of a lot of it."

Next on the list were the two Renton bodyguards who, though not British, were charged with aiding and abetting in the murder of James Kennedy, Steve Renton's manager. "The pathologist confirmed he was killed by lethal injection before he was stabbed and we learnt that the reason for killing was due to him threatening to blow the whistle on what they were doing to Judy Mendise's father and it transpired that as well as being a nymphomaniac, she was also a sadist, hence the stabbing. She knew he was already dead, but stabbed him as well. She has been arrested for murder and is awaiting deportation. The Renton's accountant, as well as being an alcoholic, was at one time a very well respected and highly qualified lawyer and accountant, but by getting involved with the New York Mafia, was not able to get out from under their control for a serious misdemeanour he committed against the New York State and so was blackmailed into working for them. How you managed to get the documents you got from him James, the FBI don't know, let alone us, but we will come to that later. He has, by way of those documents, been arrested and will also be deported and sentencing will be carried out in New York. The FBI will be making further arrests in the

States as a result of what they now hold as positive proof of corruption, theft, misappropriation of funds, non-payment of taxes and fraud. Once again, he sang like a bird and was terrified that he would be killed by the mafia and asked for protection when he comes out of prison. Coming to Peter Evans, having committed suicide, all we could do was to get his body collected by the undertaker requested by his mother and get the suicide letter he wrote to her delivered to her. As far as I am aware, after the post mortem, the result of which was suicide by poisoning, he has already had his funeral. Last but certainly not least, we have Steve Renton. If he loved his wife, then he showed little of it to us when we questioned him. He said all the connection to the mafia and the influence imposed was all down to her. He suggested that all the things he did were down to her and that all he wanted to do was be a good and famous actor. He was arrested and, like his wife, has been put in prison awaiting deportation back to America.

"Of those we interviewed, two counter charges were investigated, and both dismissed as a case of self-defence, the first one was the body guard Ivor Bocock accusing Joyce Sheen of unlawful wounding, when she smashed his face in with a heavy ashtray and the fireman Andy Good accusing Fred Baker of malicious wounding. There will be nothing further done about either of these."

He went on say that he spoke earlier of how Mr. Royston managed to get hold of the Mafia documents folder and accounts ledgers. He asked if James could tell those assembled how he had managed it. James went on to explain that Hargraves was drunk enough at the time to be almost hysterical when pressure was put on him. "When it was explained to him that he would go to prison for a long time and what the outcome would be if he did not get protection from the police or FBI when he was finally released, and that he wouldn't get that unless he came clean to me, and that I would do my best for him with the police if he gave me all the documents he had in the safe. When we had persuaded him, with Fred's assistance, we got them. Before we left him, we gave him a bottle of his own whisky and suggested he have a couple of drinks before we arrived in Southampton." Superintendent Beavis now spoke up saying they wondered why Hargraves was unconscious when they entered his cabin, but guessed what might have happened when they found the empty bottle of whisky by the chair he was collapsed in and several other empty bottles in other parts of the cabin. James went on to explain that what he had done was cruel but under the circumstances had to be done. He realised how important what they had stumbled on was directly he started looking through the papers, but did not have time to go through all of them and in any case he didn't really understand those that he did glance at; he just hoped the man was alright when he sobered up, which was confirmed by the superintendent, albeit that he was very remorseful.

This question answered, Commander Bryden asked Captain Baron, who had not said a word, if there was anything he had to say. The Captain said as part of his rescheduled leave, he was pleased to be able to get the opportunity to thank firstly Mr. Royston and Mr. Baker for everything they had done during the five day trip back from New York and also Detective Commander Bryden for the way he had organised his staff on board and in getting his ship clear of passengers as quickly as he did, so that there was no hold up in sailing on the next trip back to New York. He said it was the most arduous trip he had ever undertaken all the time he had been at sea; he had never been deprived of sleep so much, but had found the trip the most exhilarating he had ever made. He said he hoped the report he had submitted to the police, with the attachment of Mr. Royston's to his, which he had sent a copy to his head office, was helpful and that he was glad the police had tied up all the loose ends. He also hoped that there would be no come-back on James and Fred from the mafia, for he knew what a vengeful organisation they were. He also took the opportunity to ask if Mr. Royston and Mr. Baker had been called up to the Cunard office yet and perhaps they could let him and the police know what had come of it.

The commander thanked the Captain, saying he and his staff could not have been more obliging in every way and that it made their job so much easier due to it. Turning to James and Fred with great interest, he said, "Have you been to head office and what was the outcome?" James said they had and an offer made to them becoming security officers and that they had decided to go into business together and form a private detective agency and they were only waiting for their registration to come through before they were ready to start working for themselves and that Cunard would always have first call on their services. This statement was met by approval from each and every man sitting at the table and the best of luck wished to them both. Fred now spoke for the first time saying how fortunate it had been that he and James had met and that he was sure they would have a very successful business.

The meeting broke up but not before the Superintendent invited everyone down to the police officers' dining room for high tea and hoped they would be able to meet the Chief Constable if he could make the time available to join them. He did make it and once again compliments were given for the help that the police had received from them.

On leaving and saying thank you and goodbye to everyone, James and Fred left the building saying cheerio to Captain Baron when they got outside. He wished them luck with their venture and he looked forward to seeing them on any ship he was the master of. They shook hands and went their separate ways. James hailed a taxi to take them to Fleet Street from where they found their way to 'The Times' offices. At reception James asked if Ms. Joyce Sheen was in her office. The receptionist asked who they were and did they have any identity on them, and when they showed her their driving licences she said she would find out. Fred asked her not to give her their names for they had come to surprise her and hoped it would be a pleasant surprise. She phoned the extension and was asked who wanted to see her. The receptionist said it was two gentlemen that thought she would like to see them. She then said that they look the genuine article before she obviously got the OK to send them up. The receptionist smiled and told them where to go and said they should feel privileged because she would normally send somebody down here. They went to where they were directed and found the office with 'Sheen, Assistant Editor and Foreign Correspondent' on the door. The glass in the top half of the door was opaque but they could see a little movement through it. James knocked and when told to come in, opened it and both he and Fred stood on the threshold. When she saw who it was she gave a little shriek and ran across and threw her arms round their necks together. "What are you doing here?" she said.

"Looking for a job," was the reply she got.

"Please, sit down," she said, "I'm so pleased to see you."

They said that they had read the articles she had written and how explicit they were, and wondered what response she had got from them. She said after writing the first one directly she got back she was exhausted as she did not finish until three o'clock in the morning and in fact only just made the early edition front page. She said she was given a right grilling by the police before they let her leave the ship, but all to help them get their men. She said she had been in touch with Detective Superintendent Beavis and got from him what had happened to them all. James and Fred told her they had other papers after them but had managed to keep them at bay. She thanked them for that and said she had dealt with other assignments since getting back but only day jobs in Europe. She asked them if they were serious about coming for a job and when James said he and Fred had taken her and others' advice and gone into the detective business together, she said she was delighted and would keep it in mind. She said she would have liked to have introduced them to her editor but that he was out of the office. They chatted for nearly an hour; they went over what had been discussed at New Scotland Yard, James spoke of his love affair with Susan, and Fred's engagement and forthcoming marriage to Amy. They said how funny fate can be, but agreed that one should take advantage of it when it strikes. She said she must get on with her work and they likewise said they had to get home before the rush hour started and the trains get packed. They promised to send Joyce their business card when they had been printed and told her they would always be available to work for her or her paper, if Cunard weren't using them. They wished each other good luck and Joyce gave them both a peck on the cheek and told them to stay in touch.

They got back to Waterloo station to catch their trains, shaking hands once again before going to their respective platforms, agreeing to start work directly they could, but in the meantime to keep in touch.

On getting home, James changed out of his suit and got into something more casual and at six o'clock gave Susan a ring and asked her if they went to Hayling Island tonight, would Carol be able to come out to play? She said she would give her a ring to find out and if she could they could go over when he had picked her up.

He picked Susan up at the arranged time and on learning that Carol was free, drove over to pick her up too. Carol came to the door and invited them in so that Susan could say hello to her Aunt and Uncle and introduce James. Like Susan's parents, they were very nice and also took to James straight away. Carol was ready to go out, so after the introductions they went out together. Carol gave James the directions to a pub right down by the Hayling ferry where they could talk and have a few drinks. James, after saying how pleased he was to see her, wanted to know how she was after the ordeal on the ship. She told him that what had happened had kind of been shut out of her memory and she could hardly remember anything about it. James said he could remember what it had all led up to. They chatted about their holiday with their Aunt Freda and said they would definitely be going back there again, or at least Carol would be, if Susan was saving up to get married.

James said did they realise their meeting tonight was how it all started, meeting them on the ship, his meeting with their uncle Fred and how it had all panned out.

At ten thirty James dropped Carol back home and said he hoped they could have another night out soon. It was as they were driving back from Carol's house that Susan asked James to stop the car in any dark and quiet spot they came to. He stopped when he found what he thought was a suitable place and pulled off the road, turning the lights out and switching the engine off. They both knew what for and got into the back of the car. When they were comfortable Susan whispered to James that now was 'soon' and so they made passionate love, a love that they hoped would last for the rest of their lives.